I0834145

HOME
INFLUENCE
BY
GRACE AGUILAR
D. APPLETON. AND COMPANY.

HOME INFLUENCE:

A TALE

FOR

MOTHERS AND DAUGHTERS.

BY

GRACE AGUILAR.

NEW EDITION.

NEW YORK:
D. APPLETON & COMPANY,
90, 92 & 94 GRAND STREET.
1871.

TO

MRS. HERBERT TOWNSHEND BOWEN.

My Dear Friend,

Independent of the personal feelings which urged the dedication of this unpretending volume to you, I know few to whom a story illustrative of a mother's solemn responsibilities, intense anxiety to fulfil them, and deep sense of the Influence of Home, could, with more justice, be tendered. Simple as is the actual narrative, the sentiments it seeks to illustrate, are so associated with you — have been so strengthened from the happy hours of unrestrained intercourse I have enjoyed with you — that, though I ought, perhaps, to have waited until I could have offered a work of far superior merit to a mind like yours, I felt as if no story of mine could more completely belong to you. Will you, then, pardon the *unintentional* errors which I fear you, as an earnest Protestant, *may* discern, and accept this little work as a slight tribute of the warm affection and sincere esteem with which you have been so long regarded by

Your truly attached Friend,

GRACE AGUILAR.

PREFACE.

The following story will, the author trusts, sufficiently illustrate its title to require but few words in the way of preface. She is only anxious to impress two facts on the minds of her readers. The one — that having been brought before the public principally as the author of Jewish works, and as an explainer of the Hebrew Faith, some Christian mothers might fear that the present work has the same tendency, and hesitate to place it in the hands of their children. She therefore begs to assure them, that as a simple domestic story, the characters in which are all Christians, believing in and practising that religion, all *doctrinal* points nave been most carefully avoided, the author seeking only to illustrate the spirit of true piety, and the virtues always designated as the Christian virtues thence proceeding. Her sole aim, with regard to Religion, has been to incite a train of serious and loving thought toward God and man, especially toward those with whom He has linked us in the precious ties of parent and child, brother and sister, master and pupil.

The second point she is desirous to bring forward is her belief, that in childhood and youth the *spoken* sentiment is one of the safest guides to individual character; and that if, therefore, she have written more conversation than may appear absolutely necessary for the elucidation of "Home Influence," or the interest of the narrative, it is from no wish to be diffuse, but merely to illustrate her own belief. SENTIMENT is the vehicle of THOUGHT, and THOUGHT the origin of ACTION. Children and youth have very seldom the power to evince character by action, and scarcely if ever understand the mystery of thought; and therefore their unrestrained conversation may often greatly aid parents and teachers in acquiring a correct idea of their natural disposition, and in giving hints for the mode of education each may demand.

Leaving the beaten track of works written for the young, the author's aim has been to assist in the education of the HEART, believing that of infinitely greater importance than the mere instruction of the MIND, for the bright awakening of the latter, depends far more on the happy influences of the former than is generally supposed.

The *moral* of the following story the author acknowledges is addressed to mothers only, for on them so much of the responsibility of Home Influence devolves. On them, more than on any other, depends the well-doing and happiness, or the error and grief, not of childhood alone, but of the far more dangerous period of youth. A Preface is not the place to enter on their mission. The author's only wish is, to *aid* by the thoughts, which in some young mothers, anxious and eager to perform their office, her story *may* excite. To daughters, also, she hopes it may not be found entirely useless, for on them rests so much of the happiness of home, in the simple thought of, and attention to those little things which so bless and invigorate domestic life. Opportunities to evince the more striking virtues woman may never have, but for the cultivation and performance of the lesser, they are called upon each day.

CLAPTON, *January*, 1847.

MEMOIR OF GRACE AGUILAR.

Grace Aguilar was born at Hackney, June 2d, 1816. She was the eldest child and only daughter of Emanuel Aguilar, one of those merchants descended from the Jews of Spain, who, almost within the memory of man, fled from persecution in that country, and sought and found an asylum in England.

The delicate frame and feeble health observable in Grace Aguilar throughout her life displayed itself from infancy; from the age of three years, she was almost constantly under the care of some physician, and, by their advice, annually spending the summer months by the sea, in the hope of rousing and strengthening a naturally fragile constitution. This want of physical energy was, however, in direct contrast to her mental powers, which developed early and readily. She learned to read with scarcely any trouble, and, when once that knowledge was gained, her answer, when asked what she would like for a present, was, invariably, "A book," which was read, re-read, and preserved with a care remarkable in so young a child. With the exception of eighteen months passed at school, her mother was her sole instructress, and both parents took equal delight in directing her studies and facilitating her personal inspection of all that was curious and interesting in the various counties of England to which they resorted for her health.

From the early age of seven she commenced keeping a journal, which was continued with scarce any intermission throughout her life. In 1825 she visited Oxford, Cheltenham, Gloucester, Worcester, Ross, and Bath; and though at that time but nine years old, her father took her to Gloucester and Worcester cathedrals, and also to see a porcelain and pin manufactory, &c., the attention and interest she displayed on these occasions affording convincing proof that her mind was alive to appreciate and enjoy what was thus presented to her observation. Before she had completed her twelfth year, she ventured to try her powers in composition, and wrote a little drama, called Gustavus Vasa, never published, and only here recorded as being the first germ of what was afterward to become the ruling passion.

In September, 1828, the family went to reside in Devonshire for the health of Mr. Aguilar, and there a strong admiration for the beauties and wonders of nature manifested itself: she constantly collected shells, stones, sea-weed, mosses, &c., in her daily rambles; and, not satisfied with admiring their beauty, sedulously procured whatever little catechisms or other books on those subjects she could purchase or borrow, eagerly endeavoring, by their study, to increase her knowledge of their nature and properties.

When she had attained the age of fourteen, her father

commenced a regular course of instruction for his child, by reading aloud while she was employed in drawing, needle-work, &c. History was selected, that being the study which now most interested her, and the first work chosen was Josephus.

It was while spending a short time at Tavistock, in 1830, that the beauty of the surrounding scenery led her to express her thoughts in verse. Several small pieces soon followed her first essay, and she became extremely fond of this new exercise and enjoyment of her opening powers, yet her mind was so well regulated that she never permitted herself to indulge in original composition until her duties and her studies were all performed.

Grace Aguilar was extremely fond of music; she had learned the piano from infancy, and in 1831 commenced the harp. She sang pleasingly, preferring English songs, and invariably selecting them for the beauty or sentiment of the words; she was also passionately fond of dancing, and her cheerful, lively manners in the society of her young friends would scarcely have led any to imagine how deeply she felt and pondered upon the serious and solemn subjects which afterward formed the labor of her life. She seemed to enjoy all, to enter into all, but a keen observer would detect the hold that sacred and holy principle ever exercised over her lightest act and gayest hour. A sense of duty was apparent in the merest trifle, and her following out of the divine command of obedience to parents was only equalled by the unbounded affection she felt for them. A wish was once expressed by her mother that she should not waltz, and no solicitation could afterward tempt her. Her mother also required her to read sermons, and study religion and the Bible regularly; this was readily submitted to, first as a task, but afterward with much delight; for evidence of which we cannot do better than quote her own words, in one of her religious works:

"This formed into a habit, and persevered in for a life, would in time, and without labor or weariness, give the comfort and the knowledge that we seek; each year it would become lighter and more blessed; each year we should discover something we knew not before, and, in the valley of the shadow of death, feel to our heart's core that the Lord our God is Truth." *

Nor did Grace Aguilar only study religion for her own personal observance and profit. She embraced its *principles* (the principles of all creeds) in a widely-extended and truly liberal sense. She carried her practice of its holy and benevolent precepts into every minutiæ of her daily life, doing all the good her limited means would allow, finding time in the midst of her own studies, and most varied and continual occupations, to work for and instruct her poor neighbors in the country, and, while steadily venerating and adhering to her own faith, neither inquiring nor heeding the religious opinions of the needy whom she succored or consoled. To be permitted to help and comfort she considered a privilege and a pleasure; she left the rest to God; and thus, bestowing and receiving blessings and smiles from all who had the opportunity of knowing her, her young life flowed on in an almost uninterrupted stream of enjoyment, until she had completed her nineteenth year.

Alas! the scene was soon to change, and trials awaited that spirit which, in the midst of sunshine, had so

* *Women of Israel*, vol. ii. p. 43

beautifully striven to prepare itself a shelter from the storm. The two brothers of Miss Aguilar, whom she tenderly loved, left the paternal roof to be placed far from their family at school. Her mother's health necessitated a painful and dangerous operation; and from that time, for several years, alternate hopes and fears, through long and dreary watchings beside the sick-bed of that beloved mother, became the portion of her gifted child. But even this depressing and arduous change in the duties of her existence did not suspend her literary pursuits and labors. She profited by all the intervals she could command, and wrote the tale of the "Martyr," the "Spirit of Judaism," and "Israel Defended," the latter translated from the French, at the earnest request of a friend, and printed only for private circulation. The "Magic Wreath," a little poetical work, and the first our authoress ever published, dedicated to the Right Honorable the Countess of Munster, also appeared about this time.

In the spring of 1835, Grace Aguilar was attacked with measles, and never afterward recovered her previous state of health, suffering at intervals with such exhausting feelings of weakness as to become, without any visible disease, really alarming.

The medical attendants recommended entire rest of mind and body; she visited the sea, and seemed a little revived, but anxieties were gathering around her horizon, to which it became evidently impossible her ardent and active mind could remain passive or indifferent, and which recalled every feeling, every energy of her impressible nature into action. Her elder brother, who had long chosen music as his profession, was sent to Germany to pursue his studies; the younger determined upon entering the sea-service. The excitement of these changes, and the parting with both, was highly injurious to their affectionate sister; and her delight, a few months after, at welcoming the sailor boy returned from his first voyage, with all his tales of danger and adventure, and his keen enjoyment of the path of life he had chosen, together with her struggles to do her utmost to share his walks and companionship, contributed yet more to impair her inadequate strength.

The second parting was scarcely over ere her father, who had long shown symptoms of failing health, became the victim of consumption. He breathed his last in her arms; and the daughter, while sorrowing over all she had lost, roused herself once more to the utmost, feeling that she was the sole comforter beside her remaining parent. Soon after, when her brother again returned, finding the death of his father, he resolved not to make his third voyage as a midshipman, but endeavor to procure some employment sufficiently lucrative to prevent his remaining a burden upon his widowed mother. Long and anxiously did he pursue this object, his sister, whose acquaintance with literary and talented persons had greatly increased, using all her energy and influence in his behalf, and concentrating all the enthusiastic feelings of her nature in inspiring him with patience, comfort, and hope, as often as they failed him under his repeated disappointments. At length his application was taken up by a powerful friend, for her sake; she had the happiness of succeeding, and saw him depart at the very summit of his wishes. Repose, which had been so long necessary, seemed now at hand; but her nerves had been too long and too repeatedly overstrung, and when this task was done the worn and weary spirit could sustain no more, and sank under the labor that had been imposed upon it.

Severe illness followed; and though it yielded, after a time, to skilful remedies and tender care, her excessive languor and severe headaches continued to give her family and friends great uneasiness.

During all these demands upon her time, her thoughts, and her health, however, the ruling passion neither slumbered nor slept. She completed the Jewish Faith, and also prepared Home Influence for the press, though very unfit to have taxed her powers so far. Her medical attendant became urgent for total change of air and scene, and again strongly interdicted *all* mental exertion; a trip to Frankfort, to visit her elder brother, was therefore decided on. In June, 1847, she set out, and bore the journey without suffering nearly so much as might have been expected. Her hopes were high, her spirits raised; the novelty and interest of her first travels on the Continent gave her, for a very transient period, a gleam, as it were, of strength. For a week or two she appeared to rally; then, again, every exertion became too much for her, every stimulating remedy seemed to exhaust her. She was ordered from Frankfort to try the baths and mineral waters of Schwalbach, but without success. After a stay of six weeks, and persevering with exemplary patience in the treatment prescribed, she was one night seized with alarming convulsive spasms, so terrible that her family removed her the next morning with all speed back to Frankfort, to the house of a family of most kind friends, where every attention and care was lavishly bestowed.

In vain. She took to her bed the very day of her arrival, and never rose from it again; she became daily weaker, and in three weeks from that time her sufferings ceased forever. She was perfectly conscious to within less than two hours before her death, and took an affectionate leave of her mother and brother. Speech had been a matter of difficulty for some time previous, her throat being greatly affected by her malady; but she had, in consequence, learned to use her fingers in the manner of the deaf and dumb, and almost the last time they moved it was to spell upon them, feebly, "Though He slay me, yet will I trust in Him."

She was buried in the cemetery of Frankfort, one of which is set apart for the people of her faith. The stone which marks the spot bears upon it a butterfly and five stars, emblematic of the soul in heaven, and beneath appears the inscription,

"GIVE HER OF THE FRUIT OF HER HANDS, AND LET HER OWN WORKS PRAISE HER IN THE GATES."

Prov. ch. xxvi. v. 31.

And thus, 16th of September, 1847, at the early age of thirty-one, Grace Aguilar was laid to rest; the bowl was broken, the silver cord was loosed. Her life was short, and checkered with pain and anxiety, but she strove hard to make it useful and valuable, by employing diligently and faithfully the talents with which she had been endowed. Nor did the serious view with which she ever regarded earthly existence induce her to neglect or despise any occasion of enjoyment, advantage, or sociality which presented itself. Her heart was ever open to receive, her hand to give.

Inasmuch as she succeeded to the satisfaction of her fellow-beings, let them be grateful; inasmuch as she failed, let those who perceive it deny her not the meed of praise for her endeavor to open the path she believed would lead mankind to practical virtue and happiness, and strive to carry out the pure philanthropic principles by which she was actuated, and which she so earnestly endeavored to diffuse.

October, 1849.

CONTENTS.

PART I.

THE SISTERS.

PART II.

TRAITS OF CHARACTER.

PART III.

SIN AND SUFFERING.

HOME INFLUENCE.

PART I.

THE SISTERS.

CHAPTER I.

A LAUNCH.—A PROMISE.—A NEW RELATION.

In a very beautiful part of Wales, between the northern boundaries of Glamorgan and the south-eastern of Carmarthenshire, there stood, some twenty or thirty years ago, a small straggling village. Its locality was so completely concealed that the appearance of a gentleman's carriage, or, in fact, any vehicle superior to a light spring-cart, was of such extremely rare occurrence as to be dated, in the annals of Llangwillan, as a remarkable event, providing the simple villagers with amusing wonderment for weeks.

The village was scattered over the side of a steep and rugged hill; and on the east, emerging from a thick hedge of yews and larches, peeped forth the picturesque old church, whose tin-coated spire, glittering in the faintest sunshine, removed all appearance of gloom from the thick trees, and seemed to whisper, whatever darkness lingered round, light was always shining there. The churchyard, which the yews and larches screened, was a complete natural garden, from the lowly cottage flowers, planted by loving hands over many a grassy grave, and so hallowed that not a child would pluck them, however tempted by their luxuriance and beauty. A pretty cottage, whose white walls were covered with jasmine, roses, and honeysuckle, marked the humble residence of the village minister, who though in worldly rank only a poor curate, from his spiritual gifts deserved a much higher grade.

A gurgling stream ran leaping and sparkling over the craggy hill till it formed a deep, wide bed for itself along the road leading to the nearest town, embanked on one side by a tall leafy hedge, and on the other by rich grass and meadow flowers. By the side of this stream groups of village children were continually found, sometimes reaching for some particular flower or insect, or floating pieces of wood with a twig stuck upright within them as tiny fleets; but this amusement had given place the last ten days to the greater excitement of watching the progress of a miniature frigate, the workmanship of a young lad who had only very lately become an inmate of the village. All had been at length completed, sails, ropes, and masts, with a degree of neatness and beauty, showing not only ingenuity but observation; and one lovely summer evening the ceremony of launching took place. For a few minutes she tottered and reeled amid the tiny breakers, then suddenly regained her equilibrium and dashed gallantly along. A loud shout burst from the group, from all save the owner, a beautiful boy of some twelve years, who contented himself with raising his slight figure to its full height, and looking proudly and triumphantly round him. One glance would suffice to satisfy that his rank in life was far superior to that of his companions, and that he condescended from circumstances, not from choice, to mingle with them. So absorbed was the general attention that the very unusual sound of carriage-wheels was unremarked until close beside them, and then so astounding was the sight of a private carriage and the coachman's very simple question if that road led to the village, that all hung back confused. The owner of the little vessel, however, answered proudly and briefly in the affirmative. "And can you direct me, my good boy," inquired a lady, looking from the window, and smiling kindly at the abashed group, "to the residence of Mrs. Fortescue. It is out of the village, is it not?"

"Mrs. Fortescue!" repeated the boy eagerly and gladly, and his cap was off his head in a moment, and the bright sunshine streamed on a face of such remarkable beauty, and withal so familiar, that though the lady bent eagerly forward to address him, emotion so choked her voice that the lad was enabled to reply to her inquiry, and direct the coachman to the only inn of the village, and they had driven off, before words returned.

The boy looked eagerly after them, then desiring one of his

companions to meet the lady at the inn, and guide her to the cottage, caught up his little vessel, and darted off across some fields which led by a shorter cut to the same place.

It was a very humble dwelling, so surrounded by hills that their shadow always seemed to overhang it: yet within, the happy temper of a poor widow and her daughter kept up a perpetual sunshine. Three weeks previous to the evening we have mentioned, a lady and two children had arrived at Llangwillan, unable to proceed farther from the severe indisposition of the former. They were unattended, and the driver only knew that their destination was Swansea; he believed they had been shipwrecked off Pembroke, and that the poor lady was very ill when she commenced her journey, but the curious inquiries of the villagers could elicit nothing more. Mr. Myrvin, with characteristic benevolence, devoted himself to insuring, as far as he could, the comfort of the invalid; had her removed from the inn to Widow Morgan's cottage, confident that there she would at least be nursed with tenderness and care, and so near him as to permit his constant watchfulness. But a very few days too sadly convinced him, not only that her disease was mortal, but that his presence and gentle accents irritated instead of soothed. Ill-temper and self-will seemed to increase with the weakness, which every day rendered her longing to continue her journey more and more futile. It was some days before she could even be persuaded to write to the relative she was about to seek, so determined was she that she would get well; and when the letter was forwarded, and long before an answer could have been received (for twenty years ago there were no railroads to carry on epistolary communication as now,) fretfulness and despondency increased physical suffering, by the determined conviction that she was abandoned, her children would be left uncared for. In vain Mr. Myrvin assured her of the impossibility yet to receive a reply, that the direction might not even have been distinct enough, for her memory had failed her in dictating it; she knew she was deserted, she might have deserved it, but her Edward was innocent, and it was very hard on him. As self-will subsided in physical exhaustion, misery increased. A restless torturing remembrance seemed to have taken possession of her, which all the efforts of the earnest clergyman were utterly ineffectual to remove. She would not listen to the peace he proffered, and so painfully did his gentle eloquence appear to irritate instead of calm, that he desisted, earnestly praying, that her sister might answer the letter in person, and by removing anxiety prepare the mind for better thoughts.

One object alone had power to bring something like a smile to that altered but still most beautiful countenance, conquer even irritation, and still create intervals of pleasure — it was her son, the same beautiful boy we have already noticed, and whose likeness to herself was so extraordinary that it would have been almost too feminine a beauty, had it not been for the sparkling animated expression of every feature, and the manly self-possession which characterized his every movement. That he should be his mother's idol was not very surprising, for the indiscreet and lavish indulgence which had been his from birth, had not yet had power to shake his doating fondness for his mother, or interfere with her happiness by the visible display of the faults which her weakness had engendered. Caressingly affectionate, open-hearted, generous, and ever making her his first object, perhaps even a more penetrating mother would have seen nothing to dread but all to love. His uncontrolled passion at the slightest cross, his haughty pride and indomitable will toward all save her, but increased her affection. And when he was with her, which he was very often, considering that a sick close room would have been utterly repugnant to him had it not contained his mother, Mrs. Fortescue was actually happy. But it was a happiness only increasing her intensity of suffering when her son was absent. Hide it from herself as she might, the truth would press upon her that she was dying, and her darling must be left to the care of relations indeed, but utter strangers to him, and unlikely to treat him as she had done. She knew that he had, what strict disciplinarians, as she chose to regard her sister and her husband, would term and treat as serious faults, while she felt them actually virtues; and agony for him in the dread of what he might be called upon to endure, would deluge her pillow with passionate tears, and shake her slight frame as with convulsion.

The day we have mentioned, Edward had been absent longer than usual, and toward evening Mrs. Fortescue awoke from a troubled sleep to brood over these thoughts, till they had produced their usual effect in tears and sobs, the more painful to witness from the increasing physical incapacity to struggle with them.

A little girl, between ten and eleven years old, was seated on a low wooden stool, half concealed by the coarse curtain of the bed, employed in sewing some bright gilt buttons on a blue jacket. It seemed hard work for those small, delicate hands; but she did not look up from her task till roused by the too familiar sound of her mother's suffering, and then, as she raised her head, and flung back the heavy and somewhat disordered ringlets, the impulse seemed to be to spring up and try to soothe, but a mournful expression quickly succeeded, and she sat several minutes without moving. At length, as Mrs. Fortescue's sobs seemed almost to suffocate her, the child gently bent over her, saying, very timidly, "Dear mamma, shall I call widow Morgan, or can I get any thing for you?" and, without waiting for a reply, save the angry negative to the first question, she held a glass of water to her mother's lips and bathed her forehead. After a few minutes Mrs. Fortescue revived sufficiently to inquire where Edward was.

"He has gone down to the stream to launch his little frigate, mamma, and asked me to fasten these buttons on his jacket, to make it look like a sailor's meanwhile; I do not think he will be very long now."

Mrs. Fortescue made no rejoinder, except to utter aloud those thoughts which had caused her previous paroxysm, and her little girl, after a very evident struggle with her own painful timidity, ventured to say:

"But why should you fear so much for Edward, dear mamma? Everybody loves him and admires him, so I am sure my aunt and uncle will."

"Your aunt may for my sake, but she will not love or bear with his childish faults as I have done; and your uncle is such a harsh, stern man, that there is little hope for his forbearance with my poor Edward. And he is so frank and bold, he will not know how even to conceal his boyish errors, and he will be punished, and his fine spirit broken, and who will be there to shield and soothe him!"

"I may be able sometimes, mamma, and indeed, indeed, I will whenever I can," replied her child, with affecting earnestness. "I love him so very, very much, and I know he is so much better than I am, that it will be very easy to help him whenever I can."

"Will you promise me, Ellen, will you really promise me to shield him, and save him from harshness whenever it is in your power," exclaimed Mrs. Fortescue, so eagerly, that she half raised herself, and pressed Ellen to her with an appearance of affection so unusual, and a kiss so warm, that that moment never passed from the child's mind, and the promise she gave was registered in her own heart, with a solemnity and firmness of purpose little imagined by her mother, who, when she demanded it, conceived neither its actual purport nor extent; she only felt relieved that Edward would have some one by him, to love him and enable him to conceal his errors, if he should commit any.

Had she studied and known the character of Ellen as she did that of her son, that promise would perhaps never have been asked; nor would she so incautiously and mistakenly have laid so great a stress upon *concealment*, as the only sure means of guarding from blame. From her childhood Mrs. Fortescue had been a creature of passion and impulse, and maternity had unhappily not altered one tittle of her character. In what manner, or at what cost, Ellen might be enabled to keep that promise, never entered her mind. It had never been her wont, even in days of health, to examine or reflect, and present weakness permitted only the morbid indulgence of one exaggerated thought.

For several minutes she lay quite silent, and Ellen resumed her seat and work, her temples throbbing, she knew not why, and a vain longing to throw her arms round her mother's neck, and entreat her only for one more kiss, one other word of love; and the consciousness that she dared not, caused the hot tears to rush into her eyes, and almost blind her, but she would not let them fall, for she had learned long ago, that while Edward's tears only excited soothing and caresses, hers always called forth irritation and reproof.

"Joy, joy! Mother, darling!" exclaimed an eager voice, some minutes afterward, and Edward bounded into the room, and throwing himself by his mother's side, kissed her pale cheek again and again. "Such joy! My ship sailed so beautifully, I quite longed for you to see it, and you will one day when you get well and strong again; and I know you will soon now, for I am sure aunt Emmeline will very soon come, and then, then, you will be so happy, and we shall all be happy again!"

Mrs. Fortescue pressed him closer and closer to her, returning his kisses with such passionate fondness, that tears mingled with them, and fell upon his cheek.

"Don't cry, mamma, dear! indeed, indeed, my aunt will soon come. Do you know I think I have seen her and spoken to her too?"

"Seen her, Edward? You mean you have dreamed about her, and so fancy you have seen her;" but the eager, anxious look she fixed upon him evinced more hope than her words.

"No, no, mamma; as we were watching my ship, a carriage passed us, and a lady spoke to me, and asked me the way to the cottage where you lived, and I am sure it is aunt Emmeline from her smile."

"It cannot be," murmured his mother, sadly; "unless —" and her countenance brightened. "Did she speak to you, Edward, as if she knew you, recognized you, from your likeness to me?"

"No, mamma, there was no time, the carriage drove off again so quickly; but, hush! I am sure I hear her voice down stairs, and he sprung up from the bed and listened eagerly. "Yes, yes, I am right, and she is coming up; no, it's only widow Morgan, but I am sure it is my aunt by your face," he added, impatiently, as Mrs. Morgan tried by signs to beg him to be more cautious, and not to agitate his mother. "Why don't you let her come up?" and springing down the whole flight of stairs in two bounds, he rushed into the little parlor, caught hold of the lady's dress, and exclaimed, "You are my aunt, my own dear aunt; do come up to mamma, she has been wanting you so long, so very long, and you will make her well, dear aunt, will you not?"

"Oh, that I may be allowed to do so, dear boy!" was the painfully agitated reply, and she hastened up the stairs.

But to Edward's grief and astonishment, so little was he conscious of his mother's exhausted state, the sight of his aunt, prepared in some measure as she was, seemed to bring increase of suffering instead of joy. There was a convulsive effort for speech, a passionate return of her sister's embrace, and she fainted. Edward in terror flung himself beside her, entreating her not to look so pale, but to wake and speak to him. Ellen, with a quickness and decision, which even at that moment caused her aunt to look at her with astonishment, applied the usual restoratives, evincing no unusual alarm, and a careless observer might have said, no feeling; but it was only a momentary thought which Mrs. Hamilton could give to Ellen, every feeling was engrossed in the deep emotion with which she gazed on the faded form and altered face of that still beloved though erring one; who, when she had last beheld her, thirteen years previous, was bright, buoyant, lovely as the boy beside them. Her voice yet, more than the proffered remedies, seemed to recall life, and after a brief interval the choking thought found words.

"My father! my father! Oh, Emmeline I know that he is dead! My disobedience, my ingratitude for all his too indulgent love, killed him — I know it did. But did he curse me, Emmeline? did all his love turn to wrath, as it ought to have done? did —"

"Dearest Eleanor," replied Mrs. Hamilton, with earnest tenderness, "dismiss such painful thoughts at once; our poor father did feel your conduct deeply, but he forgave it, would have received your husband, caressed, loved you as before, had you but returned to him; and so loved you to the last moment, that your name was the last word upon his lips. But this is no subject for such youthful auditors," she continued, interrupting herself, as she met Edward's bright eyes fixed wonderingly upon her face, and noticed the excessive paleness of Ellen's cheek. "You look weary, my love," she said, kindly, drawing her niece to her, and affectionately kissing her. "Edward has made his own acquaintance with me, why did you not do so too? But go now into the garden for a little while, I am sure you want fresh air, and I will take your place as nurse meanwhile. Will you trust me?"

And the kind smile which accompanied her words gave Ellen courage to return her kiss, but she left the room without speaking. Edward required more persuasion; and the moment he was permitted he returned, seated himself on a stool at his aunt's feet, laid his head on her lap, and remained for nearly an hour quite silent, watching with her the calm slumbers which had followed the agitating conversation between them. Mrs. Hamilton was irresistibly attracted toward him, and rather wondered that Ellen should stay away so long. She did not know that Edward had spent almost the whole of that day in the joyous sports natural to his age, and that it had been many weary days and nights since Ellen had quitted her mother's room.

CHAPTER II.

GLIMPSES INTO A CHILD'S HEART.—A DEATHBED.

On leaving the cottage, Ellen hastily traversed the little garden, and entered a narrow lane, leading to Mr. Myrvin's dwelling. Her little heart was swelling high within her, and the confinement she had endured, the constant control she exercised for fear she should add to her mother's irritation, combined with the extreme delicacy of natural constitution, had so weakened her as to render the slightest exertion painful. She had been so often reproved as fretful and ill-tempered, whenever in tears, that she always checked and concealed them. She had been so frequently told that she did not know what affection was, that she was so inanimate and cold, that though she did not understand the actual meaning of the words, she believed she was different to any one else, and was unhappy without knowing why. Compared with her brother, she certainly was neither a pretty nor an engaging child. Weakly from her birth, her residence in India had increased constitutional delicacy, and while to a watchful eye the expression of her countenance denoted constant suffering, the heedless and superficial observer would condemn it as peevishness, and so unnatural to a young child, that nothing but confirmed ill-temper could have produced it. The soft, beautifully-formed black eye was too large for her other features, and the sallowness of her complexion, the heavy tresses of very dark hair, caused her to be remarked as a very plain child, which in reality she was not. Accustomed to hear beauty extolled above every thing else, beholding it in her mother and brother, and imagining it was Edward's great beauty that always made him so beloved and petted, an evil-disposed child would have felt nothing but envy and dislike toward him. But Ellen felt neither. She loved him devotedly; but that any one could love her, now that the only one who ever had, — her idolized father, — was dead, she thought impossible.

Why her heart and temples beat so quickly as she left her mother's room — why the promise she had so lately made should so cling to her mind, that even her aunt's arrival could not remove it — why she felt so giddy and weak as to render walking painful, the poor child could not have told, but, unable at length to go farther, she sat down on a grassy bank, and believing herself quite alone, cried bitterly. Several minutes passed and she did not look up, till a well-known voice inquired, —

"Dear Ellen, what is the matter? What has happened to grieve you so to-day? won't you tell me?"

"Indeed, indeed, I do not know, dear Arthur; I only feel — feel — as if I had not so much strength as I had a few days ago — and, and I could not help crying."

"You are not well, Ellen," replied her companion, a fine lad of sixteen, and Mr. Myrvin's only son. "You are looking paler than I ever saw you before; let me call my father. You know he is always pleased when he sees you, and he hoped you would have been to us before to-day; come with me to him now."

"No, Arthur, indeed I cannot; he will think I have forgotten all he said to me the last time I saw him, and, indeed, I have not — but I — I do not know what is the matter with me to-day."

And, in spite of all her efforts to restrain them, the tears would burst forth afresh; and Arthur, finding all his efforts at consolation ineffectual, contented himself with putting his arm round her and kissing them away. A few minutes afterward his father appeared.

"In tears, my dear Ellen!" he said, kindly; "your mother is not worse, I hope?"

"I do not know, sir," replied the child, as well as her tears would permit; "she has been very ill just now, for her faint was longer than usual."

"Did any thing particular occasion it?"

"I think it was seeing my aunt. Mamma was very much agitated before and afterward."

"Mrs. Hamilton has arrived then! I am rejoiced to hear it," replied Mr. Myrvin, gladly. Then sitting down by Ellen, he took one of her hands in his, and said, kindly, "Something has grieved my little girl this evening; I will not ask what it is, because you may not like to tell me; but you must not imagine evils, Ellen. I know you have done, and are doing, the duty of a good, affectionate child, nursing your suffering mother, bearing with intervals of impatience, which her invalid state occasions, and giving up all your own wishes to sit quietly by her: I have not seen you, my child, but I know those who have, and this has pleased me, and, what is of much more consequence, it proves you have not forgotten all I told you of your Father in Heaven, that even a little child can try to love and serve Him."

"But have you not told me those who are good are always happy?" inquired Ellen; "then I cannot be good, though indeed I try to be so, for I do not think I am happy, for I can never laugh and sing and talk as Edward does."

"You are not in so strong health as your brother, my dear little girl, and you have had many things to make you unhappy, which Edward has not. But you must try and remember that even if it please God that sometimes you should be more sorrowful than other children, He loves you notwithstanding. I am sure you have not forgotten the story of Joseph that I told you a few Sundays ago. God so loved him, as to give him the power of foretelling future events, and enabling him to do a great deal of good, but when he was taken away from his father and sold as a slave and cast into prison among cruel strangers, he could not have been very happy, Ellen. Yet still, young as he was, little more than a child in those days, and thrown among those who did not know right from wrong, he remembered all that his father had taught him, and prayed to God, and tried to love and obey Him; and God was pleased with him, and gave him grace to continue good, and at last so blessed him, as to permit him to see his dear father and darling brother again."

"But Joseph was his father's favorite child," was Ellen's sole rejoinder; and the tears which were checked in the eagerness with which she had listened, seemed again ready to burst forth. "He must have been happy when he thought of that."

"I do not think so, my dear Ellen," replied Mr. Myrvin, more moved than he chose to betray, "for being his father's favorite first excited the dislike and envy of his brothers, and caused them to wish to send him away. There was no excuse indeed for their conduct; but perhaps if Joseph had always remained near his father he might have been spoiled by too great indulgence, and never become as good as he afterwards was. Perhaps in his solitary prison he might even have regretted that his father had not treated them all alike, as then the angry feelings of his brothers would not have been called forth. So you see, being a favorite will not always make us happy, Ellen. It is indeed very delightful to be loved and caressed, and if we try to do our duty and love as much as we can, even if we are not sure of being loved at first, we may be quite certain that we shall be loved and happy at last. Do you understand me, my child?"

The question was almost needless, for Ellen's large eyes had never moved from his face, and their expression was so full of intelligence and meaning, that the whole countenance seemed lighted up. "Then do you think mamma will recover?" she eagerly exclaimed; "will she ever love me? — oh, if I thought so, I could never, never be naughty again!"

"She will love you, my dear Ellen," replied Mr. Myrvin, now visibly affected, "I cannot, I dare not tell you that she will recover to love you on earth, but if indeed it be God's will that she should go to Him, she will look down on you from Heaven and love you far more than she has done yet, for she will know then how much you love her."

"And will she know if I do all she wishes — if I love and help Edward?" asked Ellen, in a low, half-frightened voice; and little did Mr. Myrvin imagine how vividly and how indelibly his reply was registered in the child's memory.

"It is a question none can answer positively, Ellen, but it is my own firm belief, that the beloved ones we have lost are permitted to watch over and love us still, and that they see us, and are often near us, though we cannot see them. But even to help Edward," he continued somewhat anxiously, "you must not be tempted—"

He was interrupted by the appearance of a stranger, who, addressing him courteously, apologized for his intrusion, and noticing the children, inquired if both were his.

Mr. Myrvin replied that he could only lay claim to one; the little girl was Miss Fortescue.

"And my name is Hamilton, so I think I have an uncle's privilege was the reply; and Ellen, to her astonishment, received an affectionate embracé from the unknown relative, whom her mother's ill-judged words had taught her actually to dread. Mr. Myrvin gladly welcomed him, and, in the interest of the conversation which followed, forgot the lesson he had been so anxious to impress upon Ellen. Arthur accompanied her to the garden gate, and the gentlemen soon afterward entered the cottage together.

Days merged into weeks, and still Mrs. Fortescue lingered; but her weakness increasing so painfully from alternate fever and exhaustion that to remove her was impossible. It was the first time that Mrs. Hamilton had ever been separated from her children, and there were many disagreeables attendant on nursing a beloved invalid in that confined cottage; and with only those little luxuries and comforts that could be procured (and even these were obtained with difficulty, for the nearest town was twenty miles distant,) but not a selfish or repining thought entered Mrs. Hamilton's mind. It was filled with thankfulness, not only that she was permitted thus to tend a sister, whom neither error, nor absence, nor silence could estrange from her heart, but that she was spared long enough for her gentle influence and enduring love to have some effect in changing her train of thought, calming that fearful irritability, and by slow degrees permitting her to look with resignation and penitent hope to that hour which no human effort could avert. That Mr. Myrvin should seek Mrs. Hamilton's society and delight in conversing with her, Mrs. Fortescue considered so perfectly natural, that the conversations which took place in her sick room, whenever she was strong enough to bear them, excited neither surprise nor impatience. Different as she was, wilfully as she had always neglected the mild counsels and example of her sister, the years of separation and but too often excited self-reproach had fully awakened her to Mrs Hamilton's superiority. She had never found any one at all like her — so good and holy, yet so utterly unassuming and the strong affection, even the deep emotion in one usually so controlled, with which her sister had met her, naturally increased these feelings.

"Ah, you and Emmeline will find much to converse about," had been her address to Mr. Myrvin, on his first introduction to Mrs. Hamilton. "Talk as much as you please, and do not mind me. With Emmeline near me, I can restrain irritability which must have frightened you away. I know she is right. Oh, would to God I had always been like her!" and the suffering betrayed in the last words was a painful contrast with the lightness of her previous tone.

Mr. Myrvin answered soothingly, and for the first time his words were patiently received. From listening listlessly, Mrs. Fortescue, by slow degrees, became interested in the conversations between him and Mr. and Mrs. Hamilton, and so a change in sentiments was gradually wrought, which by any other and harsher method of proceeding would have been sought for in vain.

One evening as Mrs. Hamilton sat watching the faded countenance of her patient, and recalling those days of youth and buoyancy, when it seemed as if neither death nor care could ever have assailed one so bright and lovely, Edward, before he sought his favorite stream, threw his arms round her neck, and pressed his rosy lips on her cheek, as thus to wish her good-by.

"He will repay you for all your care, dearest Emmeline," his mother said, with a heavy sigh, as he left the room; "I know he has what you and your husband will think faults, but, oh, for my sake, do not treat him harshly; his noble spirit will be broken if you do!"

"Dearest Eleanor, dismiss all such fears. Am I not a mother equally with yourself?" and do you think when your children become mine I shall show any difference between them and my own? You would trust me even in former years, surely you will trust me now?"

"Indeed, indeed, I do; you were always kind and forbearing with me, when I little deserved it. But my poor Edward, it is so hard to part with him, and he loves me so fondly!" and a few natural tears stole down her cheek.

"And he shall continue to love you dearest Eleanor; and oh, believe me, all that you have been to him I will be. I have won the devoted affection of all my own darlings, and I do not fear to gain the love of yours; and then it will be an easy task to make them happy as my own."

"Edward's love you will very quickly obtain, if it be not yours already; but Ellen you will have more trouble with. She is a strange, cold, unlovable child."

"Are the dispositions of your children so unlike? I should not have fancied Ellen cold; she is timid, but that I thought would wear off when she knew me better."

"It is not timidity; I never knew her otherwise than cold and reserved from her birth. I never could feel the same toward her as I did toward Edward, and therefore there must be something in Ellen to prevent it."

Mrs. Hamilton did not think so, but she answered gently, "Are you quite sure, my dear Eleanor, that you have equally studied the characters of both your children? because you know there are some cases which require more study and carefulness than others."

"I never was fond of studying any thing, Emmeline, as you may remember," replied Mrs. Fortescue, painfully trying to smile, "and therefore I dare say I have not studied my children as you have yours. Besides, you know I always thought, and still think, the doctrine of mothers forming the characters of their children, and all that good people say about the importance of early impressions, perfectly ridiculous. The disposition for good or bad, loving or unloving, is theirs from the moment of their birth, and what human efforts can alter that? Why, the very infancy of my children was different; Edward was always laughing, and animated, and happy; Ellen fretful and peevish, and so heavy that she never seemed even to know when I entered the room, while Edward would spring into my arms, and shout and laugh only to see me. Now what conduct on my part could have done this? Surely I was justified in feeling differently toward such opposite dispositions; and I know I never made more difference between them than — than papa did between us, Emmeline, and I have had greater reason to be partial; you were always better than I was."

She ceased, from exhaustion, but the flush which had risen to her temples, and the trembling hands, evinced the agitation always called forth by the mention of her father, which Mrs. Hamilton, with earnest tenderness, endeavored to soothe.

"I must speak, Emmeline," she continued, natural impetuosity for the moment regaining ascendency; "how did I repay my fond father's partiality? his too great indulgence? Did I not bring down his gray hairs with sorrow to the grave? Did I not throw shame and misery upon him by my conduct to the ill-fated one he had chosen for my husband? Did I not? — oh my God, my God! Death may indeed be merciful! — my Edward might do the same by me!" and, shuddering violently, she hid her face on her sister's bosom.

It was long before Mrs. Hamilton could calm that fearful agitation, long before her whispered words of heavenly hope, and peace, and pardon — if indeed she believed — could bring comfort; but they did at length, and such fearful paroxysms returned at longer and longer intervals, and at length ceased, in the deep submission and clinging trust to which she was at last permitted to attain. Though Mrs. Hamilton was detained six weeks at Llangwillan, her devoted attendance on her sister prevented any thing more than occasional observation of the children so soon about to be committed to her care. That Edward was most engaging, and riveted her affection at once, and that Ellen was unlike any child she had ever known or seen, she could not but feel, but she was not one to decide on a mere feeling. Her present mournful task prevented all actual interference with them, except the endeavor by kindly notice to win their confidence and love. His mother's illness and his uncle's presence, besides, for the present, his perfect freedom with regard to employment, had deprived Edward of all inclination to rebel or exert his self-will, and Mr. and Mrs. Hamilton both felt that he certainly had fewer faults, than was generally the consequence of unlimited indulgence. Whether Ellen's extreme attention to her mother, her silent but ever ready help when her aunt required it, proceeded from mere cold duty, or really had its origin in affection, Mrs. Hamilton could not satisfactorily decide. Her sister had avowed partiality, but that neglect and unkindness could have been shown to such an extent by a mother as to create the cold exterior she beheld, was so utterly incomprehensible, so opposed to every dictate of maternal love, which she knew so well, that she actually could not even imagine it. She could believe in the possibility of a preference for one child more than another, but not in utter neglect and actual dislike. She could imagine that Ellen's love for her mother might be less warm than Edward's, believing, as she did, that a parent must call for a child's affection, not be satisfied with leaving all to Nature; but if it were not love that dictated Ellen's conduct, it was strange and almost unnatural, and so unpleasing, that so young a child should have such an idea of duty. But these were only passing thoughts; cost what trouble it might, Mrs. Hamilton determined she would understand her niece as she did her own children.

But though to her Ellen was a riddle, to her sister Nature was resuming her sway, too late, alas! for all save the mother's own reproaches. Her weakness had become such that days would pass when speech, save a few whispered words, was impossible; but she would gaze upon her child, as hour after hour she would sit by the bed, resisting all Edward's entreaties, and sometimes even her aunt's to go and play, and long to fold her to her heart, and confess she had been cruelly unjust, and that she did love her now almost as much as Edward, but she was much too weak to do more than feel. And Ellen remained unconscious of the change, except that now and then, as she would bring her nourishment or bend over to bathe her forehead, her mother would, as if involuntarily, kiss her cheek and murmur some caressing word. And Ellen longed to cling to her neck and say how much she loved her, but she did not dare, and she would hurry out of the room to conceal her tears, instead of returning the caress, thus unhappily confirming the idea of natural coldness.

Even the comfort of sitting by her mother was at length denied her. Mrs. Fortescue became so alarmingly and painfully ill, that Mrs. Hamilton felt it an unnecessary trial for her children to witness it, especially as they could be no comfort to her, for she did not know them. The evening of the fourth day she recovered sufficiently to partake of the sacrament with her sister and Mr. Hamilton, and then entreat that her children might be brought to her. She felt herself, what the physician had imparted to her sister, that the recovery of her senses would in all human probability be followed in a few hours by death, and her last thoughts were on them.

Edward, full of glee at being permitted to see her again, bounded joyfully into the room, but the fearful change in that beloved face so startled and terrified him, that he uttered a loud cry, and throwing himself beside her, sobbed upon her bosom. Mrs. Fortescue was fearfully agitated, but she conjured her sister not to take him from her, and her heavy eyes wandered painfully round the room in search of Ellen.

"Come to me, Ellen, I have done you injustice, my sweet child," she murmured in a voice that Ellen never in her life forgot, and she clung to her in silent agony. "I have not done my duty to you, I know — I feel I have not, and it is too late now to atone. I can only pray God to bless you, and raise you up a kinder parent than I have been! Bless, bless you both." Faintness overpowered her, and she lay for several minutes powerless, in Mrs. Hamilton's arms. Edward, in passionate grief, refused to stir from the bed; and Ellen, almost unconsciously, sunk on her knees by Mr. Myrvin.

"My own sister, bless you — for all you have been to me — all you will be to my children — may they repay you better than I have done, Emmeline! You are right, there is but one hope, our Saviour, for the sinner — it is mine —" were the broken sentences that, in a voice which was scarcely audible, and uttered at long intervals, escaped Mrs. Fortescue's lips, and then her head sunk lower on Mrs. Hamilton's bosom, and there was a long, long silence, broken only by Edward's low and half-suffocated sobs. And he knew not, guessed not, the grief that was impending. He only felt that his mother was worse, not better, as he had believed she would and must be, when his aunt arrived. He had never seen death, though Ellen had, and he had passionately and wilfully refused either to listen or to believe in his uncle's and Mr. Myrvin's gentle attempts to prepare him for his loss. Terrified at the continued silence, at the cold heavy feel of his mother's hand, as when Mr. Myrvin and the widow gently removed her from the still-supporting arm of Mrs. Hamilton, it fell against his, he started up, and clinging to his aunt, implored her to speak to him, to tell him why his mother looked so strange and white, her hand felt so cold, and why she would not speak to and kiss him, as she always did, when he was grieved.

Mrs. Hamilton raised her head from her husband's shoulder, and struggling with her own deep sorrow, she drew her orphan nephew closer to her, and said, in a low, earnest voice, "My Edward, did you not hear your mother pray God to bless you?"

The child looked at her inquiringly.

"That good God has taken her to Himself, my love; He has thought it better to remove her from us, and take her where she will never know pain nor illness more."

"But she is lying there," whispered Edward, in a frightened voice, and half hiding his face in his aunt's dress —"she is not taken away. Why will she not speak to me?"

"She cannot speak, my sweet boy! the soul which enabled her to speak, and smile, and live, was God's gift, and it has pleased Him to recall it."

"And will she never, never speak to me again? will she never kiss me — never call me her own darling, beautiful Edward again?" he almost screamed in passionate grief, as the truth at length forced itself upon him. "Mamma, mamma, my own lear, pretty, good mamma, oh! do not go away from me —

or let me go with you — let me die too; no one will love me and kiss me as you have done." And even the natural awe and terror of death gave way before his grief; he clung to the body of his mother so passionately, so convulsively, that it required actual force to remove him. And for hours his aunt and sister watched over and tried to soothe and comfort him in vain; he would only rouse himself angrily to ask Ellen how she could know what he felt; she had never loved their mother as he had — she did not know what he had lost — she could not feel as he did, and then relapse into tears and sobs. Ellen did not attempt reply. She thought, if it were such pain to her to lose her mother, who had only the last few weeks evinced affection for her, it must indeed be still more suffering to him; and though his angry words grieved and hurt her (for she knew she did love her mother most fondly, her idea of her own extreme inferiority acquitted her unconsciously of all injustice toward her, and made her believe that she had loved Edward best only because he was so much better than herself,) his very grief caused her to love and admire him still more, and to believe that she really did not feel as much as he did. And yet before they quitted Llangwillan, which they did the second day after Mrs. Fortescue's funeral, Edward could laugh and talk as usual — except when any object recalled his mother; and poor Ellen felt that though she had fancied she was not happy before, she was much more unhappy now. Her fancy naturally vivid, and rendered more so from her having been left so much to herself, dwelt morbidly on all that had passed in her mother's illness, on every caress, every unusual word of affection, and on Mr. Myrvin's assurance that she would love her in Heaven; the promise she had made to love and help Edward returned to her memory again and again, and each time with the increased determination to keep it solemnly. It was not for her mother's sake alone, and connected only with her; perhaps, had it not been for the careful instructions of her father, whom, as we shall presently see, she had cause almost to idolize, Ellen might have become indifferent to her mother and envious of Edward. But his repeated instructions, under all circumstances to love, cherish, and obey her mother had been indelibly engraved, and heightened natural feeling. She believed that to keep the promise, which had so evidently pleased her mother, would be also obeying her father, and this double incentive gave it a weight and consequence, which, could Mrs. Hamilton have known it, would have caused her great anxiety, and urged its removal. But Ellen had been too long accustomed to hide every thought and feeling to betray that which, child as she was, she believed sacred between herself and her mother. Mrs. Hamilton watched her in silence, and trusted to time and care to do their work; and by enabling her to understand her character, permit her to guide it rightly.

The morning of their intended departure was bright and sunny, and before even widow Morgan was moving, Ellen had quitted her little bed, and was in the churchyard by her mother's grave. She sat there thinking so intently, that she did not know how time passed, till she was roused by her favorite Arthur Myrvin's voice.

"Up so early, Ellen, why, I thought I should have been first to show you I had not forgotten my promise." And he displayed some choice flower-roots, which he commenced planting round the grave.

"Dear Arthur, how very kind you are; but you look so sad — what is the matter? Does not Mr. Myrvin like you to do this — pray don't, then."

"No, no, Ellen, my father said I was right, and that he would take care of the flowers also himself. I am only sorry you are going away, and to live so differently to what we do — you will quite forget me."

"Indeed, indeed I shall not, dear Arthur; I can never forget those who have been so kind to me as you and dear Mr. Myrvin; I would much rather stay here always with you, than go among strangers again, but I heard my aunt say last night, that perhaps Mr. Myrvin would let you come and see us sometimes — and you will like that, will you not?" Arthur did not seem quite sure whether he would like it or not; but they continued talking till his task was completed, and Arthur, at Ellen's earnest request, for she suddenly feared her aunt would be displeased at her having staid out so long, returned with her to the cottage; the silent kiss, however, which she received when Arthur explained what had detained them, reassured her, and bound her yet closer to the kind relative, whom, if timidity had permitted, she would already have so loved.

The novelty of his situation, the rapid and pleasant movement of his uncle's carriage, the idea of the new relations he was about to meet, and an unconfessed, but powerful feeling of his own increased consequence in being so nearly connected with wealth and distinction, all had their effect upon Edward, and his eye sparkled and his cheek glowed, as if all sorrow had entirely passed away; not that he had ceased to think of his mother, for the least reference to her would fill his eyes with tears and completely check his joy — but still delight predominated. Ellen felt more and more the wish to shrink into herself, for the farther they left Llangwillan, the more painfully she missed Mr. Myrvin and his son, and the more she shrunk from encountering strangers. Edward she knew would speedily find companions to love, and to be loved by, and he would think still less of her. Her aunt would soon be surrounded by her own children, and then how could she expect to win her love? And Ellen looked intently and silently out from the carriage-window — her uncle believed on the many-flowered hedge and other objects of interest by which they passed — his wife imagined to hide a tear that trembled in her eyes, but which she had determined should not fall.

CHAPTER III.

RETROSPECTION. — THE LOWLY SOUGHT. — THE HAUGHTY FOILED.

In order clearly to understand the allusions of the previous chapters, and the circumstances which had formed the different characters of Mrs. Hamilton and Mrs. Fortescue; it will be necessary to take a retrospective glance on their early lives. Should it be uninteresting to the more youthful of our readers, we will beg them to proceed at once to "Traits of Character," but to their elder relatives we hope the matter will prove of sufficient interest to obtain perusal.

Emmeline and Eleanor Manvers were the daughters of Lord Delmont, a nobleman whose title and rank were rather burdensome than otherwise, from the want of sufficient means to keep them up as inclination and position warranted. Lady Delmont, whose energetic, yet gentle character would have greatly ameliorated the petty vexations of her husband, died when Emmeline was only seven, Eleanor five, and Charles, her only boy, an infant of but three years old. A widow lady, Mrs. Harcourt by name, had been selected by Lady Delmont, in her last illness, as instructress and guardian of her daugh ters. Her wishes, always laws to her doating husband, were promptly fulfilled, and Mrs. Harcourt, two months after her friend's death, assumed the arduous and responsible duties for which her high character well fitted her.

With Emmeline, though there were naturally some faults to correct, an indolence and weakness to overcome, and apparently no remarkable natural aptitude for acquirement, her task was comparatively easy, for her pupil had the capabilities, not only of affection but of reverence, to a very great extent, and once loving and respecting Mrs. Harcourt, not a command was neglected, nor a wish unfulfilled. Eleanor, on the contrary, though so gifted that teaching might have been a complete labor of love — by self-will, violent passions, and a most determined want of veneration, even of common respect, a resolute opposition from her earliest years to the wishes of Mrs. Harcourt, because she was merely a governess, so much her inferior in rank, rendered the task of education one of the most difficult and painful that can be conceived — increased from the injudicious partiality of Lord Delmont. It was not indeed the culpable negligence and dislike which Eleanor afterward displayed toward her own, but originating in the fancy that Mrs. Harcourt was unjust, and Emmeline was her favorite. Lord Delmont was one of those unfortunately weak, irresolute characters that only behold the surface of things, and are therefore utterly incapable of acting either with vigor or judgment. When he did venture into the precincts of his daughters' apartments, he generally found Eleanor in sobs and tears, and Emmeline quietly pursuing her daily duties. That Mrs. Harcourt often entreated his influence with her younger pupil to change her course of conduct, he never remembered longer than the time of her expostulations lasted. Once or twice, indeed, he did begin to speak seriously, but Eleanor would throw her arms round his neck and kiss him, call him every endearing name, and beg him not to look so much like grave, cross Mrs. Harcourt, or she should think she had indeed no one to love her; and her beautiful eyes would swell with tears, and her voice quiver, so that her gratified father would forget all his reproof, and give her some indulgence to make up for the injustice and harshness she encountered in the school-room. Her power once thus experienced, of course, was never resigned. Her father's appearance in their study was always the signal for her tears, which she knew would confirm all his ideas of Mrs. Harcourt's unjust partiality.

And this idea was strengthened as they grew older, and

masters for various accomplishments somewhat lightened Mrs. Harcourt's actual labors. Emmeline's steady application and moderate abilities were lost sight of in the applause always elicited by her younger sister, whose natural gifts alike in music, languages, and drawing had full play, directly she was released, even in part, from the hated thraldom of her governess. Lord Delmont had been accustomed to hear Eleanor's beauty extolled, and now the extraordinary versatility and brilliancy of her talents became the theme of every tongue. Professors are naturally proud of a pupil who does them more than justice, and Miss Eleanor Manvers was in consequence held up in very many families, whom Lord Delmont only casually knew, and spoken of by very many again to him, knowing his weak point, and thus seeking to curry favor. Mrs. Harcourt was the only one from whom he never heard Eleanor's praises, and the only one who spoke in praise of Emmeline. It must then be wilful blindness on her part; and the father felt indignant, but in spite of himself had too much real respect for her, individually, to do more than redouble his indulgence to Eleanor. Emmeline could not complain of her father's neglect, for he was both kind and affectionate to her; but she did sometimes wish she could be quite sure that he loved her as much as her sister; and her deep affection, unsuspected by her father, rejected and laughed at by Eleanor, twined themselves closer and closer round Mrs. Harcourt and her brother Charles, on whom she actually doted, and who returned her affection with one quite as fond and warm as a happy, laughter-loving, frank-hearted boy had it in his power to bestow; yet even his holidays were times of as much suffering as joy to his sister, from the violent quarrels which were continually taking place between him and Eleanor. Emmeline, happy in herself and Mrs. Harcourt's companionship, could endure Eleanor's determined supremacy, and, except where her conscience disapproved, yielded to her. But this could not be expected from Charles, who, despite his elder sister's gentle entreaties, would stand up for what he called her rights, and declare that, when he was at home, Miss Eleanor should not lord it over the whole family. Eleanor would, of course, first quarrel with him and then appeal to her father, who without hearing the case would give her right, and harshly condemn Charles, whose high spirit revolted; and unable to bear with his father's weakness of character, as he ought to have done, would answer disrespectfully; and words succeeded words till Charles in a desperate passion would seek Emmeline's chamber, and his father, though he actually deeply loved and was very proud of his son, wished that the holidays were over, and Charles safe again at school.

Trifling as domestic disputes may seem in description, they never fail in their painful reality to banish all lasting happiness. Emmeline could bear that her father should prefer Eleanor to herself, but that he should be unjust to her darling Charles, and that Charles should increase this evil by dispute and self-will, tried her severely, and obliged her often and often to fly to the solitude of her own chamber, lest her temper also should fail, and, to defend her brother, she should forget her duty to her father. But with her, Mrs. Harcourt's lessons had indeed been blessed. The spirit of true, heartfelt piety, which she had sought to instil into her youthful charge, even more by the example of her daily life than by precepts, had become Emmeline's, young as she still was, and enabled her not only to bear up against the constant petty annoyances of her home, but the heavy trial sustained in the death of Mrs. Harcourt, just as she was looking forward to her entrance into the gay world, under her maternal guardianship, and her parting with her brother, who, not two months afterward, left her to fulfil his darling wish of going to sea.

At eighteen, then, Emmeline Manvers became the mistress of her father's establishment, and had to encounter alone, not only the suffering of bereavement — in which, though Lord Delmont sincerely respected Mrs. Harcourt, he could not sympathize, and at which, after the first shock and momentary remorse for her own conduct to so true a friend, Eleanor, if she did not actually rejoice, felt so very greatly relieved as to be irritated and angry at Emmeline's quiet sorrow — but the separation from her brother and all the cares and disagreeables of such strict economy at home, as would permit the sustaining a proper position in society, so that the necessity of economy should not even be suspected. It was this regard of appearances which so chafed and pained Emmeline's upright and independent spirit. Not that Lord Delmont, even for appearances, would go beyond his income; but still there were obliged concealments and other petty things which his daughter could not bear. Mrs. Harcourt's trial — a widow, compelled not only to teach for a subsistence, but to part with her only child, who had been adopted by a married sister, living in Italy — appeared to Emmeline's ideas of truth and honor preferable to appearing richer than they really were. But on this subject, even less than on any other, she knew there was no chance of sympathy, and so she devoted all the energies of her matured and well-regulated mind to correcting the evil as much as it lay in her individual power; and in the year which her earnest entreaties prevailed on her father to permit her remaining in quiet retirement, before she entered the world, Lord Delmont was astonished at the greater comfort and increase of dignity which pervaded his establishment. He never had chosen Mrs. Harcourt to interfere with his household concerns, believing that he conducted them himself, when in reality he was completely governed by his housekeeper and steward. Mrs. Harcourt's penetration had seen and regretted this, and had endeavored so to guide and instruct Emmeline, that when she became old enough to claim her right as mistress, the evil should be remedied. Could she have looked down on the child of her love, she would indeed have rejoiced at the beautiful fruition of her labors. Lord Delmont was not astonished and delighted only, a feeling of respect toward his gentle, his truthful child entered his heart, such as he had experienced toward none, save her mother. Emmeline would indeed have thought all her toils repaid, could she have known this, but the very feeling prevented the display of that caressing affection he still lavished on Eleanor, and the tears of his elder girl often fell thick and fast from the painful longing for one similar caress, one evidence on his part, that, though neither so beautiful, nor talented, nor engaging as Eleanor, she could yet minister to his comfort and increase his happiness.

But Emmeline's strong feeling of religion, while it enabled her to bear up against care and the constant and most painful feeling of loneliness, rendered the trial of beholding her sister's wilful course of error, if possible, still more severe. She knew that all her affectionate counsels were worse than useless, that though Eleanor could be even caressingly affectionate when it served her purpose, would even listen to her at the moment of suffering from some too hasty impulse, she had no lasting influence. And this became more and more evident as Eleanor became the almost constant companion of the Marchioness Lascelles, their only female relative. It was the evil influence of this lady which had so increased Eleanor's natural repugnance to Mrs. Harcourt's gentle sway, that for full two years before the latter's death the flattery of Lady Lascelles and Eleanor's passionate entreaties had prevailed on Lord Delmont to permit his daughter being more with her than with her sister and governess. Lady Lascelles was a woman of the world, utterly heartless, highly distinguished, and supremely fashionable. At her house all the ton of the beau-monde congregated, and scandal, frivolity, and *esprit* were the prevailing topics, diversified with superficial opinions of the literature, arts, and politics of the day, and various sentimental episodes, which the lady of the house endured for the sake of variety. Here Eleanor, even at fourteen, was made a popular idol; her extreme beauty, her vivacity, her talents, her sharpness of repartee, all were admired, extolled, and encouraged. At seventeen she was introduced and initiated into all the mysteries of an ultra-fashionable life, and very speedily added to her other accomplishments all the arts of a finished and heartless coquette.

With Lady Lascelles for her chaperon, it was not very surprising that Emmeline Manvers shrunk in pain and dread from her introduction into society; but yet she knew her social duties too well to refuse, and, by an affectation of superior sanctity, which of course would have been the charge levelled against her, throw a sneer upon those holy feelings and spiritual principles which had become part of her very being. She entered into society, but the isolation to a heart like hers of the coteries of Lady Lascelles and her friends, was indeed most painful, and aggravated by the constant dread which the contemplation of Eleanor's reckless career could not but occasion.

But Emmeline's trial of loneliness was happily not of very long duration. At a ball, which was less exclusive than the assemblages of Lady Lascelles, the attention of both sisters was attracted to a young man, by name Arthur Hamilton — Eleanor, from his distinguished appearance and extreme reserve, Emmeline, by the story attached to his name. His father had so distinguished himself in the amelioration of the peasantry and working classes in various parts of England, in addition to various services of a private and confidential nature from the home government to the courts abroad, that a viscountcy was offered to his acceptance. The message from royalty reached him on his death-bed, and though, from the faint and flickering accents with which he replied to the intended honor, it seemed as if he declined it, it was attributed to the natural feelings of a dying man, seeing the utter nothingness of earthly honors, and the title was generously proposed to his son. But Arthur Hamilton had not been the pupil and friend of his father in vain. With a calm dignity and uncompromising independence, he declared that he had neither claim nor heirship to the reward of his father's services; that he believed his parent would himself have refused it, preferring the honorable distinction of being an untitled English gentleman, to the unvalued honor of a newly-created lordship. He respectfully thanked the government for the honor they intended, but decisively refused it — that his dearest inheritance was his father's name.

Of course this most extraordinary decision was canvassed again and again in the fashionable world, meeting there with very little appreciation, because it sprang from much higher feelings than the world could comprehend. By many he was imagined very little removed from insane — by others as actuated by some ulterior motive, which would be sure to display itself some day — by all regarded with curiosity — by some few with earnest, quiet, heartfelt admiration: and of this number was not only Emmeline Manvers, but her father; who, though weak and yielding, was not worldly, and could admire honorable independence, even while some of his friends succeeded in persuading him that in this case it nearly reached romance.

Arthur Hamilton was a star creating a sensation; it signified little to Eleanor Manvers why or wherefore, but she fully resolved to conquer him and chain him, as she had already done innumerable others, victim to her charms. His very reserve deepened her ardent longing, and the difficulty only strengthened her resolution, but she tried in vain; for the first time she was completely and entirely foiled, and she disliked him accordingly — a dislike increasing to actual abhorrence — when the truth at length forced itself upon her, that he admired, conversed with, evidently sought the society of her sister, whom she chose to charge with deceit and underhand dealing, with all the violence of angry passion and mortified defeat.

Emmeline bore the storm calmly, for her conscience perfectly acquitted her. She was not indeed indifferent to Arthur Hamilton, but she had tried hard to prevent the ascendency of affection, for she had heard that he still mourned the loss of a beloved one to whom he had been for many years engaged. And deep was her thankful joy, and unexpected indeed the intensity of her happiness, when six months after their first introduction he related to her the heavy trial of his early life, and concluded by asking her if she could indeed accept a heart which had so loved another, but which was now entirely her own, and happier than he had once believed it ever could be. The very frankness of his avowal increased the feelings of reverence and regard he had already inspired, and to the great delight, and no little pride of Lord Delmont, his elder daughter, who had been by Lady Lascelles' coterie so overlooked and neglected, who had been by many for years considered a mere foil to the beauty and talent of her younger sister, was united before she was twenty, to a man who — however his high principles might have excited laughter as high-flown romance, his unbending integrity and dislike of the pleasures and amusements, but too aften the sole pursuit of the wealthy, exposed him to the charge of severity and eccentricity — was yet sought, and his connection deemed a most desirable *partie* by all and every family who had marriageable daughters.

CHAPTER IV.

RESTROSPECTIVE. — EFFECTS OF COQUETRY. — OBEDIENCE AND DISOBEDIENCE.

ELEANOR'S unfounded dislike toward Arthur Hamilton did not decrease when he became her brother-in-law; she chose to believe that he had injured her by being the only one who had remained proof against all the fascinations she had thrown in his way. Even in her childhood, if any one chanced to notice Emmeline more than herself, it was considered a mortal offence, and the person who had so offended was scarcely spoken to again. Therefore that Emmeline should be married before herself, and to the man she intended to captivate, but *not to love*, or wed, was an offence visited upon her sister by the withdrawal of her speech for six months, and on Mr. Hamilton by an insulting haughtiness of demeanor toward him, at which he only smiled; and, to her extreme annoyance, she found that even as she had failed to fascinate, she equally failed to offend. He *would* speak to her, *would* treat her with courtesy, and the quiet familiarity of an older relative — and more, actually remonstrate with her conduct whenever he thought it wrong. It was the recollection of this time, yet more than actual present feeling, which had occasioned the mistaken impressions she had infused into both her children, of the extreme severity and harshness of their uncle, thoughtlessly indeed, for the present was always all to her, and if she did think that they might one day be under his charge, she little imagined the unhappiness and mischief which their supposition of his unbending sternness might engender.

To Emmeline, the change in her young life was so marvellous, so complete — care, anxiety, loneliness, that sinking of the whole frame and heart, from the absence of appreciation and social kindness, had so departed, leaving in their stead such an intensity of quiet domestic happiness, that it was long before her full heart could believe it reality, and rest secure. She had always longed for one to reverence, to cling to, and her husband gave her room for both. As his betrothed, even before their marriage, she had been introduced to very different society to that of the marchioness; she beheld him reverenced, loved, appealed to by the wisest and the best men, often older than himself. That this man should so love, cherish, and actually reverence her — no wonder that under the magic of such feelings her character matured, displaying such engaging and unsuspected qualities, that even her husband often looked at her with astonishment, playfully asking her if she could be the same calm, almost too quiet, and seemingly too cold Emmeline Manvers whom he had first seen. Her very talents, which had seemed worthless, compared to her sister's, were called forth by her husband. She found that her voice and her touch on either piano or harp, could give him exquisite pleasure, and this once discovered, she made such improvement as almost to surprise herself. She found the sketches taken from the various lovely spots in the vicinity of their noble seat, and in which Devonshire abounds, delighted him, and when Eleanor did visit Oakwood, she was astounded at the various beautiful drawings, which evinced the employment of that leisure which she had declared must be even to the quiet Emmeline a horrid bore.

To Lord Delmont the change in his daughter was much more astonishing than to her husband. He was very often at Oakwood, (particularly when a little grandson was added to the happy party,) for his home under Eleanor's extravagant and heedless management had lost all the comfort that Emmeline had bestowed. He had begun, too, to discover that his darling, his still favorite Eleanor, was not faultless. Emmeline's generous assistance and determination to spare her father all discomfort, had concealed Eleanor's personal extravagance from him; but after her marriage, as Eleanor's fashionable amusements increased, so did the quantity and amount of her bills, which, as the young lady did not seem inclined to settle them, were sent to her father. Lord Delmont was painfully startled, and with his usual want of judgment spoke to Eleanor at the very moment that he felt most angry; unaccustomed to reproof from him, she retorted with equal passion, and a violent altercation ensued, which ended in Eleanor ordering the carriage, and driving to Lady Lascelles, declaring she could not think of returning home, till her father had sufficiently recovered his senses for her to do so in safety.

The interference of Emmeline at length succeeded in restoring peace, but Lord Delmont's eyes had been rudely opened, and, as is unhappily too often the case with those weak characters where over-indulgence of childhood has occasioned those annoyances of ungoverned youth, he became irritable and sometimes even harsh with Eleanor, which conduct threw her still more with Lady Lascelles. As to joining society with Mr. and Mrs. Hamilton, when they were in London, Eleanor would not hear of it. But to her sister's great joy, and some surprise, she accepted an invitation to Oakwood a short time after little Percy's birth; and, still more surprising, condescended to make herself agreeable. The London season had tired her, and she thought she might just as well be dull on the banks of the Dart in August, and September, as in some stupid watering-place. Mr. Hamilton, despite her dislike, which she cared not to avow, she found could be at least very entertaining; her father was more like his former self, her sister far more delightful and lovely than she ever thought she could be, and her nephew certainly a pretty little plague. Then Mr. Hamilton had a beautiful horse entirely for her use, and she rode exceedingly well, and was greatly admired. She was seized with an exploring mania, and dragged Emmeline to every old ruin and dark wood within ten miles of Oakwood. Altogether the impression she left behind her, after a two months' visit, was such as to ease Mrs. Hamilton's great anxiety, more especially as it appeared, from certain private conversations, that her affections were for the first time really engaged, and Emmeline had always fondly hoped that when that should be the case, Eleanor would become a very different person. Alas! penetrative as she was, she had not yet learned her sister's character; simply because utter heartlessness in any woman she could not comprehend.

Her visit to her father in London, in the winter, removed all their rising hopes, and caused such increased and intense anxiety, as so to injure her already delicate health that her husband bore her back to Oakwood a full month before they had originally intended. Whether or not Eleanor loved Lord Fitzclair, it was impossible to determine; but that he devotedly, passionately loved her, was only too evident, not only to the world, but to herself; and this once confirmed, she left no method untried to torment, and so, as she declared, to try if his affections were worth having. He was half an Italian, and had inherited all the strong, fierce passions of that country, without one atom of self-control. Mr. Hamilton knew him well, far better than he knew himself, and conjured him to withdraw from the society of one who could never make him happy, and whose capricious conduct was so likely to render him desperate and miserable; he reasoned, entreated in vain. "She only wants to try the strength of my love," was his sole reply; "and were she to torment health and life away, it will never change—she will be mine yet."

And to the astonishment of Mr. and Mrs. Hamilton, two months afterward he proposed in form, and actually was accepted, with the sole condition that their engagement should be kept secret till it should please Eleanor to name the wedding day, which could not be at least for six or eight months.

This engagement might have eased anxiety, but the condition increased it, especially, as instead of coming to Oakwood as Emmeline had asked and hoped, the latter part of the summer and autumn was to be spent in Cheltenham with a very gay party, in which Eleanor was still of course the star. Mrs. Hamilton entered the nursery one morning earlier than usual, for her infant had not been well the night before, and she had already experienced the care as well as the joy of a mother. Her babe was better, and as he lay smilingly and happily in her lap, and watched the eager movements of his brother, she was only sensible of pleasure. The nurse had arranged the chairs in a long line, that Master Percy might, with their help, walk the whole length of the large and airy room. The feat mightily pleased the little gentleman, who, having acquired the venerable age of fifteen months, liked better to feel his feet than crawl on the floor, or be carried about on any limbs but his own. Every two or three paces he stood nearly alone, and burst into a loud merry laugh, which was always echoed by a crow of joy from his little brother.

"Take care, Percy, love, don't fall and frighten mamma," said his young mother, who was watching him with such pleasure as to send for his father to share it. When her son, to prove how well he obeyed her commands to take care, stood for a second without any support, and then ran quite alone across the room, and with a yet louder laugh hid his rosy face in her lap. Mrs. Hamilton fondly kissed the little nestling head, and at that moment her husband entered the room. 'Dearest Arthur," she eagerly exclaimed, "I was actually foolish enough to send for you. Herbert seems quite well; I was, it seems, needlessly alarmed, and Percy has this moment—" She stopped in sudden terror, for there was an ex pression on her husband's countenance of such unusual agitation, that though he tried to smile when he heard her words, she could not conquer her alarm, more than to say, in a caressing voice to her little boy—

"Will not Percy run to papa, and ask him why he looks so sad?"

The child looked up in her face, and then, as his father held out his arms to him, let go his mother's dress, and obeyed her. Mr. Hamilton caught him to his heart, held him for above a minute, kissed him fondly, and left the nursery without uttering a single word.

"Let me take Master Herbert, ma'am," said the head nurse respectfully, for she saw that her mistress's unexpressed alarm had nearly overpowered her; and in a few minutes Emmeline was with her husband, whose agitation was so excessive, that even his wife's presence, for the moment, had scarcely power to calm him.

The tale was soon told. Eleanor's conduct since her engagement had been such as to excite the displeasure, not of her father alone, but actually of the marchioness; who, though a weak and worldly woman, had yet some idea of propriety. As a near relation of Lord Delmont, Eleanor's engagement with Lord Fitzclair was of course told to her, and again and again she warned her that she was going too far, and might lose her lover before she was aware of it; but Eleanor only laughed at her, and at last won her over to the belief that it was certainly better to cure Fitzclair of his jealous tendency *before* marriage than afterward. Lord Delmont's reproofs she was wont to silence, by invariably making them the signal of mortifying and annoying Lord Fitzclair still more than usual. Yet still at times she relented, and so strengthened the love she had excited, so enhanced her own fascinations, that all the agony he had endured and was still, he knew, to endure, by an incomprehensible contradiction, riveted her power and hastened his own doom. Weak in all things but his love, he could not demand as his actual right the publication of their engagement. Eleanor vowed if he did till she permitted him, she would have nothing more to say to him. She knew, though she did not say it, that once made known, a chain would be thrown round her actions, which she did not choose to endure. And father, lover, and friend, all feeling she was wrong, and the first and last repeatedly telling her so, had yet neither of them the resolution to contend with her, and compel the proper course.

A month of their visit to Cheltenham so passed, when Eleanor's attention was arrested by a new actor on the scene. She had begun to tire of her present satellites, and a young military captain, whose furlough from India had just expired, and whose pale face, somewhat melancholy expression, and very elegant figure, presented a new object for conquest impossible to be resisted; and it was unhappily only too easily achieved. She made no secret of her admiration, speaking of him in such terms to her intended husband as to excite anew every jealous feeling. It was easy for Captain Fortescue to discover Fitzclair was his rival; but believing himself decidedly the object of Eleanor's preference, he increased his attentions, little imagining the storm he was exciting, the more fearful from its determined suppression. Lord Delmont interfered several times, not only by reproaches to Eleanor, but by determined coldness to her new suitor. Finding at length that her encouragement actually neared a criminal extent, and after a desperately stormy interview, he solemnly declared that if she did not dismiss Captain Fortescue at once, he would shame her in the face of the whole world, by proclaiming her engagement with the young marquis. Eleanor in equal anger declared that if he threatened, so too could she; and if he tormented her any more she would prevent all publication of her engagement by herself snapping it asunder, and pledging her faith to Captain Fortescue. This was too much even for Lord Delmont. Declaring if she did so, a father's heaviest malediction should fall on her head, he hastily left her; and Eleanor very composedly went to prepare for an excursion on horseback with Fortescue, Fitzclair, and others.

When Lord Delmont's passions were once roused, even his ordinarily slender judgment entirely forsook him, and he did that which at another time, knowing Fitzclair as he did, he would have shrunk from. He sought him, while still exasperated, upbraided him for his weakness in permitting Eleanor's unprincipled conduct, and warned him that, if he did not adopt some strong measures to prevent it, he would certainly lose her entirely.

The young man heard him without reply; but his face grew livid, and he clenched his hand till the blood started from the nails, and in this mood of concentrated passion joined the riding party. The exercise itself is, to some temperaments, unusually exciting, and the determined coldness of Eleanor to himself, and the eagerly-received devotion of Fortescue, maddened him. He demanded an interview with her on their return home struggled to speak calmly, expostulated, and, finally, reproached. Eleanor, already irritated, and, beyond all, that her lover, in general so obsequious and humble, should dare to call her to account for mere amusement, combined with the recollection of Captain Fortescue's flattering vows and willing homage, excited her to an extent of which she was herself unconscious, inasmuch as she firmly believed, whatever she might say then, a few soft words would speedily obliterate. She told him that really his jealous temperament was beyond all endurance; that he certainly must intend her to despise and abhor him; and that the contrast he presented to Captain Fortescue was such as to make her most heartily wish to put an end to their engagement, as she felt quite sure it must only end in misery for both; and, without waiting for a reply, she haughtily brushed by him, and disappeared.

Of the extent of Fitzclair's passion Eleanor had not the least idea, and this is saying a great deal, for she generally exaggerated her own power. She believed she had inflicted pain, but not as much as he deserved; and determined that she would torment him yet more at the ball that evening. But to her extreme mortification he did not appear, and there was a vague dread on her spirits as she retired for the night, which prevented any thing like rest. His absence had excited surprise in all, especially Lady Lascelles, who knew that to leave Eleanor entirely to the attentions of young Fortescue was so unprecedented as to bode no good. But the wildest conjectures were far from reality. The very next morning all Cheltenham was thrown into the most painful excitement by the incomprehensible and most extraordinary fact of the suicide of Lord Fitzclair; by what occasioned, plunged into such mystery that nothing but sudden aberration of mind was imagined, a belief justified by the very peculiar temperament and manners of the young nobleman during his sojourn with them. His will, a valuable present, with a few lines of regard to his faithful attendant, and a letter addressed to Arthur Hamilton, Esq., were the sole evidences that the awful deed had not been committed without some preparation; but as that was often the case with madness itself, it excited no remark.

The state of Eleanor's mind, when these awful tidings were communicated to her, which they were by her father, in his agitation and anger, without the least preparation, we leave our readers to imagine. Hardened, heartless, wilful as she was, she was still a woman, and a very young one, and till Captain Fortescue appeared, had loved, as far as it was in her nature, Lord Fitzclair. To believe that she had nothing to do with his miserable end was an attempt so vain and hollow, that even she shrunk from the hopeless struggle to realize it; remorse, in all its torturing, unmitigated anguish, took possession of her, but instead of leading her to penitence, and thence the hope of peace, it urged her to a course of action from which she imagined there was no withdrawing; and which must in time, by removing her from all painful associations, lessen her present misery.

For three days and nights she never quitted her own apartment, and then joined her usual circles without the smallest evidence of the internal agony which was still hers. It was very easy to displace paleness by artificial roses, and her gay smiles and joyous sallies were tempered only by a judiciously-expressed horror when the late event was discussed before her, supposed natural to one who had known him so intimately; but the hours of loneliness which followed this conduct in society were terrible indeed. By a strange contrariety of feeling, her better nature longed for Emmeline, and her artificial, which had, alas! only too forcibly become her natural self, felt as if she would leave the kingdom rather than encounter the mild, sorrowful glance of those penetrating eyes.

Lord Delmont was himself in a most pitiable condition; even minor evils had always been great to him, and the effect of this, the wish to take Eleanor away from Captain Fortescue's increased and annoying attentions, and yet the dread that doing so would connect her with Fitzclair's death, so distracted him as to render him really ill — information which instantly brought Mr. and Mrs. Hamilton to Cheltenham.

Some young wives and mothers might have felt it hard that their domestic enjoyment should so continually have been disturbed and annoyed from the faults of others; but Emmeline had been accustomed to trace every thing that created personal suffering to the highest source, and feel that it was good for her, or it would not be; a conviction that enabled her to bear with and still to love the erring one that was the visible cause of pain.

Eleanor was at a gay ball the night of her arrival, and Mrs Hamilton requested she might not be informed of it till the following day. About half an hour before her usual hour of rising after such scenes, she entered her sister's room. All around her lay the ornaments of the previous evening, looking so strange, gaudy, and faded in the darkened room, and judged by the calmer feelings of the morning. A sensation of intense depression crept over Emmeline as she gazed, increasing as she looked on the face of the sleeper, which, divested of its unnatural bloom, looked so fearfully wan and haggard. Her beautiful hair lay in tangled masses on her damp brow, and as Emmeline gently tried to remove it, Eleanor started and awoke.

"Is it already time to get up?" she said languidly, and only half unclosing her eyes; "I feel as if I had not slept at all. Am I dreaming?" she added, starting up, "or have I slept in one place, and awoke in another? Am I at Oakwood?"

"No, dearest Eleanor; will you not welcome me to Malvern House?"

The voice, the look, seemed to thrill through her; her temples were throbbing, her heart weighed down, as it always was when she first awoke, with an undefinable sense of guilt and pain; she tried to be cold, proud, reserved, but it would not do, and she suddenly flung her arms round her sister's neck, and burst into agonized tears.

It was a most unexpected greeting, and Mrs. Hamilton argued hopefully from it. Alas! the unwonted softening only lasted one brief half hour. She left her at Eleanor's entreaty while dressing, and when she returned, though the reckless girl told her with a half smile that she was ready for her lecture, for she could only have come from Oakwood to give her one; and that however severe her words might be, she could not alter her tone, that must be kind, in spite of herself. Yet Emmeline could not succeed in convincing her how wrongly, how cruelly she had acted. Eleanor would persist that she was not in the least to blame, and that poor Fitzclair's fearful end was only owing to his own violent passions; in fact, that he must have been out of his mind, and that, though it was certainly very dreadful, she had perhaps escaped a very terrible doom; but speak as she might, Emmeline was not deceived as to the agony she was actually enduring. Finding, however, that all her gentle efforts were useless, that even the perusal of Fitzclair's brief lines to her husband — which Eleanor insisted on seeing, and in which he deplored his madness in not having followed his advice, and flown from her presence, and bade him take his forgiveness to her, and say, that the means he had adopted would, he trusted, dissolve their engagement to her satisfaction — had no effect, save in causing her to turn so deadly pale, that her sister was convinced nothing but an almost supernatural effort of pride preserved her from fainting. She desisted; hoping against hope that Eleanor would yet repent and become a different being. She knew harshness would only harden, and so she tried to prevail on her father to treat her as usual, but this Lord Delmont could not do. It is strange how often we find those parents who have been over-indulgent to childhood, unusually harsh to the faults of youth. Weak characters, also, when driven to anger, are always more violent than firmer ones; and, certainly, Eleanor's continued haughtiness and coldness, as if she were the injured one, did not tend to calm him.

And his angry feelings were unfortunately but too soon aggravated by a proposal in form from Captain Fortescue for the hand of Eleanor. Without a moment's delay he despatched a decided and almost insulting refusal to the young soldier, and then sought his daughter, and vented on her the anger and vexation which overpowered him, upbraiding her not only with the death of Fitzclair, but for having dared so to encourage young Fortescue as to give him courage for his audacious proposal. To his astonishment, he was heard without any attempt at reply; but he would have been startled, could he have seen the pallid cheek, compressed lip, and clenched hand with which, when he had left her, Elearnor muttered—

"Father, if it be sin to leave you, be it on your own head. I would have wedded with your consent, had you permitted it; but now my destiny is fixed. There is no peace in England: at least let me be spared the agony of breaking another loving heart."

Nearly three weeks rolled on, and Eleanor's extraordinary submission, and even in some degree withdrawal from society, (for which Mrs. Hamilton's arrival was a good excuse,) caused her father's irritation against her almost entirely to subside. That she passed several hours each day apart from her sister, excited no surprise. Emmeline was thankful even for her change of deportment, but nothing confidential ever again passed between them. That reports were floating about, connecting the names of Miss Manvers and the late Lord Fitzclair, seemed little heeded by Eleanor, though they caused natural vexation to her family. About this time an invitation arrived for Eleanor from a lady of rank, slightly known to her father, and living ten miles from Cheltenham, in a beautiful villa, at which she expected a select party of fashionables to ruralize for a week or two. There was nothing in the note to excite the dread that weighed on Mrs. Hamilton's spirits, as Eleanor carelessly threw it to her for her perusal, but she would not express it, as Lord Delmont seemed inclined that Eleanor should accept it, knowing that the lady was much too exclusive for Captain Fortescue to join her guests, and believing that Eleanor's apparent indifference to the visit originated from that cause. Telling her he was so gratified by her having devoted so many evenings to her sister, he added, she had his full consent to go if she liked, as he could better spare her than when Emmeline returned to Oakwood. She quietly thanked him, but evinced no particular pleasure.

The day before her intended departure, the sisters were sitting together, and little Percy, who now ran firmly without any falls, was playing about the room. He had already displayed a high spirit and passionate temper, with their general accompaniment, self-will, even in trifles, that Mrs. Hamilton felt would render her task a trying one; but she was as firm as she was gentle, and faced the pain of contradicting her darling bravely: —

"Do not touch that, Percy, love," she said, as her little boy stretched out his hand toward a beautiful but fragile toy, that stood with other knickknacks on a low table. The child looked laughingly and archly toward her, and withdrew his hand, but did not move from the table.

"Come here, Percy, you have not played with these pretty things for a long time;" and she took from her work-box some gayly colored ivory balls, which had been his favorite playthings, but just at present they had lost their charm, and the young gentleman did not move.

Mrs. Hamilton knelt down by him, and said quietly:

"My Percy will not disobey mamma, will he?"

"Me want that;" he replied, in the pretty coaxing tone of infancy; and he twined his little round arms caressingly round her neck.

Mrs. Hamilton felt very much tempted to indulge him, but she resisted it.

"But that is not a fit plaything for you, love; besides, it is not mine, and we must not touch what is not ours. Come and see if we cannot find something just as pretty, that you may have."

And after some minutes' merry play in her lap his mother hoped he had forgotten it; but the little gentleman was not, he thought, to be so governed. The forbidden plaything was quietly grasped, and he seated himself on the ground, in silent but triumphant glee.

Surprised at his sudden silence, Mrs. Hamilton looked toward him. It was his first act of decided disobedience, and she knew she must not waver. Young as he was, he had already learned to know when she was displeased, and when she desired him very gravely to give her the toy, he passionately threw it down, and burst into a violent fit of crying. His nurse took him struggling from the room, and Mrs. Hamilton quietly resumed her work; but there was such an expression of pain in her countenance, that Eleanor exclaimed,

"Emmeline! I have been watching you for the last half hour, and I cannot comprehend you. Do explain yourself."

"I will if I can;" and Mrs. Hamilton looked up, and smiled.

"Why would you not let that poor little Percy have that toy?"

"Because it would have been encouraging his touching or taking every thing he sees, whether proper for him or not."

"But he could not understand that."

"Not now, perhaps; but I wish him to know that when I speak, he must obey me. It is, I think, a mistaken doctrine, that we ought to give children a *reason* for all we desire them to do. Obedience can then never be prompt, as it ought to be. And, in fact, if we wait until they are old enough to understand the reasons for a command, the task will be much more difficult, from the ascendency which wilfulness may already have obtained."

"But then why were you so cruel as to send the poor child up-stairs? Was it not enough to take the toy from him?"

"Not quite; for him to remember that he must not touch it again."

"And do you really think he will not?"

"I can only hope so, Eleanor; but I must not be disheartened if he do. He is an infant still, and I cannot expect him to learn such a difficult lesson as obedience in one, two, or six lessons."

"And will he love you as much as if you had given it to him?"

"Not at the moment, perhaps, but when he is older he will love me more. And it is that hope which reconciles me to the pain which refusing to indulge him costs me now."

"And voluntarily you will bear the pain which had almost brought tears into the eyes of the severe and stoical Mrs. Hamilton!" exclaimed Eleanor.

"It was a foolish weakness, my dear Eleanor, for which my husband would have chidden me; but there must be pain to a mother if called upon to exert authority, when inclination so strongly points to indulgence."

"Well, if ever I have any thing to do with children, I certainly shall not be half as particular as you are, Emmeline. I really cannot imagine what harm gratifying myself and Percy could possibly have done."

"If ever you have children, my dear Eleanor, may you have strength of mind and self-control sufficient to forget self, and refuse the gratification of the present moment for the welfare of future years!"

Mrs. Hamilton spoke impressively, and something, either in her words or tone, caused the blood to rush into Eleanor's cheeks, and she hastily walked to the window; then, as abruptly returning, she kissed her sister, a very rare token of affection, and declaring she was much too good for her to understand, quitted the room.

The following day, dressed for her visit, and only waiting for the carriage, Eleanor, accompanied by Mrs. Hamilton and her little boys, entered the same apartment. Though not in general fond of nursing, Eleanor had taken Herbert in her arms, and was playing with him with unusual fondness; Percy, who had not seen the tempting plaything since his banishment the preceding day, the moment his eye caught it, to the astonishment of Eleanor, ran up to his mother, and lisping, "Me no touch that — Percy good boy now," held up his little face lovingly to hers, and with a very pardonable feeling of delight, Mrs. Hamilton lifted him up and covered him with kisses. The feelings which thrilled through Eleanor at that moment she might indeed have found it difficult to explain, but she was so conscious of a change of countenance as to hide her face on Herbert's head. It might have been obedience and disobedience brought so suddenly and strangely in contrast — and who were the actors? an infant and herself. For a minute she recovered, stricken with sudden and agonized remorse; but it was too late, she had gone too far, and the announcement of the carriage was a relief from that bitter moment of painful indecision. Placing her baby nephew in his nurse's arms, she said, caressingly, "Will not Percy give Lina some of those kisses as well as mamma?" The child threw one little arm round her neck, and the other round that of his mother, and then burst into a merry laugh at thus seeing himself as it were a link between them. Never had it seemed to Eleanor that she had loved and admired her sister as she did at that moment; all the neglect, unkindness, she had shown her, all the sarcasm and satire, of which, either before or behind her, she had so often made her the victim, combined with an intense, but how painfully vain longing to have resembled her in the remotest degree, rather than be the character which had never before appeared so degraded, so hateful — almost overpowered her — a convulsive sob escaped her as she clasped Emmeline in a close embrace, and almost choked her hurried good-by! Lord Delmont and Mr. Hamilton were in the hall, and the former was surprised and delighted at the warmth with which his usually reckless child returned his kiss and farewell; the carriage drove off leaving unusual hope and cheerfulness behind it. Alas! in one short fortnight every rising hope was blighted, Emmeline's momentary dread fulfilled, and Lord Delmont experiencing, in all its agony,

> "How sharper than a serpent's tooth it is,
> To have a thankless child!"

CHAPTER V.

A HEART AND HOME IN ENGLAND. — A HEART AND HOME IN INDIA.

From the moment Arthur Hamilton returned to Cheltenham with the painful intelligence that he had arrived at Leith only in time to witness the departure of the beautiful vessel which contained Captain Fortescue and the exquisitely lovely bride who had, it seemed, turned the heads of all the usually quiet Scotsmen who had seen her, Lord Delmont gradually sunk. The agony of losing her forever — for so he regarded her departure for, and residence in India for an indeterminate time — conquered every other feeling. Her conduct had caused emotions of anguish far too deep for the relieving sensation of anger. The name of the lady from whose house and by whose connivance she had eloped, he was never heard to breathe; but, if ever casually mentioned before him, every feature would become convulsed, and he would instantly leave the room. Often and often he accused his own harshness as the cause of driving her from him, and then came, with overwhelming bitterness, the thought that if he had lately been harsh, surely the recollection of all the indulgent fondness he had shown demanded some gratitude in return. If she had but written, had but expressed one wish for his continued love, one regret for his present pain! But no letter came, and the contending but all-depressing emotions so completely under mined a constitution never very strong, and already worn by care, that when another and still heavier trial came, he sunk at once beneath it.

Though Eleanor had been his favorite, his feelings of pride and hope had greatly centred in his son, whose career, in five years' active service on board a man-of-war had been such as to raise him already to a lieutenancy, and excite every gratifying emotion, not only in his immediate family, but in a large circle of admiring friends. Mrs. Hamilton's love for her brother had naturally increased, strong as it always had been, even in childhood — and the visits which Charles had been enabled to make to Oakwood, brief in duration as they were compelled to be, had always been fraught with heartfelt, joyous happiness, not only to herself but to her husband. The pain and anxiety attendant on Eleanor's elopement, and the dread of its effects on Lord Delmont, had for two or three months been the sole subject of thought; but at length, and, like a fearful flash bringing a new sorrow to light, it pressed upon them that it was long after the period that intelligence of Charles ought to have been received. Still hoping against hope, not only the Delmont family, but all who had friends and relatives on board the Leander, imagined that she might have drifted from her course, or been engaged on some secret and distant expedition, but that intelligence concerning her would and must soon come. Alas! after months of agonizing suspense, information was received that several planks and masts, bearing evidence of fire as well as water, and some sea-chests, bearing names, only too soon recognized as those of some of the Leander's crew, had been cast off the coast of Barbary, and there could be no more doubt that death or slavery — that fearful slavery which the bombardment of Algiers had so displayed to European eyes — was the portion of all those beloved ones, for whom so many aching hearts and eyes had watched and wept in vain. It was a trial so terrible that Mrs. Hamilton felt at first as if even submission had departed from her; and she could almost have rebelled in spirit against the inscrutable decree, that had consigned one so free from vice and evil, so full of happiness and worth, to a doom so terrible. Much as she had loved and reverenced her husband before, she seemed never to have felt his worth and tenderness till then. It was his sympathy, his strength, that recalled her to a sense of her duty, and gave her power to endure, by a realization once more of that submissiveness to a Father's will, which had never before failed her. But time, though it softened the first anguish, had no power over the memories of this brother, not even when the increasing cares and joys of maternity so fully engrossed her, that the present and the future of her children appeared to have banished all of her own past.

Lord Delmont did not survive the mournful tidings of the certain wreck of the Leander above two months; but his released spirit did not meet that of his son. Charles was not dead. He toiled as a slave long years in living death before there was even a partial amelioration of his sufferings. But no tidings of him ever came; a young child of three years old, a distant branch of the Manvers family, became Lord Delmont.

Years rolled on, and Mrs. Hamilton's lot was so full of tranquil happiness, so fraught with innumerable daily joys of a loving wife and devoted mother, that her prayer was ever rising for guidance and gratitude, that prosperity might not unfit her for the dark days of trial and adversity, when they should come. That she had cares as well as joys could not be otherwise, when so intensely anxious to bring up her children with more regard to their spiritual and moral welfare than even the cultivation of their intellect. She was one of those who thought still more of the training of the heart than of the mind, believing that were the first properly awakened, the latter would need little incitement to exertion. Two girls had been the sole addition to her family.

One other wish, and one of many years' standing, Mrs. Hamilton had it in her power to fulfil. From childhood she had been accustomed to think of Lucy Harcourt as one, to whom it might one day be in her power to return the heavy debt of gratitude she owed her mother; she had been accustomed to correspond with her from very early years; Mrs. Harcourt delighting in creating a mutual interest between her pupil and the child from whom circumstances had so sadly separated her. When therefore an event of a very painful nature to Miss Harcourt's individual feelings compelled her — as the only hope of regaining peace, and strengthening her for the arduous duty of instruction, which she knew, as a single woman, was her sole source of independent subsistence — she had no scruple in accepting that friendship which Mrs. Hamilton had so warmly proffered. A very few days of personal intercourse sufficed for mutual conviction, that correspondence had not deceived in the favorable impressions of either. Miss Harcourt found, indeed, the friend her aching spirit needed; and Mrs. Hamilton, long before the months of repose which she had insisted should forestall the commencement of exertion were over, rejoiced in the conviction that the daughter of her beloved and regretted friend was indeed well fitted for that position in her family — her helper in the moral and intellectual training of her daughters — which her vivid fancy had often pictured as so filled. They were indeed but infants when Miss Harcourt arrived; but Mr. and Mrs. Hamilton found means to overrule the honorable scruples which, on the part of Lucy, seemed at first against their plan, and in her gradually returning health and peace, Mrs. Hamilton not only rejoiced, but felt gratefully thankful that the wish of so many years' standing, and which had seemed so little likely to be fulfilled, was absolutely accomplished, and she could prove how deeply she had loved and mourned her truly maternal friend. It is astonishing how often, if an earnest, heartfelt desire for the gratification of some good feeling or for the performance of some good deed be steadily and unvaryingly held before us, without any regard to its apparent impossibility, its accomplishment is at length obtained. It is supposed to be only done so in books, but this is a mistaken supposition, arising from the simple fact of individuals so often forgetting their own past, and failing steadily to pursue one object, regardless of the lapse of years. If they looked into themselves more often and more carefully, if they sought consistency in desire and pursuit, they would often be startled at their connection, and that it is not so useless to *wish* and *seek*, when both are of such a nature as can be based on and strengthened by prayer, as it may seem. Human life presents as many startling connections and contingencies as romance — only as the *actors* not the *observers* of this world's busy scene, we cannot trace them as we do in books.

The thought of Eleanor was the only dark shade in Mrs. Hamilton's life. She had written to her often, but communication with India was not then what it is now, and her letters might not have reached their destination; especially as being in active service, Captain Fortescue was himself constantly changing his quarters. Whatever the cause (for Eleanor's letters, Mrs. Hamilton thought, might also have miscarried,) she heard nothing of her till the hurried epistle commenced by her sister, and finished by Mr. Myrvin, brought the startling intelligence that she was a widow and dying, unable to reach Oakwood, where she had hoped at least to have sufficient strength to bring her children, and implore for them protection and love, and conjuring Mrs. Hamilton to come to her without delay. The letter, imperfectly directed, had been days on its journey and it was with the most melancholy forebodings Mr. and Mrs. Hamilton had started for Llangwillan.

But though it was not till many years after Edward and Ellen Fortescue became inmates of her family that Mrs. Hamilton became acquainted with all the particulars of their childhood, it is necessary that our readers should be rather more enlightened; otherwise the character of Ellen may be to them as unnatural and as incomprehensible as it was to her aunt.

That Eleanor could realize true happiness in a marriage entered into only because she could not bear the torture of her own thoughts, and her constant dread of the world's contumely, was not likely. At first, indeed, it was a very delightful thing to find herself the object not only of devotion to her husband (whom, could she entirely have forgotten Fitzclair, she might have really loved,) but a still more brilliant star in India than she had even been in England. Though Captain Fortescue was often engaged in marches and countermarches, where Eleanor sometimes, though very rarely, accompanied him, still there were intervals of rest for him in the larger cities, where his wife ever shone preëminent. For the first three or four years, the pride he felt in seeing her so universally admired, in the greater attention he received for her sake, compensated for, or concealed the qualities, which, as a soldier's wife, he had fondly believed she would possess. But as his health, always delicate, became more and more undermined, and compelled him to relinquish society, at least in a great measure, and to look for the quiet pleasures of domestic life, he found, and bitter was that first awakening, that his wishes, his comfort, were of no importance. She could not resign the pleasures of society — of still being enabled to pursue the dangerous amusement of her girlhood (though so guardedly that not a rumor against her ever found breath,) for the dulness of her home. Yet still he loved her; and when Eleanor, with all the fascinating playfulness of her former self, would caress and try to persuade him to go out with her, and not sit moping at home, and that if he would, she would behave just as he liked, and if he did not care to see her surrounded, as she knew she was, by red coats, she would dismiss them all, and devote herself to him — but indeed she could not stay at home — he would feel that it would be cruel indeed to chain such a being to his side, and sometimes make the exertion (for which he was little fitted) to accompany her; at others, with kind words and indulgent love, permit her to follow her own wishes, and remain alone. But little did he think the real reason that Eleanor could not rest in quiet at home. The recollection of Lord Fitzclair was at such times so fearfully vivid, that the very agony she had endured when first told of his fearful end would return in all its intensity; the thought: Had her father really cursed her for her disobedience, and was it that forever hovering round her, preventing any thing like lasting happiness! And yet, by a strange contradiction, while the idea of her father's curse shook her whole frame at times with convulsive sobs, pride, that most fatal ingredient of her character, utterly prevented all attempt on her part to communicate with her relations. She said, as they had made no effort to conciliate, she would not; and yet the longing for Emmeline sometimes became actually painful.

Eleanor was never intended for the heartless, reckless being she had tried to become. It was a constant and most terrible struggle between the good and evil parts of her nature, and though the evil triumphed — in the determination that nothing should change her course of action, nothing compel her to acknowledge she had ever been in the wrong, and was really not the perfect creature which flattery was ever ready to pour into her ear — the good had yet so much power as to make her miserable, by the conviction, that she was not what she might have been — that she never could be happy — that every pleasure was hollow, every amusement vain. Again and again the memories of Emmeline's gentle, sustaining, ever-active piety would come before her, as if beseeching her to seek the only fount of peace; but so terrible was the self-reproach, the anguish which the thought called up, that she always turned from it with a shudder, resolved that religion was never meant for such as herself, and that its restrictions should never enter her mind, or its dictates pass her lips.

With the awakening intelligence of her son, however, there seemed one pleasure not wholly hollow — one enjoyment without the shadow of alloy; and she grasped it with an avidity and a constancy, that in a character generally so wavering and inconsistent was almost incredible. That her son was from his earliest infancy the image of herself, might have added strength to the feeling; but the intense love, almost idolatry, she felt toward him, increasing with his growth, did much toward banishing the unpleasant feelings of remorse and home-sickness. She devoted herself to her boy, not judiciously indeed, for she was not one to practise self-denial in education; and as Edward's disposition was not one to cause her annoyance, even from over-indulgence, there was not even the check of his ill temper or rudeness toward herself, to whisper the fearful evil she was engendering.

What was the emotion which had so riveted her to her son, it might have been difficult to ascertain; it could scarcely have been the mere instinct of maternity, for then it would have extended to her daughter; but as complete as was her indulgence to Edward, so was her neglect of Ellen.

Colonel Fortescue (for he had gradually attained that rank) had borne, without complaint, neglect of himself; nay, it had not had power in the least degree to diminish his love, though it might have awakened him to the consciousness that his wife was indeed not perfect. Her devotion to Edward, even undertaking the toilsome task of instruction, had delighted him; for, at first, having been much from home, he was not conscious of the lonely fate of his little girl; but when the truth became evident, that she was an object almost of dislike — that she was left entirely to the tender mercies of a hireling, and Eleanor only alluded to her, to contrast her peevishness and stupidity with Edward's happiness and intellect, all the father was roused within him, and, for the first time, he felt and expressed serious displeasure. He acknowledged that his son might, indeed, be superior in beauty and talent, but he would not allow that Ellen's affections were less warm, or her temper less capable of guidance. To him, and to all who had in the least attended to childhood, Ellen's face, even from infancy, expressed not ill-temper, but suffering. Continually ill, for she inherited her father's constitution, the poor little infant was constantly crying or fretful; which Eleanor, never having known what illness was, attributed at once to a naturally evil temper which annoyed her. The nurse, as ignorant as she was obsequious, adopted the same opinion; and, before she was even three years old, harshness, both by nurse and mother, had been constantly used, to make Ellen as good a child as her brother.

In vain did the Colonel, when he became aware of this treatment, remonstrate that it was the illness of the poor child — neither obstinacy nor ill-temper: his wife would not understand him, and at length he sternly and peremptorily declared, that as she had her will with Edward, he would have his with Ellen, and that no chastisement should be inflicted. If she did wrong, he was to be told of it, and if necessary he would reprove her, but he would allow no other interference. Mrs. Fortescue made not the least objection, believing that as her husband had thus taken her in charge, she was exonerated from all blame if she left her entirely to him.

Only too quickly did the poor child discover that the lovely being whom she called mother, and whom she loved so fondly, had no love, no caress for her. Repeated punishment, though it had only extended to her fifth year, had completely crushed the gentle, tender spirit, that had required such judicious nursing; and combined with physical suffering, instead of deadening the feelings, as in some dispositions it would have done, had rendered them morbidly acute — an effect which constant loneliness naturally deepened. Her father's love and caresses had caused her to cling to him so passionately, that every word he said, every request he made her, was treasured and thought upon, when he was away from her, with a tenacity many would have fancied unnatural in a child. He taught her, though his heart often bled as he did so (for what claim had her mother upon the feelings he sought to inculcate,) to love, honor, and obey her mother in all things — that if she did so, she would be as happy as Edward in time; and Ellen, though she did not understand him, obeyed. But Colonel Fortescue little imagined the evil which was accruing from these very natural lessons.

Ellen learned to believe that, as her mother never noticed her, except in accents of anger or irritation, it must be her own fault. She longed to be beautiful and buoyant as Edward; and that she was neither, marked her in her own young mind as so inferior, it was no wonder her mother could not caress or love her. Had Edward presumed on his favoritism, and been unkind or neglectful, she might, perhaps, have envied more than she loved him; but his disposition was naturally so noble, so open-hearted, so generous, that he always treated her with affection, and would share with her his playthings and sweets, even while he could not but believe her in all things his inferior; and that as such, of course, her wishes could never cross with his. Poor child, she scarcely knew what it was to wish, except that she might cling to her mother as she did to her father, and that she could but be good and beautiful enough to win her love! The lesson of concealment of every feeling is but too easily and too early learned. Tears do not flow even from childhood, when always rudely checked, and angrily reproved. Affection cannot display itself unless called forth; and so the very outward seeming of children is more in a parent's hand than mere superficial observers may believe: and Mrs. Fortescue blamed and disliked the cold inanimate exterior which she had never tried to warm.

Ellen's extreme difficulty in acquiring knowledge, compared with Edward's extraordinary quickness, only confirmed her painful conviction of her great inferiority, the impossibility of her ever winning love — and the consequent increased intensity of her affection for her father and brother, who loved her notwithstanding. That the child herself could not have defined these sensations is true; but that they had existence, even before she was nine years old, and that they influenced many years of her after-life, causing error and suffering, and rendering Mrs. Hamilton's task one of pain and difficulty, before these mistaken influences could be eradicated, is equally so. The power over early years is so immense, its responsibility so extensive, its neglect or abuse may indeed make the earnest thinker tremble; less, perhaps, for the actual amount of general evil, for that circumstances in after life are sometimes graciously permitted to avert, but for individual suffering and individual joy — and especially is this the case in the training of girls. More enduring in their very fragility than boys, they may be compared to those precious metals which fire and water and pressure have no power to break, but simply to draw out to a thinner and thinner thread, dwindling more and more, but to its last spider-woven fineness capable of tenuity and vitality. While boys, like men, are often crushed at once — the frame of the one and the spirit of the other equally unable to endure.

CHAPTER VI.

DOMESTIC DISCORD AND ITS END.

The displeasure of her husband, his reproaches for her conduct to Ellen, by causing some degree of annoyance, increased Mrs. Fortescue's feelings of dislike toward the object who had caused it, and this was soon afterward heightened by self-reproach.

A malignant fever broke out in the British settlement where Colonel Fortescue was stationed; his wife and children were with him, and, dreadfully alarmed, Eleanor determined to remove with her children to some less unhealthy spot. The Colonel willingly consented; but before their hasty preparations were concluded Ellen sickened. Alarm for Edward, however, so engrossed the mother, that she appeared incapable of any other thought. In vain Colonel Fortescue urged that his son would be safe with the friends who had promised to take charge of him, and who were on the point of leaving the city; that there were none on whom he could depend so to tend the little sufferer as not to require a guiding head, and she knew how impossible it was for him to be with his child as his heart prompted. He urged, entreated, commanded in vain, Mrs. Fortescue was inexorable. She declared that the idea of her son being away from her at such a time would drive her mad; and as for duty, one child demanded her care as much as another; that her husband might not care about thus exposing her to infection, but she really thought, for Edward's sake, it was her duty to take care of herself. It might be nothing to the Colonel or Ellen whether she lived or died, but to Edward it was a great deal; and so as she must choose between them, she would go with him who loved her best, and who would be miserable without her. The haughty, angry tone with which she spoke, the unjust taunt, roused every indignant feeling, and Colonel Fortescue said more in that moment of irritation than he could have believed possible. But it only awakened the cold, sustaining pride which Eleanor always called to her aid when conscience smote her, and she departed with her son, hardening every better feeling, and rousing anger against her husband and child to conquer the suffering of self-reproach. But when many miles from the city of death, and there were no fears for Edward, anxiety and wretchedness so assailed her, that pride itself gave way. To communicate with the infected city was difficult, and very infrequent, and again and again did she wish that she had remained.

During the continuance of Ellen's illness her father's anguish was indeed terrible. Every leisure moment he spent by her side, moistening her parched lips, bathing her burning forehead, and listening to the plaintive accents of delirium with an acuteness of suffering, that injured his own health more than he had the least idea of. The attendants were really both kind and skilful, but the Colonel fancied, when he was not with her, she was neglected, and in still greater suffering; and the struggle between his duties and his child was almost more than he could bear. He had never been a religious man — never known what it was to pray, except in the public services of his regiment: but now prayer, earnest, heartfelt, poured from him; and the thankfulness to God, which so overpowered him when she was pronounced out of danger, as to compel him to weep like a child, planted a sense of a Father's infinite love and infinite compassion within him, which was his sole sustainer the short remainder of his life.

Eleanor's letters, few as they were, had in some degree soft ened his anger toward her; but as he beheld the ravages of disease on his poor child's face and form, rendering her still less attractive than she had been, and perceived that bodily weakness had extended to her mind, and often and often forced tears from her eyes and momentary complainings, he trembled lest Eleanor should find still more to dislike and reprove; and often his heart bled as Ellen would ask with tears, for her dear mamma, adding, plaintively, "Mamma never kisses me or loves me as she does Edward; but I like to be near her, and look at her dear beautiful face, and wish I was good and pretty enough for her to love me. Why does she never come to me? — and why may I not go to her?"

And what could the Colonel reply, except that her mother feared Edward would take the infection, and therefore she was obliged to go with him to some place of safety? And his child was satisfied, repeating so fondly her delight that her dear, dear Edward had been saved from being as ill as she was, that her father clasped her closer and closer to his heart, feeling the intrinsic beauty of a disposition that, instead of repining that she was left alone to suffer, could rejoice that her brother had been spared.

Colonel Fortescue obtained a few weeks' leave, that he might take his child to the seaside as recommended, ere she joined her mother. And alone with him, gradually regaining a moderate degree of strength, Ellen was very happy; but such bright intervals were indeed few and far between. There was no change in her mother's conduct toward her, when reunited. Her heart had indeed risen to her lips as she again beheld the child so nearly lost; and had she followed impulse, she would have clasped her in her arms and wept over her, but that would have seemed tacitly to acknowledge that she had been wrong, and had suffered from it; and so she refrained, causing suffering to herself, anguish to her child, and pain to her husband, all from that fell demon, pride. She only chose to remember that it was Ellen who had been the cause of her husband's anger — Ellen, the constant subject of contention between them — Ellen, always causing the pang of self-reproach: and so how was it possible that she could love her?

About a year after Ellen's dangerous illness, when she was nearly ten, and Edward just eleven, Colonel Fortescue was ordered to take command of some troops to be stationed at a fort, whose vicinity to some hostile natives rendered it rather a post of danger. The wives and children of the officers were permitted to accompany them, if they wished it, and, except in the

Colonel's own family, there had been no hesitation in their choice. The Colonel was strangely and painfully depressed as with some vague dread, and all his affection for his wife had returned with such force as to make him shrink in unusual suffering from the idea of leaving her; and conquering reluctance, for he felt as if she would not accede, he implored her to accompany him, confessing he felt ill and unhappy, and shrank from a separation. His wife looked at him with astonishment; he had never asked nor thought of such a thing before, she said, in their many brief partings, and she really could not understand him. The place was decidedly unhealthy, and Edward must not be exposed to its malaria; besides which, she had promised him to go to a juvenile ball, which was given by an English family of rank, in a fortnight's time, and she could not possible disappoint him; and why her husband should wish for her in such a place she could not imagine, but she knew she should die of terror before she had been there a week. Not a word did the Colonel utter in reply, but he felt as if an ice-bolt had struck his heart and frozen it at once. He fixed his eyes upon her, with a strange, sad, reproaching look, which haunted her till her death, and turning from her, sought the room where Ellen was preparing her lessons for the joyful hour when he could attend to her. As she sprung toward him with a cry of glee, he clasped her to his bosom, without the power of uttering a sound, save a groan so deep and hollow, that the child's unusual glee was checked, and she clung to him in terror; and when he could tell her that he was about to leave her, and for an indefinite time, her passionate grief seemed almost to comfort him, by its strong evidence of her childish love.

"Let me go with you, papa, dear papa! oh! I will be so good — I will not give you any trouble, indeed, indeed I will not. Pray, pray, take me with you, dear, dear papa!" And she looked in his face so beseechingly, that the colonel had no strength to resist, and fondly kissing her, he promised that if Mrs. Cameron would permit her to join her little family, she should go with him; and, to Ellen's intense thankfulness, the permission was willingly accorded.

Mrs. Fortescue had indeed replied, when her husband briefly imparted his intention, that he certainly must intend Ellen to be ill again, by exposing her to such an unhealthy climate; and that if she were, he must not be angry if she refused to go and nurse her, as it would be all his weak indulgence, and no fault of hers. The Colonel made no answer, and, irritated beyond measure at his manner, Eleanor parted from her husband in coldness and in pride.

The fortnight passed, and Mrs. Fortescue felt as if her own youth were indeed renewed, the longings for universal admiration again her own; but now it was only for her son, and her triumph was complete; many and lovely were the youthful beings called together on that festive night, seeming as if England had concentrated her fairest and purest offspring in that far distant land; but Edward, and his still lovely mother, outshone them all. That she was herself admired as much, if not more, than she had ever been in her palmy days of triumph, Eleanor scarcely knew; her every feeling was centred in her boy, and consequently the supercilious haughtiness which had so often marred her beauty in former days was entirely laid aside, and maternal pride and pleasure gratified to the utmost, added a new charm to her every movement and every word. She heard the universal burst of admiration which greeted her, as to oblige Edward she went through a quadrille with him, and never in her whole career had she felt so triumphant, so proud, so joyous. During the past fortnight she had often been tormented by self-reproach, and her husband's look had disagreeably haunted her; but this night not a fleeting thought of either the Colonel or Ellen entered her mind, and her pleasure was complete.

Tired with dancing, and rather oppressed with the heat, Eleanor quitted the crowded ball-room, and stood for a few minutes quite alone in a solitary part of the veranda, which, covered with lovely flowers, ran round the house. The music in the ball-room sounded in the distance as if borne by the night breeze in softened harmony over the distant hills. The moon was at the full, and lit up nearly the whole garden with the refulgence of a milder day. At that moment a cold chill crept over the heart and frame of Eleanor, causing her breath to come thick and gaspingly. Why, she knew not, for there was nothing visible to cause it, save that, in one part of the garden, a cluster of dark shrubs, only partly illuminated by the rays of the moon, seemed suddenly to have assumed the shape of a funeral bier, covered with a military pall. At the same moment the music in the ball-room seemed changed to the low wailing plaint and muffled drums, the military homage to some mighty dead. And if it were indeed but excited fancy, it had a strange effect, for Eleanor fainted on the marble floor.

That same afternoon Colonel Fortescue, with some picked men, had set off to discover the track of some marauding natives, who for some days had been observed hovering about the neighborhood. Military ardor carried him farther than he intended, and it was nearly night, when entering a narrow defile, a large body of the enemy burst upon them, and a desperate contest ensued. The defile was so hemmed in with rock and mountain, that though not very distant from the fort, the noise of the engagement had not been distinguished. Captain Cameron was quietly sitting with his wife and elder children, awaiting without any forebodings the return of the Colonel. Though it was late, Ellen's fears had been so visible, that Mrs. Cameron could not send her to bed; the child seemed so restless and uneasy that the Captain had tried to laugh her out of her cowardice, as he called it, declaring that her father would disown her if she could not be more brave. Hasty footsteps were at length heard approaching, and Ellen started from her seat and sprung forward, as the door opened; but it was not the Colonel, only a sergeant, who had accompanied him, and whose face caused Captain Cameron to exclaim, in alarm, "How now, Sergeant Allen, returned and alone; what has chanced?"

"The worst those brown devils could have done!" was the energetic reply. "We've beaten them, and we will beat them again, the villains! but that will not bring *him* back — Captain — Captain, the Colonel's down!"

The Captain started from his chair, but before he could frame another word, Ellen had caught hold of the old man's arm, and wildly exclaimed, "Do you mean — do you mean, pray tell me, Sergeant Allen! — Have the natives met papa's troop, and have they fought? — and — is he hurt — is he killed?" The man could not answer her — for her look and tone, he afterward declared to his comrades, went through his heart, just for all the world like a sabre-cut; and for the moment neither Captain nor Mrs. Cameron could address her. The shock seemed to have banished voice from all save from the poor child principally concerned.

"Stay with me, my dear Ellen!" Mrs. Cameron at length said, advancing to her, as she stood still clinging to the sergeant's arm: "the Captain will go and meet your father, and if he be wounded, we will nurse him together, dearest! Stay with me."

"No, no, no!" was the agonized reply; "let me go to him, he may die before they bring him here, and I shall never feel his kiss or hear him bless me again. He told me he should fall in battle — oh! Mrs. Cameron, pray let me go to him."

And they who knew all which that father was to his poor Ellen, could not resist that appeal. The sergeant said the

Colonel was not dead, but so mortally wounded they feared to move him. It was a fearful scene. Death in its most horrid form was all around her; her little feet were literally deluged in blood, and she frequently stumbled over the dusky forms and mangled and severed limbs that lay on the grass, but neither sob nor cry escaped her till she beheld her father. His men had removed him from the immediate scene of slaughter, and tried to form a rough pallet of military cloaks, but the ghastly countenance, which the moon's light rendered still more fixed and pallid, the rigidity of his limbs, all seemed to denote they had indeed arrived too late, and that terrible stillness was broken by the convulsed and passionate sobs of the poor child, who, flinging herself beside him, besought him only to open his eyes, to look upon her once more, to call her his darling, and kiss her once, only once again: and it seemed as if her voice had indeed power to recall the fluttering soul. The heavy eyes did unclose, the clenched hand relaxed to try and clasp his child, and he murmured feebly —

"How came you here, my poor darling Ellen? are friends here? — is that Cameron's voice?" The Captain knelt down by him and convulsively pressed his hand, but he could not speak.

"God bless you, Cameron! Take my poor child to her mother — implore her — to — and it is to-night, this very night — she and my boy are happy — and I — and my poor Ellen —" A fearful convulsion choked his voice, but after a little while he tried to speak again —

"My poor child, I have prepared you for this; but I know you must grieve for me. Take my blessing to your brother, tell him to protect — love your mother, darling! she must love you at last — a ring — my left hand — take it to her — oh! how I have loved her — God have mercy on her — on my poor children!" He tried to press his lips again on Ellen's cheek and brow, but the effort was vain — and at the very moment Mrs. Fortescue had stood transfixed by some unknown terror, her husband ceased to breathe.

It was long before Ellen rallied from that terrible scene. Even when the fever which followed subsided, and she had been taken, apparently perfectly restored to health, once more to her mother and brother, its recollection so haunted her, that her many lonely hours became fraught with intense suffering. Her imagination, already only too morbid, dwelt again and again upon the minutest particular of that field of horror; not only her father, but the objects which, when her whole heart was wrapped in him, she seemed not even to have seen. The ghastly heaps of dead, the severed limbs, the mangled trunks, the gleaming faces all fixed in the distorted expressions with which they died — the very hollow groans and louder cry of pain which, as she passed through the field, had fallen on her ear unheeded, returned to the poor child's too early awakened fancy so vividly, that often and often it was only a powerful though almost unconscious effort that prevented the scream of fear. Her father's last words were never forgotten; she would not only continue to love her mother because he had desired her to do so, but because *he had so loved her*, and on her first return home this seemed easier than ever to accomplish. Mrs. Fortescue, tortured by remorse and grief, had somewhat softened toward the child who had received the last breath of her husband; and could Ellen have overcome the reserve and fear which so many years of estrangement had engendered, and given vent to the warmth of her nature, Mrs. Fortescue might have learned to know, and knowing, to love her — but it was then too late.

So torturing were Mrs. Fortescue's feelings when she recalled the last request of her husband, and her cruel and haughty refusal; when that which had seemed so important, a juvenile ball — because not to go would disappoint Edward — became associated with his fearful death, and sunk into worse than nothing — she had parted with him in anger, and it proved forever; — that even as England had become odious to her, twelve years before, so did India now; and she suddenly resolved to quit it, and return to the relatives she had neglected so long, but toward whom she now yearned more than ever. She thought and believed such a complete change would and must bring peace. Alas! what change will remove the torture of remorse!

Though incapable of real love, from her studied heartlessness, it was impossible for her to have lived twelve years with one so indulgent and fond as Colonel Fortescue, without realizing some degree of affection, and his unexpected and awful death roused every previously dormant feeling so powerfully, that she was astonished at herself, and in her misery believed that the feeling had only come to add to her burden — for what was the use of loving now? and, determined to rouse herself, she made every preparation for immediate departure; but she was painfully arrested. The selfish mother had fled from the couch of her suffering child, and now a variation of the same complaint laid her on a bed of pain. It was a desperate struggle between life and death; but she rallied, and insisted on taking her passage for England some weeks before her medical attendant thought it advisable. The constant struggle between the whisperings of good and the dominion of evil, which her whole life had been, had unconsciously undermined a constitution naturally good; and when to this was added a malignant disease, though brief in itself, the seeds of a mortal complaint were planted, which, ere the long voyage was concluded, had obtained fatal and irremediable ascendency, and occasioned those sufferings and death which in our first chapters we described.

To Edward, though the death of his father had caused him much childish grief, still more perhaps from sympathy with the deep suffering of his mother, than a perfect consciousness of his own heavy loss, the *manner* in which he died was to him a source of actual pride. He had always loved the histories of heroes, military and naval, and gloried in the idea that his father had been one of them, and died as they did, bravely fighting against superior numbers, and in the moment of a glorious victory. He had never seen death, and imagined not all the attendant horrors of such a one; and how that Ellen could never even hear the word without shuddering he could not understand, nor why she should always so painfully shrink from the remotest reference to that night, which was only associated in his mind with emotions of pleasure. In the tedious voyage of nearly six months (for five-and-twenty years ago the voyage from India to England was not what it is now,) the character of Edward shone forth in such noble coloring as almost to excuse his mother's idolatry, and win for him the regard of passengers and crew. Captain Cameron had impressed on his mind that he now stood in his father's place to his mother and sister; and as the idea of protecting is always a strong incentive to manliness in a boy, however youthful, Edward well redeemed the charge, so devoting himself not only to his mother, but to Ellen, that her affection for him redoubled, as did her mistaken idea of his vast superiority.

His taste had always pointed to the naval in preference to the military profession, and the voyage confirmed it. Before he had been a month on board he had become practically an expert sailor — had learned all the technical names of the various parts of a ship, and evinced the most eager desire for the acquirement of navigation. Nor did he fail in the true sailor spirit, when, almost within sight of England, a tremendous storm arose, reducing the vessel almost to a wreck, carrying her far from her destined moorings, and compelling her, after ten days' doubt whether or not she would reach land in safety, to anchor in Milford Haven, there to repair her injuries, ere she could be again seaworthy.

The passengers here left her, and Mrs. Fortescue, whose illness the terrors of the storm had most alarmingly increased, was conveyed to Pembroke in an almost exhausted state; but once on land she rallied, resolved on instantly proceeding to Swansea, then cross to Devonshire, and travel direct to Oakwood, where she had no doubt her sister was. But her temper was destined to be tried still more. The servant who had accompanied her from India, an Englishwoman, tired out with the fretful impatience of Mrs. Fortescue during the voyage, and disappointed that she did not at once proceed to London, demanded her instant discharge, as she could not stay any longer from her friends. The visible illness of her mistress might have spared this unfeeling act, but Eleanor had never shown feeling or kindness to her inferiors, and therefore, perhaps, had no right to expect them. Her suppressed anger and annoyance so increased physical suffering, that had it not been for her children she must have sunk at once; but for their sakes she struggled with that deadly exhaustion, and set off the very next morning, without any attendant, for Swansea. They were not above thirty miles from this town when, despite her every effort, Mrs. Fortescue became too ill to proceed. There was no appearance of a town or village, but the owners of a half-way house, pitying the desolate condition of the travellers, directed the postboy to the village of Llangwillan; which, though out of the direct road, and four or five miles distant, was yet the nearest place of shelter. And never in her whole life had Mrs. Fortescue experienced such a blessed sensation of physical relief, as when the benevolent exertions of Mr. Myrvin had installed her in widow Morgan's humble dwelling, and by means of soothing medicine and deep repose in some degree relieved the torture of a burning brain and aching frame. Still she hoped to rally, and obtain strength sufficient to proceed; and bitter was the anguish when the hope was compelled to be relinquished. — With all that followed, our readers are already acquainted, and we will, therefore, at once seek the acquaintance of Mrs. Hamilton's own family, whose "Traits of Character" will, we hope, illustrate other and happier home influences than those of indiscreet indulgence and culpable neglect.

PART II.

TRAITS OF CHARACTER.

CHAPTER I.

YOUTHFUL COLLOQUY — INTRODUCING CHARACTER

The curtains were drawn close, the large lamp was on the table, and a cheerful fire blazing in the grate; for though only September, the room was sufficiently large, and the evenings sufficiently chill, for a fire to add greatly to its aspect of true English comfort. There were many admirable pictures suspended on the walls, and well-filled book-cases, desks, and maps, stands of beautiful flowers, and some ingenious toys, all seeming to proclaim the apartment as the especial possession of the young party who were this evening busily engaged at the large round table which occupied the centre of the room. They were only four in number; but what with a large desk piled with books and some most alarming-sized dictionaries, which occupied the elder of the two lads, the embroidery frame of the elder girl, the dissected map before her sister, and two or three books scattered round the younger boy, the table seemed so well filled that Miss Harcourt had quietly ensconced herself in her own private little corner, sufficiently near to take an interest, and sometimes join in the conversation of her youthful charge; but so apart as to be no restraint upon them, and to enable her to pursue her own occupations of either reading, writing, or working uninterruptedly. Could poor Mrs. Fortescue have glanced on the happy group, she certainly might have told her sister, with some show of justice, that there was such an equal distribution of interesting and animated expression (which is the great beauty of youth,) that she could not have known the trial of having such a heavy, dull, unhappy child as Ellen. Mrs. Hamilton, indeed, we rather think, would not have considered such a trial, except as it proved ill-health and physical pain in the little sufferer; and, perhaps her increased care and tenderness (for such with her would have been the consequence of the same cause which had created her sister's neglect) might have removed both the depression of constant but impalpable illness, and the expression of heaviness and gloom. Certain it is, that her own Herbert had, with regard to delicate health, given her more real and constant anxiety than Eleanor had ever allowed herself to experience with Ellen; but there was nothing in the boy's peculiarly interesting countenance to denote the physical suffering he very often endured. Care and love had so surrounded his path with blessings, that he was often heard to declare, that he never even wished to be as strong as his brother, or to share his active pleasures, he had so many others equally delightful. Whether it was his physical temperament, inducing a habitude of reflection and studious thought much beyond his years, or whether the unusually gifted mind worked on the frame, or the one combined to form the other, it would be as impossible to decide with regard to him as with hundreds of others like him; but he certainly seemed, not only to his parents, but to their whole household, and to every one who casually associated with him, to have more in him of heaven than earth; as if indeed he were only lent, not given. And often and often his mother's heart ached with its very intensity of love, causing the unspoken dread — how might she hope to retain one so faultless, and yet so full of every human sympathy and love! The delicate complexion, beautiful color of his cheeks and lips, and large soft, very dark blue eye, with its long black lash, high, arched brow, shaded by glossy chestnut hair, were all so lit up with the rays of mind, that though his face returned again and again to the fancy of those who had only once beheld it, they could scarcely have recalled a single feature, feeling only the almost angelic expression of the whole.

His brother, as full of mirth and mischief, and as noisy and laughter-loving as Herbert was quiet and thoughtful, made his way at once, winning regard by storm, and retaining it by his frank and generous qualities, which made him a favorite with young and old. Even in his hours of study, there was not the least evidence of reflection or soberness. As a child he had had much to contend with, in the way of passion, pride, and self-will; but his home influence had been such a judicious blending of indulgence and firmness on the part of both his parents, such a persevering inculcation of a strong sense of duty, religious and moral, that at fifteen his difficulties had been all nearly overcome; and, except when occasional acts of thoughtlessness and hasty impulse lured him into error and its painful consequences, he was as happy and as good a lad as even his anxious mother could desire.

The elder of his two sisters resembled him in the bright, dark, flashing eye, the straight intellectual brow, the rich dark brown hair and well-formed mouth; but the expression was so different at present, that it was often difficult to trace the likeness that actually existed. Haughtiness, and but too often ill-temper, threw a shade over a countenance, which when happy and animated was not only attractive then, but gave a fair promise of great beauty in after years. The disposition of Caroline Hamilton was in fact naturally so similar to that of her aunt, Mrs. Fortescue, that Mrs. Hamilton's task with her was not only more difficult and painful in the present than with any of the others, but her dread of the future at times so overpowering, that it required all her husband's influence to calm her, by returning trust in Him, who had promised to answer all who called upon Him, and would bless that mother's toils which were based on, and looked up alone, to His influence on her child, and guidance for herself.

The blue-eyed, fair-haired, graceful, little Emmeline, not only the youngest of the family, but from her slight figure, delicate, small features, and childish manner, appearing even much younger than she was, was indeed a source of joy and love to all, seeming as if sorrow, except for others, could not approach her. She had indeed much that required a carefully guiding hand, in a yielding weakness of disposition, indolent habit in learning, an unrestrained fancy, and its general accompaniment, over-sensitiveness of feeling, but so easily guided by affection, and with a disposition so sweet and gentle, that a word from her mother was always enough. Mrs. Hamilton had little fears for her, except, indeed, as for the vast capability of individual suffering which such a disposition engendered, in those trials which it was scarcely possible she might hope to pass through life without. There was only one safeguard, one unfailing comfort, for a character like hers, and that was a deep ever-present sense of religion, which untiringly, and yet more by example than by precept, her parents endeavored to instil. Greatly, indeed, would both Mr. and Mrs. Hamilton have been astonished, had they been told that the little girl, Ellen Fortescue, who to both was such an enigma, and who was seemingly in all things so utterly unlike their Emmeline, was in natural disposition *exactly the same;* and that the vast difference in present and future character simply arose from the fact, that the early influences of the one were sorrow and neglect, and of the other, happiness and love.

"I wonder whether mamma and papa will really come home to-night;" observed Caroline, after several minutes of unbroken silence, all seemingly so engrossed in their own occupations as to have no inclination to speak. "And if they do, I wish we could know the exact time, I do so hate expecting and being disappointed."

"Then neither wonder nor expect, my sage sister," replied Percy, without, however, raising his head or interrupting his writing; "and I will give you two capital reasons for my advice. Firstly, wonder is the offspring of ignorance, and has two opposite effects on my sex and on yours. With us it is closely connected with philosophy, for we are told in 'wonder all philosophy begins, in wonder it ends, and adoration fills up the inter space;" but with you, poor weak creatures, the only effect it produces is increased curiosity, of which you have naturally a more than adequate supply. Secondly, if you begin to wonder and except, and speculate as to the ayes and noes of a contingency to-night, you will not cease talking till mamma really does appear; and then good-by to my theme, for to write while your tongue is running, is impossible. So pray, take my advice, on consideration that you have had as good a sermon from me as my reverend brother Herbert can ever hope to give."

"I do not think mamma and papa will be quite satisfied if he do not give us a much better one, even the very first time he attempts it;" rejoined Emmeline, with a very arch look at her brother.

"What, you against me, Miss Emmy! and beginning to talk too. You forget what an important personage I am, during papa's absence especially; and that as such, I am not to be insulted with impunity. So here goes — as a fresh exercise for your patience!" And he mingled all the fixed and unfixed parts of her map in most bewildering confusion, regardless of her laughing entreaty to let them alone.

"You have tried a very bad way to keep me quiet, Percy," continued Caroline; "you must either explain why wonder may not equally have the same good effect on us as on you, or retract your words entirely. You know you would not have expressed such a contemptuous opinion, if mamma had been present."

"My mother is such a very superior person, that when she is present her superiority extends over her whole sex, Caroline; even you are safe, because, as her child, it is to be hoped that one of these days you may be something like her; exactly, I do not expect—two such women as my mother can not exist."

"As if your opinion were of such importance, Percy," replied Caroline haughtily; "it really is very little consequence to me whether you think me like mamma or not."

"It is to me, though," rejoined Emmeline, earnestly; "I would rather be like mamma than like anybody else, and I should like Percy to think I was, because then he would love me still more."

"Bravo, my little Em; spoken almost as well as I could myself; and, as a reward, as soon as this most annoying piece of erudition is accomplished, I will help you with your map. Why, you silly little thing, you have put Kamschatka as the terra firma of South America; no doubt that ice and snow would be very welcome there, but how the Americans would stare to see the fur-clad Kamschatkans such near neighbors. That's it, go on, puzzle away till I can help you. And you Miss Caroline, retain your contempt of my opinion, and may you never repent it."

"I thought you told me not to talk, Percy," replied his sister; "and I should like to know who is talking the most, you or I? You will not finish what you are doing before the bell rings for prayers, if you go on in this way."

"That proves how little you know the extent of my powers. I have only to make a clean copy of these learned reflections. Why, in the name of all the gods, were there such provokingly clever people as Seneca, Cicero, Pliny, and a host of others! or, if they must be wise, why did they not burn all the written wisdom, instead of leaving it as a means of torture in the hands of learned pedagogues, yclept schoolmasters, and as a curse on those poor unfortunates whose noddles are not wise enough to contain it."

"I should be very sorry if all the ancient authors were thus annihilated," observed Herbert, looking up from his book with a bright smile. "I should lose a great deal of enjoyment even now, and still more by-and-by, when I know more."

"Ay, but my dear fellow, your head is not quite so like a sieve as mine. Yours receives, contains, digests, and sends forth the matter improved by your own ideas; but as for mine, the matter undoubtedly enters, but runs out again, and only leaves behind that which is too large and gross to pass through. No, no, Bertie, your head and minė are not related even in the twentieth degree of consanguinity, however nearly connected their masters may be. Hush! not a word; I have only one line more; what a wise man that was to be sure, who said, 'Otiosum esse quam nihil agere' — better to be idle than doing nothing. Don't shake your head and laugh, Emmy. Vale! never did I say good-by so willingly. Hurrah! mamma and papa may come home when they like now. Cast your eye over it Herbert; just tell me if it looks correct, and then vale books — vale pens — vale desk for to-night!" He placed his writing on his brother's open book, threw his dictionary and grammar high in air, and dexterously caught them as they fell, piled up his books, closed his desk, and then, with a comical sigh of relief, flung himself full length on a sofa.

"Now that you have finished your task, Percy, perhaps you will have the kindness to inform us why at this time of the evening you have been writing Latin?" inquired Caroline.

"And open my wound afresh! However, it is quite right that Miss Harcourt should know that, if I am ill from over-study to-morrow, it is her doing."

"Mine!" answered Miss Harcourt, laughing; "pray explain yourself, young man, for I am so perfectly innocent as not even to understand you."

"Did you not this morning give me a message to Lady Helen Grahame?"

"I did; you passed her house on your way to Mr. Howard's."

"Well, then, if you had not given me the message, much as I felt disinclined to pore over musty books and foolscap paper, from the extreme loveliness of the morning, I should have nerved myself to go straight on to the Rectory. Lady Helen was not visible, so I tarried, believing your message of vital importance, and Annie came to me — by-the-by, what a little woman that child is; Emmeline, you are a baby to her. I wonder she condescends to associate with you."

"I do not think she is at all fond of me — Caroline is her friend," replied Emmeline; "but what can Annie have to do with your Latin?"

"A great deal — for she talked and we walked, and time walked too, and by the time I had seen Lady Helen, it was two hours later than I ought to have been with Mr. Howard.

On I went, feeling not particularly comfortable; but though it is clear logic that if Miss Harcourt had not sent me to Lady Helen's I should not have been led into temptation; I was magnanimous enough not to mention her, but to lay the whole blame of my non-appearance, on my own disinclination for any study but that of nature. Mr. Howard looked grave and sorrowful — I wish to heaven he was more like any other schoolmaster; that look and tone of his are worse than any rod! — and to redeem my lost time in the morning, I was desired to write a Latin theme on a letter of Pliny's this evening. And now that I have satisfied all your inquiries, please satisfy mine. Is there any chance of mamma's coming home to-night?"

"Every probability," replied Miss Harcourt. "It only depends on your cousin, who is so very delicate, that if she were too fatigued, Mr. Hamilton would remain at Exeter to-night, and proceed here early to-morrow."

"Well, my little cousin, though I have not the pleasure of knowing you, I hope you will be so kind as to let mamma come on to-night, for we have been too long without her, and I long to resign to papa his robes of office, for they sit mightily like borrowed plumes upon me. Mamma writes of Ellen and Edward — I wonder what they are like! Come, Tiny, paint them for me — your fertile fancy generally fills up the shadow of a name."

"I cannot, Percy, for I am afraid my pictures would not be agreeable."

"Not agreeable!" repeated Percy and Miss Harcourt together. "Why not?"

Emmeline hesitated, then answered ingenuously, "We are so very, very happy together, that I do not feel quite sure that I am glad my cousins are going to live with us."

"What! are you afraid I shall love Ellen more than you, Emmy?" exclaimed her brother, starting up and sitting on her chair; "do not be alarmed, Tiny; no cousin shall take your place."

"Indeed I am not afraid of that, Percy, dear," she replied, looking so fondly in his face, that he gave her a hearty kiss. "I cannot tell why I should feel half sorry that they are coming, but I am quite sure I will do all I can to make them happy."

"You could not do otherwise if you were to try, Tiny. Come, Caroline, what say you? We have all been thinking about them, so we may as well give each other the benefit of our thoughts."

"Suppose I do not feel inclined to do so?"

"Why we must all believe you are ashamed of them," replied Percy, quickly, "and if you are, I know who has made you so. I would lay any wager, the whole time you have been with Lady Helen Grahame, since mamma has been away, she has been talking of nothing else — look, look, she is blushing — I am right."

"And if she did," replied Caroline, very much provoked, "she said nothing that I am ashamed of repeating. She knew my aunt before she went to India, and I am sure if her children are like her, they will be no agreeable additions to our family."

"Bravo, Caroline! you really are an apt pupil; Lady Helen's words and manner completely! but you may have one comfort; children are not always like their parents, and if they are as unlike Lady Helen's description of my poor aunt (which by the way she had no right to give, nor you to listen to) as you are at this moment unlike mamma, we shall get on capitally, and need have no fears about them."

"Percy you are intolerably disagreeable!"

"Because I speak the sad, sober truth? Caroline, do pray, get rid of that dawning-ill temper, before mamma comes; it will not be a pleasant welcome home."

"I am not ill-tempered, Percy: I suppose I may have my own opinion of Ellen and Edward, as well as all of you," replied his sister angrily.

"But do not let it be an unkind one, without knowing them, dear Caroline," observed Herbert gently; "it is so very difficult to get rid of a prejudice when once it has entered our minds, even when we know and feel that it is a wrong one. I am sure if we only thought how sad it is that they have neither father nor mother to love them, and are coming all among strangers — born in a strange land too — we should find quite enough to think kindly about, and leave all wonder as to what they will be like, till we know them. I dare say we shall often have to bear and forbear, but that we have to do with each other, and it will only be one brother and sister more."

"Brother and sister! I am sure I shall not think of them so, Herbert, however you may. My father might have been a nobleman, and who knows any thing of theirs?"

"Caroline, how can you be so ridiculous!" exclaimed Percy, with a most provoking fit of laughter. "Their father served and died for his king — as our grandfather did; and had he lived might have been offered a title too — and their mother — really I think you are very insulting to mamma: her sister's children I should imagine quite as high in rank as ourselves!"

"And even if they were not — what would it signify?" rejoined Herbert. "Dear Caroline, pray do not talk or think so; it makes me feel so sorry, for I know how wrong it is — we might have been in their place."

"I really cannot fancy any thing so utterly impossible," interrupted Caroline, "so you may spare the supposition, Herbert."

"It is no use, Bertie; you must bring the antipodes together, before you and Caroline will think alike," interposed Percy, perceiving with regret the expression of pain on his brother's face, and always ready to guard him either from physical or mental suffering, feeling instinctively that, from his extraordinary mind and vivid sense of duty, he was liable to the latter, from many causes which other natures would pass unnoticed.

Miss Harcourt did not join the conversation. It had always been Mrs. Hamilton's wish that in their intercourse with each other, her children should be as unrestrained as if they had been alone. Had Caroline's sentiments received encouragement, she would have interfered; but the raillery of Percy and the earnestness of Herbert she knew were more likely to produce an effect than any thing like a rebuke from herself, which would only have caused restraint before her in future. It was through this perfect unrestraint that Mrs. Hamilton had become so thoroughly acquainted with the several characters of her children. That Caroline's sentiments caused her often real pain was true, but it was far better to know them, and endeavor to correct and remove them, by causing education to bear upon the faults they revealed, than to find them concealed from her by the constant fear of words of reproof.

To remove Herbert's unusual seriousness, Percy continued, laughingly —

"Miss Harcourt, what are your thoughts on this momentous subject? It is no use asking Herbert's, we all know them without his telling us; but you are almost the principally concerned of the present party, for Ellen will bring you the trouble of another pupil."

"I shall not regret it, Percy; but only shall rejoice if I can in any way lessen your mother's increased charge. As for what your cousins will be like, I candidly tell you I have scarcely thought about it. I have no doubt we shall find them strange and shy at first; but we must do all we can to make them feel they are no strangers.'

"And now, then, it only remains for the right honorable me to speak; and really Emmy and Herbert and you have told my story, and left me nothing. I do not know whether I am pleased or not, but I am very sorry for them; and it will be capital if this Master Edward turns out a lad of spirit and mischief, and not over-learned or too fond of study — one, in fact, that I can associate with, without feeling such a painful sensation of inferiority as I do when in company with my right reverend brother."

"Dear Percy, do not call me reverend," said Herbert, appealingly: "I feel it almost a mockery now, when I am so very far from being worthy to become a clergyman."

"You are a good fellow, Bertie; and I will not tease you, if I can help it — but really I do not mean it for mockery; you know, or ought to know, that you are better now than half the clergymen who have taken orders, and as much superior to me in goodness as in talent."

"Indeed I know no such thing, Percy; I am not nearly so strong in health as you are, and am therefore naturally more fond of quiet pleasures: and as for talent, if you were as fond of application as of frolic, you would leave me far behind."

"Wrong, Bertie, quite wrong! but think of yourself as you please, I know what everybody thinks of you. Hush! is that the sound of a carriage, or only the wind making love to the old oaks?"

"The wind making love, Percy!" repeated Emmeline, laughing; "I neither hear that, nor the carriage wheels kissing the ground."

"Well done, Tiny! my poetry is beaten hollow; but there — there — I am sure it is a carriage!" and Percy bounded from the table so impetuously as nearly to upset it, flung back the curtain, and looked eagerly from the window.

Herbert closed his book to listen; Emmeline left her nearly-completed map, and joined Percy; Caroline evidently tried to resume serenity, but, too proud to evince it, industriously pursued her work, breaking the thread almost every time that she drew out the needle.

"It is nothing, Percy; how could you disappoint us so?" said Herbert, in a tone of regret.

"My good fellow, you must be deaf — listen! nearer and louder — and, look there, Emmeline, through those trees, don't you see something glimmering? that must be the lamp of the carriage."

"Nonsense, Percy, it is a glowworm."

"A glowworm! why, Emmeline, the thought of seeing mamma has blinded you. What glowworm ever came so steadily forward? No? there is no mistake now. Hurrah, it *is* the carriage: here Robert, Morris, Elias, all of you, to the hall! to the hall! The carriage is coming down the avenue." And with noisy impatience, the young gentleman ran into the hall, assembled all the servants he had named, and others too, all eager to welcome the travellers; flung wide back the massive door, and he and Herbert both were on the steps several minutes before the carriage came in sight.

CHAPTER II.

THREE ENGLISH HOMES, AND THEIR INMATES.

If more than the preceding conversation were needed to reveal the confidence and love with which Mr. and Mrs. Hamilton were regarded by their children, the delight, the unrestrained expressions of affection, with which by every one of the young party they were received, would have evinced it still more clearly. Herbert was very speedily on his favorite seat, a low stool at his mother's feet. Emmeline, for that one half hour at least, assumed her still unresigned privilege, as the youngest and tiniest, to quietly slip in her lap; Percy was talking to his father, making Edward perfectly at home, saying many kind words to Ellen, and caressing his mother, all almost at the same moment. Caroline was close to her father, with her arm round his neck; and Miss Harcourt was kindly disrobing Ellen from her many wraps, and making her lie quietly on a sofa near her aunt; who, even in that moment of delightful reunion with her own, had yet time and thought, by a few judicious words, to remove the undefinable, but painful sensation of loneliness, which was creeping over the poor child as she gazed on her bright, happy-looking cousins; and thought if to her own mother Edward's beauty and happiness had made him so much more beloved than herself, what claim could she have on her aunt? Ellen could not have said that such were the thoughts that filled her eyes with tears, and made her heart so heavy; she only knew that much as she had loved her aunt during the journey, her kiss and kind words at that moment made her love her more than ever.

Never had there been a happier meal at Oakwood than the substantial tea which was speedily ready for the travellers. So much was there to hear and tell: Percy's wild sallies; Caroline's animated replies (she had now quite recovered her temper); Herbert's gentle care of Ellen, by whom he had stationed himself (even giving up to her his usual seat by his mother); Emmeline's half shy, half eager, efforts to talk to her cousins; Mr. and Mrs. Hamilton's earnest interest, all combined, long before the meal was concluded, to make Edward feel perfectly at his ease, and very happy, and greatly to remove Ellen's unacknowledged dread. The time passed so quickly, that there was a general start when the prayer bell sounded, though it was nearly two hours after the usual time.

"Are you prepared for to-night, my boy?" Mr. Hamilton asked of Herbert, as they rose to adjourn to the library, where, morning and evening, it had been the custom of the Hamilton family for many generations, to assemble their whole household for family devotion.

"Yes, papa; I was not quite sure whether you would arrive to-night."

"Then I will not resume my office till to-morrow, Herbert, that I may have the gratification of hearing you officiate," replied his father, linking his son's arm in his, and affectionately glancing on the bright blush that rose to the boy's cheek.

There was a peculiar sweetness in Herbert Hamilton's voice, even in speaking; and as he read the service of the lessons for the evening, adding one or two brief explanations when necessary, and more especially when reading, or rather praying, the beautiful petitions appropriated to family worship, there was an earnest solemnity of tone and manner, presenting a strange contrast, yet beautiful, combining with the boyish form and youthful face, on which the lamp, suspended over the reading-desk, shed such a soft and holy light. The occasional prayer which was added to the usual evening service, was always chosen by the reader; and Mr. and Mrs. Hamilton were surprised and affected at the earnestness with which their almost angel boy selected and read over one peculiarly bearing on the events of that evening; the introduction of their orphan relatives, for compassion and blessing on them, and grace for increased kindness and forbearance in their intercourse with one another — Miss Harcourt, his brother and sisters, knew well to what he alluded, and all but one responded with earnestness and truth

Caroline could not enter into Herbert's feelings even at that moment: it was a great effort even to prevent a feeling of irritation, believing that he directly pointed at her, and determining that as neither he nor any one else had any right to interfere with her private thoughts, and that they could do harm to none while confined to her own breast, she resolved not to overcome them, and so could not join with any fervor in the prayer.

To Edward all was strange. While the graces of his body and mind had been most sedulously cultivated, he had never been taught even the public ordinances of religion, much less its inward spirit. His mother had often and often felt a pang of reproach, at thus neglecting that which an inward voice would whisper was most essential; but she was wont to silence the pang by the determined idea, that she was neither worthy nor able to give him such solemn lessons, and that it would come by instinct to him in after years. There was time enough for him to think of such things. He had been now and then to church, but it was a mere form, regarded as a weary duty, from which he escaped whenever he could. The present scene, then, completely bewildered him. He had always fancied himself superior to any of the boys he had associated with; but as he looked at and listened to Herbert, who seemed at most only two years older than himself, he became sensible of a very strange and disagreeable, but a very decided feeling of inferiority; and then, too, it was so incomprehensible, the servants all joining them, a class of people whom in India he had been taught so to consider his inferiors, that even to speak with them was a species of degradation; and he was destined to be still more surprised, for before they left the library, he heard his aunt and uncle address them all, and say a few kind words, and make inquiries after their families to each.

To Ellen that evening service recalled some of Mr. Myrvin's instructions, and seemed to help her to realize those new thoughts and feelings, which she had learned, for the first time, in Wales. Her father had, indeed, the last year of his life tried to give her some ideas of religion; but having only so very lately begun to think seriously himself, he felt diffident and uncertain of his own powers, and so left an impression more of awe toward the subject than of love, which to a disposition such as Ellen's was unfortunate.

A very short time sufficed for Percy and Emmeline to introduce their cousins to all the delights and mysteries of their dear old home; and Oakwood Hall was really a place for imagination to revel in. It was a large castellated mansion, fraught with both the associations of the past, and the comforts of the present. The injuries which the original mansion had received during the civil war of Charles I., had, when the family returned at the Restoration, caused much of the old house to be pulled down, and replaced with larger rooms, and greater conveniences for a modern dwelling-house, retaining, however, quite sufficient of the past to throw interest around it.

The wings were still flanked with turrets, which were Percy's and Emmeline's delight; and the many stair-cases, leading into all sorts of nooks and corners — and the small and most uncomfortable rooms, because some of them happened to be hung with tapestry, and had those small narrow windows sunk in deep recesses — were pronounced by both far more enjoyable than the beautiful suit of rooms forming the centre of the mansion, and the dwelling of the family. These were only saved from being disagreeably modern — Percy would declare — by their beautiful richly-polished oaken panels, and by the recesses which the large windows still formed, making almost a room by themselves. The hall, too, with its superb sweep of staircase and broad carved oaken balustrade, leading to a gallery above, which opened on the several sleeping apartments, and thus permitting the full height of the mansion, from base to roof, to be visible from the hall. The doors visible in the gallery opened mostly on dressing-rooms, or private sitting-rooms, which led to the large, airy sleeping-rooms, to which the servants had access by back staircases leading from their hall; and so leaving the oaken staircase and gallery entirely to the use of the family, and of many a game of noisy play had that gallery been the scene. There had been a beautiful little chapel adjoining the mansion, but it was mercilessly burned to the ground by the infatuated Puritans, and never restored; the venerable old church of the village henceforth serving the family of the hall.

Situated on the banks of the Dart, whose serpentine windings gave it the appearance of a succession of most lovely lakes, Nature had been so lavish of her beauties in the garden and park, especially in the magnificent growth of the superb oaks, from which the estate took its name, that it was not much wonder Mrs. Hamilton, always an intense lover of nature, should have become so attached to her home, as never to feel the least inclination to leave it. She did not wish her girls to visit London till a few months before Caroline was old enough to be introduced, to give them then finishing masters; and to that time she of course always looked, as demanding from her part of the year to be spent in town. The career of Eleanor, the recollections of the frivolity and error into which her own early youth had been thrown, had given her not only a distaste, but an actual dread of London for her girls, till such principles and associations had been instilled which would enable them to pass through the ordeal of successive seasons without any change of character or feeling. Her sons, since their tenth year, had more than once accompanied their father to the metropolis; but though these visits were always sources of enjoyment, especially to Percy, they never failed to return with unabated affection to their home, and to declare there was no place in England like it.

Mr. Hamilton, though in neither profession nor business, was far from being an idle man. His own estate was sufficiently large, and contained a sufficient number of dependents, for whose mortal and immortal welfare he was responsible, to give him much employment; and in addition to this, the home interests and various aspects of his country were so strongly entwined with his very being — that, though always refusing to enter Parliament, he was the prompter and encourager of many a political movement, having for its object amelioration of the poor, and improvement of the whole social system; closely connected with which, as he was, they gave him neither public fame nor private emolument. He acted in all things from the same single-hearted integrity and high honor which caused him to refuse the title proffered to his father. Her husband's connection with many celebrated characters, and her own correspondence, and occasional visits from her friends to Oakwood, prevented Mrs. Hamilton's interest from too complete concentration in her home, as, in her first retirement, many feared. She had, too, some friends near her, whose society gave her both pleasure and interest; and many acquaintances who would have visited more than she felt any inclination for, had she not had the happy power of quietly pursuing her own path, and yet conciliating all.

The Rev. William Howard had accepted Mr. Hamilton's eagerly-proffered invitation to become his rector, and undertake the education of his boys, from very peculiar circumstances. He had been minister of a favorite church in one of the southern towns, and master of an establishment for youths of high rank, in both which capacities he had given universal satisfaction. The reprehensible conduct of some of his pupils, carried on at first so secretly as to elude his knowledge, at length became so notorious as to demand examination. He had at first refused all credence, but when proved, by the confused replies of all, and half confession of some, he briefly and emphatically laid before them the enormity of their conduct, and declared that, as confidence was entirely broken between them, he would resign the honor of their education, refusing to admit them any longer as members of his establishment. In vain the young men implored him to spare them the disgrace of such an expulsion; he was inexorable.

This conduct, in itself so upright, was painted by the smarting offenders in such colors, that Mr. Howard gradually but surely found his school abandoned, and himself so misrepresented, that a spirit less self-possessed and secure in its own integrity must have sunk beneath it. But he had some true friends, and none more active and earnest than Mr. Hamilton. A very brief residence at Oakwood Rectory removed even the recollection of the injustice he had experienced; and he himself, as pastor and friend, proved a treasure to high and low. Ten other youths, sons of the neighboring gentry, became his pupils, their fathers gladly following in Mr. Hamilton's lead.

About a mile and a half across the park was Moorlands, the residence of Lady Helen Grahame, whose name had been so often mentioned by the young Hamiltons. Her husband Montrose Grahame, had been Arthur Hamilton's earliest friend, at home, at college, and in manhood. Lady Helen the youngest daughter of a marquis, had been intimate with Emmeline and Eleanor Manvers from childhood, and had always admired and wished to resemble the former, but always failed, she believed, from being constituted so differently; others might have thought from her utter want of energy and mental strength. The marriage at first appeared likely to be a happy one, but it was too soon proved the contrary. Grahame was a man of strict, perhaps severe principles; his wife, though she never did any thing morally wrong, scarcely knew the meaning of the word. Provoked with himself for his want of discrimination, in imagining Lady Helen so different to the being she really was; more than once discovering that she did not speak the exact truth, or act with the steady uprightness he demanded, his manner became almost austere; and, in consequence, becoming more and more afraid of him, Lady Helen sunk lower and lower in his esteem.

Two girls and a boy were the fruits of this union. Lady Helen had made a great many excellent resolutions with regard to their rearing and education, which she eagerly confided to Mrs. Hamilton, but when the time of trial came, weakness and false indulgence so predominated, that Grahame, to counteract these evil influences, adopted a contrary extreme, and, by a system of constant reserve and severity, became an object of as much terror to his children as he was to his wife. But he did not pursue this conduct without pain, and never did he visit Oakwood without bitter regret that his home was not the same.

Mr. and Mrs. Hamilton had often tried to alter the aspect of affairs at Moorlands; the former, by entreating Grahame to be less severe; the latter, by urging Lady Helen to a firmer mode of conduct. But those friendly efforts were as yet entirely useless. Grahame became a member of Parliament, which took his family to London for five or six months in the year — a particularly agreeable change to Lady Helen, who then associated with her sisters, whose families were conducted much on the same fashion as her own, but unfortunately only increasing the discomfort of Moorlands when they returned to it. And this was the more to be regretted, from the fact that both Grahame and his wife were full of good intentions, and had the one been more yielding, and the other more firm, there might have been no small share of happiness for both.

But heavy as Lady Helen thought her trial in the want of her husband's confidence and love, and which she had greatly brought upon herself, it was light in comparison with that of Mrs. Greville, another near neighbor and valued friend of Mrs. Hamilton. She had loved and married a man whose winning manners and appearance, and an ever-varying flow of intelligent conversation, had completely concealed, till too late, his real character. Left at a very early age his own master, with a capital estate and large fortune; educated at a very large public school, at which he learned literally nothing but vice, and how effectually to conceal it; courted and flattered wherever he went, he became vain, overbearing, and extravagant; with no pursuit but that of gambling in all its varieties, even hunting and shooting could not be thoroughly enjoyed without some large bets depending on the day's sport: his thoughts from boyhood were so completely centred in self, that he had affection for nothing else. He had indeed fancied he loved Jessie Summers, when he had so successfully wooed her; but the illusion was speedily dispelled, and repeatedly he cursed his folly for plaguing himself with a wife. His first child, too, was a girl and that annoyed him still more; and when, the next year, a boy was granted, he certainly rejoiced, but it was such rejoicing as to fill his wife's heart with an agony of dread; for he swore he would make his boy as jovial a spirit as himself, and that her namby-pamby ideas should have nothing to do with him.

It was indeed a difficult and painful task Mrs. Greville had to perform. Though her husband would spend weeks and even months at a time away, the impressions she so earnestly and prayerfully sought to instil into her son's heart were, or appeared to be, completely destroyed by her husband's interference the whole time of his sojourn at his home. It was his pleasure to thwart her every plan, laugh at her fine notions, make a mockery of all that was good, and holy, and self-denying; and all in the presence of his children; succeeding in making Alfred frequently guilty of disrespect and unkindness, but failing entirely with Mary, who, though of such a fragile frame and gentle spirit that her father's visits almost always caused her a fit of illness, so idolized her suffering but never-murmuring mother, that she only redoubled her attention and respect whenever she saw her more tried than usual. This conduct, of course, only made her an object, equally with her mother, of her father's sneers and taunts, but she bore it with the true spirit of a martyr. Suffering was doing for her what Herbert Hamilton was naturally — making her spiritual and thoughtful far beyond her years, and drawing her and Herbert together with such a bond of mutual reverence and sympathy, that to talk to him was her greatest consolation, and to endeavor to lessen her sorrows one of his dearest pleasures.

Alfred was not naturally an evil-disposed boy, and, when his father was from home, seldom failed either in respect or obedience. Mrs. Greville possessed the rather rare combination of extreme submissiveness with a natural dignity and firmness. which enabled her to retain the reverence and sympathy of her friends and her household, without once stopping to receive their pity. It was generally supposed, by those who did not know her personally, that she was one of those too soft and self-denying characters who bring on themselves the evils they deplore; but this in Mrs. Greville's case was a very great mistake. It was impossible to associate even casually with her, without feeling intuitively that she suffered deeply, but the emotion such conviction called was respect alone.

As anxious and as earnest a parent as Mrs. Hamilton herself, Mrs. Greville failed not to inculcate the good in both her children, and still more forcibly, when they became old enough to observe, by example than by precept. But with Alfred there must have been an utter hopelessness as to the fruit of her anxious labors, had she not possessed that clinging, single-hearted trust which taught her that no difficulty should deter from a simple duty, and that nothing was too hard for Him who — if He saw that she shrunk not from the charge and responsibility which, in permitting her to become a mother, he had given, and did all she could to counteract those evil influences, for the removal of which she had no power — would, in His own good time, reward, if not on earth — with Him in Heaven; and so untiringly, as unmurmuringly, she struggled on.

CHAPTER III.

HOME SCENE. — VISITORS. — CHILDISH MEDITATIONS.

The part of the day which, to Emmeline Hamilton was the happiest of all, was that in which she and Caroline, and now, of course, Ellen, were with their mother alone. Not that she particularly liked the very quiet employment of plain work, which was then their usual occupation, but that she could talk without the least restraint either about her lessons, or her pleasures, or her thoughts, and the stories or histories she had been reading, and if she thought wrong no one ever corrected her so delightfully, so impressively as "mamma." The mornings, from three to four hours, according as their age and studies required, were always under the control of Miss Harcourt, with such visits from Mrs. Hamilton as gave an increased interest to exertion, and such interruption only as permitted their practice and lessons in music, which three times a week Mrs. Hamilton had as yet herself bestowed. The dressing-bell always rung at half-past three, and dinner was at four, to allow the lads' return from Mr. Howard's, whose daily lessons commenced at nine and concluded at three. From half-past one to half-past three, in the very short days, was devoted to recreation, walking, or driving, and in the longer, to Emmeline's favorite time — an hour at work with her mother, and the remainder to the preparation of lessons and exercises for the next day, which in the winter occupied from five to six. From six to seven in the same generally gloomy season they read aloud some entertaining book with their mother and Miss Harcourt, and seven was the delightful hour of a general reunion at tea and signal for such recreation till nine as they felt inclined for;

their brothers having been employed for Mr. Howard part of the time between dinner and tea, with sufficient earnestness to enjoy the rest and recreation afterward, quite as buoyantly and gladly as their sisters; and many a merry dance enlivened their winter evenings.

In the summer, of course, this daily routine was frequently varied by most delightful excursions in the country. Mrs. Hamilton earnestly longing to implant a love of Nature and all its fresh, pure associations in the minds of her children while yet young, knowing that once obtained, the pleasures of the world would be far less likely to obtain too powerful dominion. That which the world often terms romance, she felt to be a high, pure sense of poetry in the Universe and in Man, which she was quite as anxious to instil as many mothers to root out. She did not believe that to cultivate the spiritual needed the banishment of the matter of fact; but she believed, that to infuse the latter with the former would be their best and surest preventive against all that was low and mean; their best help in the realization of a constant unfailing piety. For the same reason she cultivated a taste for the beautiful, not only in her girls, but in her boys — and beauty, not in arts and nature alone, but in character. She did not allude to beauty of merely the high and striking kind, but to the lowly virtues, struggles, faith, and heroism in the poor — their forbearance and kindness to one another — marking something to admire, even in the most rugged and surly, that at first sight would seem so little worthy of notice. It was gradually, and almost unconsciously, to accustom her daughters to such a train of thought and sentiment, that she so particularly laid aside one part of the day to have them with her alone; ostensibly, it was to give part of their day to working for the many poor, to whom gifts of ready-made clothing are sometimes much more valuable than money; but the *education* of that one hour she knew might, for the right cultivation of the heart, do more than the mere *teaching* of five or six, and that education, much as she loved and valued Miss Harcourt, she had from the first resolved should come from her alone.

To Emmeline this mode of life was so happy, she could not imagine any thing happier. But Caroline often and often envied her great friend Annie Grahame, and believed that occasional visits to London would make her much happier than remaining all the year round at Oakwood, and only with her own family. She knew the expression of such sentiments would meet no sympathy at home, and certainly not obtain their gratification, so she tried to check them, except when in company with Annie and Lady Helen; but her mother knew them, and, from the discontent and unhappiness they so often engendered in her child, caused her both pain and uneasiness. But she did not waver in her plans, because only in Emmeline they seemed to succeed: nor did she, as perhaps some over-scrupulous mothers would have done, check Caroline's association with Miss Grahame. She knew that those principles must be indeed of little worth, which could only actuate in retirement, and when free from temptation. That to prevent intimacy with all, except with those of whom she exactly approved, would be impossible, if she ever meant her daughters to enter the world; and therefore she endeavored so to obtain their unrestrained confidence and affection, as to be regarded, both now and when they were young women, as their first, best, and truest friend; and that end obtained, intimacies with their young companions, however varied their character, she felt would do no permanent harm.

"Dear, dear mamma!" exclaimed Emmeline, one morning about a week after her parents' return, and dropping her work to speak more eagerly, "you cannot think how delightful it does seem to have you at home again; I missed this hour of the day so very much; I did not know how much I loved it when I always had it, but when you were away, every time the hour came I missed you, and longed for you so much that — I am afraid you will think me very silly — I could not help crying."

"Why, how Percy must have laughed at you, Emmy!"

"Indeed, he did not, mamma; I think he felt half inclined to cry too, the first day or two that he came home from Mr. Howard's, and could not rush up into your dressing-room, as he always does. He said it was a very different thing for you to go from home, than for him to go to London, and he did not like it at all; nor Herbert, nor Caroline, neither; though they did not say so much about it."

"I did not miss mamma after the first, quite so much as you did, Emmeline," replied her sister, ingenuously; "because when Lady Helen returned from London, she made me go there so often, and as I know you never refuse me that indulgence, mamma, and Miss Harcourt did not object, I was glad to do so."

"I have only one objection, my dear Caroline, and I think you know what that is."

"That whenever I am with Annie I think and wish more

about going to London, mamma; I am afraid I do; but indeed I try to think that you must know what is better for me, and try not to be discontented, though sometimes I know I do not succeed," and her eyes filled with tears.

"I am satisfied that you endeavor to trust my experience, my love; I am quite aware of all the difficulties you have to encounter in doing so, and therefore your most trifling conquest of self is a great source of comfort to me. I myself should feel that the pain of increased discontent, and so of course increased difficulty in conquering its constant accompaniment, ill temper, would more than balance the pleasure of Annie's society, and so not indulge in the one so often at the expense of the other; but of that you are yourself the best judge, and you know in such a case I always permit you to be a free agent. But what has become of Mary, Emmeline? I begged Mrs. Greville to let you be as much together as possible during my absence; did not her society afford you some pleasure?"

"Oh, yes, mamma, a great deal; but unfortunately Mr. Greville was at home almost all the time you were away, and poor Mary could not often leave her mother, and I don't feel as if it were quite right for me to go so often there, when he is at home. I am sure Mrs. Greville and Mary must both feel still more uncomfortable when any one is there to see how unkind he is, and hear the cruel things he says. Oh, how I do wish I could make poor Mary more happy!"

"She would tell you that affection is a great comfort to her, Emmy."

"Yours and Herbert's may be, mamma, because you are both so much better and wiser than I am; but I can do so little, so very little."

"You can be and are a great source of interest to her, my dear; and when we wish very much to make another person happy, you may be quite sure that the most trifling act gives pleasure; but Ellen looks very much as if she would like to know who this Mary is, that is so tried — suppose you tell her."

Emmeline eagerly obeyed, painting her friend in such glowing colors, that Ellen felt, however tried she might be, a person so good and holy must be happy, notwithstanding; besides, to be loved so by Mrs. Hamilton and Herbert, discovered to her mind such superior qualities, that she almost wondered how Emmeline could speak of her so familiarly, and think of her as her own particular friend. But the conversation on her, and then on other topics, so interested her, that she was almost as sorry as her cousin, when it was interrupted by a visit from Lady Helen Grahame and her daughter.

"Returned at length, dearest Emmeline!" was the former's lively greeting, and evincing far more warmth of manner than was usual to her. "Do you know, the banks of the Dart have seemed so desolate without their guardian spirit, that the very flowers have hung their heads, and the trees are withered?"

"I rather think the change of season, and not my absence, has been the cause of these melancholy facts," replied Mrs. Hamilton, in the same tone; "but even London will not change your kind thoughts for me, Helen."

"Nay, I must follow the example of my neighbors, rich and poor, whom you may appeal to as to the fact of your absence causing terrible lamentation; ask this naughty little girl too, who scarcely ever came to see me, because she had so many things to do to please mamma; but forgive me," she added, more seriously, as she glanced on the deep mourning of her friend, and indeed of all the group; "what a cold, heartless being you must believe me to run on in this way, when there has been so sad a cause for your absence — poor Eleanor!"

"I trust we may say happy Eleanor, my dear Helen; mercy has indeed been shown to her and to me — but we will talk of this another time. Annie," she continued, addressing Miss Grahame, who was already deep in conversation with Caroline, "I have another little girl to introduce to you, whom I hope you will be as friendly with as with Caroline and Emmeline."

The young lady turned round at the words, but her sole notice of Ellen, who had come timidly forward, was a haughty stare, a fashionable courtesy, and a few unintelligible words, which caused Emmeline to feel so indignant, that it was with difficulty she kept silence, and made Ellen so uncomfortable, that it was with even more than her usual shyness, she received Lady Helen's proffered hand.

"And why not introduce her to me too, Emmeline? I knew your mother when she was little older than you are, my dear; so I hope you will learn to know and to like me as fast as you can."

Ellen might have found courage to reply for there was an interest attached to all who had known her mother; but as she raised her eyes to speak, she again encountered Annie's rude and disagreeable stare, and the words died on her lips. The young party were, however, soon all in the garden, for Mrs. Hamilton never made any scruple in dismissing her children, when she wished to speak on subjects she did not choose them to hear; and she was anxious so to relate Eleanor's illness and change of sentiment, as to remove the impressions which her early career had left on Lady Helen's memory.

"It must be nearly time for my brothers to be returning; shall we go and look for them, Ellen? I dare say Edward will have a great deal to tell you," was Emmeline's affectionate address, as Annie and Caroline turned in a different direction; and generally judging others by herself, she thought that being Edward's first day of regular attendance on Mr. Howard, Ellen would like to know all about it as soon as possible, and they proceeded accordingly.

"Well, how do you like your new cousins, what are they like?" inquired Miss Grahame, the moment she had Caroline entirely to herself.

"Edward I think I may like very much; he is so affectionate and so good-natured, and as merry and full of fun as Percy. And he is so handsome, Annie, I think even you would admire him."

"Then altogether he must be very unlike his sister. I never saw a girl so plain, and I am sure she looks as if no fun could exist near her."

"Mamma says we must remember how short a time has elapsed since poor aunt's death, and also that Ellen is not strong enough to be very lively."

"That does not at all account for her looking cross. I am sure she has nothing to be ill-tempered about; there are few girls in her situation who would have made one of your family, as she will be. Mamma said it would be a very anxious thing for Mrs. Hamilton."

"Mamma did seem to think so," replied Caroline, thoughtfully; "but I fancy you are wrong, Annie. Ellen has not yet given any proof of ill-temper."

"She has had no time, my dear; but no one can be deceived by such a face. My cousin, Lady Adelaide Maldon, told me she could always judge people by their faces. But do you like her as well as her brother, Caroline?"

"Ask me that question this day month, my dear Annie; I can not answer you now, for I really do not know. I certainly do not see any thing particularly striking in her yet—I do not understand her; she is so dreadfully shy or timid, and so very inanimate, one cannot tell whether she is pleased or sorry. To tell you the real truth, I am afraid I shall not like her."

"Why afraid?"

"Because mamma would be so sorry were she to know it. I know she wishes us to love one another."

"Nonsense, Caroline. Mrs. Hamilton cannot be so unreasonable as to expect you to love everybody alike."

"Mamma is never unreasonable," replied Caroline, with spirit; "and I do wish, Annie, you would treat Ellen exactly as you do us."

"Indeed, I shall not. What is Colonel Fortescue's daughter to me? Now don't be angry, Caroline, you and I are too old friends to quarrel for nothing: I shall certainly hate Ellen altogether, if she is to be a subject of dispute. Come, look kind again;" and the caress, with which she concluded, restored Caroline's serenity, and other subjects were discussed between them.

Annie Grahame was a few months younger than Caroline Hamilton, (who was nearly thirteen,) but from having been emancipated from the nursery and school-room at a very early age, and made her mother's companion and confidant in all her home vexations — very pretty and engaging — she was very much noticed, and her visits to her titled relations in London, by causing her to imitate their fashionable manners, terms of speech, thoughts on dress, and rank, &c., made her a woman many years before her time; and though to Lady Helen's family and to Lady Helen herself this made her still more agreeable, from becoming so very companionable; to Mrs. Hamilton, and to all, in fact, who loved childhood for childhood's sake, it was a source of real regret, as banishing all the freshness and artlessness and warmth which ought to have been the characteristics of her age. Her father was the only one of her own family who did not admire — and so tried to check — this assumption of fine ladyism, on the part of his daughter; but it was not likely he could succeed, and he only estranged from him the affections of his child.

Annie Grahame had a great many fashionable acquaintances in London, but she still regarded Caroline Hamilton as her favorite friend. Why, she could not exactly tell, except that it was so very, very delightful to have some one in the country to whom she could dilate on all the pleasures of London, display her new dresses, new music, drawings, work, &c. (not however considering it at all necessary to mention that her work and drawings were only *half* her own, and Caroline was much too truthful herself to imagine it, and her mother too anxious to retain that guileless simplicity to enlighten her, as she was well capable of doing.) Annie's quick eye discovered that at such times Caroline certainly envied her, and she imagined she must be a person of infinite consequence to excite such a feeling, and this was such a pleasant sensation, that she sought Caroline as much as possible during their stay at Moorlands. Of Mrs. Hamilton, indeed, she stood in such uncomfortable awe, though that lady never addressed her except in kindness, that as she grew older, it actually became dislike; but this only increased her intimacy with Caroline, whom she had determined should be as unlike her mother as possible; and as this friendship was the only one of his daughter's sentiments which gave Mr. Grahame unmixed satisfaction, he encouraged it by bringing them together as often as he could.

Emmeline and Ellen, meanwhile, had pursued their walk in silence, both engrossed with their own thoughts (for that children of eleven years, indeed of any age, do not think, because when asked what they are thinking about their answer is invariably "Nothing," is one of those mistaken notions which modern education is, we hope, exploding.) Emmeline was so indignant with Annie that she felt more sure than ever that she did not and could never like her. "She is always talking of things mamma says are of such little consequence, and is so proud and contemptuous, and I am afraid she does not always tell the exact truth. I wonder if it is wrong to feel so toward her; one day when I am quite alone with mamma, I will ask her," was the tenor of her meditations.

But Ellen, though Annie's greeting had caused her to shrink still more into herself, and so produced pain, was not thinking only of her. The whole of that hour's intimate association with Mrs. Hamilton had puzzled her; she had doted on her father — she was sure she loved her aunt almost as dearly, but could she ever have given words to that affection as Emmeline had done, and as Edward always did? and so, perhaps, after all, she did not feel as they did, though the wish was so strong to caress her aunt, and sit as close and lovingly by her as Herbert and Emmeline and even Edward did, that its very indulgence seemed to give her pain. Then Caroline's confession too — could she ever have had courage to confess the indulgence of a feeling which she knew to be wrong — and all her aunt had said both to Caroline and Emmeline so fastened on her mind as to make her head ache, and she quite started when a loud shout sounded near them.

"It is only Percy," said Emmeline laughing; I dare say he and Edward are running a race or having some sort of fun." And so they were; laughing, shouting, panting, they came full speed, darting in and out the trees in every variety of mathematical figures their ingenuity could frame; but as soon as

Percy's restless eye discovered Emmeline, he directed his course toward her, exclaiming, "Holla, Edward, stop running for to-day: come here, and let us be sober. Why, Tiny, what brings you and Ellen out now? It is not your usual time."

"Ellen, Ellen, I have had such a happy day; I like Mr. Howard more than ever (he had only seen him twice before.) I am sure I shall get on with him, and he will teach me astronomy and navigation too, so I shall not be ashamed to go to sea next year; I shall learn so much first."

"Let me walk home with you, dear Edward, and do tell me every thing you have done and are going to do," asked Ellen, clinging to his arm, and looking in his face with such an expression that there was little trace of ill-temper. Emmeline meanwhile had made her brother a party in her indignation against Annie's pride, which he termed insolence, vowing he would make her feel it. And as they came in sight of her and Caroline, he called out to Ellen, who, all her timidity returning, tried to draw Edward into another walk.

"Not there, not there, Miss Nelly, you are not going to cut me in that fashion. You have talked quite enough to Edward and must now come to me. Edward, there's mamma; off with you to tell your tale of delight to her." And Edward did not wait a second bidding, leaving Ellen to Percy, who threw his arm affectionately round her, and began talking to her so amusingly that she could not help laughing, and so devoted did he appear to her, that he had only time to greet Miss Grahame, with a very marked and polite bow, and passed on. He wished to provoke, and he succeeded, for Annie was always particularly pleased when the handsome, spirited Percy Hamilton paid her any attention, and that he should be so devoted to his little pale, disagreeable-looking cousin, as not even to give her a word, annoyed her as much as he desired.

Edward's hasty progress to his aunt was slightly checked at seeing a stranger with her, but when he was introduced he made his bow with so much of his mother's grace, that, combined with the extraordinary likeness, and her feelings already interested in Mrs. Hamilton's account of her sister's sufferings and death, Lady Helen could not for the moment speak except to exclaim, "Oh, how that look recalls the past! I could almost fancy poor Eleanor herself stood before me."

"Did you — did you know my mother, madam?" said Edward, with so much eagerness that his cheeks crimsoned and his voice trembled. "Were you one of mamma's" — but he could not finish the sentence, and leaning his head against his aunt, he burst into tears.

"Poor child!" said Lady Helen pityingly, as Mrs. Hamilton pressed him closer to her, and stooped down to kiss his forehead without speaking; and that sudden and unexpected display of feeling contrasted with Ellen's painful shyness, stamped at once and indelibly Lady Helen's opinion of the two orphans.

CHAPTER IV.

VARIETIES.

A FEW days more brought Mrs. Greville and Mary to well-come their friends, and Ellen had again the pain of being introduced to strangers; but this time it was only the pain of her own shyness, for could she have overcome that feeling, she might have felt even pleasure. As it was, the gentle voice and manner with which Mrs. Greville addressed her, and the timid, yet expressive glance of Mary told of such sympathy and kindness, that she felt attracted toward both, and could quite enter into Emmeline's enthusiastic admiration of her friend; not, however, believing it possible that she herself could ever be worthy to win Mary's regard. Taught from such a very early age to believe herself so far inferior to Edward, such characters as Herbert and Mary appeared to her so exalted, that it was quite impossible they could ever think of her; the constant little acts of unobtrusive kindness that her cousin showed her, she attributed to his extreme goodness, not from the most trifling merit in herself. She did indeed love him very dearly, the best next to her aunt; but so much of reverence mingled with it, that she was almost more reserved with him than with the others. But Herbert was naturally reserved himself in words, and so he did not think any thing about it, except to wish and endeavor to make his little cousin happier than she seemed.

When contrasting Mary Greville with Annie Grahame, as she was rather fond of doing, Emmeline became so afraid she was disliking the latter more than she ought to do, that she never rested till she made an opportunity to confess all her feelings to her mother, and beg her to tell her if they were very wrong, and if she ought to like her.

"I am not so unconscionable as to expect you to like every

one with whom you associate, my dear little girl," replied her mother, fondly, for there was something in Emmeline's guileless confidence irresistibly claiming love. "All we have to do when we find nothing that exactly sympathizes with our own feelings, or our own ideas of right and wrong, is to try and find out some reason for their being so different; some circumstance that may have exposed them to greater temptations and trials, for you know I have often told you pleasure and amusements, if too much indulged in, are a much greater trial to some than sorrow and pain. Now, Annie has had a great many more temptations of this kind than you or Mary, and we cannot expect one so very young entirely to resist them."

"Do you mean, mamma, her going out so much in London?"

"Yes, love; she is very much noticed, and so perhaps thinks a little more of appearance and dress and pleasure than is quite necessary."

"But Lady Helen need not take her out so much, if she did not like. Do you think she is quite right to do so?" asked Emmeline, very thoughtfully.

"We must never pronounce judgment on other people's actions, my little girl. I think it better not to interrupt your present quiet and I hope happy life, and therefore I do not take you or Caroline to London; but Mr. Grahame is obliged to be there for several months, and Lady Helen very naturally would not like to be separated either from him or her children And then she has such a large family, and Annie so many young relations, that you see Lady Helen could not keep her children quite as free from temptation as I do mine, and we should be more sorry for Annie than blame her individually, however we may not like her faults. Do you understand me, my dear?"

"Oh, yes, mamma, and I am so glad I took courage to tell you all I felt. I am afraid I have encouraged many unkind thoughts about her, and I am quite sorry now, for I see she cannot help them as much as I thought she could. I do not think I could ever make her my friend, but I will try very much not to dislike and avoid her."

"And that is all that is required of you, my love. When I tell you that our Father in Heaven commands us to love one another, and to avoid all unkindness in thought and deed, I do not mean that He desires us to love all alike, because He knew it would be neither for our happiness nor good that it should be so, but only to prevent the too great influence of prejudice and dislike. We might think such feelings can do no harm, because only confined to our own minds, but they would be sure gradually to lead us to taking pleasure in listening to their dispraise, and joining in it, and to seeing and talking only of their faults, forgetting that if we had been circumstanced exactly as they are, we might have been just the same; and this is the feeling David condemns in one of the Psalms we read this morning. Are you tired of listening to me, dearest, or shall we read it over again together?"

Emmeline's only answer was to run eagerly for her little Bible, and with glowing cheeks and sparkling eyes listen to her mother, as she turned to the fifteenth Psalm, and reading it through, particularly pointed out the third verse, and so explained it, as easily and happily to satisfy her child as to the Divine authority for all that she had said, and to stamp them still more forcibly on her memory.

"And now I do not mean to talk to you any more, my darling," she said, kissing the little earnest face upturned to hers. "You have heard quite enough to think about, and I am sure you will not forget it, so go and play; Ellen must be wondering what has become of you." And again full of glee, the happy child bounded away, exclaiming, as she did so, "Poor Annie, I am glad I am not exposed to such temptations, for I am sure I should not be able to resist them either."

But though any one who had seen her the next half hour might have fancied that a serious thought or sober task could not approach her, neither the conversation nor the Psalm was forgotten; with Herbert's explanatory assistance, she not only found the Psalm, but committed it to memory; and the second Sunday after her conversation with her mother, repeated it so correctly and prettily to her father, as to give her the delight of his caressing approbation. Learning correctly by rote was always her greatest trial, for her vivid fancy and very versatile powers occasioned her actual lessons to be considered such drudgery, as to require a great effort on her part to retain them. The sense, indeed, if she understood it, she learned quickly enough; but she preferred her own language to any one's else, and Mrs. Hamilton had some difficulty in making her understand that in time of study she required *correctness*, and not fancy; and that the attention which was necessary to conquer the words as well as the sense of the lesson, was much more important and valuable, however disagreeable it might seem, than the facility of changing the language to something prettier than the original.

When, therefore, as in the present case, she voluntarily undertook, and conquered really a difficult task for a little lively girl, her parents had no scruple in giving the only reward she cared for — their approbation. It was in the bestowal of praise Mrs. Hamilton was compelled to be almost painfully guarded. She found that the least expression of unusual approbation caused Caroline to relax in her efforts, thinking she had done quite enough, and perniciously increasing her already too exalted ideas of herself. While to Emmeline it was the most powerful incentive to a continuance in improvement, and determined conquest of her faults. There was constantly a dread on the mother's heart, that Caroline would one day accuse her of partiality, from the different measure of her approbation which she was compelled to bestow; and yet painful as it was to persevere under such an impression, the future welfare of both was too precious to be risked for the gratification of the present.

She was watching with delight Emmeline's unrestrained enjoyment of her father's caresses and lively conversation, in which Percy as usual joined — for Tiny, as he chose to call her, was his especial pet and plaything — when she was startled by a low and evidently suppressed sob near her; Ellen was bending over a book of Bible-stories which Herbert had lent her, and her long ringlets completely concealed her face; Miss Harcourt and Caroline both looked up surprised, but a rapid sign from Mrs. Hamilton prevented their making any remark. Herbert fixed his eyes pityingly on his little cousin, as if wishing but not liking to address her. Edward was the only one of the party who moved. He was busily engaged in examining a large Noah's ark, and speculating as to its resemblance to a ship, and its powers of floating; but after a few minutes' apparent thought he left it, and sitting down on Ellen's chair, put his arm round her, and begged her to find a picture of Noah's ark, and see if it were at all like the toy. Cheered by his affection, she conquered with a strong effort the choking in her throat, and turned to the page, and tried to sympathize in his wonder if it really were like the vessel in which Noah was saved, and where he could have put all the animals. Mrs. Hamilton joined them, and without taking more notice of Ellen's very pale cheeks and heavy eyes, than gently to put back the thick tresses that seemed to annoy her by their weight, gave them so much interesting information on the subject and so delighted Edward with allowing him to drag down several books from the library to find out all they said about it, that two hours slipped away quite unconsciously; and Ellen's very painful feeling had been so soothed, that she could smile, and join Emmeline in making all the animals walk in grand procession to their temporary dwelling.

But Mrs. Hamilton did not forget the child's involuntary evidence of suffering, and vainly tried to imagine what at that moment could have caused it. Herbert seemed to think about it, too, for the next day she heard him ask Edward —

"If he knew why his sister always looked so sad? — if he thought it was because she was not yet reconciled to Oakwood?"

"It is not that," was Edward's reply: "she has always looked and seemed sad, as long as I can remember her. One reason may be, she was always ill in India, and papa was often telling me how very much she suffered, and how patiently she bore it; and then, too, she knew I was poor mamma's favorite, (his voice trembled,) and that used to make her very unhappy; but I do not know why she is so very sad now, unless she is ill again, and that no one can tell, for she never will complain."

"Was your sister such a constant sufferer then?" inquired his aunt. "Come here, and tell me all you can about her, Edward. I wish I could know more about both your lives in India."

Edward, with eager willingness, communicated all he knew, though, from his being so constantly with his mother, and Ellen so much left with her father and herself, that all was little enough; adding, however, that after her very dangerous illness, when she was eight years old he perfectly well remembered hearing some celebrated physician say to his father she would probably feel the effects of it all her life.

"It was a very long time before mamma permitted me to see her," added Edward, "and when I did, I remember being almost frightened, she was so altered, so pale, and thin, and weak; and then she was very ill after poor papa's death; but since then she has never complained, and never kept her bed; but I know she is often in pain, for when I have touched her forehead sometimes, it has burnt my hand like fire."

This childish explanation certainly told Mrs. Hamilton more than she had known before; but that Ellen had witnessed the fearful scene of her father's death was still concealed. Edward, as he grew older, though he did not know why, seemed to shrink from the subject, particularly that he had been at a ball the same awful night.

A few days afterward, as Mrs. Hamilton was crossing the

large hall on her way to the school-room — for so, spite of Percy's determination that it should receive the more learned and refined appellation of studio, it was still called — she overheard Caroline's voice, exclaiming in angry impatience —

"Indeed, I shall not, I have enough to do with my own lessons, without attending to other people's. It is your idleness, Ellen, not the difficulty of your lesson; for I am sure it is easy enough."

"For shame, Caroline!" was Emmeline's indignant reply. "She is not idle, and I am sure her lesson is not so easy; I wish I could explain it properly."

"You know Miss Harcourt herself said she was careless or idle to-day, and she must know. I am not going to lose my hour of recreation to help those who won't help themselves."

"How can you be so ill-natured, so unkind!" began Emmeline; but Ellen's beseeching voice interrupted her —

"Do not quarrel with your sister on my account, dearest Emmeline; I dare say I am very stupid, but my head does feel confused to-day; pray do not mind me, dear Emmy; go with Caroline, aunt Emmeline will not like your remaining in."

Caroline had already quitted the room, and in her haste ran against her mother, who she instantly perceived had heard all she said. With a deep blush, she turned as to reënter the school-room, but Mrs. Hamilton stopped her —

"No," she said, gravely, "if you are only to act kindly for fear of my reproof, it will do no good either to yourself or Ellen. I could scarcely have believed it possible you should so have spoken, had I not heard it. Go and amuse yourself as you intended; I rather think had you given up a little of your time to help your cousin, you would have experienced more real pleasure than you will now feel all day."

"Dear mamma, will *you* help Ellen?" asked Emmeline, very timidly, for though at Ellen's reiterated entreaty she had left her, she felt it almost disrespect to run across the hall while her mother was speaking; and the thought suddenly crossed her that, as she was quite sure Ellen was not idle though Miss Harcourt thought she was, her mother, by assisting her, might save her from increased displeasure.

"Yes, dearest, if necessary; I have heard enough to satisfy me that you would if you could; and so I will, for your sake." And Emmeline ran away, quite happy, to try all she could to soothe Caroline, whose self-reproach had as usual terminated in a fit of ill-temper and anger against Ellen, instead of against herself.

Mrs. Hamilton entered the school-room, and stood by Ellen so quietly that the child did not perceive her. Her attention was completely absorbed in her book; but after a few minutes she suddenly pushed it from her, and exclaiming almost passionately:

"I *cannot* learn it, try all I can! and Miss Harcourt will be so very, very angry"—and she gave way, for the first time since her arrival at Oakwood, to a violent burst of tears.

"What is this very, *very* difficult lesson, my little Ellen!" inquired her aunt, kindly taking one hand from her face. "Tell me, and we shall be able to learn it together, perhaps."

"Oh, no, no! it is because I am so very stupid; Miss Harcourt has explained it to me twice, and I know, I know, I ought to understand it—but—"

"Well, then, never mind it to-day. We can all learn much better some days than others, you know; and I dare say to-morrow you will be able to conquer it."

"But Miss Harcourt is already displeased, and she will be still more so, if I leave it without her permission," replied the sobbing girl, longing, but not daring, to throw her arms round her aunt's neck, and lean her aching head against her bosom.

"Not if I beg a reprieve," replied her aunt, smiling; "but you must not let it make you so very unhappy, Ellen. I am afraid it is not only your lesson, but that you are ill, or unhappy about something else. Tell me, dearest, what can I do to make you more happy, more at home?"

"Oh, nothing, nothing!" replied Ellen, struggling with her tears. "Indeed I am happier than I ever thought I could be; I must be very ungrateful to make you think I am unhappy, when you are so good and so kind. My head ached to-day, and that always makes me feel a wish to cry; but indeed I am not unhappy, and never when you kiss me and call me your Ellen, whatever I may feel when you are not by;" and, as if frightened at her own confession, she hid her face in her aunt's dress.

Mrs. Hamilton lifted her into her lap, and kissed her without speaking.

"You must learn to love me more and more then, my Ellen," she said, after a pause, "and when you are feeling ill or in pain, you must not be afraid to tell me, or I shall think that you only fancy you love me."

"Oh, no, it is not fancy; I never loved any one as I do you—except papa—my own darling, good papa!" the word was almost choked with sobs. "He used to fondle me and praise me, and call me his darling Ellen, as uncle Hamilton did Emmeline last Sunday; and when I was ill, so ill they said I should die, he never left me, except when his military duties called him away; and he used to nurse me, and try to amuse me, that I might forget pain and weakness. Oh, I shall never, never forget that dreadful night!" and she closed her eyes and shuddered, as the horrid scene of blood and death flashed before her.

"What dreadful night, my poor child?" inquired Mrs. Hamilton, soothingly, after doubting whether or not it would be better for Ellen to pursue such an evidently painful theme, and no longer requiring an explanation of her emotion the previous Sabbath.

"The night poor papa was killed; — oh, there were so many horrid forms on the grass, the natives and poor papa's own men, and they looked so ghastly in the moonlight, and the grass was covered with blood and limbs and heads that had been shot off; and there were such cries and groans of pain — I see it, I hear it all again so often before I go to sleep, and when my head feels as it does to-day, and fancy I hear poor papa's last words, and feel his kiss as he lay bleeding, bleeding slowly to death, and his voice was so strange, and his lips so cold!"

"But how came you in such a dreadful scene, my poor Ellen? who could have permitted such a little child to be there?"

"Because I wished it so very much; I knew he would die before they could bring him to me, and I did so want to feel his kiss and hear his voice once more. Oh, aunt Emmeline! shall I never see him again? I know he cannot come to me; but shall I, oh, shall I ever be good enough to go to him?" And she looked up in her aunt's face with such a countenance of beseeching entreaty, that Mrs. Hamilton's eyes filled with tears, and it was a full minute before she could speak; but when she did, Ellen felt more relieved and comforted, than on the subject of her father's death she had ever felt before. From her mother not being able to bear the subject even partially alluded to, and from having no one to whom she could speak of it, it had taken a still stronger hold of her imagination; and whenever she was unusually weak, and her head aching and confused, it became still more vivid. The very visible sympathy and interest of her aunt, and the gentle words in which she tried to turn the child's thoughts from that scene of horror to the happiness of her father in Heaven, and an assurance that, if she tried to do her duty, and to love and serve God, and trust in His mercy to render her efforts acceptable, she would rejoin him, seemed to remove the mass of tangled thought within her young mind. Her head, indeed, still ached very painfully, and her eyes seemed as if they would close, notwithstanding all her efforts to keep them open; but when she awoke from a long quiet sleep, on the sofa in Mrs. Hamilton's dressing-room, where her aunt had laid her, and found that kind friend still watching over her, the little heart and temples had ceased to throb so quickly, and she felt better and happier.

Mr. Maitland, the medical friend of the family, confirmed the opinion which Edward had said their physician in India had given of his sister's state of health. He did not, he said, consider her liable to serious illness, or of a constitution that would not endure; but that he feared it would be some years before she knew the blessing of really good health, and be constantly subject to that lassitude, severe headache, and the depression of the whole system thence proceeding, which must prevent the liveliness and quickness of acquirement natural to most children. He thought the evil had been very greatly increased by want of sufficient care in early years, and the unwholesome climate in which she had so long lived, that he wondered her mother had not been advised to send her over to England, adding, with a smile, he was quite sure Mrs. Hamilton would not have refused the charge, anxious as it might have been. And earnestly, not only on account of the child's physical but mental health, did Mrs. Hamilton wish that such had been the case, and that she had had the care of her niece from earliest infancy; and how much more would she have wished this, had she known that Mrs. Fortescue had really been advised to do with Ellen as Mr. Maitland had said; but that believing it merely an idle fancy, and persisting, too, in her own headstrong idea, that it was ill-temper, not illness, which rendered Ellen so disagreeable, she would not stoop so to conquer her unfortunate pride as to ask such a favor of her relatives, and to whom else could she appeal? Colonel Fortescue had none but distant cousins. She did satisfy a qualm of conscience by once suggesting to her husband — as her own idea, however, not as that of an experienced physician — that as he fancied Ellen was always ill, she might be better in England; but, as she expected, not only his intense love for his little girl rose up against the idea of separation, but his pride revolted from sending her to claim the pity of relatives who had so completely cast off her parents; yet had he been told it was absolutely necessary for her health and so greatly for her happiness, he would not have hesitated to sacrifice every thought of self. But Eleanor, satisfied that she had done her duty, and delighted that in one respect he was quite as proud as she was, never again referred to the subject, and the physician who had thus advised, from his constant removals, he never chanced to meet.

Great, indeed, was the amount of childish suffering which this selfish decision, on the part of her mother, occasioned Ellen. We do not mean the pain of constant languor itself, though that in its full amount our happy healthful young readers cannot have the least idea of: they, perhaps, think it almost a pleasant change, the care, and petting, and presents so often lavished on a brief decided illness; but that is a very different thing to that kind of suffering which only so affects them as to be dull and heavy, they do not know why, and to make it such a very difficult task to learn the lessons others find so easy; and such a pain sometimes to move, that they are thought slow and unwilling, and perhaps even idle, when they would gladly run, and help, and work as others; and so weak sometimes, that tears start at the first harsh or unkind word, and they are thought cross, when they do not in the least feel so; and this, not for a few weeks, but, with few exceptions, the trial of months and even years.

And this was Ellen's — which not even the tenderest and most unfailing care of her aunt could entirely guard her from. It is a most difficult thing for those who are strong and healthy themselves to understand and always bear with physical suffering in others. Miss Harcourt, though in general free from any thing like prejudice, and ardently desirous to follow up her own and Mrs. Hamilton's ideas of right and wrong, could not so govern her affections as to feel the same toward Ellen as she did toward Edward and the children she had lived with and taught so long. Her task with Ellen required more patience and forbearance and care than with either of the others, and sometimes she could not help believing and acting toward her as if it were wilful idleness and carelessness, not the languor of disease.

With the recollection and evidence of Herbert, who had been delicate from his birth, and who was yet of such a remarkably gifted mind, and so bright in aspect, so sweet in temper, that illness seemed to have spiritualized instead of deadened every faculty, she could not understand, as Mrs. Hamilton did, the force of circumstances in producing from nearly the same cause two such different effects, nor how it was that complete neglect had engendered more evils than indiscreet indulgence; but that it appeared to have done so, was unhappily only too evident not only to Miss Harcourt but to Mrs. Hamilton. It seemed almost surprising, and certainly a proof of a remarkably good disposition, that Edward appeared so free from great faults, and of such a warm, generous, frank, and *seemingly* unselfish nature, so open to conviction and to all good impressions, that, except occasional fits of violent passion, there really was, as far as his aunt and uncle could perceive, nothing to complain of. They did not know that he stood in such awe of Mr. Hamilton, from his mother's lessons of his exceeding sternness, that he exercised the greatest control over himself; and he was so excessively fond of Mr. Howard, and his days glided by in such varied and delightful employment, that there was no temptation to do wrong, except certain acts of trifling disobedience, of more consequence from the self-will they betrayed than the acts themselves, but which might have been sources of anxiety to his aunt, and lessened her confidence in him had she known them; but she did not, for Ellen not only constantly concealed, but she was the sufferer for him, and so brought reproof and suspicion on herself, which, could the truth have been known, might have been averted. But truth of act as well as word had never been impressed on Edward; and, therefore, though he was constitutionally too brave to utter a falsehood, too honorable to shield himself at the expense of another, if he knew that other suffered, he had been too long taught to believe that Ellen was his inferior, and must always give up to him, to imagine that he was ever acting deceitfully or unmanfully in permitting her to conceal his acts of disobedience.

There was so much to love and admire in Edward, that neither Mr. nor Mrs. Hamilton imagined the real weakness of his character — that those lovable qualities all sprung from natural impulse, unsustained by any thing like principle. The quickness and apparent fervor with which he received the religious impressions they and Mr. Howard sought so earnestly tc instil, in the short time that was allowed them before he entered the navy, they augured so hopefully from, that not only his preceptor and uncle, but his ever-anxious aunt, looked forward to his career with scarcely a doubt as to its probity and honor.

Ellen caused her infinitely more anxiety. There was a disregard to truth, a want of openness and candor, which, though Mrs. Hamilton believed the effects of neglect and extreme timidity, both her husband and Miss Harcourt feared were natural. Much, indeed, sprung from the poor child's mistaken idea of the nature and solemnity of the promise she had made her mother, and her constant watchfulness and determination to shield Edward. For the disregard to truth, her mother had, indeed, alone been answerable. Ellen's naturally very timid character required the inculcation of a high, firm principle, to enable her so to conquer herself as to speak the truth, even if she suffered from it. It was only, indeed, in extreme cases of fear — and never to her father that she had ever spoken falsely; but to Mrs. Hamilton's high principles, which by extreme diligence and care she had so successfully imparted to her own children, even concealment was often an acted untruth, and of this fault and equivocation Ellen was but too often guilty, exciting Miss Harcourt's and Caroline's prejudices yet more against her. The latter, with all her faults, never swerved from the rigid truth, and had a strong contempt and dislike toward all those who did — except her friend Annie, who, as she always took care to speak the truth to her, she did not suspect of being less careful than herself. Emmeline, who had had some difficulty in restraining her love of exaggeration, and also in so conquering her own timidity and fear as always to speak the truth, only pitied Ellen, but did not love her the less.

Of course, it was not till some months had passed that these lights and shadows of character in the orphans, and in the opinions they called forth in those around them, could be discovered; but notwithstanding she stood almost alone in her opinion, notwithstanding there was very little outward evidence that she was correct, Mrs. Hamilton believed there was a great deal more in her niece than was discernible. She seemed to possess a strength, almost an intensity, of feeling and warmth of affection, which, if properly guided, would effectually aid in removing the childish errors engendered by neglect; and it was this belief which not only enabled her to bear calmly the anxiety and care, and often pain, which those faults and their compelled correction occasioned, but actually to love her niece, if possible, still more than Edward, and very nearly with the same amount of quiet but intense affection which she felt for her own children.

CHAPTER V.

A YOUNG GENTLEMAN IN A PASSION. — A WALK. — A SCENE OF DISTRESS.

One very fine morning in May, Mrs. Hamilton invited Edward to join her in a walk, intending also to call at Moorlands and Greville Manor on their way. The lads were released for a few days from their attendance on Mr. Howard, that gentleman having been summoned on some clerical business to Exeter. Percy was to accompany his father on an equestrian excursion; Herbert had been commissioned by Emmeline some days before to take some books to Mary Greville, and had looked forward himself to spending a morning with her. Edward, delighted at being selected as his aunt's companion, prepared with haste and glee for his excursion. Robert was, however, unfortunately not at hand to give him a clean pair of shoes (he had already spoiled two pair that morning by going into the stream which ran through the park to sail a newly-rigged frigate,) and angry at the delay, fearing that his aunt would not wait for him, he worked himself into such a violent passion, that when Robert did appear he gave vent to more abusive language than he had ever yet ventured to use, concluding by hurling both his discarded shoes at the domestic, who only escaped a severe blow by starting aside, and permitting them to go through the window.

"Robert, leave the room: I desire that you will not again give your assistance to Master Fortescue till he knows how to ask it," was Mrs. Hamilton's most unexpected interference, and Edward so startled at her voice and look, that his passion was suddenly calmed.

"Finish your toilet, and when you have found your shoes and put them away, you may join me in the breakfast-room, Edward. I only wait your pleasure."

And never did Edward leave her presence more gladly. Shame had suddenly conquered anger; and though his chest still heaved and his cheeks were still flushed, he did not utter another word till nearly a quarter of a mile on their walk.

Twice he had looked up in his aunt's face as if about to speak, but the expression was so very grave, that he felt strangely afraid to proceed. At length he exclaimed —

"You are displeased with me, dear aunt; but indeed I could not help feeling angry."

"I am still more sorry than displeased, Edward; I had hoped you were learning more control, and to know your duty to a domestic better. Your uncle — "

"Oh, pray do not tell him!" implored Edward, "and I will ask Robert's pardon the moment I go home."

"I certainly shall not complain of you to him, Edward, if my arguments can convince you of your error; but if you are only to ask Robert's pardon for fear of your uncle, I would rather you should not do so. Tell me the truth; if you were quite sure your uncle would know nothing about it, would you still ask Robert's pardon?"

Edward unhesitatingly answered "No!"

"And why not?"

"Because I think he ought to ask mine for keeping me waiting as he did, and for being insolent first to me."

"He did not keep you waiting above five minutes, and that was my fault, not his, as I was employing him; and as for insolence, can you tell me what he said?" Edward hesitated.

"I do not remember the exact words, but I know he called me impatient, and if I were, he had no right to tell me so."

"Nor did he. I heard all that passed, and I could not help thinking how very far superior was Robert, a poor country youth, to the young gentleman who abused him."

The color rose to Edward's temples, but he set his teeth and clenched his hand, to prevent any farther display of anger; and his aunt, after attentively observing him, continued —

"He said that his young master Percy never required impossibilities, and though often impatient, never abused him. You heard the word, and feeling you had been so, believed he applied it to yourself."

"But in what can he be my superior?" asked Edward, in a low voice, as if still afraid his passion would regain ascendency.

"I will answer your question by another, Edward. Suppose any one had used abusive terms toward you, and contemptuously desired you to get out of your sight, how would you have answered?"

"I would have struck him to the earth," replied Edward, passionately, and quite forgetting his wished for control. "Neither equal nor superior should dare speak so to me again.'

And what prevented Robert acting in the same manner?" Do you think he has no feeling?—that he is incapable of such emotions as pain or anger?"

Edward stood for a minute quite still and silent.

"I did not think any thing about it," he said, at length; "but I certainly supposed I had a right to say what I pleased to one so far beneath me."

"And in what is Robert so far beneath you?"

"He is a servant, and I am a gentleman in birth, rank—"

"Stop, Edward! did you make yourself a gentleman? Is it any credit to you, individually, to be higher in the world, and receive a better education than Robert?"

Edward was again silent, and his aunt continued to talk to him so kindly yet so earnestly, that at length he exclaimed—

"I feel I have indeed been wrong, dear aunt; but what can I do to prove to Robert I am really sorry for having treated him so ill?"

"Are you really sorry, Edward, or do you only say this for fear of your uncle's displeasure?"

"Indeed, I had quite forgotten him," replied Edward, earnestly; "I deserve his anger, and would willingly expose myself to it, if it would redeem my fault."

"I would rather see you endeavor earnestly to restrain your passions my dear boy, than inflict any such pain upon you. It will be a great pleasure to me if you can really so conquer yourself as to apologize to Robert; and I think the pain of so doing will enable you more easily to remember all we have been saying, than if you weakly shrink from it. The life you have chosen makes me even more anxious that you should become less passionate—than were you to remain longer with me; I fear you will so often suffer seriously from it."

"I very often make resolutions never to be in a passion again," returned Edward, sorrowfully; "but whenever any thing provokes me, something seems to come in my throat, and I am compelled to give way."

"You will not be able to conquer your fault, my dear Edward, without great perseverance; but remember, the more difficult the task, the greater the reward; and that you *can* control anger I have, even during our walk, had a proof."

Edward looked up surprised.

"Did you not feel very angry when I said Robert was your superior?"

"Yes," replied Edward, blushing deeply.

"And yet you successfully checked your rising passion, for

fear of offending me. I cannot be always near you; but, my dear boy, you must endeavor to remember that lesson I have tried to teach you so often—that you are never *alone*. You cannot even think an angry thought, much less speak an abusive word and commit the most trifling act of passion, without offending God. If you would but ask for His help, and recollect that to offend Him is far more terrible than to incur the displeasure of either your uncle or myself, I think you would find your task much easier, than if you attempted it, trusting in your own strength alone, and only for fear of man."

Edward did not make any reply, but his countenance expressed such earnest thought and softened feeling, that Mrs. Hamilton determined on not interrupting it by calling at Moorlands as she had intended, and so turned in the direction of Greville Manor. They walked on for some little time in silence, gradually ascending one of those steep and narrow but green and flowery lanes peculiar to Devonshire; and on reaching the summit of the hill, and pausing a moment by the little gate that opened on a rich meadow, through which their path lay, an exclamation of "How beautiful!" burst from Edward.

Fields of alternate red and green sloped down to the river's edge, the green bearing the glistening color peculiar to May, the red from the full rich soil betraying that the plough had but lately been there, and both contrasting beautifully with the limpid waters, whose deep azure seemed to mock the very heavens. The Dart from that point seemed no longer a meandering river: it was so encompassed by thick woods and fertile hills, that it resembled a lake, to which there was neither outlet nor inlet, save from the land. The trees all presented that exquisite variety of green peculiar to May, and so lofty was the slope on which they grew, that some seemed to touch the very sky, while others bent gracefully over the water, which their thick branches nearly touched. The hills themselves presented a complete mosaic of red and green; the fields divided by high hedges, from which the oak and elm and beech and ash would start up, of growth so superb as to have the semblance of a cultivated park, and not of natural woodland.

Greville Manor, an Elizabethan building, stood on their right, surrounded by its ancient woods, which, though lovely still, Mr. Greville's excesses had already shorn of some of their finest timber. Some parts of the river were in complete shade from the overhanging branches, while beyond them would stretch the bright blue of heaven: in other parts, a stray sunbeam would dart through an opening in the thick branches, and shine like a bright spot in the surrounding darkness; and farther on, the cloudless sun so flung down his full refulgence, that the moving waters flashed and sparkled like burning gems.

"Is it not beautiful, dear aunt? Sometimes I feel as if I were not half so passionate in the open air as in the house; can you tell me why?"

"Not exactly, Edward," she replied, smiling; "but I am very pleased to hear you say so, and to find that you can admire such a lovely scene as this. To my feelings, the presence of a loving God is so impressed upon his works — we can so distinctly trace goodness, and love, and power, in the gift of such a beautiful world, that I feel still more how wrong it is to indulge in vexation, or care, or anxiety, when in the midst of a beautiful country, than when at home; and perhaps it is something of the same feeling working in you, though you do not know how to define it."

"But *you* can never do or feel any thing wrong, dear aunt," said Edward, looking with surprised inquiry in her face.

"Indeed, my dear boy, I know that I very often have wrong thoughts and feelings; and that only my Father in Heaven's infinite mercy enables me to overcome them. It would be very sad, if I were as faulty, and as easily led into error, as you and your cousins may be, when I have had so many more years to think and try to improve in; but just in the same way as you have duties to perform and feelings to overcome, so have I; and if I fail in the endeavor to lead you all in the better and happier path — or feel too much anxiety, or shrink from giving myself pain, when compelled to correct a fault in either of you, I am just as likely to incur the displeasure of our Father in Heaven, as you are when you are passionate or angry; and perhaps still more so, for the more capable we are of knowing and doing our duty, the more wrong we are when we fail in it, even in thought."

There was so much in this reply to surprise Edward, it seemed so to fill his mind with new ideas, that he continued his walk in absolute silence. That his aunt could ever fail, as she seemed to say she had and did, and even still at times found it difficult to do right, was very strange; but yet somehow it seemed to comfort him, and to inspire him with a sort of courage to emulate her, and conquer his difficulties. He had fancied that she could not possibly understand how difficult it was for him always to be good; but when he found that she could do so even from her own experience, her words appeared endowed with double force, and he loved her, and looked up to her more than ever.

Ten minutes more brought them to the Gothic lodge of the Manor, and instead of seeking the front entrance, Mrs. Hamilton led the way to the flower-garden, on which Mrs. Greville's usual morning-room opened by a glass door.

"Herbert was to tell Mary of our intended visit; I wonder she is not watching for me as usual," observed Mrs. Hamilton, somewhat anxiously; and her anxiety increased, as on nearing the half open door she saw poor Mary, her head leaning against Herbert, deluged in tears. Mrs. Greville was not there, though the books, work, and maps upon the table told of their morning's employment having been the same as usual. Herbert was earnestly endeavoring to speak comfort, but evidently without success; and Mary was in general so controlled, that her present grief betrayed some very much heavier trial than usual.

"Is your mother ill, my dear Mary? What can have happened to agitate you so painfully?" she inquired, as at the first sound of her voice the poor girl sprung toward her, and tried to say how very glad she was that she had come just then; but the words were inarticulate from sobs; and Mrs. Hamilton, desiring Edward to amuse himself in the garden, made her sit down by her, and told her not to attempt to check her tears, but to let them have free vent a few minutes, and then to try and tell her what had occurred. It was a very sad tale for a child to tell, and as Mrs. Hamilton's previous knowledge enabled her to gather more from it than Mary's broken narrative permitted, we will give it in our own words.

Mr. Greville had been at home for a month, a quarter of which time the good humor which some unusually successful bets had excited, lasted; but no longer. His amusement then consisted, as usual, in trying every method to annoy and irritate his wife, and in endeavoring to make his son exactly like himself. Young as the boy was — scarcely twelve — he took him to scenes of riot and feasting, which the society of some boon companions, unhappily near neighbors, permitted; and though Alfred's cheek became pale, his eye haggard, and his temper uneven, his initiation was fraught with such a new species of excitement and pleasure, that it rejoiced and encouraged his father in the same measure as it agonized his mother, and, for her sake, poor Mary.

That morning Alfred had declared his intention of visiting a large fair, which, with some races of but ill repute, from the bad company they collected, was to be held at a neighboring town, and told his father to prepare for a large demand on his cash, as he meant to try his hand at all the varieties of gaming which the scene presented. Mr. Greville laughed heartily at what he called the boy's right spirit, and promised him all he required; but there was a quivering on her mother's lip, a deadly paleness on her cheek, that spoke volumes of suffering to the heart of the observant Mary, who sat trembling beside her. Still Mrs. Greville did not speak till her husband left the room; but then, as Alfred was about to follow him, she caught hold of his hand, and implored him, with such a tone and look of agony, only to listen to her, for her sake to give up his intended pleasure; that, almost frightened by an emotion which in his gentle mother he had scarcely ever seen, and suddenly remembering that he had lately been indeed most unkind and neglectful to her, he threw his arms round her neck, and promised with tears that if it gave her so much pain, he would not go; and so sincere was his feeling at the moment that, had there been no tempter near, he would, in all probability, have kept his word. But the moment Mr. Greville heard from his son his change of intention and its cause, he so laughed at his ridiculous folly, so sneered at his want of spirit in preferring his mother's whims to his father's pleasures, that, as could not fail to be the case, every better feeling fled. This ought to have been enough; but it was too good an opportunity to vent his ill-temper on his wife, to be neglected. He sought her, where she was superintending Mary's lessons, and for nearly an hour poured upon her the most fearful abuse and cutting taunts, ending by declaring that all the good she had done by her saintly eloquence was to banish her son from her presence, whenever he left home, as in future Alfred should be his companion; and that he should begin that very day. Mrs. Greville neither moved nor spoke in reply; and the expression of her countenance was so sternly calm, that poor Mary felt as if she dared not give way to the emotion with which her heart was bursting.

Mr. Greville left the room, and they heard him peremptorily desire the housekeeper to put up some of Master Alfred's clothes. In a perfectly composed voice Mrs. Greville desired Mary to proceed with the exercise she was writing, and emulating her firmness, she tried to obey. Fortunately her task was writing, for to have spoken or read aloud would, she felt, have been impossible. So full half an hour passed, and then hasty footsteps were heard in the hall, and the joyous voice of Alfred exclaiming —

"Let me wish mamma and Mary good-by, papa."

"I have not another moment to spare," was the reply. "You have kept me long enough, and must be quicker next time; come along, my boy."

The rapid tread of horses' hoofs speedily followed the sullen clang with which the hall-door closed, and as rapidly faded away in the distance. With an irresistible impulse, Mary raised her eyes to her mother's face; a bright red flush had risen to her temples, but her lips were perfectly colorless, and her hand tightly pressed her heart; but this only lasted a minute, for the next she had fallen quite senseless on the floor. Her poor child hung over her almost paralyzed with terror, and so long did the faint last, that she was conveyed to her own room, partially undressed, and laid on her bed before she at all recovered. A brief while she had clasped Mary to her bosom, as if in her was indeed her only earthly comfort, and then in a faint voice desired to be left quite alone. Mary had flung herself on the neck of the sympathizing Herbert Hamilton (who had arrived just in the confusion attendant on Mrs. Greville's unusual illness,) and wept there in all the uncontrolled violence of early sorrow.

Mrs. Hamilton remained some time with her afflicted friend, for so truly could she sympathize with her, that her society brought with it the only solace Mrs. Greville was capable of realizing from human companionship.

"It is not for myself I murmur," were the only words that in that painful interview might have even seemed like complaint; "but for my poor child. How is her fragile frame and gentle spirit to endure through trials such as these; oh, Emmeline, to lose both, and through their father!"

And difficult indeed did it seem to realize the cause of such a terrible dispensation; but happily for Mrs. Greville, she could still look up in love and trust, even when below all of comfort as of joy seemed departed; and in a few days she was enabled to resume her usual avocations, and, by an assumption of cheerfulness and constant employment, to restore some de gree of peace and happiness to her child.

Neither Herbert nor Edward seemed inclined to converse on their walk home, and Mrs. Hamilton was so engrossed in thought for Mrs. Greville, that she did not feel disposed to speak either. Herbert was contrasting his father with Mary s, and with such a vivid sense of his own happier lot, that he felt almost oppressed with the thought, he was not, he never could be, grateful enough; for, what had he done to be so much more blessed? And when Mr. Hamilton, who, wondering at their long absence, had come out to meet them, put his arm affectionately round him, and asked him what could possibly make him look so pale and pensive, the boy's excited feelings completely overpowered him. He buried his face on his father's shoulder, and burst into tears; and then leaving his mother to explain it, for he felt quite sure she could, without his telling her, darted away and never stopped till he found himself in the sanctuary of his own room; and there he remained, trying to calm himself by earnest thought and almost unconscious prayer, till the dinner-bell summoned him to rejoin his family, which he did, quiet and gentle, but cheerful, as usual.

Edward did not forget the thoughts of the morning, but the struggles so to subdue his pride as to apologize to Robert, seemed very much more difficult when he was no longer hearing his aunt's earnest words; but he *did* conquer himself, and the fond approving look, with which he was rewarded, gave him such a glowing feeling of pleasure as almost to lessen the pain of his humiliation.

CHAPTER VI.

CECIL GRAHAME'S PHILOSOPHY. — AN ERROR AND ITS CONSEQUENCES. — A MYSTERY AND A CONFIDENCE.

A FEW days after the events of the last chapter, Mrs. Hamilton, accompanied by Percy, called at Moorlands. Cecil Grahame was playing in the garden, and Percy remained with him, his good-nature often making him a companion, though there was nearly six years' difference in their age.

"Are you going to T— on Thursday, Percy? There will be such fine doings. Races and the county fair, and wild beasts and shows, and every thing delightful; of course, you will go?"

"I do not think it at all likely," replied young Hamilton.

"No!" repeated Cecil, much astonished. "Why, I was only saying the other day how much I should like to be as old as you are; it must be so delightful to be one's own master."

"I do not consider myself my own master yet, Cecil. Sometimes I wish I were; at others, I think I am much better as I am. And, as for this fair, Mr. Howard will be back to-morrow, so there is no chance of my going."

"Why is there no such thing as the possibility of a holiday, Percy?" replied Cecil, with great glee; "or perhaps," he added, laughing, "your papa is like mine, and does not allow such freaks; thinks it wrong to go to such places, acting against morality, and such out-of-the-way ideas."

"Are these Mr. Grahame's opinions?" inquired Percy, almost sternly.

"Why ye — yes — why do you look at me so, Percy? I am sure I said no harm; I only repeated what I have heard mamma say continually."

"That is not the very least excuse for your disrespect to your father; and if he think thus, I wonder you should talk of going to the races; you cannot have his permission."

"Oh, but mamma has promised if I am a good boy till then, and she can manage it, I shall go; for she cannot see any harm in it. And as for waiting for papa's permission — if I did, I should never go anywhere. He is so unkind, that I am always afraid of speaking or even playing, when he is in the room."

"You are a silly boy, Cecil," replied young Hamilton; "Believe me, you do not know your best friend. I should be very sorry to feel thus toward my father."

"Oh! but yours and mine are very different sort of people. Your papa never punishes you, or refuses you his permission, when you wish particularly to do any thing, or go anywhere."

"If papa thinks my wishes foolish, or liable to lead me into error, he does refuse me without scruple, Cecil. And though I am old enough now, I hope, so to conduct myself as to avoid actual punishment: when I was as young as you are, papa very frequently punished me, both for my violence and pride."

"But then he was kind to you afterward. Now I should not so much mind papa's severity when I am naughty, if he would only be kind, or take some notice of me when I am good. But has Mr. Hamilton told you not to go to the races?"

"Not exactly: he has merely said he thinks it a day most unprofitably wasted; and that the gambling and excesses, always the attendant of races, are not fit scenes for young persons. Were I to take my horse and go, he would not, perhaps, be actually displeased, as I am old enough now, he says, in some things, to judge for myself; but I should be acting against his principles, which, just now, I am not inclined to do, for I am sure to suffer from it afterward."

"Well, all I can say, is, that when I am as old as you are, Percy, I shall certainly consider myself under no one. I hope I shall be at Eton by that time, and then we shall see if Cecil Grahame has not some spirit in him. I would not be tied down to Oakwood, and to Mr. Howard's humdrum lessons, as you are, Percy, for worlds."

"Take care that Cecil Grahame's spirit does not effervesce so much, as to make him, when at Eton, wish himself back at Moorlands," replied Percy, laughing heartily at his young companion's grotesque attempts at self-consequence, by placing his cap dandily on his head, flourishing his cane, and trying to make himself look taller. Cecil took his laugh, however, in good part, and they continued in amicable conversation till Mrs. Hamilton summoned Percy to attend her home.

Our readers have, perhaps, discovered that Percy, this day was not quite as lively as usual. If they have not, his mother did; for, strange to say, he walked by her side silent and dispirited. His thoughtlessness very often led him into error and its disagreeable consequences; and, fearing this had again been the case, she playfully inquired the cause of his most unusual abstraction. He colored, but evaded the question, and successfully roused himself to talk. His mother was not anxious, for she had such perfect confidence in him, that she knew if he had committed error, he would redeem it, and that his own good feelings and high principles would prevent its recurrence.

It so happened, however, that young Hamilton, by a series of rather imprudent actions, had plunged himself into such a very unusual and disagreeable position, as not very well to know how to extricate himself from it, without a full confession to his father; which, daringly brave as in general he was, he felt almost as if he really had not the courage to make. One of Mr. Hamilton's most imperative commands was, that his sons should never incur a debt, and, to prevent the temptation, their monthly allowance was an ample one, and fully permitted any recreative indulgences they might desire.

Now Percy was rather inclined to extravagance, from thoughtlessness and a profuse generosity, which had often caused him such annoyance as to make him resolve again and again to follow his father's advice, and keep some accounts of his expenditure, as a slight check on himself. The admiration for beauty in the fine arts, which his mother had so sedulously cultivated, had had only one bad effect; and that was that his passion for prints and paintings, and illustrated and richly-bound volumes, sometimes carried him beyond bounds, and very often occasioned regret, that he had not examined the letter-press of such works, as well as their engravings and bindings. He had given orders to Mr. Harris, a large fancy stationer, librarian, and publisher of T—, to procure for him a set of engravings, whose very interesting subjects and beautiful workmanship Mr. Grahame had so vividly described to him, that young Hamilton felt to do without them till his father or he himself should visit the metropolis, and so judge of their worth themselves, was quite impossible. The order was given without the least regard to price. They arrived at the end of the month, and the young gentleman, to his extreme astonishment, discovered that his month's allowance had been so expended, as not to leave him a half-quarter of the necessary sum. What to do he did not very well know. Mr. Harris had had great difficulty in procuring the prints, and of course he was bound in honor to take them. If he waited till he could pay for them, he must sacrifice the whole of one month's allowance, and then how could he keep free from debt till the next? As for applying to his father, he shrank from it with actual pain. How could he ask his ever kind and indulgent parent to discharge a debt incurred by such a thoughtless act of unnecessary extravagance? Mr. Harris made very light of it, declaring that, if Mr. Percy did not pay him for a twelvemonth, it was of no consequence; he would trust him for any sum or any time he liked. But to make no attempt to liquidate his debt was as impossible as to speak to his father. So, after a violent struggle with his pride, which did not at all like the idea of betraying his inability to pay the whole, or of asking a favor of Mr. Harris, he agreed to pay his debt by instalments, and so in two or three months, at the very latest, discharge the whole.

One week afterward he received his month's allowance, and, riding over directly to the town, relieved his conscience of half its load. To have only half his usual sum, however, for monthly expenditure, caused him so many checks and annoyances as to make him hate the very sight of the prints whose possession he had so coveted; but he looked forward to the next month to be free at least of Mr. Harris — the idea of disobedience to his father in incurring a debt at all, causing him more annoyance than all the rest.

Again the first day of the month came round, and putting the full sum required in his purse, he set off, but on his way encountered such a scene of distress, that every thought fled from his mind, except how to relieve it. He accompanied the miserable half-famished man to a hut in which lay a seemingly dying woman with a new-born babe, and two or three small half-starved, half-naked children — listened to their story, which was really one of truth and misfortune, not of whining deceit, poured the whole contents of his purse into their laps, and rode off to T—, to find, not Mr. Harris but Mr. Maitland, and implore him to see what his skill would do for the poor woman. He encountered that gentleman at the outskirts of the town, told his story, and was so delighted at Mr. Maitland's willing promise to go directly, and also to report the case to those who would relieve it, that he never thought of any thing else till he found himself directly opposite Mr. Harris's shop, and his bounding heart sunk suddenly down, as impelled by a weight of lead. The conviction flashed upon him that he had been giving away money which was actually not his own; and the deed which had been productive of so much internal happiness, now seemed to reproach and condemn him. He rode back without even seeking Mr. Harris, for what could he tell him as the reason of his non-payment? Certainly not his having given it away.

The first of May, which was his birthday, he had been long engaged to spend with some young men and lads who were to have a grand game of cricket, a jovial dinner, an adjournment to some evening amusement, and, to conclude the day, a gay supper, with glees and songs. Mr. Hamilton had rather wished Percy to leave the party after dinner, and had told him so, merely, however, as a preference, not a command, but giving him permission to use his own discretion. Percy knew there would be several expenses attendant on the day, but still he had promised so long to be one of the party, which all had declared would be nothing without him, and his own inclinations so urged him to join it, that it seemed to him utterly impossible to draw back, especially as he could give no excuse for doing so. How could he say that he could not afford it? when he was, or ought to have been, nearly the richest of the party and what would his father think?

He went. The day was thoroughly delightful, and so exciting, that though he had started from home with the intention of leaving them after dinner, he could not resist the pleadings of his companions and his own wishes, and remained. At supper alone excitement and revelry seemed to have gained the upper hand, and Percy, though steady in entirely abstaining from all excess, was not quite so guarded as usual. A clergyman had lately appeared at T—, whose appearance, manners, and opinions had given more than usual food for gossip, and much uncharitableness. His cloth indeed ought to have protected him, but it rather increased the satire, sarcasm, and laughter which he excited. He was brought forward by the thoughtless youths of Percy's party, quizzed unmercifully, made the object of some clever caricatures and satires, and though young Hamilton at first kept aloof, he could not resist the contagion. He dashed off about half-a-dozen verses of such remarkably witty and clever point, that they were received with roars of applause, and an unanimous request for distribution; but this he positively refused, and put them up, with one or two other poems of more innocent wit, in which he was fond of indulging, into his pocket.

The day closed, and the next morning brought with it so many regrets, and such a confused recollection of the very unusual excitement of the previous evening, that he was glad to dismiss the subject from his mind, and threw his satire, as he believed, into the fire. In fact, he was so absorbed with the disagreeable conviction that he could only pay Mr. Harris a third of his remaining debt, trifling as in reality it was, that he thought of nothing else. Now Mr. Harris was the editor and publisher of rather a clever weekly paper, and Percy happened to be in his parlor waiting to speak to him, while he was paying a contributor.

"I wish my head were clever enough to get out of your debt in that comfortable way," he said, half laughing, as the gentleman left them together.

"I wish all my customers were as desirous of paying their large debts as you are your small one," was Mr. Harris's reply. "But I have heard something of your clever verses, Mr. Percy; if you will let me see some, I really may be able to oblige you, as you seem so very anxious to have nothing more to do with me—"

"In the way of debt, not of purchases, Mr. Harris; and I assure you, I am not thinking so much about you, as of my own disobedience. I will send you my papers, only you must give me your word not to publish them with my name."

"They will not be worth so much," replied Mr. Harris, smiling.

"Only let me feel they have helped to discharge my debt, or at least let me know how much more is wanted to do so, and I will worship the muses henceforth," replied Percy, with almost his natural gayety, for he felt he wrote better verses than those Mr. Harris had been so liberally paying for; and the idea of feeling free again was so very delightful, that, after receiving Mr. Harris's solemn promise not to betray his authorship, he galloped home, more happy than he had been for some days.

Mr. Harris had said he must have them that evening, and Robert was leaving for the town as his young master entered the house. He hastily put up his portfolio, and sent it off. His conscience was so perfectly free from keeping any thing that he afterward had cause to regret, that he did not think of looking them over, and great was his delight, when a few lines arrived from Mr. Harris, speaking in the highest terms of his talent, and saying, that the set of verses he had selected, even without the attraction of his name, would entirely liquidate his trifling debt.

For the next few days Percy trod on air. He had resolved on waiting till the poem appeared, and then, as he really had discharged his debt, take courage and confess the whole to his father, for his idea of truth made him shrink from any farther concealment. He hoped and believed that his father would regard the pain and constant annoyance he had been enduring so long, as sufficient penalty for his disobedience, and after a time give him back the confidence, which he feared must at his first confession be withdrawn.

What, then, was his grief, his vexation, almost his despair, when he recognized in the poem selected, the verses he thought and believed he had burned the morning after they were written; and which in print, and read by his sober self, seemed such a heartless, glaring, cruel insult, not only on a fellow-creature, but a minister of God, that he felt almost overwhelmed. What could he do? Mr. Harris was not to blame, for he had made no reservation as to the contents of his portfolio. His name, indeed, was not to them, and only having been read lightly once to his companions of that hateful supper — for so he now felt it — almost all of whom were not perfectly sober, there was a chance of their never being recognized as his, and as their subject did not live near any town where the paper was likely to circulate, might never meet his eye. But all this was poor comfort. The paper was very seldom seen at Oakwood, but its contents were often spoken of before his parents, and how could he endure a reference to those verses, how bear this accumulation of concealment, and, as he felt, deceit, and all sprung from the one thoughtless act of ordering an expensive and unnecessary indulgence, without sufficient consideration how it was to be paid. To tell his father, avow himself the author of such a satire, and on such a subject, he could not. Could he tell his mother, and implore her intercession? that seemed like a want of confidence in his father -- no — if he ever could gain courage to confess it, it should be to Mr. Hamilton alone; but the more he thought, the more, for the first time, his courage failed. It was only the day before his visit to Lady Helen's that he had discovered this accumulation of misfortune, and therefore it was not much wonder he was so dispirited. Two days afterward Herbert, with a blushing cheek and very timid voice, asked his father to grant him a great favor. He was almost afraid to ask it, he said, but he hoped and believed his parent would trust his assurance that it was for nothing improper. It was that he might be from home next day unattended for several hours. He should go on horseback, but he was so accustomed to ride, and his horse was so steady, he hoped he might be allowed to go alone. Mr. Hamilton looked very much surprised, as did all present. That the quiet, studious Herbert should wish to give up his favorite pursuits, so soon, too, after Mr. Howard's return, and go on what appeared such a mysterious excursion, was something so extraordinary, that various expressions of surprise broke from his sisters and Edward. Percy did look up, but made no observation. Mr. Hamilton only paused, however, to consult his wife's face, and then replied —

"You certainly have mystified us, my dear boy; but I freely grant you my consent, and if I can read your mother's face aright, hers is not far distant. You are now nearly fifteen, and never once from your birth has your conduct given me an hour's pain or uneasiness; I have therefore quite sufficient confidence in your integrity and steadiness to trust you, as you wish, alone. I will not even ask your intentions, for I am sure they will not lead you into wrong."

"Thank you, again and again, my own dear father. I hope I shall never do any thing to forfeit your confidence," replied Herbert, so eagerly that his cheeks flushed still deeper, and his eyes glistened; then throwing himself on the stool at his mother's feet, he said, pleadingly, "Will you, too, trust me, dearest mother, and promise me not to be anxious, if I do not appear till after our dinner-hour? — promise me this, or I shall have no pleasure in my expedition."

"Most faithfully," replied Mrs. Hamilton, fondly. "I trust my Herbert almost as I would his father; I do not say as much for this young man, nor for that," she added, playfully laying her hand on Percy's shoulder, and laughing at Edward, who was so excessively amused at the sage Herbert's turning truant, that he was giving vent to a variety of most grotesque antics of surprise. Percy sighed so heavily that his mother was startled.

"I did not intend to call such a very heavy sigh, my boy," she said. "In an emergency I would trust you quite as implicitly as Herbert; but you have often yourself wished you had his steadiness."

"Indeed I do, mother; I wish I were more like him in every thing," exclaimed Percy, far more despondingly than usual.

"You will be steady all in time, my boy, I have not the very slightest fear; and as I like variety, even in my sons, I would rather retain my Percy, with all his boyish errors, than have even another Herbert. So pray do not look so sad, or I shall fancy I have given you pain, when I only spoke in jest."

Percy threw his arm round her waist, and kissed her two or three times, without saying a word, and when he started up and said in his usual gay tone, that as he was not going to turn truant the next day, he must go and finish some work, she saw tears in his eyes. That something was wrong, she felt certain, but still she trusted in his candor and integrity, and did not express her fears even to her husband.

The morrow came. Percy and Edward went to Mr. Howard's, and Herbert at half-past nine mounted his quiet horse, and after affectionately embracing his mother, and again promising care and steadiness, departed. He had risen at five this morning, and studied till breakfast so earnestly that a double portion was prepared for the next day. He had said, as he was starting, that, if he might remain out so long, he should like to call at Greville Manor on his way back, take tea there, and return home in the cool of the evening.

"Your next request, my very modest son, will be, I suppose, to stay out all night," replied Mrs. Hamilton; and that certainly will be refused. This is the last to which I shall consent — off with you, my boy, and enjoy yourself."

But Herbert did not expect to enjoy himself half as much as if he had gone to Mr. Howard's as usual. He did not like to mention his real object, for it appeared as if the chances were so much against its attainment, and if it were fulfilled, to speak about it would be equally painful, from its having been an act of kindness.

The day passed quietly, and a full hour before prayers, Herbert was seen riding through the grounds, and when he entered the usual sitting-room, he looked so happy, so animated that, if his parents had felt any anxiety — which they had not — it would have vanished at once. But though they were contented not to ask him any questions, the young party were not, and except by Percy, (who seemed intently engaged with a drawing,) he was attacked on all sides, and, to add to their mirth, Mr. Hamilton took the part of the curious, his wife that of her son.

"Ah, mamma may well take Herbert's part," exclaimed the little joyous Emmeline; "for of course she knows all about it; Herbert would never keep it from her."

"Indeed I do not!" and "Indeed I have not even told mamma!" was the reply from both at the same moment, but the denial was useless; and the prayer-bell rung, before any satisfaction for the curious could be obtained, except that from half-past six Herbert had been very quietly at Mrs. Greville's.

That night, as Percy sat in gloomy meditation in his own room, before he retired to bed, he felt a hand laid gently on his shoulder, and looking up, beheld his brother —

"Have you lost all interest in me, Percy?" asked Herbert, with almost melancholy reproach. "If you had expressed one word of inquiry as to my proceedings, I should have told you all without the slightest reserve. You have never before been so little concerned for me, and indeed I do not like it."

"I could not ask your confidence, my dear Herbert, when for the last three months I have been wanting in openness to you. Indeed, annoyed as I am with my own folly, I was as deeply interested as all the rest in your expedition, though I guessed its object could be nothing but kindness; but how could I ask your secret when I was so reserved with you."

"Then do not let us have secrets from each other any longer, dearest Percy," pleaded Herbert, twining his arm round his neck, and looking with affectionate confidence in his face. "I do not at all see why my secret must comprise more worth and kindness than yours. You talk of folly, and I have fancied for some days that you are not quite happy; but you often blame yourself so much more than you deserve, that you do not frighten me in the least. You said, last night, you wished you were more like me; but, indeed, if you were, I should be very sorry. What would become of me without your mirth and liveliness, and your strength and ever-working care to protect me from any thing like pain, either mentally or bodily? I should not like my own self for my brother at all."

"Nor I myself for mine," replied Percy, so strangely cheered, that he almost laughed at Herbert's very novel idea, and after listening with earnest interest to his story, took courage and told his own. Herbert in this instance, however could not comfort him as successfully as usual. The satire was the terrible thing; every thing else but that, even the disobedience of the debt, he thought might be easily remedied by an open confession to his father; but that unfortunate oversight in not looking over his papers before he sent them to Mr. Harris, the seeming utter impossibility to stop their circulation, was to both these single-hearted, high-principled lads something almost overwhelming. It did not in the least signify to either that Percy might never be known as their author. Herbert could not tell him what to do, except that, if he could but get sufficient courage to tell their father, even if he could not help them he was sure it would be a great weight off his mind, and then he gently reproached him for not coming to him to help him discharge his debt; it was surely much better to owe a trifle to his brother than to Mr. Harris.

"And, to gratify my extravagance, deprive you of some much purer and better pleasure!" replied Percy, indignantly. "No, no, Bertie; never expect me to do any such thing; I would rather suffer the penalty of my own faults fifty times over! I wish to heaven I were a child again," he added with almost comic ruefulness, "and had mamma to come to me every night, as she used to do, before I went to sleep. It was so easy then to tell her all I had done wrong in the course of the day, and then one error never grew into so many; but now — it must be out before Sunday, I suppose — I never can talk to my father as I do on that day, unless it is; — but go to bed, dear Herbert; I shall have your pale cheeks upon my conscience to-morrow, too!"

CHAPTER VII.

MR. MORTON'S STORY. — A CONFESSION. — A YOUNG PLEADER. — GENEROSITY NOT ALWAYS JUSTICE.

"Do you remember, Emmeline, a Mr. Morton, who officiated for Mr. Howard at Aveling, five or six weeks ago?" asked Mr. Hamilton of his wife, on the Saturday morning after Herbert's mysterious excursion. The family had not yet left the breakfast-table.

"Perfectly well," was the reply; "poor young man! he's ap

pearance and painful weakness of voice called for commiseration too deeply not to be remembered."

"Is he not deformed?" inquired Miss Harcourt; "there was something particularly painful about his manner as he stood in the pulpit."

"He is slightly deformed now; but not five years ago he had a graceful, almost elegant figure, though always apparently too delicate for the fatiguing mental duties in which he indulged. He was of good family, but his parents were suddenly much reduced, and compelled to undergo many privations to enable him to go to Oxford. There he allowed himself neither relaxation nor pleasure of the most trifling and most harmless kind; his only wish seemed to be to repay his parents in some degree the heavy debt of gratitude which he felt he owed them. His persevering study, great talent, and remarkable conduct, won him some valuable friends, one of whom, as soon as he was ordained, presented him with a rich living in the North. For nine months he enjoyed the most unalloyed happiness. His pretty vicarage presented a happy, comfortable home for his parents, and the comforts they now enjoyed, earned by the worth of their son, amply repaid them for former privations. One cold snowy night he was summoned to a poor parishioner, living about ten miles distant. The road was rugged, and in some parts dangerous; but he was not a man to shrink from his duty for such reasons. He was detained eight hours, during which time the snow had fallen incessantly, and it was pitchy dark. Still believing he knew his road, he proceeded, and the next morning was found lying apparently dead at the foot of a precipice, and almost crushed under the mangled and distorted carcass of his horse."

An exclamation of horror burst from all the little group, except from Percy and Herbert; the face of the former was covered with his hands, and his brother seemed so watching and feeling for him, as to be unable to join the general sympathy. All, however, were so engrossed with Mr. Hamilton's tale, that neither was observed.

"He was so severely injured, that for months his very life was despaired of. Symptoms of decline followed, and the inability to resume his ministerial duties for years, if ever again, compelled him to resign his rich and beautiful living in Yorkshire; and he felt himself once more a burden on his parents, with scarcely any hope of supporting them again. Nor was this all; his figure, once so slight and supple, had become so shrunk and maimed, that at first he seemed actually to loathe

the sight of his fellows. His voice, once so rich and almost thrilling, became wiry, and almost painfully monotonous; and for some months the conflict for submission to this inscrutable and most awful trial was so terrible that he nearly sunk beneath it. This was, of course, still more physical than mental, and gradually subsided, as, after eighteen months' residence in Madeira, where he was sent by a benevolent friend, some portion of health returned. The same benefactor established his father in some humble but most welcome business in London; and earnestly, on his return, did his parents persuade him to remain quietly with them, and not undertake the ministry again; but this he could not do, and gratefully accepted a poor and most miserable parish on the moor, not eight miles from here."

"But when did you become acquainted with him, papa?" asked Caroline; "you have never mentioned him before."

"No, my dear; I never saw him till the Sunday he officiated for Mr. Howard; but his appearance so deeply interested me, I did not rest till I had learned his whole history, which Mr. Howard had already discovered. He has been nearly a year in Devonshire, but so kept aloof from all but his own poor parishioners, dreading the ridicule and sneers of the more worldly and wealthy, that it was mere accident which made Mr. Howard acquainted with him. Our good minister's friendship and earnest exhortations have so far overcome his too great sensitiveness, as sometimes to prevail on him to visit the Vicarage, and I trust in time equally to succeed in bringing him here."

"But what is he so afraid of, dear papa?" innocently asked Emmeline. "Surely nobody could be so cruel as to ridicule him because he is deformed?"

"Unfortunately, my dear child, there are too many who only enter church for the sake of the sermon and the preacher, and to criticize severely and uncharitably all that differs from their preconceived ideas; to such persons Mr. Morton must be an object of derision. And now I come to the real reason of my asking your mother if she remembered him."

"Then you had a reason," answered Mrs. Hamilton, smiling; "your story has made me wonder whether you had or not."

"I must tax your memory once more, Emmeline, before my cause is told. Do you recollect, for a fortnight after the Sunday we heard him, he preached twice a week at Torrington, to oblige a very particular friend?"

"Yes, and that you feared the increased number of the congregation proceeded far more from curiosity than kindliness or devotion."

"I did say so, and my fears are confirmed: some affairs brought Morton to Torrington for two or three days this week, and yesterday I called on him, and had some hours' interesting conversation. He was evidently even more than usually depressed and self-shrinking, if I may use the word, and at length touched, it seemed, by my sympathy, he drew my attention to a poem in Harris's 'Weekly Magazine.'"

"'It is not enough that it has pleased my God to afflict me,' he said, 'but my fellow-creatures must unkindly make me the subjects of attacks such as these. There is indeed no name, but to none else but me will it apply.' I could not reply, for I really felt too deeply for him. It was such a cruel, wanton insult, the very talent of the writer, for the verses, though few in number, were remarkably clever, adding to their gall."

"I wonder Harris should have published them," observed Miss Harcourt; "his paper is not in general of a personal kind."

"It is never sufficiently guarded; and it would require a person of higher principles than I fear Harris has, to resist the temptation of inserting a satire likely to sell a double or treble number of his papers. I spoke to him at once, and bought up every one that remained; but though he expressed regret, it was not in a tone that at all satisfied me as to his feeling it, and of course, as the paper has been published since last Saturday evening, the circulation had nearly ceased. If I could but know the author, I think I could make him feel the excessive cruelty, if not the actual guilt, of his wanton deed."

"But, dear papa, the person who wrote it might not have known his story," interposed Caroline, to Edward's and Ellen's astonishment, that she had courage to speak at all; for their uncle's unusual tone and look brought back almost more vividly than it had ever done before their mother's lessons of his exceeding and terrible sternness.

"That does not excuse the ridicule, my dear child; it only confirms the lesson I have so often tried to teach you all, that any thing tending by word or deed to hurt the feelings of a fellow-creature, is absolutely wrong — wrong in the thing itself, not according to the greater or less amount of pain it may excite."

"But, my dear husband, the writer may not have been so taught. Satire and ridicule are unhappily so popular, that these verses may have been penned without any thought of their evil tendency, merely as to the *éclat* they would bring their author. We must not be too severe, for we do not know —"

"Mother! mother! do not—do not speak so, if you have ever loved me!" at length exclaimed poor Percy, so choked with his emotion, that he could only throw himself by her side, bury his face in her lap, and sob for a few minutes like a child. But he recovered himself with a strong effort, before either of his family could conquer their anxiety and alarm, and, standing erect, though pale as marble, without in the least degree attempting excuse or extenuation, acknowledged the poem as his, and poured out his whole story, with the sole exception of how he had disposed of the money, with which the second time of receiving his allowance he had intended to discharge his debt; and the manner in which he told that part of his tale, from the fear that it would seem like an excuse or a boast, was certainly more calculated to call for doubt than belief. Herbert was about to speak, but an imploring glance from Percy checked him.

Mr. Hamilton was silent several minutes after his son had concluded, before he could reply. Percy was so evidently distressed—had suffered so much from the consequence of his own errors—felt so intensely the unintentional publication of his poem—for his father knew his truth far too well to doubt his tale, and there was something so intrinsically noble in his brave confession, that to condemn him severely he felt as if he could not.

"Of wilful cruelty toward Mr. Morton, your story has certainly exculpated you," he said, as sternly as he could; "but otherwise you must be yourself aware that it has given me both grief and pain, and the more so, because you evidently shrink from telling me in what manner you squandered away that money which would have been sufficient to have fully discharged your debt six weeks ago; I must therefore believe there is still some deed of folly unrevealed. I condemn you to no punishment—you are old enough now to know right from wrong, and your own feelings must condemn or applaud you. Had you been firm, as I had hoped you were, example would not so have worked upon you, as to tempt even the composition of your satire; as it is, you must reap the consequences of your weakness, in the painful consciousness that you have deeply wounded one, who it would seem had been already sufficiently afflicted, and that confidence must for the time be broken between us. Go, sir, the hour of your attendance on Mr. Howard is passed."

Mr. Hamilton rose with the last words, and somewhat hastily quitted the room. Percy only ventured one look at his mother she seemed so grieved — so sad — that he could not bear it, and darting out of the room, was seen in less than a minute traversing the grounds in the direction of the vicarage, at such a rate that Edward, fleet as in general he was, could not overtake him. Herbert lingered; he could not bear that any part of Percy's story should remain concealed, and so told at once how his second allowance had been expended.

Mrs. Hamilton's eyes glistened. Percy's incoherence on that one point had given her more anxiety than any thing else, and the relief the truth bestowed was inexpressible. Imprudent it was; but there was something so lovable in such a disposition, that she could not resist going directly to her husband to impart it.

"You always bring me comfort, dearest!" was his fond rejoinder; "anxious as that boy's thoughtlessness must make me (for what are his temptations now to what they will be?) still I must imbibe your fond belief, that with such an open, generous, truthful heart, he cannot go far wrong. But what *are* we to do about that unfortunate poem? I cannot associate with Morton, knowing the truth and yet permit him to believe I am as ignorant of the author as himself."

"Let me speak to Percy before we decide on any thing, my dear Arthur. Is Mr. Morton still at Torrington?"

"No; he was to return to Heathmore this morning."

Mrs. Hamilton looked very thoughtful, but she did not make any rejoinder,

In the hour of recreation Emmeline, declaring it was much too hot for the garden, sought her mother's private sitting-room, with the intention of asking where she could find her father. To her great delight, the question was arrested on her lips, for he was there. She seated herself on his knee, and remained there for some minutes without speaking — only looking up in his face with the most coaxing expression imaginable.

"Well, Emmeline, what great favor are you going to ask me?" said Mr. Hamilton, smiling; "some weighty boon, I am quite sure."

"Indeed, papa, and how do you know that?"

"I can read it in your eyes."

"My eyes are treacherous tell-tales then, and you shall not see them any more," she replied, laughing, and shaking her head till her long bright ringlets completely hid her eyes and blushing cheeks. "But have they told you the favor I am going to ask?"

"No," replied her father, joining in her laugh; "they leave that to your tongue."

"I can read more, I think," said Mrs. Hamilton; "I am very much mistaken, if I do not know what Emmeline is going to ask."

"Only that — that — " still she hesitated, as if afraid to continue, and her mother added —

"That papa will not be very angry with Percy; Emmeline, is not that the boon you have no courage to ask?"

A still deeper glow mounted to the child's fair cheek, and throwing her arms round her father's neck, she said, coaxingly and fondly —

"Mamma has guessed it, dear papa! you must, indeed, you must forgive him — poor fellow! he is so *very* sorry, and he has suffered so much already — and he did not throw away his money foolishly, as you thought; he gave it to some very poor people — and you are always pleased when we are charitable; pray forget every thing else but that, and treat him as you always do, dear papa — will you not?"

"I wonder which is most certain — that mamma must be a witch, or Emmeline a most eloquent little pleader," said Mr. Hamilton, caressingly stroking the ringlets she had disordered, "and suppose, after to-day, I do grant your request — what then?"

"Oh, you will be such a dear, darling, good papa!" exclaimed Emmeline, almost suffocating him with kisses, and then starting from his knee, she danced about the room in a perfect ecstasy of delight; "and Percy will be happy again, and we shall all be so happy. Mamma, dear mamma, I am sure you will be glad too."

"And now, Emmeline, when you have danced yourself sober again, come back to your seat, for as I have listened to and answered you, you must listen to and answer me."

In an instant she was on his knee again, quite quiet and attentive.

"In the first place, do you think Percy was justified making Mr. Morton an object of satire at all, even if it should never have left his own portfolio?"

"No, papa, and I am quite sure, if he had not been rather more excited — and — and heedless than usual — which was very likely he should be, you know, papa, after such a day of nothing but pleasure — he would never have done such a thing; I am sure he did not think of hurting Mr. Morton's feelings; he only wanted to prove that he was quite as clever as his companions; and that was very natural, you know, when he *is* so clever at such things. But my brother Percy willingly ridicule a clergyman! no, no, dear papa, pray do not believe it."

"Well defended, my little girl; but how do you justify his disobeying my commands, and incurring a debt?"

Emmeline was silent. "He was very wrong to do that, papa; but I am sure, when he ordered the engravings, he did not intend to disobey you, and you know he is naturally very — I mean a little impatient."

"Still on the defensive, Emmeline, even against your better judgment. Well, well, I must not make you condemn your brother; does he know what an eloquent pleader he has in his sister?"

"No, papa; and pray do not tell him."

"And why not?"

"Because he might think it was only for my sake you forgave him, and not for his own; and I know I should not like that, if I were in his place."

"He shall know nothing more than you desire, my dear little girl," replied her father, drawing her closer to him, with almost involuntary tenderness. "And now will you try and remember what I am going to say. You wish me only to think of Percy's kind act in giving his money to the poor people; but I should have been better pleased in this case, had he been more *just*, and not so generous. I know it is not unfrequently said by young persons, when they think they are doing a charitable act, and can only do it by postponing the payment of their debts — 'Oh, Mr. So-and-so has plenty of business, he can afford to wait for his money, but these poor creatures are starving.' Now this is not generosity or charity, but actual injustice, and giving away money which is literally not their own. I do not believe Percy thought so, because I have no doubt he forgot Mr. Harris, at the time, entirely; but still, as it was a mere impulse of kindness, it does not please me quite so much as it does you."

"But it was charity, papa, was it not? You have said that whenever we are kind and good to the poor, God is pleased with us; and if Percy did not intend to wrong Mr. Harris, and only thought about relieving the poor family, was it not a good feeling?"

"It was; but it might have been still worthier. Suppose Percy had encountered this case of distress when on his way to order his engravings, and to enable him to relieve it as he wished, he had given up the purchasing them. That he found he could not afford the *two*, and so gave up the one mere *individual* gratification, to succor some unhappy fellow-creatures; would not that have been still worthier? and by the conquest of his own inclinations rendered his charity still more acceptable to God? Do you quite understand me, Emmy?"

"I think I do, dear papa; you mean that, though God is so good, He is pleased whenever we are charitable, He is still better pleased when to be so gives us a litttle pain."

"Very well explained, my little girl; so you see in this instance, if Percy had been just before he was generous, and then to be generous, had denied himself some pleasure, his conduct would not have given us or himself any pain, but have been quite as worthy of all the praise you could bestow. And now I wonder how mamma could have discovered so exactly what favor you had to ask?"

"Oh, mamma always knows all my feelings and wishes, almost before I know them myself, though I never can find out how."

"Shall I tell you, Emmeline? Your mother has devoted hours, weeks, months, and years to studying the characters of all her children; so to know them, that she may not only be able to guide you in the path of good, but to share all your little joys and sorrows, to heighten the one and guard you from the other. Ought you not to be very grateful to your Father in Heaven for giving you such a mother?"

His child made no answer in words, but she slipped from his knee, and darting to her mother, clasped her little arms tight round her neck, and hid her glowing cheeks and tearful eyes in her bosom. And from that hour, as she felt her mother's fond return of that passionate embrace, her love became religion, though she knew it not. Her thoughts flew to her cousins and many others, who had no mother, and to others whose mothers left them to nurses and governesses, and seemed always to keep them at a distance. And she felt, How could she thank and love God enough? Nor was it the mere feeling of the moment, it became part of her being, for the right moment had been seized to impress it.

CHAPTER VIII.

AN UNPLEASANT PROPOSAL.—THE MYSTERY SOLVED.—A FATHER'S GRIEF FROM A MOTHER'S WEAKNESS.—A FATHER'S JOY FROM A MOTHER'S INFLUENCE.

MEANWHILE the young heir of Oakwood had passed no very pleasant day. His thoughts since Mr. Howard's return had been so preoccupied, that his studies had been unusually neglected; so much so, as rather to excite the displeasure of his gentle and forbearing preceptor. The emotion of the morning had not tended to steady his ideas, and a severe reproof and long imposition was the consequence. Not one word did he deign to address Herbert and Edward, who, perceiving him leave the Vicarage with every mark of irritation, endeavored, during their walk home, to soothe him. His step was even more rapid than that in which he had left home, and he neither stopped nor spoke till he had reached his father's library, which, fortunately for the indulgence of his ire in words, was untenanted. He dashed his cap from his brow, flung his books with violence on the ground, and burst forth—

"Am I not a fool—an idiot, thus to torment myself, and for one act of folly, when hundreds of boys, at my age, are entirely their own masters? do what they please—spend what they please—neither questioned nor reproved—and that poem—how many would glory in its authorship, and not care a whit whom it might wound. Why am I such a fool, as to reproach myself about it, and then be punished, like a school-boy, with an imposition to occupy me at home, because I did not choose to learn in the hours of study?—Not choose! I wish Mr. Howard could feel as I have done to-day, nay, all this week; and I challenge him to bore his head with Greek and Latin! But why am I so cowed as to feel so? Why cannot I have the same spirit as others—instead of being such a slave—such a—"

"Percy!" exclaimed Mrs. Hamilton, who, having sought him the moment she heard the hall-door close, had heard nearly the whole of his violent speech, and was almost alarmed at the unusual passion it evinced. Her voice of astonished expostulation checked his words, but not his agitation; he threw himself on a chair, leaning his arms upon the table, buried his face upon them, while his whole frame shook. His mother sat down by him, and laying her hand on his arm, said gently —

"What is it that has so irritated you, my dear Percy? What has made you return home in such a very different mood to that in which you left it? Tell me, my boy."

Percy tried to keep silence, for he knew if he spoke he should, as he expressed it, be a child again, and his pride tried hard for victory. Even his father or Herbert at that moment would have chafed him into increased anger, but the almost passionate love and reverence which he felt for his mother triumphed over his wrath, and told him he was much more unhappy than angry; and that he longed for her to comfort him, as she always had done in his childish griefs; and so he put his arms round her, and laid his head on her shoulder and said, in a half-choked voice, —

"I am very unhappy, mother; I feel as if I had been every thing that was bad, and cruel, and foolish, and so it was a relief to be in a passion; but I did not mean you to hear it, and cause you more grief than I have done already."

"You have been very thoughtless, very foolish, and not quite so firm as we could have wished, my own dear boy, but I will not have you accuse yourself of any graver faults," replied Mrs. Hamilton, as she lightly pushed back the clustering hair from his heated forehead, and the gentle touch of her cool hand seemed as restorative as her soothing words; and Percy, as he listened to her, as she continued speaking to him in the same strain for some little time, felt more relieved than five minutes before he thought possible, and more than ever determined that he would never act so thoughtlessly; or, if he were tempted to do so, never keep it concealed so long again. Mrs. Hamilton's anxious desire with him was, always to do justice to his better qualities, at the same time that she blamed and convinced him of his faults. It was a very delicate thing, and very difficult to succeed in, perhaps impossible to minds less peculiarly refined, and hearts less intensely anxious than Mrs. Hamilton's; but no difficulty, no failure, had ever deterred her — and in Percy she was already rewarded. He was of that high, fine spirit, that any unjust harshness would have actually confirmed in error — any unguarded word bring argument on argument, and so, for the mere sake of opposition, cause him to abide in his opinions, when the acknowledgment of his being right in some things, produced the voluntary confession of his error in others.

"And now about these unfortunate verses, my dear boy; I

am not quite clear as to their fate, how it happened that you did not destroy them directly you returned home."

"I fully intended, and believed I had done so, mother, but the whirl of that night seemed to extend to the morning, and I dressed and prepared for Mr. Howard in such a hurry (I had overslept myself, too) that though I had quite resolved they should not pollute my pocket-book any longer, I had no time to look over my papers — thought I could not be mistaken in their outside — burnt those I really wished to keep, and threw those which have caused me all this pain into my portfolio. If I had but been firm enough to have followed my father's advice, and left my companions before supper! — or, if I did join them, had not been so weak, so mad, as to yield to the temptation, but adhered to my principles, notwithstanding they might have been laughed at, I might have been spared it all; but I was so excited, so heated, with a more than sufficient quantity of wine, that I did not know what I was about — not its extent of wrong, at least."

"And you have suffered enough for an evening's excitement, my poor boy; but I am sure you would atone for it, if you could."

"Atone for it, mother! I would give all I possess to cancel that odious poem, and blot it from Mr. Morton's memory, as from my own."

"And I think you can do both, Percy."

He looked at her in utter bewilderment.

"Do both, mother!" he repeated.

"Yes, my boy! it is a painful remedy, but it would be an effectual one. Seek Mr. Morton, and tell him yourself your whole story."

Percy crimsoned to the very temples.

"Do not ask me such a thing, mother," he answered very hurriedly; "I cannot do it."

"You think so at this moment, my dear boy; I am not at all astonished that you should, for it will be very humiliating, and very painful; and if I could spare you either the humiliation or the pain, yet produce the same good effects, I need not tell you how gladly I would; but no one can remove the sting of that poem from Mr. Morton's sensitive feelings but yourself; and I am quite sure if you will allow yourself a little time for quiet thought, you will agree with me."

"But why should I inflict such pain upon myself, granting I deserve it?" answered Percy, still much heated; "when, though my poem is the only one that has unfortunately met his eye, the others were quite as galling and my companions quite as much to blame — why should I be the sufferer?"

"Because, by many errors, you have brought it on yourself. Your companions did indeed act very wrongly, but are we quite sure that the principles which your father and Mr. Howard have so carefully impressed upon you, have been as carefully impressed upon them? and in such a case are not you the more responsible? They had evidently no inward check to keep them from such an amusement; you had, for you have acknowledged that you kept aloof at first, *knowing it was wrong*, and only yielded from want of sufficient firmness. Inflict the pain of an avowal upon yourself, my boy and its memory will help you in future from yielding to too great weakness — and the act prove to us that, though for a moment led into great error, you are still as brave and honest as we believe you."

Percy did not reply, but his countenance denoted an inward struggle, and his mother added —

"Suppose, as is very likely, Mr. Morton becomes intimate here, how can you, with your open, truthful heart, associate with him, with any comfort or confidence even though perfectly satisfied that we would not betray you, and that he would never know the truth? You may fancy now that you could, but I know my Percy better; but I must not talk to you any more, for the dressing-bell rang some minutes ago. Remember, my dear boy, that I lay no command on you to seek Mr. Morton; I have only told you that which I believe would restore you to happiness and atone for your faults, more effectually than any thing else; but you are quite at liberty to act as you think proper."

She left the room as she spoke, but Percy remained for some few minutes longer in deep thought, and when he prepared for dinner, and joined his family, it was still in the same unbroken silence. Mr. Hamilton took no notice of him, and two or three times the little affectionate Emmeline felt the tears rising to her eyes, for she could not bear to see that brother, who was in general the life of the family group, so silent and abstracted.

Sliding after him, as he quitted the room after dinner, she took his hand, and looked coaxingly in his face, longing, but not daring to tell him her father's promise, for fear he should discover her share in the transaction.

"Well, dear Emmy?"

"Are you going to take a walk, Percy? — let me go with you."

"I do not think I am, love. I may be going to ride."

"To ride!" repeated the little girl; "will it be worth while?"

"You forget, Emmy, it is summer now, I have full four hours before prayers; but do not say any thing about my intentions, Emmeline, for I do not know them myself yet."

He kissed her forehead and left her, and a few minutes afterward she was summoned to join her mother, Caroline, and Ellen, in a walk. They sauntered through the grounds in the direction of the northern lodge, which opened on the road leading to Dartmoor; when, not a quarter of an hour after they had left the house, they were overtaken by Percy, riding at what seemed almost a hand gallop, but he had time as he passed his mother to gracefully doff his cap, and her fond heart throbbed, as she caught the expression of his flushed, but earnest face. He was out of sight in another moment, followed by Robert, who was the lads' constant attendant.

Before they had concluded their walk, they met Mrs. Greville and Mary, and returned with them to the house. Emmeline, who had not seen Mary for nearly a fortnight, was in an ecstasy of enjoyment, and Ellen always felt it a real pleasure quietly to walk by Mary's side, and answer the many questions with which she always contrived to interest her. On entering the house, Mr. Hamilton, Herbert, and Edward joined them, and Mrs. Hamilton was somewhat surprised at the even more than ordinary warmth with which her son was greeted by her friends, and at the flush which stained his cheek at Mrs. Greville's first words —

"You were not too much fatigued last Thursday, I hope, my dear Herbert?" she inquired, and as she looked at him, her eyes glistened in tears.

"Oh, not in the least," he replied instantly, and as if he would exceedingly like to change the subject; but Mrs. Greville, turning to Mrs. Hamilton, continued —

"Will you forgive me, Emmeline, if I confess that my visit this evening was more to inquire after your son, than even to see you. I was so anxious to know that he had suffered no inconvenience from his unusual, and I am sure fatiguing, exertion."

"I suppose I must no be jealous, as you are so candid," replied Mrs. Hamilton, smiling; "but I feel very much inclined to be so, finding that you are more in my son's confidence than I am myself. I know Herbert was from home on Thursday, but I was not aware of any particular exertion on his part."

"Did you not know then where he went?" exclaimed Mary and her mother at the same moment; and the former continued, with unusual eagerness, "Did you not know that he went to the races, to try and hear something of Alfred? and that by hunting about both the fair and the race-ground — scenes which I know he so much dislikes — he actually found him, and amused him so successfully, that he kept him with him all day. Papa was so engaged that he had no time to look after Alfred, who, from being left entirely to himself, might have sought the worst companions; I cannot think what charm Herbert used, but Alfred was quite contented to be with him; they dined together, and —"

"He brought me what, next to my boy himself, was the greatest consolation I could have," interposed Mrs. Greville, her voice so faltering, that tears almost escaped, — "a few lines which, he assures me, Alfred thought of writing himself, telling me, he could not bear to think he had left home without kissing me, and that, though he was so happy with his father, that he could not wish to return home, he still loved me and Mary very, very much, and would continue to love us, and come and see us, whenever he could. Oh, Emmeline, can you not imagine the relief of such a letter, of hearing of him at all? and it was all through the kindness, the goodness of your boy!"

When Mrs. Greville and Mary had first begun to speak, Herbert tried to retreat; but Edward placing himself against the door, so that to open it was impossible, and Caroline and Emmeline, both at once catching hold of him, to keep him prisoner, egress was not to be thought of; so, in laughing despair, he broke from his sisters, flung himself on his usual seat, his mother's stool, and almost hid himself in her dress.

"It must have been a relief, indeed," answered Mr. Hamilton; "and rejoiced am I that my quiet Herbert thought of such a plan. Look up, Master Shamefaced, and tell us the reason of your most extraordinary mystery on this occasion. Why did you so carefully conceal your intentions from your mother and myself?"

"Because, papa, I feared you might not approve of them; I hardly dared think about it myself, for it seemed as if I were doing actually wrong in disregarding your principles, for only the *chance* of effecting good. I know, if I had mentioned my wish to find Alfred, or hear something about him, you would not have refused my going; but then mamma must have known it, and she would have been anxious and uncomfortable, if I had not appeared the very moment I had named; would you not?" he continued, looking up in her face with that expression of affection, which very few, even comparative strangers, had power to resist.

"I should indeed, my dear boy; I fear I should have condemned your scheme as a very wild one, and really am glad you thought so much of my comfort, as not to tell me more than you did. So I must not even be jealous, Jessie, but rather propose a vote of thanks to you and Mary for solving the mystery. I do not think Herbert ever excited so much curiosity and speculation, in his life, before."

The entrance of Mr. Grahame changed the current of the conversation, greatly to Herbert's relief, for he did not at all like being thus brought forward. Austere as Grahame was at home, he was always welcomed with pleasure by the young Hamiltons, who never could understand why Annie and Cecil should so fear him. That something unusual had annoyed him, Mr. Hamilton perceived at the first glance; but he took no notice, for Grahame seemed to find relief in talking gayly to the young people.

"And where is my friend Percy?" he inquired, as he joined the happy group at tea, and Percy was still absent. Mr. Hamilton repeated the question in some surprise; but his wife replying that he had gone to ride, and might not be back yet, the subject dropped.

After tea, Mrs. Greville and Mary, attended by Herbert and Edward, returned to the Manor; and the little girls went to finish some business for the next day, and amuse themselves as they liked. Grahame remained alone with his friends, who at length drew from him the cause of his solicitude. He had, that morning, discovered that, notwithstanding his positive commands, Cecil had gone to the prohibited places of amusement. His wife had prevaricated when he questioned her; at one moment almost denying her connivance at the boy's disobedience, at another unconsciously acknowledging it, by insisting that there was no harm in it; and if Grahame would persist in so interfering with his children's amusements, he must expect to be disobeyed. If such were his home, where was he to look for truth, honor, and affection? What would be his son's after career, if such were the lessons of his childhood? He had punished him severely, but there was little hope of its producing any good effect, when his wife was yet more to blame than his child. It would only alienate the boy's affections still more from him. Yet what could he do? Could he let such disobedience and untruthfulness — for Cecil had denied his having been at the races — pass unnoticed? He had shut himself up in his library the remainder of the day; but at length, unable to bear his own thoughts, had walked over to

Oakwood, feeling sure, if peace were to be found, he should find it there.

Their sympathy it was easy for Mr. and Mrs. Hamilton to give — for they felt it sincerely — but to advise was both delicate and difficult. To interfere in a household is not the part even of the most intimate friends. And when Lady Helen herself encouraged the boy in his disobedience, and showed him an example of equivocation, what could be said? Grahame could not bear the idea of a public school for a boy scarcely eleven, and whose home influence was so injurious, and Mr. Hamilton could not advise it. He tried, therefore, merely to raise the depressed spirits of his friend, bringing forward many instances, when even the best training failed; and others where the faults of childhood were subdued by circumstances, and became fair promising youth. Grahame shook his head despondingly.

"You can scarcely be a fit judge of my trial, Hamilton," he said; "you have known nothing but the blessing of hand-in-hand companionship, in the training of your children, as in every thing else. There must be *unity* between father and mother, or there is little hope of joy in their offspring for either; were my wife only in some things like yours — but I see I must not speak so," he added hurriedly, as he met a glance of reproach from Mrs. Hamilton, and he turned to address the two lads, who at that instant entered from their walk. The bell for prayers rung soon afterward, and Grahame rose to say good night.

"Nay, stay with us," said Mr. Hamilton, earnestly. "Why should the call for devotion be the signal for separation? join us, Grahame. It is not the first time by very many that we have prayed together."

Grahame yielded without an instant's hesitation. Still Percy had not returned, and his mother became dreadfully anxious. Her husband, at her request, waited a quarter of an hour, but reluctantly; for he was more particular that every member of his household should assemble at the stated hour of prayer, than in any othor point relating to his establishment. Scarcely, however, had the first word been said, when Percy and Robert entered, and the former, with a very rapid, but noiseless step, traversed the large room, and kneeled in his accustomed place. In vain did Mrs. Hamilton try to keep her thoughts fixed on the service. Had he really been to Mr. Morton, and if he had, how had he been received? had his fine spirit been soothed or irritated? and a thousand other nameless but natural fears thronged her heart. But one look on her son as he rose reassured her; his cheek was flushed with rapid riding, but his dark eye sparkled, and he looked more bright and joyous than he had done for weeks. He advanced without hesitation to Mr. Hamilton the moment the domestics had quitted the library and said, eagerly, but still respectfully —

"Will you, too, forgive me, my dear father? Mr. Morton knows the whole truth, and has not only pardoned my cruel folly, but assured me, that I have more than atoned for the pain my hateful verses inflicted; that he will laugh at them himself, and declare he knows their author as a most particular friend — which he hopes you will permit me to become — whenever he has the opportunity; for that such notice of them will be the surest way to consign them to oblivion. I have endured so much pain the last few weeks that I do not think I shall be so thoughtless and weak in a hurry again. Will you try me once more?"

Astonished and touched, far more than he was ever in the habit of allowing himself to feel, much less to display, Mr. Hamilton had some difficulty in replying; but his words were even more than satisfactory to his son's eager heart, for he answered earnestly —

"Pray, do not give me any praise for my courage, papa; I am quite sure, if it had not been for mamma's suggestion, I never could have done it. It might have crossed my mind, but I fear pride would not have permitted me to listen to it; but when mamma put the case before me as she did, I could not prevent my conscience from feeling the truth of all she said, and if I had not followed her advice, I should have been more miserable still. Dearest mother," he continued, as he turned with even more than his usual affection to receive her nightly embrace, "you have made me so happy! how can I thank you?"

If she made him happy, he certainly had returned the blessing, for Mrs. Hamilton had seldom felt more exquisite pleasure than she did at that moment; and her little Emmeline, though she could not quite understand all her mother's feelings, felt, in her way, almost as glad.

"Well, Mrs. Hamilton, will not your son's words confirm mine?" said Mr. Grahame trying to speak cheerfully when the young party had retired, and he was again alone with his friends. "Can he go far wrong with such a friend?"

"Indeed, he has done me more than justice, and himself not

enough. When I left him, I had scarcely a hope that my very disagreeable advice would be followed; besides, Mr. Grahame," she added, more playfully, "it was not from disagreeing with you on a mother's influence that my look reproached you, you know well enough what it meant; and I still say, that even now, if you would but be less reserved and stern, would but see Helen's many better qualities, as clearly as you do her faults, you might still win her to your will even with regard to your children."

"Not now, Mrs. Hamilton, it is too late; but you have no idea how your look transported me back to years past," he added evidently resolved to change the subject, "when I actually almost feared to approach you. Do you remember, Hamilton, when I told you, if Miss Manvers had a fault, she was too cold?"

"I shall not easily forget the incidents of that night," replied Mr. Hamilton, with a fond glance towards his wife. "Poor Eleanor, when her conduct that evening fell under my lash, I little thought her orphan children would be living under my roof, and to me almost like my own."

"And one her very image," observed Grahame. "Does either resemble her in mind or disposition?"

"Edward almost as much in mind as in personal beauty," replied Mrs. Hamilton. "But not in all points of his disposition. Ellen does not resemble her poor mother in any thing."

"Is she like her father?"

"I did not know him sufficiently to judge, but I fancy not.—In fact, I hardly yet understand Ellen."

"Indeed!" answered Grahame, smiling; "is your penetrative genius here at fault?"

"I fear it is," she answered, in the same tone; "Ellen is my youngest child—and that which has been my successful help five times, has become blunted at the sixth, and refuses to aid me further."

"Grahame, do not heed her," interposed her husband, laughing; "she fancies there is something extraordinary about Ellen, which she cannot comprehend; and I feel certain that imagination has been playing with my wife's sober judgment, and that our little niece is a very ordinary child, only rather more sad and quiet than is usual at her age, which may be easily accounted for by her early trials and constant ill-health. So I solve what my wife pronounces a mystery. She has so few fancies, however, that I do not quarrel with this, for it has all the charm of novelty."

There were more than usual subjects of thougnt on the minds of all the young inmates of Oakwood, before they went to sleep that night. Percy's, Herbert's, and Emmeline's were all peculiarly happy and peaceful. Caroline's were not so agreeable. Praise lavished on others never gave her pleasure: the question would always come, Why did she not receive it too? It was very hard that she so seldom received it, and self-love was always ready to accuse her parents of some degree of partiality, rather than herself of unworthiness. But these thoughts only came when she was alone; the moment she heard her father's voice, or met her mother's smile, they fled from her till they were pertinaciously recalled.

Ellen thought mostly of Herbert. She had been as curious as the rest to know where he had been, though she had not said so much about it. But that it was for some good, kind deed she had never doubted.

"No wonder Mary loves him so much," she said internally: "but how can I ever hope he will love one so often naughty as I am. If Edward be so much superior, what must Herbert be? How I wish I were his sister, and then he would love me, deserving or not."

That poor Ellen was often thought, as she expressed it, "naughty" was true; and it was this mingling of many apparent faults, especially disregard to her aunt's commands, and but too often endeavor to conceal and equivocate, instead of an open confession, with a sorrow and repentance too deep and painful for her years, that so fairly bewildered Mrs. Hamilton, and really, as she had told Mr. Grahame, prevented her from understanding Ellen. If she could but have known of that unfortunate promise, and the strong hold it had taken of the child's vived imagination; that by dwelling on it she had actually made herself believe that, by always shielding Edward from blame or punishment, she was obeying and making her mother love her from heaven, and so, still more deepening her father's affection for her; and that this idea enabled her to bear the suffering of that most painful of all punishments, her aunt's displeasure, Mrs. Hamilton would have left no means untried to remove such a mistaken impression, and no doubt would have succeeded; but she had not the slightest conception of the real origin of her niece's incomprehensible contradictions. She had believed and hoped the influences of her earlier life would disappear before the quiet, wholesome routine of the present, and often and often she found herself fearing that it could not be only maternal neglect, but actual disposition, at fault. When convinced of the great importance of truth, Ellen frequently, instead of attempting to conceal what Edward might have heedlessly done, actually took it upon herself, not being able to define that in such self-sacrifice she was also forfeiting truth; or, if she did believe so, it was also clear, that to tell the real truth to her aunt and betray Edward, was breaking her solemn promise to her mother; and, either way, she was doing wrong. To describe or define the chaos in the poor child's mind, from these contending feelings, would be almost as impossible to us as it was to herself. She only knew that she was often naughty when she most wished to be good; that her aunt must think she did not care for her displeasure; when it made her so very unhappy, that she was scarcely ever in disgrace without being ill. That she never could feel happy, for even when "good" there always seemed a weight hanging over her, and therefore she must be different to, and worse than anybody else. Little do mere superficial observers know the capabilities for joy or suffering in a young child's heart, the exquisitely tender germ which is committed to us; the awful responsibility which lies in the hands of adults, for the joy or grief, good or evil, as the portion of a child! Happily for Ellen, Mrs. Hamilton's love was as inexhaustible as her patience, or her niece might have been still more unhappy, for few would have so understood and practised the delicate and difficult task of constantly being called upon to correct, and yet to love.

Our young readers must not think Edward very cowardly and very dishonorable, always to let his sister bear the penalty of his faults. He had never been taught, and therefore could not understand, the imperative necessity, when guilty of heedlessness or disobedience, boldly to step forward, whether others were injured or not, and avow it. He did not understand how not to say any thing about it, unless he was asked, could be a want of truth.

It was also Mrs. Hamilton's constant custom never to mention to the members of her family, who might have been absent at the time, any thing of fault or disgrace which had fallen under her own immediate jurisdiction, unless their nature absolutely demanded it; and the absence of the young offenders from the happy family circle, either at meals or hours of recreation, when such an unusual proceeding was necessary, in consequence, never excited any remark, but a very general feeling of regret. Edward, therefore, scarcely ever heard the actual cause of his sister's disgrace, and sometimes did not even know she had incurred it. He did, indeed, when she was sometimes absent, feel very uncomfortable; but his immovable awe of his really indulgent uncle (an impression of his mother's creating, quite as strong as Ellen's idea of the sanctity of her promise) caused him to adopt every means of removing the uncomfortable consciousness that he was far more to blame than Ellen, but the right one, a fearless inquiry as to why she was punished, and an open avowal that it was he who had either led her into error, or was the real offender. His thoughts on Percy's conduct were very different to those of his cousins.

"No!" he exclaimed, almost aloud, in the energy of his feelings, "no! I would have suffered any thing, every thing, rather than have done this — seek Mr. Morton, humble myself by avowing the truth to him, and ask his pardon for a mere clever joke, that Percy ought to have been proud of, instead of regretting! If I did not know him well, I should believe him a craven milk-and-water lad, without a particle of the right spirit within him. What could have possessed him? — my uncle's look must have frightened him out of his sober senses: to be sure it was very terrible; poor mamma was, indeed, right as to his unbending sternness; but I think I could have dared even his anger, rather than beg Mr. Morton's pardon, when there really was no necessity." And sleep overtook him, with the firm conviction resting on his mind, that though in some things Percy might be his equal, yet in manliness and spirit, he (Edward) was decidedly the superior.

CHAPTER IX.

TEMPTATION AND DISOBEDIENCE. — FEAR. — FALSEHOOD AND PUNISHMENT.

It was the Christmas vacation — always a happy season in the halls of Oakwood. The previous year, the general juvenile party with which Mr. and Mrs. Hamilton indulged their children on the first or sixth of January, as circumstances permitted, had not taken place on account of Mrs. Fortescue's death, and was therefore this year anticipated with even more than usual joy. Caroline and Emmeline were never permitted to go to indiscriminate parties. Two or three, really confined to children, their mother allowed their joining, with Miss Harcourt, in the course of the year, but their own ball was always considered the acme of enjoyment, especially now that Caroline began to fancy herself very much too old for only children's parties. Annie went almost everywhere with Lady Helen, and quite laughed at the idea of joining children; and Caroline this year began to wish most intensely that her mother would take her out to grown-up parties too, and lost all relish for the pleasant parties she had enjoyed. Mrs. Hamilton never obliged her to go out with Emmeline and Ellen, if she really did not wish it; but Caroline could not get any farther in considering herself a woman.

The week before Christmas, Mr. and Mrs. Hamilton did not allow to be all holiday and amusement. The season was to their feelings of religion, one of earnest, intense thankfulness, and they wished to make it equally so to their children — a source of joy and hope indeed, but the joy and hope of Heaven, not the mere amusements and pleasures of earth. They had thought long and tried earnestly to make their children so to love serious things, as never to associate them with gloom or sadness — never to fancy that to be truly and spiritually religious demanded a relinquishment of the joys and pleasures and innocent happiness of their age, and admirably had they succeeded. Christmas week was always anticipated with quiet gladness, for they were still more with their father and mother; and the few serious readings and lessons they had, were from and with them alone; Miss Harcourt's time was then entirely her own. As soon as Christmas-day was passed, the young party, with the sole exception of two hours' work by themselves, in the morning or some part of the day if the mornings were wanted — (for Mrs. Hamilton never permited *all* duty to be suspended, believing — and her children had experienced the wisdom of the belief — that pleasure and recreation were infinitely more enjoyable after the performance of some duty, however brief and easy, than had they nothing to do but to amuse themselves all day) — were allowed to be just as free, happy, and noisy as they pleased; and the exuberance of their innocent happiness would have been envied by many, who might have thought the quiet routine of their usual life irksome indeed.

Edward Fortescue was looking forward with the greatest delight to becoming a midshipman in the course of the following year. He hoped, indeed, it would be in a very few months; but his uncle and Mr. Howard had only told him to work on as hard as he could, for the summons might come for him to join at a very short notice, and it would be very dreadful, if the commission should be refused because his guardians did not think him forward enough in his various studies to leave them. They had looked very mischievous when they had told him this, and Edward had enjoyed the joke, and resolved they should not have any such amusement. He would go to sea, if he worked night and day for the privilege; and he really did so well, that his uncle gave him great praise, which was as unexpected and delightful as his anger was terrible.

It happened that on the morning after Christmas-day, Edward and Ellen were quite alone in the school-room; the former was in one of his most impatient moods, for at his own request, his uncle was to examine him in a favorite study, and one of the necessary books was wanting. He had read it a few evenings previous, but something had crossed him, and in a desperate passion he had flung the book from him, and where it fell he neither knew nor cared. Caroline and Emmeline had already gone on an expedition to some poor people, with their mother; Ellen had asked and received permission to put some seeds in her little garden, Percy having kindly promised to show her where, and to do some harder work in it for her. He was, however still engaged with his father, and would be, he had told her, for perhaps an hour longer, but he would be sure to come to her then; and, to employ the interval, she had intended to work hard at a purse she was making for him. Edward, however, entirely engrossed her, and for nearly half an hour they hunted in every nook and corner of the room, at length —

"I see it! I see it! Edward," Ellen exclaimed, adding, however, in a very desponding tone, "But what shall we do? we cannot get it."

"Why not?" answered Edward impatiently; where is it, Ellen?"

"Behind that stand of flowers," she replied, pointing to one that filled a corner of the room and which, though it was winter, was filled with some beautiful flowering geraniums of all colors, and some few rare myrtles in full flower.

"There!" said Edward joyfully; "Oh, that is very easily moved — I shall get it in a minute."

"But you know aunt Emmeline desired us not to touch it," implored Ellen, clinging to his arm; "and the flowers are almost all Caroline's. Dear Edward — pray do not move it."

"Stuff and nonsense, Ellen! How is aunt to know any thing about it? and what do I care about the flowers being Caroline's; they may be whose they like, but they shall not prevent my getting my book."

"But it will be disobeying aunt, Edward — pray, pray, don't; you know how displeased she was with Emmeline last week for a much more trifling disobedience than this will be. And if any thing should happen to the flowers, Caroline will be so angry."

"And what do I care for Caroline's anger," retorted Edward, impatiently; "My uncle's indeed is something to care about, and if I don't get my book and go to him directly, I shall have it. I don't like to disobey aunt, but in this case there is no help for it. I am sure I can reach it without doing any harm; besides, I *must* get my book — I cannot do without it."

"Then only wait till aunt comes home, or at least let me ask uncle if we may move it, dear Edward; do let me go — I will not be a minute."

"And so betray my being in a passion the other day, and get me a reproof for that, and for my carelessness into the bargain! Nonsense, Ellen; I will get it, and you must help me, for I have not a moment to lose."

"No, Edward! indeed, indeed, I cannot touch it," she replied imploringly, and shrinking back.

"Say, rather, you wish to get me into disgrace, and perhaps prevented from going out this evening, and to-morrow, and Friday too!" exclaimed Edward, irritated beyond all forbearance; "and the other day you were so very sorry I was going from home so soon — much you must care about me, that you cannot do such a trifling thing as this to oblige me! I hate deceit."

Ellen made no reply, though the tears started to her eyes; but as usual her firmness deserted her. The heavy stand was carefully moved a little forward, without injuring any of the plants; the book was obtained, and at that moment the voice of Percy was heard exclaiming —

"Edward! Edward! what are you about? papa has been expecting you the last half-hour; he says if you do not come directly, you will not have time to do all you wish — what can you be about?"

Edward did not wait to hear much more than his name, but darted off, leaving his sister to push back the stand. Ellen felt almost sure she could not do it by herself; but how was she to act? To ask assistance would not only be confessing her own disobedience, but inculpating her brother, and really, perhaps, deprive him of the enjoyments he anticipated, and so confirm his unkind words. She tried to replace it, and thought she had quite succeeded; but as she moved it, one of the myrtles fell to the ground, and its beautiful blossom hung on the stalk, preserved from being quite broken off only by three or four delicate fibres. It was Caroline's favorite plant; one she so cherished and tended, that Percy called it her petted child; and poor Ellen stood paralyzed; she raised the pot mechanically, and rested the broken head of the flower against the still uninjured sprig, and it looked so well and natural, that the thought for a moment darted across her mind that after all it might not be discovered. Then came all her aunt's lessons of the many ways of acting an untruth without words, and, therefore, even if it should not be discovered, it was no comfort; but could she, dared she, voluntarily confess what must appear a wilful disobedience? If her aunt had been at home, she might in that first moment have gained the necessary courage; but she was not expected back for two or three hours, and Ellen sat with her face buried in her hands, only conscious of misery, till her cousin's joyous voice called out from the hall —

"Come along, Nelly, I have kept you long enough; Tiny would never have left me quiet so long; but there is no tiring your patience. However, I will make up for it now."

And glad to escape from her own thoughts, she hastily collected the various seeds, and ran after him. And Percy was so active, so obliging, so amusing in his queer ways of working and talking, that she almost forgot the impending trial, till she met her aunt and cousins at luncheon. Edward had been so intent, so happy at his business with his uncle, that he had never cast a thought as to how the stand got back; and after lunch he had to go for a row on the river, and after dinner to attend a lecture on astronomy, which, that night and the one following, was to be given in the Town-hall in T—. His uncle and Percy and Herbert were to accompany him, and so, that he should give a thought to any thing disagreeable, was not likely.

The day wore on; Ellen's little courage had all gone, and she almost unconsciously hoped that nothing would be discovered. Mr. Hamilton and the lads departed at six, and Mrs. Hamilton proposed adjourning to her daughters' room, to finish an entertaining book that they were reading aloud. She had noticed, with her usual penetration, that all day Ellen evidently shrunk from her eye, and felt quite sure something was wrong again; but she asked no questions, fearing again to tempt equivocation. Caroline's passionate exclamation that somebody had broken her beautiful flower, drew the attention of all to the stand, and one glance sufficed to tell Mrs. Hamilton that it had been moved. Her anxious suspicions at once connected this with Ellen's shrinking manner, and she turned to ask her if she knew any thing about it. But Ellen had disappeared; and she rang the bell, and inquired of the only domestics whose department ever led them into the room, if they could explain the accident. But neither of them could; all uniting in declaring, that in the morning the myrtle was quite perfect.

"Ellen was at home, mamma; she must know something about it. Percy said they did not begin gardening till more than an hour after we were gone," exclaimed Caroline, whose temper was sorely tried by this downfall of all her cares. "I dare say she did it herself — spiteful thing! — and has gone to hide herself rather than confess it — it is just like her!"

"Stop, Caroline, do not condemn till you are quite certain; and do not in your anger say what is not true. Ellen has given no evidence as yet of being spiteful or mischievous. Emmeline, go and tell your cousin that I want her."

The child obeyed. Miss Harcourt had continued working most industriously at the table, without uttering a word, though Mrs. Hamilton's countenance expressed such unusual perplexity and pain, that it would have seemed kinder to have spoken. One look at Ellen convinced her aunt, and she actually paused before she spoke, dreading the reply almost as much as the child did the question. It was scarcely audible; it might have been denial, it certainly was not affirmative, for Miss Harcourt instantly exclaimed —

"Ellen, how can you tell such a deliberate falsehood? I would not tell your aunt, for I really wished you to have the opportunity of in some degree redeeming your disobedience; but I saw you move back the stand, and your sinful attempt at concealment by replacing the broken flower — and now you dare deny it?"

"I did not replace the flower with the intention of concealing it," exclaimed Ellen, bursting into tears; for that one unjust charge seemed to give back the power of speech, though the violent reproach and invective which burst from Caroline prevented any thing further.

"I must beg you to be silent, Caroline, or to leave the room, till I have done speaking to your cousin," said her mother, quietly; "the fate of your flower seems to make you forget that I have never yet permitted disrespect or any display of temper in my presence."

"But what right had Ellen to touch the stand?"

"None — she has both disobeyed and again tried to deceive me; faults which it is my duty to chastise, but not yours to upbraid. Answer me, Ellen, at once and briefly; your fault is known, and, therefore, all further equivocation is useless. Did you move that flower-stand?"

"Yes," replied the child, almost choked with sobs, called forth the more from the contrast which her aunt's mildness presented to Miss Harcourt's harshness, and Caroline's violent anger, and from the painful longing to say that her first disobedience was not entirely her own fault.

"Did you remember that I had expressly forbidden either of you to attempt to move it?"

"Yes," replied Ellen again, an exclamation at the apparent hardihood of her conduct escaped from both Miss Harcourt and Caroline.

"And yet you persisted, Ellen; this is indeed a strange contradiction to your seemingly sincere sorrow for a similar fault a few months back. What did you move it for?"

For full a minute Ellen hesitated, thus unhappily confirming the suspicion that when she did reply it was another equivocation

"To get a book which had fallen behind."

"I do not know how a book could have fallen behind, unless it had been put or thrown there, Ellen; you said, too, that you did not replace the broken flower for the purpose of concealment. I hardly know how to believe either of these assertions. Why did you leave the room just now?"

"Because — because — I knew you would question me, and — and — I felt I should not have courage to speak the truth — and I knew — you would be so — so displeased." The words were scarcely articulate.

"I should have been better satisfied, Ellen, if your fear of my displeasure had prevented the committal of your first fault, not to aggravate it so sinfully by both acted and spoken untruths. Painful as it is to me in this season of festivity and enjoyment to inflict suffering, I should share your sin if I did not adopt some measures to endeavor at least to make you remember and so avoid it in future. I have told you so very often that it is not me you mostly offend when you speak or act falsely, but God himself — who is Truth — that I fear words alone will be of no avail. Go to your own room, Ellen; perhaps solitude and thought, when your brother and cousins are so happy and unrestrained, may bring you to a sense of your aggravated misconduct better than any thing else. You will not leave your apartment, except for the hours of devotion and exercise — which you will take with Ellis, not with me —

till I think you have had sufficient time to reflect on all I have said to you on this subject."

Ellen quitted the room without answering; but it was several minutes before Mrs. Hamilton could sufficiently conquer the very painful feelings which her niece's conduct and her own compelled severity excited, to enter into her daughters' amusements; but she would not punish them for the misconduct of another; and, by her exertions, temper to Caroline, and cheerfulness to Emmeline (whose tears of sympathy had almost kept peace with Ellen's of sorrow,) gradually returned, and their book became as delightful a recreation as it had been before.

Great was Edward's grief and consternation when he found the effects of what was actually in the first instance his fault; but he had not sufficient boldness to say so. His aunt had expressly said it was the untruth that had occasioned her greatest displeasure; that if the disobedience had been confessed at once, she would, in consideration of the season, have forgiven it with a very slight rebuke. "Now," he thought, "it is only the disobedience in which I am concerned, and if I confess it was mostly my fault, it won't help Ellen in the least — so what is the use of my acknowledging it? Of course, if she wishes it, I will; but how could she tell such a deliberate story?"

That he was acting one of equal deliberation, and of far more culpability, if possible — for he was permitting her to bear the whole weight of his fault — never struck him; if it did, he did not at all understand or believe it. He went to his sister, and offered to confess his share in her fault, and when — as he fully expected — she begged him not, that it could do her no good, and perhaps only get him punished too, his conscience was so perfectly satisfied, that he actually took upon himself to ask her how she could be so foolish and wrong as, when she was asked, not to allow that she had moved it at once —

"It would have been all right, then," he said; and added, almost with irritation, "and I should not have been teased with the thought of your being in disgrace just now, when I wanted so much to enjoy myself."

"Do not think about me, then, Edward," was his sister's reply; "I know the untruth is entirely my own fault, so why should it torment you; if I could but always tell and act the truth, and not be so very, very frightened — oh, how I wonder if I ever shall!" and she leaned her head on her arms, which rested on the table, so despondingly, so sorrowfully, that Edward felt too uncomfortable to remain with her. He was satisfied that he could not help her; but the disagreeable thought would come, that if he had not tempted her to disobey, she would have had no temptation to tell an untruth, and so he sought a variety of active amusements to get rid of the feeling. The continuation of the entertaining astronomical lecture, too, was so very delightful, and Thursday and Friday morning brought so many enjoyments, that he almost forgot her, till startled back into self-reproach by finding that she was not to accompany them on Friday evening to Mr. Howard's, whose great pleasure was to collect young people around him, and whose soiree in the Christmas holidays, and whose day in the country at midsummer, were anticipated by girls and boys, great and small, with such delight as to pervade the whole year round. Caroline never refused to join Mr. Howard's parties, though they were "juvenile;" and Percy always declared they were as unlike any other person's as Mr. Howard was unlike a schoolmaster. Ellen had so enjoyed the day in the country, that, timid as she was, she had looked forward to Friday with almost as much delight as Emmeline.

In vain Emmeline, Edward, Percy, Herbert, and even Mr. Hamilton entreated, that she might be permitted to go. Mrs. Hamilton's own kind heart pleaded quite as strongly, but she remained firm.

"Do not ask me, my dear children," she said, almost as beseechingly as they had implored; "I do assure you it is quite as much, if not more pain to me on this occasion to refuse, as it is for you all to be refused. If it were the first, second, or even third time that Ellen had disregarded truth, I would yield for your sakes; and in the hope that the indulgence would produce as good an effect as continued severity; but I cannot hope this now. The habit, is, I fear, so deeply rooted, that nothing but firmness in inflicting pain, whenever it is committed, will succeed in eradicating it. God grant I may remove it at last."

The tone and words were so earnest, so sad, that not only did her children cease in their intercession, but all felt still more forcibly the solemn importance of the virtue, in which Ellen had so failed, from the effect of her conduct upon their mother. She was always grieved when they had done wrong, but they never remembered seeing her so very sad as now. Edward, indeed, could scarcely understand this as his cousins did; but as his aunt still only alluded to the untruth, the qualm of con-science was again silenced, for he had only caused the disobedience. Emmeline asked timidly if she might remain with Ellen, and Edward followed her example, thinking himself very magnanimous in so doing; but both were refused — and surely he had done enough!

All went — Mr. and Mrs. Hamilton and Miss Harcourt, as well as the young people; and it was such a happy evening! First, there was the orrery, that Mr. Howard had prevailed on the lecturer to display first at his house, and Edward was almost wild in his delight; and then there were some games and intellectual puzzles, that made them all think, as well as enjoy; and then there were some music and singing and dancing, and every thing was so quiet and orderly, and yet so full of youthful enjoyment, that it was not much wonder there was no longer any room for a sorrowful thought, in any of the young party from Oakwood. Mrs. Hamilton alone thought of Ellen, and again and again accused herself of too great harshness for, perhaps, after all, it might have no better effect than kindness; but what could she do? She almost envied the quiet, unruffled unconcern of less anxious guardians; but for her to feel indifferent to her responsibility was impossible. Ellen was so often unwell that her absence did not occasion so much remark as her brother's or either of her cousins' would. "Mamma did not wish her to come," was the answer she had desired the children to give to any inquiries, and her character for indulgence was so generally known, that no one suspected any thing more than indisposition. Annie Grahame's dislike to Ellen might have made her more suspicious, but she was not there. Cecil and Lilla were, with their father, but Miss Grahame did not condescend to attend Mr. Howard's "juvenile" parties; and Caroline, though she would not have allowed it, even to herself, was both happier, and much more inclined to enjoy herself, with the amusements and society offered to her when Annie was not at a party, than when she was.

The next night, to Ellen's disposition, was a greater trial than the Friday. She neither expected, nor hardly wished to be allowed to go to Mr. Howard's, though, as the affectionate Emmeline had come to wish her good night, and with tears in her eyes repeated the regrets that she was not to go, she felt the bitter disappointment more than in the morning she had thought possible; but Saturday night it had been her aunt's custom, from the time she had been at Oakwood, to visit her daughters and niece before they went to sleep, and prepare them for the Sabbath's rest and enjoyment, by an examination of their conduct during the past week, and full forgiveness of any thing that had been wrong. When younger, Mrs. Hamilton had attended to this duty every night; but wishing to give them a habit of private prayer and self-examination, independent of her, she had, after Emmeline was twelve years old, set apart the Saturday night, until they were fifteen — old enough for her to relinquish it altogether. It had been such a habit with her own children, that they felt it perfectly natural; but with Ellen and Edward, from their never having been accustomed to it as young children, she had never felt the duty understood by them, or as satisfactorily performed by herself as with her own. Still, Ellen looked forward to this night as the termination of her banishment; for great indeed was the offence whose correction extended over the Sabbath. Ellen could not remember one instance since she had been at Oakwood, when she heard the doors of her cousins' rooms successively close, and her aunt's step retreating, without approaching hers, and she did, indeed, believe herself irreclaimably wicked, or her kind, good aunt, would, at least, have come to her. Mrs. Hamilton had purposely refrained from indulging her own inclinations, as well as comforting Ellen, hoping still more to impress upon her how greatly she had sinned. The impossibility of her perfectly comprehending her niece's character, while the poor child felt it such a sacred duty to victimize herself, made her far more severe than she would have been, could she have known her real disposition; but how was it possible she could believe Ellen's grief as deep and remorseful as it seemed, when a short time afterward she would commit the same faults? Her task was infinitely more difficult and perplexing than less anxious mothers can have the least idea of.

CHAPTER X.

PAIN AND PENITENCE. — TRUTH IMPRESSED, AND RECONCILIATION. — THE FAMILY TREE.

In feverish dreams of her parents, recalling both their deaths, and with alternate wakefulness, fraught with those deadly incomprehensible terrors which some poor children of strong imagination know so well, Ellen's night passed; and the next morning she rose, with that painful throbbing in her throat and temples, which always ended with one of those intense and exhausting headaches to which she had been so subject, but which her aunt's care and Mr. Maitland's remedies had much decreased, both in frequency and violence. She went to church however, with the family, as usual.

"Remain out, Edward!" Percy exclaimed, as they neared the house; "the old year is taking leave of us in such a glorious mood, that Tiny and I are going to ruralize and poetize till dinner — will you come with us? — and you, Ellen?"

Ellen withdrew her arm from her brother's, saying, as she did so —

"Go, dear Edward, I am very tired, and would rather not."

"Tired, and with this short walk; and you really do look as if you were — what is the matter, Ellen? you are not well."

His sister did not reply, but shrinking from the look which Mrs. Hamilton, who was passing at the moment, fixed earnestly upon her, she ran into the house.

Edward again felt uncomfortable; in fact, he had done so, so often since the Tuesday morning, that his temper was not half so good as usual. He did not choose to acknowledge, even to himself, that the uncomfortable feeling was self-reproach, and so he vented it more than once in irritation against Ellen, declaring it was so disagreeable she should be in disgrace just then.

It was Mr. and Mrs. Hamilton's custom always to dine on Sundays at half-past one, to allow those of their household who were unable to attend divine service in the morning to go in the afternoon. With regard to themselves and their children they pursued a plan, which many religionists might, perhaps, have condemned, and yet its fruits were very promising. Their great wish was to make the Sabbath a day of love, divine and domestic; to make their children look to it with joy and anticipation throughout the week as a day quite distinct in its enjoyment from any other; and for this reason, while their children were young, they only went to church in the morning, the afternoons were devoted to teaching them to know and to love God in His works as well as Word, and their evenings to such quiet but happy amusements and literature, as would fill their young hearts with increased thankfulness for their very happy lot. As they grew older, they were perfectly at liberty to do as they pleased with regard to the afternoon church. Herbert, whose ardent desire to enter the ministry increased with his years, generally spent the greater part of Sunday with Mr. Howard, with his parents' glad and full consent. The contemplation of serious things was his greatest happiness, but Mr. and Mrs. Hamilton did not expect that all their other children were to be like him. They were contented, and intensely thankful also, to perceive that diverse as were their characters, still the constant sense of God's presence and of His infinite love was active and earnest in them all, inciting love and reverence for Herbert, even though they could not sympathize with him entirely. Another peculiarity of Mr. Hamilton consisted in his permitting no *Sunday* schools at Aveling and his other villages. The Saturday afternoons were set apart instead of the Sunday. He wished his wife and daughters, when they were old enough, to superintend them, and help the children in preparing for the Sunday services and Sunday enjoyments; but he particularly disliked the system of overwork on a day of rest, which could not fail to be the case, if there were schools to attend to twice or three times a day, as well as church.

It being the last day of the old year, Mr. Howard had expressed a wish that Percy and Edward as well as Herbert should attend church that afternoon, and the lads, without the least reluctance, consented; Mr. Hamilton and Miss Harcourt were going too, and Caroline and Emmeline, of their own accord, asked permission to accompany them. Ellen's pale, suffering face had so haunted her aunt, that she could not think of any thing else, and remained for a very much longer time than was usual to her character in a state of indecision. The next night was her children's ball, and it was, too, the first day of the new year — always in her happy circle a festival of joy and thankfulness. Ellen's face certainly looked as if she had suffered quite enough to prevent the recurrence of her fault, but so it had always done, and yet, before she could possibly have forgotten its consequences, she failed again. Mrs. Hamilton sat for some time, after her children had left her, in meditation, trying to silence the pleadings of affection, and listen only to reason, as to whether continued severity or returning kindness would be the more effective, and save both Ellen and herself any further pain.

To the child herself physical suffering was so increasing as gradually to deaden mental, till at last it became so severe, that she felt sick and faint. She knew the medicine she was in the habit of taking when similarly suffering, and the lotion which her aunt applied to her forehead, and which always succeeded in removing the excessive throbbing, were both in Mrs. Hamilton's dressing-room; but it seemed quite impossible that she could get at them, for she did not like to leave her room without permission, nor did she feel as if she could walk so far, her head throbbing with increased violence with every step she took. At length she summoned sufficient courage to ring the bell, and beg Fanny to ask Ellis to come to her. The girl, who had been already dreadfully concerned that Miss Ellen had eaten no dinner, and on Sunday too! gave such an account of her, that the housekeeper hastened to her directly, and begged her to let her go for her mistress — it was so lucky she had not gone to church — but Ellen clung to her, imploring her not.

"Dear, dear Ellis, get me the medicine, and bathe my forehead yourself; I shall get well then in an hour or two, without giving my aunt any trouble: pray, pray, don't tell her. I scarcely feel the pain when she is nursing and soothing me; but I do not deserve that now, and I am afraid I never shall."

"But indeed, Miss Ellen, she will be displeased if I do not. Why, only the other morning she was quite concerned that I had not told her Jane was ill directly, and went herself two or three times every day to see she had every thing proper and comfortable."

"But that is quite different, dear Ellis; do get the lotion; I feel as if I could not bear this pain much longer without crying; you can tell her afterward, if you think you ought."

And seeing that farther argument only increased the poor child's sufferings, Ellis promised, and left her. Ellen leaned her forehead against the side of her little bed, and held the curtain tightly clasped, as if so to prevent the utterance of the hysteric sob that would rise in her throat, though she did not know what it was. But the wholly unexpected sound of Mrs. Hamilton's voice saying, close by her, "I am afraid you have one of your very bad headaches, Ellen," so startled her, as to make her raise her head suddenly; and the movement caused such agony, that, spite of all her efforts, she could not prevent an almost convulsive cry of pain.

"My dear child! I had no idea of pain like this; why did you not send for me? We have always prevented its becoming so very violent by taking it in time, my Ellen."

"Miss Ellen would not let me go for you, madam," rejoined Ellis, who, to her mistress's inexpressible relief, was close at hand with the remedies she wanted, and she repeated what the child had said.

"Again your old mistake, Ellen. I would so much, so very much rather hear you say you were *resolved* to deserve my love, than that you did not merit it. Why should you not deserve it as well as your brother and cousins, if you determined with all your heart to try and not do any thing to lessen it? Nothing is so likely to prevent your even endeavoring to deserve it, as the mistaken fancy that you never shall; but you are too unwell to listen to me now; we must try all we can to remove this terrible pain, and then see if we can bring back happiness too."

And for above an hour did Mrs. Hamilton, with the most patient tenderness, apply the usual remedies, cheered by finding that, though much more slowly than usual, still by degrees the violence of the pain did subside, and the hysterical affection give way to natural and quiet tears. Exhaustion produced a deep though not very long sleep, and after watching her some few minutes very anxiously, Mrs. Hamilton sat down by her bed, and half unconsciously drew toward her Ellen's little Bible, which lay open on the table, as if it had been only lately used. Several loose papers were between the leaves; her eyes filled with tears as she read on one of them a little prayer, touching from the very childishness of the language and imperfect writing, beseeching her Father in Heaven in His great mercy to forgive her sin, and give her courage to speak the truth, to help her not to be so frightened, but to guide her in her difficult path. Mrs. Hamilton little guessed how difficult it was, but she hoped more from the effects of her present penitence than she had done yet. She had copied, too, several verses from the various parts of the Old and New Testament which were condemnatory of falsehood, and her aunt felt no longer undecided as to her course of action.

"You have employed your solitary hours so well, my dear Ellen," she said, as, when the child awoke and looked anxiously toward her — she kissed her cheek with even more than her usual fondness — "that I scarcely require your assurance of repentance or promises of amendment. When you have taken some coffee, and think you are well enough to listen to me, I will read you an illustration of the fearful sin of falsehood from the Old Testament, which I do not think I have yet pointed out to you. Ananias and Sapphira, I see you remember."

And when Ellen had taken the delicious cup of coffee, which her aunt had ordered should be ready for her directly she awoke, and sat up, though her head was still so weak it required the support of a pillow, yet she seemed so revived, so almost happy, from the mesmeric effect of that warm, fond kiss, that her aunt did not hesitate to continue the lesson she was so anxious to impress, while the mind and heart were softened to receive it. She turned to the fourth chapter of the second book of Kings, and after briefly relating the story of Naaman — for she did not wish to divert Ellen's attention from the one important subject, by giving any new ideas — she read from the 20th verse to the end, and so brought the nature of Gehazi's sin and its awful punishment, at the hand of God himself (for the prophet was merely an instrument of the Eternal, he had no power in himself to call the disease of leprosy on his servant) to Ellen's mind, that she never forgot it.

"Do you think Elisha knew where he had been, and what he had done, before he asked him?" she ventured timidly to inquire, as her aunt ceased; "Gehazi had told a falsehood already to Naaman. Do you think God punished that or his falsehood to Elisha?"

"Most probably he punished both, my love. Elisha no doubt knew how his servant had been employed in his absence, in fact he tells him so" — and she read the 26th verse again — "but he asked him whence he had come, to give him an opportunity for a full confession of his first sin, which then, no doubt would, after some slight rebuke, have been pardoned. It was a very great fault at first, but the mercy of God was then, as it is now, so infinite so forgiving, that, had Elisha's question recalled Gehazi to a sense of his great guilt and excited real repentance, his punishment would have been averted. But his aggravated and repeated falsehood called down on him a chastisement most terrible even to think about. Leprosy was not merely a dreadful disease in itself, but it cut him off, from all the blessings and joys not only of social life but of domestic; because, as God had said it should cleave to his seed as well as to himself, he could never find any one who would dare to love him, and he must have been compelled to lonely misery all his life."

"It was a very dreadful punishment," repeated Ellen, fearfully.

"It was, dearest; but it was merciful, notwithstanding. If God had passed it by, and permitted Gehazi to continue his sinful course, without any check or chastisement that would recall him to a sense of better things, and a wish to pursue them, he might have continued apparently very happy in this life, to be miserable forever in the next; to be banished forever from God and His good angels; and would not that have been still more dreadful than the heaviest suffering here? In those times God manifested his judgments through His prophets directly. That is not the case now, but he has given us His Word to tell us, by history as well as precept, those things that are pleasing to Him, and those which excite His anger; and which, if not corrected while we are in this world, will cause our condemnation when our souls appear before Him in judgment, and when we cannot correct them if we would. Now children, and even young people, cannot know these things as well as their parents and guardians can, and if we neglect to teach them right and wrong, God is more angry with us than with them, as He tells Ezekiel." She read from the 18th to the 22d verse of the third chapter, and explained it, so that Ellen could clearly understand it, and then said, "And now, my dear Ellen, can you quite understand and quite feel why I have caused you so much pain, and been, as I dare say you have felt, so very, very severe?"

Ellen's arms were round her neck in a moment, and her head cradled on her bosom, as her sole reply, for she felt she could not speak at first, without crying again.

"I wish I could remember that God sees me wherever I am," she said, after a short pause, and very sadly. "I am so frightened when I think of anybody's anger, even Caroline's, that I cannot remember any thing else."

"Did you notice the Psalm we read the day before yesterday, my dear Ellen, in the morning lesson?"

The child had not; and her aunt turning to the 129th, read the first twelve and the two last verses carefully with her, adding—

"Suppose you learn one verse for me every morning, till you can repeat the whole fourteen perfectly, and I think that will help you to remember it, my Ellen, and prove to me that you really are anxious to correct yourself; and now one word more, and I think I shall have talked to you quite enough."

"Indeed, indeed I am not tired, dear aunt," replied Ellen, very earnestly; "I feel when you are talking to me as if I never could be naughty again. Oh! how I wish I never were."

"I am not so unconscionable as to expect you to have no faults, my dear child; all I wish you to attend to, is more obedience to my commands. I have not said any thing about your disobedience, because your untruth was of still more consequence, but that grieved me too, for disobedience to me is also disobedience to God, for He has commanded you to obey your parents and guardians; and as you said you remembered I had told you not to move the flower-stand, I cannot imagine what could have induced you so wilfully to disobey me."

Ellen looked up in her face with such earnest, wistful eyes that Mrs. Hamilton felt puzzled; but as she did not speak and laid her head again on its resting place, to hide the tears that rose, her aunt merely added —

"But as I do not wish to inflict any further pain, I will not say any thing more about it; only remember, that though I may be displeased if you disobey me again, an instant and full confession will soon gain my forgiveness; and that though I will never doubt your word, still, if I discover another untruth, it will and must oblige me to adopt still severer measures, painful as it will be to myself. Do not tremble so, my Ellen, you know you can prevent it; and remember too that whenever you fail in truth, you punish me as well as yourself;" and Mrs. Hamilton fondly kissed her as she spoke.

Light steps and a ringing laugh at that moment sounded in the passage, and Emmeline, though she certainly did ask if she might enter, scarcely waited for an answer, before she bounded in, the very personification of health and joy.

"Mamma, papa wants to know if we may not have tea to-night, and if we may not have Ellen's company too?"

"It is New Year's Eve," pleaded another joyous voice, and Percy's brown head just intruded itself through the half-opened door; "and our tree will not be half enjoyable unless we are all there."

"I had really forgotten your tree, my dear children, but I am glad papa and you all have remembered it. Come in, Percy; Ellen will, I dare say, admit you into her room."

"He raced me all around the gallery, mamma, declaring he would give you papa's message, or so take away my breath, that even if I outstripped him, I should not be able; but I have. you see sir."

"Only because I did not know whether it was quite proper to enter a young lady's room. But do come, mamma; Mr. Howard is with us as usual, and we are all *au desespoir* for you and our little Ellen — she *may* come, I can read it in your eyes."

"Are you well enough, my love? Do you think this poor little head will permit you to join us?" asked Mrs. Hamilton, anxiously for the sudden joy that gleamed in Ellen's eyes at the idea of joining the family, told what the disappointment would be if she could not.

"It does not hurt me at all if I can rest it, aunt; but I am afraid it will not let me walk," she added, sorrowfully, as the attempt to walk caused it to throb again.

"Never mind, Nelly, even if you cannot walk; you shall make use of my pedestrian powers," replied Percy, joyously;

"rest your head on my shoulder — that's it — I should make a capital nurse I declare; should I not, mamma?"

And gayly answering in the affirmative, his mother could scarcely prevent a throb of pride, as she looked on his fine manly face, beaming with benevolent kindness on his little cousin, whom he had tenderly lifted in his arms, and checked his boisterous mirth and rapid stride to accommodate her.

"You are not quite so light as Tiny, but she is all air; I expect she will evaporate some day: never mind your hair, it does very well."

"Stop, I will smooth it in a moment," exclaimed Emmeline, eagerly; "it is Sunday, Percy, she shall look well."

"You had better let me do it, Emmy," said her mother, smiling; "your cousin's head can only bear very tender handling to-night. There, that will do — and I am quite ready to attend you."

The lights, the joyous voices, even her uncle's kind greeting, almost overpowered poor Ellen; as Percy, still preserving his character of an admirable nurse, laid her carefully on a couch in the sitting-room, where not only tea was waiting, but the celebrated family tree, which Mrs. Hamilton's anxiety and Ellen's sorrow had caused them both to forget, was displayed with even more than usual taste and beauty.

Mr. Hamilton, when young, had been a great deal with his father in Germany, Denmark, and Sweden, and brought from the first and latter country certain domestic observances which had especially pleased him, as so greatly enhancing the enjoyments of home, and helping to a right understanding between parents and children, by increasing their mutual love and confidence. The family tree, or Christmas Tree, as it was called, was one of these, and from their earliest years it had been one of the children's greatest delights on New Year's Eve. Of course, as they grew older, and their taste improved, the tree itself, its suspended presents, and its surrounding decorations increased in beauty, and it had never been prettier than it was this year. The whole of the preceding afternoon had the young artists labored in preparing it, for of course, as the next day was Sunday, it was obliged to be all finished by the Saturday night; the servants, eager in all things to enhance the happiness of those whose parents made them so happy, did not care what trouble they took to help them. They always selected the room in which there was a very lofty and very deep oriel window, in the centre of which recess (which was almost as large as a moderately sized room) they placed *the* tree, which was a very large, gracefully-cut spruce fir; it was placed in a tub filled with the same soil as that in which the tree grew, so that by watering and care it remained fresh for some time. The tub which contained it was completely hidden by the flowering shrubs that were placed round it, rising in an expanding pyramid, by means of several flower-stands, till the recess seemed one mass of leaf and flower; among which the superb scarlet geranium, that in Devonshire grows so luxuriantly all through the winter, shining against its own beautiful leaf, the brilliant berries of the holly, with their dark glistening branches, the snow-berry and flowering myrtle, shone preëminent. Small lamps glittered through the flowers, and were suspended in sufficient profusion from the pendent branches of the tree to half reveal and half hide the various gifts and treasures that were there deposited; and altogether the effect, from every part of the room, was really striking.

The tree always remained till after their ball, but, the interchange of gifts which took place on New Year's Eve, causing so many peculiarly happy and home feelings, was confined to the family group; Mr. Howard always included. Many weeks before had each individual worked at his own secret undertaking. If it could not all be done in private, no questions were ever asked, and each helped the other to keep it at least from their parents till the eventful night itself. They formed so large a party altogether, as little tokens of affection between the brothers and sisters were also exchanged, that the tree was quite loaded, and many a time had Mr. and Mrs. Hamilton discovered some trait of character or some ruling fancy, even in such a simple thing as the manufacture and presentation of home gifts. Their own idea of family ties was so strong and so holy, that one great aim in the education of their children was to make them not only *love* each other, but have thought and attention for individual feelings and wishes, and so heighten feeling by action, not depend entirely on natural ties. Mrs. Hamilton had known many young persons who were lavish in attentions and even presents to friends, but never imagined that their own home circle had the first and strongest claim to kindness, whether of word or deed. She knew that affections and thought lavished on comparative strangers never radiated on home, but that when given to home *first*, they shed light and kindliness far and near.

Their tea was indeed a mirthful one; Ellen had been very fearful of meeting Mr. Howard, for she thought he must have been told how naughty she had been; but if he had, there was nothing in his manner to say so; for he shook hands with her and even kissed her most kindly, and told her, laughingly, that she must be quite well by the next night, or how was she to dance? That he thought it would be a good thing if Emmeline could give her a little of her dancing mania, as she hardly ever only walked, even when she called herself quite sober. Edward, every passing thought of self-reproach banished by his sister's return to favor, was in the wildest spirits; Percy and Emmeline seemed to have laid a wager who could say the wittiest things and laugh the most. Herbert was very quiet, but looking as happy as the rest, and quite entering into their mirth, and showing all sorts of little gentle attentions to Ellen, who had seemed to shrink from his eye, more than from all the others. Caroline fully entered into the spirit of the evening, but neither she nor Miss Harcourt took the same notice of Ellen as the rest. The person who was to act the Wizard's part, and by means of a long wand detach the various treasures from the tree, and carry them to the owners whose names they bore, was always chosen by lot; and great was the delight of the young party, when this night the office fell on Mr. Howard. No one seemed more pleased than himself, performing it with such a spirit of enjoyment and originality, that a general vote declared him the very choicest wizard they had ever had. To enumerate all the contents of that marvellous tree would be impossible. Their parents' gifts to each of them were not in the tree, but always given afterward; but great was the delight, when, after a terrible tussle to detach a large roll of cloth, down it came, right on Mr. Howard's head, and almost enveloped him with its folds, and proved to be a beautiful cover, which he had long desired for a favorite table in his drawing-room; at the embroidered border of which, not only the three girls, but Mrs. Hamilton and Miss Harcourt had all worked, as a joint offering of love and respect. This good man was so charmed, that he declared he would not use his wand again till he had full five minutes to admire it. Then there was a very pretty, comfortable pair of slippers, worked by Caroline and Emmeline for their father, and a pair of braces worked by Ellen, all accompanied by some most ludicrous, but very clever verses from Percy. Edward, who was very ingenious, had turned a very pretty stand for his uncle to put his watch in at night; and manufactured two little vessels out of cork for his aunt, so delicately, and neatly, that she promised him they should stand on the mantelpiece of her dressing-room, as long as they would last. Caroline had knitted her mother a very pretty bag, and Emmeline and Ellen had collected for her a variety of leaves throughout the year, and arranged them with great taste, both as to grouping and tinting, in a sort of small herbal, with two or three lines of poetry, selected and carefully written by each alternately, attached to each page. Mrs. Hamilton was excessively pleased, as she was also with a portfolio formed by drawings from both her boys, and tastefully made up by Miss Harcourt; and with their gifts to their father, a correct and most beautifully written out Greek poem, which Mr. Hamilton had several months, if not more than a year before, expressed a wish to possess, but the volume which contained it was so scarce, and so expensive from the quantity of uninteresting matter in which the gem was buried, that he had given up all thought of it. Herbert, however, had not, and never rested from the time his father spoke, till he had found and copied it — a task of no small difficulty, for the original was in many parts almost entirely effaced, and, if Herbert had not been an admirable Greek scholar, and a quick imaginator as to what it ought to be, Mr. Howard himself had said he could not have succeeded. The writing of the Greek character was most beautiful, and Percy, in imitation of the ancient missals, had designed and painted an elegant illuminated border round it, and a beautiful cover forming a thin volume, so valuable, their father delighted them by saying, that he would not exchange it for twenty of the most precious volumes in his library. Such evidences of the home influence they had given, in permitting leisure for the cultivation of taste and imagination, teaching them the beautiful, and opening innumerable resources of enjoyment within themselves, and thence allowing them to enhance the pleasures of others, were indeed most gratifying to those earnest and affectionate guardians. From their earliest years they had been taught, that to give the greatest amount of pleasure to their parents, their gifts must be all, or at least have something in them, of their own workmanship, and to enable them to do this, the lads had been taught in their hours of recreation to use all sorts of tools, visiting and knowing something of a variety of handicrafts; and the girls to work and draw, and even bring the stores of Nature to their aid when needed, as in the present case, with Emmeline and Ellen's tasteful gift.

Our young readers must call upon their own imagination as to the other treasures of this valuable tree; for, as they would, no doubt, like to know what sort of New Year's gifts Mr. and Mrs Hamilton had in store for their children (for Miss Harcour; too, for they never omitted her,) we really must not linger round it any longer. Poor Ellen, indeed, had the pain of feeling that her fault and its consequences had prevented the completion of her purse for Percy, and a chain for Edward, and her cheek burned very painfully, when Mr. Howard, after exhausting the tree, exclaimed —

"Nothing from Ellen for Percy and Edward. Young gentlemen, have you been receiving any gifts in secret? — out with them if you have — it is against all law and propriety."

"We shall receive them next week, most potent conjurer, as you ought to have known without inquiring," answered Percy, directly; and bending over Ellen, by whom he chanced to be standing, he said, kindly, "Never mind, Nelly, you will have time to finish them both next week."

"Do not say 'never mind,' my dear boy, though I admire and sympathize in your kind care of your cousin's feelings," said his mother, in the same low tone, as only to be heard by him and Ellen. (Mr. Howard was very quick-sighted, and he took Percy's jest and turned off all further notice of his words.) "Even such a little thing as this in Ellen's case is pain, and can only be felt as such; we do not lessen it by denying it, my Ellen, do we?"

"I would rather feel it, if it would help me to remember," was Ellen's earnest and humble reply; adding, "but I thank you, dear Percy — you are so kind."

"Not a bit," was his laughing answer. "Why, what in the world is this?" he added; "I thought the tree was exhausted."

"So it is, but this was hid at its root," replied Mr. Howard, "and though it is directed to Caroline, it is somewhat too heavy for my wand, and must reach her in a more natural way."

"Why, it is my flower, my own beautiful flower, or one exactly like it, at least," exclaimed Caroline, joyfully, as, removing a hollow pyramid of green and white paper, a myrtle was discovered of the same rare kind, and almost in as beautiful flower as the one whose death had caused such increased coldness in her feelings toward Ellen. "How did it come who could have procured it for me?"

"Ellis sent for it at my request, dear Caroline," answered Ellen. "She said they were to be purchased from the gardener at Powderham, and if it were possible to send any one so far, she would endeavor to get one for me; she told me yesterday she had succeeded, and I thought she gave it you, as I begged her, directly; I had no opportunity to tell you before, but I was so very, very sorry I had hurt your flower."

"Ellis was very wise to put it among the pretty things of this evening, instead of obeying you," said her uncle, kindly; "and I really am glad that your great desire to replace it made her think of sending for it, for though I meant to have given Caroline another, I had so many things on my mind this week that it escaped me; and I know they are so much sought for, Wilson has scarcely ever one on hand."

"Indeed, papa, you were much too kind to think about it at all," said Caroline, very earnestly. "I am afraid, if you knew how very cross and unkind the loss of the other made me, you would have withdrawn your idea of such indulgence. I am very much obliged to you, Ellen," she continued much more cordially than she had yet spoken to her cousin; "I did not deserve it even from you, for I worked myself into such an ill-temper, as almost to believe you did it purposely, and I had no right to think that."

It did indeed bear out its language, that pretty flower, for, with this one coldness removed — though Mrs. Hamilton's trembling heart dared not hope it would be lasting — love now reigned preëminent. Every happy feeling increased when in the presents from their parents each recognized something that had been wished for, though they never remembered expressing it. Mr. and Mrs. Hamilton were always united in these New Year's gifts, though tokens of approval or occasional indulgences were often given separately. There were a set of most beautiful engravings for Percy, which for the last three or four months he had been most anxious to possess; but with the recollection of former folly very fresh in his memory, he had actually succeeded in driving them from his mind, and gave them up as unattainable, till he was richer, at least. For Herbert there was a fine edition of the Greek tragedians in their original, as beautiful a work of art, in its "getting up," as Percy called it, as its letter-press, which to Herbert was beyond all price. Edward was almost wild, as his uncle and aunt telling him he was fourteen next March, and might not be with them next New Year's eve, presented him with a treasure coveted beyond all other, a gold watch. (His father's had been given by his mother as a parting gift to Captain Cameron.) Mr. Howard declared that it was much too good for a sailor, and would be lost his first voyage; he had much better hand it over to the Rectory, promising to take every care of it; but looking so mischievous, Edward vowed it should not get near his hand. For Caroline was a most complete and elegantly fitted-up embroidery-box, which quite charmed her, for it was exactly like, if not more tasteful and complete, than one Annie Grahame had brought from London, and which she had wondered, Caroline could "exist" without. As Mr. and Mrs. Hamilton found that she could not only comfortably "exist," but much as she admired and had at first so coveted it, as to have a hard battle with discontent, she had never even hinted that it might be useful. As they perceived that her mind was so happily engrossed by the idea of the pleasure her gifts would bestow, as not to cast a thought upon Annie's superior box, they indulged themselves and their child, and were more than repaid by the beaming look of delight with which it was received. For Emmeline was a parcel almost as large as herself, Percy declared. "A drawing-box all to yourself, Tiny! Thank goodness! My chalks and pencils have some chance of being let alone; I really ought to thank mamma and papa quite as much, if not more, than you, considering that in giving you a new possession they have preserved me an old one, which I began to suspect would desert me piece by piece. What, more?" he continued, laughing at his sister's almost scream of delight, as she undid the covering of a book, and found it to be the complete poem of the "Lady of the Lake," extracts of which she had read in the reviews, and so revelled in them, child as she was, as to commit them all to memory, with scarce an effort, only longing to know the whole story.

"And now, Nelly, what is your secret? still larger than Tiny's; what can it be? Come, guess; I have you in my power, for you are not strong enough to race me as Em would, and so I will be more merciful. What of all things would you like the best? — one, two, three guesses, and then I'll relieve you; I want to know if papa and mamma have looked into your secret chamber of wishes, as they have done in all of ours."

"Do not be afraid of guessing, Ellen; you are so very quiet, that your secret chamber of wishes, as Percy calls it, is more concealed than any of the others," said her uncle, smiling; "I am always obliged to refer to your aunt."

"Come, Nell, speak or I will indict you as unworthy of any thing. What did you say? a desk! Hurrah! then, there it is; and what a beauty — rosewood and mother-of-pearl — just fitted for an elegant young lady. How could mamma have found out so exactly? You have used the old shabby thing Herbert lent you, as quietly and contentedly as if there could not be a better. Do let us examine it!" and he dragged a table to her sofa, and displayed to the delighted child all its fittings-up, and its conveniences, and the pretty pen-holder and pencil-case, and fancy-wafers, and sealing-wax, and a little gold seal with her own name, and every thing that could possibly be thought of. "And even a secret drawer," exclaimed Percy, quite proud of the discovery. "Do look, Ellen; why, you can keep all sorts of secrets there, for no one would be as clever as I am to find out the spring without being told, and of course I should not betray it;" and he laughingly sent away everybody while he explained to Ellen the spring. For some little while longer did the young party examine and reëxamine and talk of their own and each other's treasures. And then Mr. Hamilton bade them remember, that, though it was New Year's Eve, it was Sunday evening, too,* and that he had deferred the hour of evening prayer till ten, that they might have time to keep both, and so not lose the sacred music which was always part of their Sunday recreation, to put away their things, and adjourn to their music-room. And he was obeyed in a very few minutes; for, though they might have preferred lingering and talking where they were, what exertion could be too great for those who so thought of, so cared for them?

Returning happiness had had such a beneficial effect, that, though Ellen still looked pale enough for her aunt not to feel quite comfortable about her, she could walk without any return of pain, and in one or two hymns even join her voice with her cousins', though it was weaker than usual. However small in appearance the talent for music, still Mrs. Hamilton cultivated it, in her boys as well as her girls, simply for the sake of giving them home resources and amusements that could be pursued together; she thought it such a mistaken notion in education to imagine that only perfection was worth attaining in the fine arts, and that, if there were not talent enough for that, it was better not attempted. Many a home might have envied the feelings with which old and young, to the lowest domestics, sought their pillows that night; for Mr. and Mrs. Hamilton, so lavish in their indulgence to their children, never forgot that for their domestics and retainers there were also claims on New Year's Eve; and the servants' hall, and every cottage which called Mr. Hamilton landlord, had vied in happiness with his own.

* While passing through the press, the scene of the Family Tree has been strongly objected to by a valued Christian friend, as being enacted on the Sunday evening. It was too late then to repair the error. The author can only express her sincere regret for a fault originating in an insufficient knowledge of the Christian feeling toward the Sabbath, and most earnestly trusts the error may be pardoned.

Mrs. Hamilton had visited Ellen the last thing, to see that she was quite comfortable, and that there was no return of pain; and she was almost startled, and certainly still more bewildered as to how such a depth of feeling could exist with such a real childish liability to error, and why it should be so carefully concealed, by the way in which Ellen clung to her, as she bent over her to wish her good night, with the same unrestrained affection as her own Emmeline did so often, with the only difference, that with the latter it seemed always to spring from the very exuberance of happiness, which could only be thus displayed. With Ellen, this night, it appeared like some deep, quiet feeling, almost of devotion, and as if — though Mrs. Hamilton's sober reason tried to persuade her imagination that it was too much meaning to attach to a mere embrace — she would thus tell her how intensely she felt, not only the indulgence of that evening, but the true kindness and watchful love which had caused the preceding sorrow. She might have thought, as no doubt many of our readers will, that Ellen was much too young and too childish, to contrast her system of treatment with her poor mother's; that she felt her soothing care in her hours of physical suffering — her indulgent love making no distinction between her and her cousins — still the more keenly and gratefully, from the recollection of her own mother's constant preference of Edward, and utter neglect of her; and that this contrast so deepened the love she bore her aunt, that it exceeded in intensity even that borne toward her by her own children. — Adults will think this all very fanciful, and perhaps interesting, but wholly improbable. Mrs. Hamilton herself would have banished the idea, as too imaginary to be entertained seriously for a moment, as any guide for her conduct. Ellen herself could not have explained or told herself that so she felt; and yet, notwithstanding, all we have written *was* there, and was the real prompter of that almost passionate embrace.

"Bless you, my darling!" was Mrs. Hamilton's fond reply, instead of permitting the child to perceive the surprise it excited in herself; and Ellen sunk to sleep, almost more happy than ever in her little life she had felt before.

CHAPTER XI.

THE CHILDREN'S BALL.

If the thought of their promised ball were the first that entered the minds of the young party at Oakwood, as they opened their eyes on New Year's day, it was not very unnatural. Percy gloried in the anticipation of being master of the ceremonies, and in conducting the whole affair with such inimitable grace and gallantry, that every one should declare it was far superior to any party, old or young, of the season, except Mr. Howard's; that was beyond him, he said, for he could not put Mr. Howard's head on his shoulders. Herbert anticipated the enjoyment of Mary Greville's society, talking to and dancing with her undisturbed, and to hearing the almost universal remark, what a sweet girl she was. Edward did not exactly know what he expected, but he was in such a mood of hilarity and mischief, that the servants all declared Master Fortescue was "*mazed.*" To Caroline their ball was almost always (though unconfessedly) the happiest evening in the year. She knew she was handsome — Annie Grahame had told her how very much she would be admired in London, and that if she were not her very dearest friend, she should envy her beauty terribly. She often in secret longed painfully for admiration and homage; and child as she still was in years, yet at her own house, and as Mr. Hamilton's eldest daughter, in addition to her real attractions, she always received both in sufficient measure, as to satisfy even herself. She delighted in those evenings when it so chanced that her brothers had young friends with them, making no hesitation in confessing that she very much preferred conversing with boys than with girls, there was so much more variety, more spirit; and though her mother's heart would actually tremble at the fearful ordeal which an introduction to the pleasures of the world would be to such a character, still she would not check the open expression of such sentiments by reproving them as wrong, and not to be encouraged. She knew that though education might do much, very much, it could not make natural characters all alike; nor, in fact, did she wish it. She did not grieve and complain that, with all her efforts she could not make Caroline give her as little trouble and anxiety as Emmeline, nor did she imagine that she should see the effect of her earnest prayers and cares all at once, or without constant relapses in the cherished object of her care. She did all she could to counteract a tendency which, situated as she would be when she entered life, must, without some strong, high principle, lead to suffering, and, perhaps, to sin — for what is coquetry? But she indulged in no idea of security, never believed that because she had so tried, so striven to sow the good seed, it could not fail to bring forth good fruit. She knew many trials might be in store for her; for how might she hope to pass through life blessed as she was then? It might please her Father in Heaven to try her faith and duty through those she loved so intensely; but if she failed not in her task, he would bring her joy at last.

To Emmeline the idea of dancing was quite enough to be the acme of enjoyment. The only drawback was, that in the intervals of rest, there was to be a little music, and though her mother had excused her at Mr. Howard's, she knew that if any body expressed a wish to hear her at her own house, play she must; and at those times she was half sorry she had chosen to learn the harp instead of the piano, as Caroline played so well on the latter instrument nobody would care to hear her; but the harp was rather a novelty, and no little girl who was coming played it, and so she was sadly afraid there was no escape for her, and that was very disagreeable, but she would not think about it till the time came; the dancing to such music as that which Mr. Hamilton had ordered from Plymouth was joy enough.

Ellen though rather afraid of so many strangers, could not resist the general contagion of anticipated enjoyment. She did not indeed wake with the thought of the ball, but with the determination to learn the verse of the Psalm her aunt had pointed out, and go and say it to her in her dressing-room before she went down. And as the first verse was very short she learned two, and repeated them without missing a word, and so as if she quite understood them, that her aunt was very much pleased; and then Ellen could think of and join her brother's and cousins' delight, even though Mrs. Hamilton was obliged to be what she called very cruel, but what Ellen knew was very kind, though it did seem a restraint, and keep her very quiet all day, instead of letting her run about from room to room, as Emmeline and Edward, and even Percy did, for fear of another headache; and so well did quietness succeed, that she looked and was unusually well, and so was almost lively by the evening.

Just before dinner, Percy, who had gone to ride because he said he was sure he should get into some scrape if he did not give a natural vent to his spirits, galloped back in company with a gentleman, whose presence seemed to occasion him still greater excitement.

"Where is my mother? and is my father at home?" he asked impatiently, flinging his horse's rein to Robert, desiring him to take every care of the gentleman's horse, as he should not let him leave Oakwood that night; and rushing across the hall threw open the door of their common sitting-room, and exclaimed —

"Mother, give me a vote of thanks and praise for my invincible eloquence! — Here is this anchorite, this monk of the moor, who, when I first encountered him, seemed so doughty a denier of my wishes, actually conquered — led a slave to your feet; reward me by throwing all the fascinations you possibly can in his way, that he may only dream of his cold ride and desolate cottage on Dartmoor to-night."

"Be quiet, madcap!" replied Mrs. Hamilton, rising with very evident pleasure, and coming forward with extended hand; "your noisy welcome will not permit mine to be heard. This is indeed a pleasure, Mr. Morton," she added, addressing the young clergyman with that earnest kindness, which always goes to the heart, "and one that Mr. Hamilton will most highly appreciate — if, as I trust, the chains my son has thrown over you, are not so heavy as to become painful."

"I should rather fear the pain will be in casting them off, Mrs. Hamilton, not in the wearing them," replied Mr. Morton, almost sadly; "it is the knowledge, that mingling as often in your home circle as Mr. Hamilton and my friend Percy desire, would wholly unfit me for the endurance of my loneliness, that keeps me so aloof, believe me. Inclination would act a very different part, but there was no resisting such eloquence and such happiness as his to-day," he continued, more gayly.

And Mr. Hamilton and Herbert entering as he spoke, their greeting was quite as warm and eager as Percy's and his mother's, and Mr. Morton gave himself up, for the evening at least, to enjoyment. His own generous nature had been particularly struck by Percy's manly conduct with regard to his satire, and different as were their characters, a warm friendship from that moment commenced between them. It was impossible to resist Percy's warm-heartedness of word and deed; and that he would sometimes leave his luxurious home and stay two or three days with Mr. Morton, seeming actually to enjoy the rude cottage and its desolate localities, and spread such a spirit of mirth within and around, that it was no wonder the afflicted young man looked to his society as almost his greatest pleasure, especially as he felt he dared not too often accept Mr. Hamilton's continually-proffered invitation. Oakwood was the home which had been his *beau idéal* for long years, but which now seemed wholly unattainable. He felt himself doomed to solitude and suffering, and the struggle for content and cheerfulness was always more painful after he had been with his friends.

When all preparations for the evening were concluded, even the respective toilets completed, Percy and Emmeline found it impossible to resist trying the spring, as they called it, of the oaken floors, (whence the carpets had been removed,) and amused themselves by waltzing in the largest circle they could make. The beautiful suit of rooms were all thrown open, and perceiving Caroline standing by the piano in an adjoining apartment, Percy called out —

"Play us a waltz, Caroline, there's a love; the very liveliest you can find, Tiny and I want to try the boards while we can enjoy them to perfection, that is, when we are the only persons in the room."

"You must excuse me, Percy," she replied somewhat pettishly; "I should think you would have dancing enough in the course of the evening; and what will our friends think, if they come and find me playing?"

"Think? why, that you are very obliging, which at present you are not," answered Percy, laughing; "never mind, Emmy; let us try what our united lungs will do."

"You may if you like, Percy, but really I am not clever enough to dance and sing at the same time — I should have no breath left," was her joyous rejoinder.

"Come and dance, Caroline, if you will not play," exclaimed Edward, who after decorating his button-hole with a sprig of holly, seemed seized with Percy's dancing-mania. "Do give me an opportunity of practising the graces before I am called upon to display them."

"My love of dancing is not so great as to attempt it without music, so practise by yourself, Edward," was Caroline's quick reply.

"Without spectators, you mean, Lina," observed her brother, very dryly; and as Emmeline begged him not to tease her, he asked —

"What has put her in this ill-humor, Emmy?"

"Oh, I don't know exactly; but if you let her alone, she will soon recover it."

"Well, to please you, I will; for you look so pretty to-night, I cannot resist you."

"Take care, Percy, if you try to turn my head with such speeches, I shall go to Edward, and punish you by not waltzing with you," said his little sister, shaking her head at him with a comic species of reproach.

"That's right, Emmy; do not take flattery even from a brother," said her father, coming forward with a smile; "but will you not tire yourself by dancing already?"

"Oh, no, papa; I feel as if I could dance all night without stopping."

"Not with me, Emmeline," rejoined Percy, shrugging his shoulders with horror at the idea; "I should cry you mercy, before one half the time had elapsed."

"But if you are not to be tired, will you not spoil your dress, and disorder all these flowing curls," continued Mr. Hamilton, "and surely that will be a great misfortune."

"Indeed it will not, papa; Percy has surely too much regard for me, to wilfully hurt my frock, and if my hair should be so troublesome as to get out of order, Fanny will rearrange it in a few minutes."

"If you wish to cause alarm on that score, my dear father," said Percy, with marked emphasis, "You must go to Caroline, not to Emmeline. Thank goodness, I have one sister above such petty misfortunes."

"Are you not too hard upon Caroline, Percy?"

"Yes, papa, he is indeed; do not mind what he says," answered Emmeline, very eagerly; but Percy said, impetuously—

"I am not, Emmeline. I would lay any wager that something has gone wrong with her dressing, to-night, and so made her pettish. Her frock is not smart enough, or she does not wear the ornaments she wished, or some such thing."

Caroline had fortunately quitted the music-room, or this speech would not have tended to restore her serenity; but before Mr. Hamilton could reply, Edward, who had been to seek Ellen, burst into the room exclaiming —

"Now, Percy, we may have a proper waltz; aunt Emmeline says we may have just one before any one comes, and here she is to play for us, and Ellen for my partner," and they enjoyed it in earnest. Mr. Hamilton watched them for a few minutes, and then went to seek his elder girl.

She was alone in a little room prepared for refreshments tastefully arranging some beautiful flowers in a bouquet. She looked up as he entered, and so smiled that her fond father thought Percy must be wrong, for there certainly seemed no trace of ill-temper.

"Why are you not with your brothers and sister in the drawing-room, my dear? and why did you just now refuse your brother such a trifling favor as playing a waltz?" he asked, but so kindly, that Caroline, though she blushed deeply, instantly replied —

"Because, papa, my temper was not quite restored; I went into the music-room to try mamma's remedy of solitude for a few minutes, but Percy spoke to me before I had succeeded. I know I answered him pettishly, but indeed, papa," she added, looking up earnestly in his face, "indeed he is very provoking sometimes."

"I know he is, my love; he does not always know how to time his jokes, or to make sufficient allowance for dispositions not exactly like his own; but tell me, what first occasioned temper so to fail that solitude was necessary."

Caroline's blush became still deeper, and she turned away her head saying, very hesitatingly —

"For such a very, *very* silly reason, papa, that I do not like to tell you."

"Nay, my dear, do not fear that I shall either laugh at or reproach you. If you feel yourself how very silly it was, I am not afraid of its gaining too great ascendency, even if you fail again."

"It was only — only — that I was not quite satisfied with the dress mamma desired me to wear to-night, papa; that was all, indeed."

"You wished, perhaps, to wear a smarter one, my love," replied her father, kissing her glowing cheek so affectionately, that the pain of her confession was instantly soothed; "but indeed, I think mamma has shown a much better taste. It requires more care than you are yet perhaps aware of, to dress so exactly according to our age and station, as to do ourselves justice, and yet excite no unpleasant feelings in those of a lower, and no contempt in those of a higher grade. Many of our friends who are coming to-night could not afford to dress their children as we might ours, and do you not think it would be both inhospitable and unkind, by being over-dressed, to excite any unpleasant feeling of inferiority in their minds, when actually none exists? for difference of fortune alone can never constitute inferiority. I am wizard enough to guess that was mamma's reason for your being attired so simply and yet so prettily to-night, and equally wizard enough to guess your reason for wishing to be smarter — shall I tell it you?" he added, playfully. "Because you fancy Miss Grahame will be attired in such a very fashionable London costume, that yours will appear so very plain and so childish. I see by that conscious smile, I have guessed correctly; but, indeed, I would not exchange my dear ingenuous Caroline, even were she attired in the cottager's stuff frock, for Annie Grahame, did she bring worlds as her dowry. And as you like ornaments, wear this," he added, tastefully twining a superb sprig of scarlet geranium in the rich dark hair that shaded Caroline's noble brow; "and if mamma inquires, tell her your father placed it there, as a token of his approbation, for temper conquered and truth unhesitatingly spoken — spite of pain."

Caroline's brilliant eye sparkled with a more delightful sense of pleasure than any triumph of dress could have bestowed, and in answer to her father's inquiry, for whom she had arranged such a beautiful bouquet, she said —

"It is for mamma, dear papa — Emmeline is always before me; but I think the idea of to-night's enjoyment has so bewildered her, that she has forgotten it, so I may just have time to present it before any one comes," and she hastened with her father to the drawing-room, where she found Mrs. Greville and her two children (for Alfred was at home for a few months,) in addition to Mr. Morton and their own family group; and the young clergyman could not but admire the natural grace with which Caroline, after warmly welcoming her guests, presented her flowers to her mother. It was a very little thing, but the joys and griefs of home are almost all made up of little things and Mrs. Hamilton was pleased, not from the attention alone, but that it proved, trifling as it was, that the annoyance and discontent which her command had occasioned in her child had left no unkind feeling behind them; and the manner with which she received it made Caroline very happy, for she had inwardly feared her ill-temper not only deserved, but had excited her mother's displeasure.

Emmeline's look of disappointment and self-reproach at her own unusual forgetfulness was so irresistibly comic, that Percy and Edward burst into an immoderate fit of laughter, which the former only checked to ask Caroline where she had been, and what she had done, to produce such an extraordinary change for the better in her appearance in so short a time

" Oh, you have no right to my secrets, Percy," was her perfectly good-humored reply; "I do not think I shall answer you, except by having the charity to refer you to papa, who has produced the change."

"By means of this pretty flower, then, I imagine," said Mrs. Hamilton; "its power I do not pretend to know, but the taste with which it is placed might vie with that of the most fashionable artists of the metropolis. Mrs. Greville do unite with me in congratulating Mr. Hamilton on his new accomplishment."

The rapid succession of arrivals prevented any further remark, and very speedily the inspiring sound of the beautiful music, which was stationed in a sort of antechamber between the drawing-room and ball-room, removed any thing like stiffness or reserve which the younger guests might have at first experienced among themselves. After two or three quadrilles, the spirit of enjoyment seemed to reign alone, not only among the dancers themselves, but even those who sat out and talked, either from preference or because the sets were full. Percy, his brother, and cousin, were so active, so universal in their attention and politeness, that all had the same measure of enjoyment; there was no sitting down four or five times consecutively for any one, and therefore neither weariness nor dissatisfaction. Where there is a great desire in the givers of a party to make every one as happy as themselves, and thoroughly to enjoy it, they seldom fail to succeed. And there was such a variety of amusements in the various rooms that were thrown open, suitable for all ages — from the mammas and papas to the youngest child, that it was scarcely possible to feel any thing but pleasure. Very many sets had been formed and danced before the Grahame family appeared, and as Caroline glanced at her friend and even at her little sister, it required a very vivid recollection of her father's words to prevent a feeling of false shame, while Annie looked at Emmeline and even her favorite Caroline for a few minutes with almost contempt.

"People talk so very much of Mrs. Hamilton's taste," she thought, "but she can have none in dress, that's certain — why no one could distinguish her daughters from the poorest gentleman's here! — But no one can mistake my rank. Thank goodness, there is not a dress like mine — how it will be envied!"

If looks were evidence of envy, Annie had them to her heart's content, but how would she have been mortified, could she have read the secret meaning of those looks, the contrast drawn between the manners and appearance of Lady Helen's daughters and those of the Honorable Mrs. Hamilton. Lady Helen herself, indeed, when she saw Caroline and Emmeline, was quite provoked that she had been so weak as to permit, and even encourage Annie, to select her own and her sister's costume.

"You are so late," said Mrs. Hamilton, as she came forward to greet them, "that I almost gave you up, fearing I don't exactly know what. I do hope nothing unpleasant has occasioned it."

"Oh no," was Mr. Grahame's reply, and it was almost bitter; "only Miss Grahame was so dreadfully afraid of being unfashionably early, that her mother did not choose to come before — indeed, my patience and my little Lilla's was so exhausted that we thought of leaving Cecil to be their beau, and coming alone an hour ago." Lady Helen's look of entreaty at Mrs. Hamilton was answered by her saying directly —

"I suppose Annie was thinking of her London parties, and forgot how completely Gothic we are as to hours and every thing else in Devonshire. But you must try and forget such superior pleasures to-night, my dear girl," she added, jestingly, though the young lady felt it rather uncomfortably as earnest, "or I fear you will find but little amusement." Alfred Greville at that moment came to claim Annie as his partner, and she gladly joined him, for though Mrs. Hamilton had "certainly no taste in dress," she never felt quite at her ease in her presence. Cecil and Lilla were soon provided with little partners, and dancing with much more real delight than their sister.

It was scarcely possible for any one, much less a parent, to look at Caroline that night without admiration. She was so animated, so graceful, so pleasing, and as such completely the centre of attraction (and really without any effort on her part) to all the gentlemen, young or old, in the room. The lads congregated round her, and it was rather a difficult task to keep clear of offence, when so very many more entreated her to dance than the length of the evening permitted; but she managed to talk to all, and yet not to neglect any of her own sex, for she always refused to dance, if she fancied her being in a quadrille prevented any couple who had not danced so much, and at those times contrived to conciliate five or six instead of only one. Emmeline took charge of the younger children, often refusing to dance with older boys, who would have made her much pleasanter partners, that she might join the little quadrille and set them all right.

"I am really glad to see Ellen among us to-night, and seeming truly to enjoy herself," said Mrs. Greville, addressing Mrs Hamilton, who was standing rather apart at the moment, watching Caroline with such mingled feelings of pride and dread, that she was quite glad when her friend's voice disturbed her train of thought. "She looked so ill in church yesterday, that I half feared we should not see her. I told her I was quite grieved that she was too unwell to be at Mr. Howard's last Friday, and—"

"What did she say?" inquired Mrs. Hamilton, anxiously.

"That it was not illness which prevented her; but she looked so confused and pained that I changed the subject directly, and the smile soon came back."

"You touched on a very painful theme," replied Mrs. Hamilton, with real relief; "Ellen and I were not quite as good friends as we usually are, last week, and my poor little girl felt my severity more than I imagined or meant. I gave her to your dear Mary's especial care to-night, for she is so timid, that left quite to herself, I was afraid it would be more pain than pleasure. Mary has taken my hint most admirable, for Ellen seems quite happy."

"It would be rather hard, if your little niece's were the only sad face in this scene of enjoyment; surely, if ever there were happiness without alloy, it is here."

"If you think so, Mrs. Greville, you will agree with my friend Morton, who has just been half poetizing, half philosophizing on this scene," said Mr. Hamilton joining them, with the young clergyman leaning on his arm. "He says there is something singularly interesting in watching the countenances and movements of children, and in tracing the dawnings of respective characters."

"You are not one of those, then, who think childhood a mere negative species of existence," rejoined Mrs. Greville.

"Indeed I do not; there is much more pleasure to me in watching such a scene, than a similar one of adults. It is full of that kind of poetry, which, from the beauty and freshness of the present, creates a future of happiness or sorrow, good or evil, as something in each countenance seems dimly to foretell. How many will be the longing thoughts thrown back in after years upon to-night!"

"Do you think, then, childhood the happiest season of life?"

He answered in the affirmative, but Mr. Hamilton shook his head.

"I differ from you, my good friend," he said. "Childhood feels its griefs as bitterly as those of maturer years. We are apt to think it was all joy in the retrospect, perhaps because it has not the anxiety and cares of riper years, but sorrow itself is felt as keenly. From reason not being perfectly formed, the difficulty to control self-will, to acquiesce in the to them incomprehensible wishes of parents or guardians, the restraint they are often compelled to use, must be all trials even to well-regulated children, and to those subject to the caprices of weakness, indolence, neglect, indulgence at one time, and tyranny at another, feelings disbelieved in, and therefore never studied or soothed — the little heart thrown back upon itself — Morton, believe me, these are trials as full of suffering, and as hard to be endured, as those which belong to manhood."

"You may be right," replied Morton; "but do you not think there is an elasticity in childhood which flings off sorrow, and can realize happiness sooner than older years?"

"Undoubtedly, and most happy it is that they are so constituted, else what would become of them? their susceptibilities for either joy or sorrow are equally quick. If the former did not balance the latter, how would their tender frames and quick affections bear their burden? The idea that childhood is in itself the happiest season in life is so far mischievous, that it prevents the necessary care and watchfulness, which alone can make it so. But we must not philosophize any more, for it has made us all grave. I see my wife is addressing Miss Grahame, and I think it is for music. Come, Morton, take Mrs. Greville to the music-room, and woo melody instead of poetry for the next half hour. Miss Grahame promises to be a very fair musician, so you will be charmed."

They adjourned to the music-room, where Percy had already gallantly conducted Annie; and several of the guests, young and old, seconded the move. Annie Grahame really played remarkably well, so far as execution and brilliancy were concerned, and Mrs. Hamilton was delighted at the expression of Grahame's face as he listened to his child and the applause she excited. "Why will he not try to win his home-affections," she thought, "when he is so formed to enjoy them? and why, why has Helen so indolently, so foolishly cast away her happiness?" was the thought that followed at the contrast which Lady Helen's face presented to her husband's; she knew Annie played well, she had heard it from very superior judges, and how could it concern her what the present company thought?

A very pretty vocal duet from the two sisters followed, and

soon afterward Caroline approached the music-stand, near which Percy and Mr. Morton were talking, and Percy, with his usual love of provoking, exclaimed —

"You surely are not going to play after Miss Grahame, Caroline. If your powers deserted you a few hours ago, and prevented the execution of a waltz, they would certainly do you a charity in deserting you completely now."

Caroline's cheek burned, but she answered, with spirit —

"Mamma desired me to oblige my friends, Percy; and she would not do so, if she thought I should disgrace myself or her."

"Do not heed your brother, Miss Hamilton," interposed Mr. Morton, taking the music from her, and offering her his arm to lead her to the piano. "I have had the pleasure of hearing you often, and those who cannot find an equal, if not superior charm in your playing to Miss Grahame's do not deserve to listen."

"Nay, you must be flattering, Mr. Morton; think of Annie's advantages."

"Indeed, my dear Miss Hamilton, yours exceed hers; no master's heart is in his pupil's progress, as a mother's in her child's, even should she not teach, but merely superintend."

Caroline was seated at the instrument as he spoke, and there was something in his few words touching a right chord; for as she began to play she certainly thought more of her mother than any one else; and determined, if possible, that others should think with Mr. Morton, forgetting at the moment that very few, except their own immediate circle, knew whose pupil she was, not imagining that the mistress of Oakwood and its large possessions could have time or inclination for any part of the education of her daughters. Morton was certainly right as to the amount of admiration, equalling, if not surpassing, that bestowed on Miss Grahame; there was a soul, a depth of expression and feeling, in Caroline's far simpler piece, that won its way to the heart at once, and if it did not surprise as much, it pleased more, and excited an earnest wish to listen to her again.

"Does not your younger daughter play?" inquired a lady, who had been much attracted with Emmeline.

"Very little, compared with her sister," replied Mrs. Hamilton; she is not nearly so fond of it, and therefore does not devote so much time to its acquirement just yet."

"Do you think it right to permit children to follow their own inclinations with regard to their education?" asked another, rather stern-looking lady, with much surprise.

"Only with regard to their accomplishments; my Emmeline is as fond of drawing as Caroline is of music, and therefore I indulge her by permitting her to give more time to the one than to the other."

"But do you think natural taste can be traced so early? that it can be distinguished from idleness or perverseness?"

"Indeed, I do," replied Mrs. Hamilton, earnestly. "If a child be allowed leisure to choose its own pursuits, and not always confined to the routine of a schoolroom, natural taste for some employment in preference to another will, I think always display itself. Not that I would depend entirely on that, because I think it right and useful to cultivate a taste for all the fine arts, only giving more time to that which is the favorite. My niece has shown no decided taste for any particular pursuit yet; but I do not neglect the cultivation of accomplishments on that account; if, in a few years, a preference manifests itself, it will be quite time enough to work hard at that particular branch."

"Is that pretty little harp used by either of your daughters?" inquired the first speaker. "It looks very much as if it were the especial property of my engaging little friend."

"Your guess is correct," replied Mrs. Hamilton, smiling. "Emmeline was quite sure she should hate music, if she must learn the great ugly piano. If she might only have a harp, she would do all she could to learn, and she really has."

"And may we not hear her?"

"When the room is not quite so full; she has not half her sister's confidence, and so large an audience would frighten away all her little powers; but I will promise you a very sweet song instead," she added, as Herbert approached, and eagerly whispered some request. "That is, if my persuasions can prevail on my young friend; Mrs. Greville, must I ask your influence, or will mine be enough?"

"What, with Mary? I rather think, your request in this case will be of more weight than mine;" and a few minutes afterward Mrs. Hamilton led the blushing, timid girl in triumph to the piano. Her voice, which was peculiarly sweet and thrilling, though not strong, trembled audibly as she commenced; but Herbert was turning over the leaves of her music, his mother was standing close beside her, and after the first few bars her enthusiastic spirit forgot the presence of all, save those she loved, and the spirit of her song.

Mrs. Hamilton never listened to and looked at her at such moments without a trembling foreboding she vainly struggled to overcome. There was something in those deep blue, earnest eyes, the hectic color that with-the least exertion rose to her cheek, the transparency of complexion, the warm and elevated spirit, the almost angel temper and endurance in her peculiarly tried lot, that scarcely seemed of earth; and never was that sad foreboding stronger than at that moment, as she looked round the crowd of young and happy faces, and none seemed to express the same as Mary's. She could scarcely command her voice and smile sufficiently to warmly thank her young favorite as she ceased; but Mary was more than satisfied by the fond pressure of her hand.

This little interruption to the actual business of the evening only increased the zest and enjoyment, when dancing recommenced. Even the call to supper was obeyed with reluctance, and speedily accomplished, that they might return the sooner to the ball-room. The hours had worn away, it seemed, on gossamer-wings, and as each happy child felt assured that the delight could not last much longer, the longing to dance to the very last moment seemed to increase. Emmeline's excitable spirit had thrown off all alloy, for it was quite impossible any one would think of asking her to play now; she had arranged all the remaining couples — for the room had begun very much to thin — for the favorite haymaker's country dance,* and accepting Edward as her own partner, and being unanimously desired to take the top, led off her young friends with such spirit and grace, and so little semblance of fatigue, that it certainly appeared as if she would verify her own words, and dance all night.

Miss Grahame had declared it was much too great a romp, and declined joining it. Caroline, who would have enjoyed it, more out of politeness to her friend than inclination, sat down with her, and a cheerful group of some of the older lads, and one or two young ladies, joined them. Herbert and Mary finding the quadrille for which they were engaged, changed to a dance for which, though they had quite the spirit, they had not the physical strength, enjoyed a quiet chat instead, and Ellen seated herself by her favorite Mary, declining, from fatigue, Alfred Greville's entreaty that she would second Emmeline.

"I declare I could dance myself with that merry group," exclaimed Mr. Grahame, after watching them some time, and all his austerity banished by the kindly spirit of the evening.

* A country dance, the author believes, peculiar to Devonshire, for she has never seen it danced elsewhere.

"Mrs. Hamilton, Mrs. Greville, do one of you take pity on me, and indulge my fancy."

Both ladies laughingly begged to be excused, offering, however, to introduce him to a partner.

"No; it must be one of you or none at all. That little sylph of yours, Mrs. Hamilton, seems inclined to dance for you and herself too. What a pretty couple she and that handsome cousin of hers make! And there goes my little Lilla — I do hope I may have one really happy child. What, tired, Percy — compelled to give up — absolutely exhausted?"

"Indeed I am," answered Percy, who had waltzed his partner very cleverly out of the line, and, after giving her a seat, threw himself on a large ottoman.

"Mother, if you do not put a stop to Emmeline's proceedings, her strength will entirely fail, and down she and Edward will go, and the rest follow, just like a pack of cards. Do, pray, prevent such a catastrophe, for I assure you it is not in the least unlikely."

The gravity with which he spoke caused a general laugh; but Mrs. Hamilton, feeling by the length of time the fatiguing dance had lasted, there was really some truth in his words, desired the musicians to stop; causing an exclamation of regret and disappointment from many youthful lips, and Emmeline and Edward ran up to her, to entreat that they might go on a little longer. Mrs. Hamilton, however, refused; and Edward yielded directly, but Emmeline was so much excited, that obedience was most unusually difficult; and when her mother desired her to sit down quietly for ten minutes, and then come to the music-room, as Mrs. Allan most particularly wished to hear her play before she left, she answered, with more petulance than she was at all aware of —

"I am sure I cannot play a note now — it will be no use trying."

"Emmeline!" exclaimed her mother, adding, gravely, "I am afraid you have danced too much, instead of not enough."

The tone, still more than the words, was enough; poor Emmeline was just in that mood when tears are quite as near as smiles; her own petulance seemed to reproach her too, and she suddenly burst into tears. Many exclamations of sympathy and condolence burst from her mother's friends: — "Poor child!" "She has over-tired herself!" "We cannot expect her to play now!" — but Mrs. Greville saying, with a smile, that her little friend's tears were always the very lightest April showers, successfully turned the attention of many from her; while Mrs. Hamilton taking her hand from her face, merely said, in a low voice —

"Do not make me more ashamed of you, Emmeline. What would papa think if he were to see you now?" Her little girl's only answer was to bury her face still more closely in her mother's dress, very much as if she would like to hide herself entirely; but on Mrs. Allan saying, very kindly —

"Do not distress yourself, my dear. I would not have asked to hear you play, if I had thought you would dislike it so much. I dare say you are very tired, and so think you will not succeed."

She raised her head directly, shook back the fair ringlets that had fallen over her face, and though the tears were still on her cheeks and filling her eyes, she said, with a blending of childish shyness and yet courageous truth, impossible to be described —

"No, ma'am, I am not too tired to play — I did not cry from fatigue, but because I was angry with mamma for not letting me dance any more, and angry with myself for answering her so pettishly; and because — because — I thought she was displeased, and that I deserved it."

"Then come and redeem your character," was Mrs. Hamilton's only notice of a reply that actually made her heart throb with thankfulness, that her lessons of truth were so fully understood and practised by one naturally so gentle and timid as her Emmeline: while Mrs. Allan knew not what to answer, from a feeling of involuntary respect. It would have been so easy to escape a disagreeable task by tacitly allowing that she was too tired to play; and what careful training must it have been to have so taught truth.

Mrs. Allan would not ask you before, because she knew you did not like to play while the room was so very full; therefore, ought you not to do your very best to oblige her?"

Emmeline looked timidly up in her mother's face to be quite sure that her displeasure had subsided, as her words seemed to denote; and quite satisfied, her tears were all checked, and taking Mrs. Allan's offered hand, she went directly to the music-room.

Mrs. Hamilton lingered to desire Herbert (who had come up to know the cause of his sister's sudden tears) to form the last quadrille, and reserve a place, if he possibly could, for Emmeline, as they would not begin till she had done. Her little girl was playing as she rejoined her, and it really was a pretty picture, her fairy figure with her tiny harp, and her sweet face seeming to express the real feeling with which she played. There was no execution in the simple Highland air, but her vivid imagination lent it a meaning, and so, when fairly playing, she did not mind it. Mrs. Allan had lost a little girl just at Emmeline's age, who had also played the harp, and there was something in her caress and thanks, after she had done, that made Emmeline stand quietly at her side, without heeding the praises that were lavished round her. Herbert at that moment appeared with one of the young Allans.

"Come, Emmy, we are only waiting for you; Mr. Allan says you have not favored him to-night, and he hopes you will now."

"Pray, do," added Mrs. Allan, as her son gayly pleaded his own cause; Emmeline only waited to read her mother's consent in her eyes, for she thought that she ought not to dance any more; and in another minute the joyous music had resounded, and she was dancing and chatting as gayly and happily as if there had been no interruption to her joy.

"And you will leave all these delights to imprison yourself in a man-of-war?" asked Mr. Grahame, jestingly, of Edward, while waiting for his wife and daughters, who were the last departures, (much to Annie's horror, for it was so unfashionable to be quite the last,) to be cloaked and shawled.

"Imprison!" was his very indignant reply, "and on the wide, free, glorious ocean! flying on the wings of the wind wherever we please, and compelling the flag of every land to acknowledge ours! No, Mr. Grahame; you landsmen don't know what liberty is, if you talk of imprisonment in a ship! We take our home wherever we go, which you landsmen cannot do, though you do so poetize on the maternal properties of Old Mother Earth."

"Only hear him, Hamilton," exclaimed Grahame, laughing heartily; "any one would think he had been a sailor all his little life. You talk boldly now, my boy, but you may change your tone when you have once tried the cockpit."

"I do not think I shall," answered Edward, earnestly; "I know there are many hardships, and I dare say I shall find them more disagreeable than I can possibly imagine; but I shall get used to them; it is so cowardly to care for hardships."

"And is it no grief to give up all the pleasures of land?"

"I exchange them for others more delightful still."

"And the sea is to be your sister, uncle, aunt, and cousins — altogether?"

"Yes all," replied Edward, laughing; adding, as he put his

arm affectionately round Ellen, "my sister has so many kind friends that she will be able to spare me till I am old enough to do all a brother ought."

"You are a good fellow, Edward, and I see I must not talk of parting, if I would preserve this evening's pleasure unalloyed," Grahame said, as he laid his hand kindly on Ellen's head, and then turned to obey the summons of his wife.

The young party, no doubt, felt that it would be infinitely more agreeable to sit up all night, and talk of the only too quickly concluded enjoyment, than to retire to their respective pillows; but the habits of Oakwood were somewhat too well regulated for such dissipation, though, no doubt, their *dream-land* that night, was peopled with the pleasant shadows of reality, and, according to their respective sources of enjoyment, brought back their evening's happiness again and again.

CHAPTER XII.

EFFECTS OF PLEASURE. — THE YOUNG MIDSHIPMAN. — ILL TEMPER, ITS ORIGIN AND CONSEQUENCES.

THE return to the quiet routine of work, and less exciting recreation after the Christmas pleasures, was of course a trial to all our young friends. Not so much to the boys, as to their sisters; Percy's elastic spirits found pleasure in every thing, being somewhat too old to care for his studies, or feel them now as a restraint. Herbert only exchanged one kind of happiness for another. Edward looked to every month that passed, as bringing nearer the attainment of his wishes; and he was so fond of Mr. Howard, and so quick at learning, and such a favorite with all his schoolfellows, that he did not care at all when the time of work came again. Ellen and Emmeline both found it very difficult to like their lessons again; especially the latter, who felt as if work and regularity were most particularly disagreeable things, and sometimes was almost in despair as to her ever enjoying them again; but she tried very hard to overcome indolence, and never give way to petulance, and succeeded, so as to win her the delight of both her parents' approbation. Indulgence always made her feel as if no effort on her part was too great to prove how much she felt it; and when any one, old or young, experiences this sort of feeling, they need never be afraid but that they will succeed in their efforts, painful and hard as they may at first seem. It was not so difficult for Ellen as for Emmeline, because she was less able to realize such an intensity of pleasure. She seemed safer when regularly employed; and besides, to work hard at her respective studies, was one of the very few things which she could do to prove how much she loved her aunt; and accustomed from such early childhood to conquer inclination, and, in fact, never to fancy pleasure and indulgence were her due, there was happiness enough for her even in their more regular life: but to Caroline the change was actually unbearable. While admiration and praise only incited Emmeline to greater exertions, they caused Caroline completely to relax in hers, and to give, in consequence, as much trouble and annoyance as she had received pleasure. The perseverance in her various studies, especially in music, the unceasing control over her temper, which *before* the holidays she had so striven for, had now entirely given way. It was much less trouble for her to learn than Emmeline, there fore her studies with Miss Harcourt were generally well performed; but the admiration she had excited made her long for more, and believe herself a person deserving much more consideration and respect than she received from her own family. These thoughts persisted in, of course produced and retained ill-temper; which, as there was no longer any fear of her being debarred by its indulgence from any pleasure, she made no attempt to overcome. The praise bestowed on her music, made her fancy herself a much greater proficient than she really was, and though her love of music was great, her love of praise was greater; and so she not only relaxed in her practice, but inwardly murmured at the very little praise she received from her mother.

"How can you give mamma so much trouble, Caroline, when you know you can do so much better?" Herbert exclaimed, one day, when an attack of weakness, to which he was liable, had confined him to a sofa.

Mrs. Hamilton, after giving her usual hour's lesson, in which Caroline had chosen to do nothing, had left her in very evident displeasure, and even Herbert was roused to most unusual indignation.

"What is the use of practising day after day?" was her angry reply; "I am sure I should play just as well if I practised less."

"You did not think so a month ago, Caroline."

"No, because then I had something to practise for."

"And have you nothing now? — Is mamma's approbation nothing? — Is the pleasure you give all of us, by your talent for music, nothing? — Oh, Caroline, why will you throw away so much real gratification, for the vain desire of universal admiration?"

"There surely can be no harm, Herbert, in wishing to be universally loved and admired."

"There is, when it makes you discontented and unhappy, and blind to the love and admiration of your home. What is the praise of strangers worth, compared to that of those who love you best?"

"There is not much chance of my receiving either at present," was the cold reply.

"Because you will not try for the one most easily and happily obtained and even without thinking of praise, how can you be so ungrateful, as to repay all mamma's care and trouble by the indolence, coldness, and almost insolence, you have shown to-day? How few mothers of her rank would — "

"You may spare your sermon, Herbert; for at this moment I am not disposed either to listen to or profit by it," interrupted Caroline, and she left the room in anger. A faint flush rose to the pale cheek of her brother, but he quickly conquered the natural irritation, and sought his mother, by every fond attention on his part, to remove the pain of Caroline's conduct.

This continued for about a fortnight, at the end of which time, Caroline suddenly resumed her music with assiduity, and there were no more ebullitions of ill-temper. Herbert hoped his expostulations were taking effect; Mrs. Hamilton trusted that her child was becoming sensible of her past folly, and trying to conquer it, and banish its memory herself: both, however, were mistaken. Annie Grahame had imparted to her friend, in strict confidence, that her mother intended giving a grand ball about the end of February, and meant to entreat Mrs. Hamilton, as a personal favor, to let Caroline be present. Caroline little knew the very slight foundation Annie had for this assertion. Lady Helen had merely said, *perhaps* she would ask; and this was only said, because she was too indolent and weak to say "No" at once. Not that she had any unkind feeling toward Caroline, but simply because she was perfectly certain Mrs. Hamilton would not consent, and to persuade as earnestly as Annie wished was really too much trouble.

Caroline's wishes in this instance triumphed over her better judgment, for had she allowed herself to think soberly, she ought to have known her mother's principles of action sufficiently, not to entertain the slightest hope of going.

The invitations (three weeks' notice) for her parents and brothers came. In them she did not expect to be included, but when above a week passed, and still not a word was said, disappointment took the place of hope, and it was only the still lingering belief that she might go, even at the last moment, that prevented the return of ill-temper.

Now Lady Helen really had asked, though she did not persuade; and Mrs. Hamilton thanked her, but, as she expected, decidedly refused. "Caroline was much too young," she said, "for such a party. Did she know any thing about being asked?" Lady Helen said, with truth, that she had not mentioned the subject to her, and had desired Annie to be equally silent.

Mrs. Hamilton quite forgot that Miss Grahame was not famous for obedience, and, relying on her friend's assurance, determined on not saying any thing to Caroline about it; wishing to spare her the pain which she knew her refusal would inflict. As it happened, it would have been better if she had spoken. The weather had prevented Caroline from seeing Annie, but she was quite sure she would not deceive her; and her proud heart rebelled against her mother, not only for refusing Lady Helen's request, but for treating her so much like a child, as to hide that refusal from her. Under the influence of such thoughts, of course, her temper became more and more difficult to control and as a natural consequence, anger and irritation against her mother, and self-reproach for the indulgence of such feelings increased, till she became actually miserable.

It happened that about this time Miss Harcourt left Oakwood for a week, on a visit to an invalid friend at Dartmouth. Mrs. Hamilton had given her full liberty, promising that her pupils should lose nothing by her absence. She left on the Saturday, and the Thursday was Lady Helen's ball. On the Monday, Mr. Hamilton detained Edward, as he was leaving the library, after morning prayers, and told him that he had received a letter, which he thought might chance to interest him. Ten minutes afterward, Edward rushed into the breakfast-room, in a state of such joyous excitement that he could scarcely speak.

"Wish me five, ten, twenty thousand joys!" he exclaimed, springing from chair to chair, as if velocity of movement should bring back speech. "In one month the Prince William sails, and I am to meet her at Portsmouth, and be a sailor, a real sailor; and to-morrow fortnight uncle says we are to start for London, and have ten days there to see all the fine sights, and then go to Portsmouth, and see all that is to be seen there, and then — and then — "

"Take care you do not lose your wits before you leave Oakwood," interposed Percy, laughing heartily. "I should not at all wonder, before you go, that you will be fancying the river Dart the Atlantic, and set sail in a basket, touch at all the islets you may pass, imagining them various cities, and finally land at Dartmouth, believing it Halifax, your destined port — that will be the end of your sailorship, Edward, depend upon it."

"I rather think I should stand a chance of being ducked into my sober senses again, Percy, unless wicker be waterproof, which I never heard it was."

"But I have, though," eagerly interrupted Emmeline; "the Scots and Picts invaded England in wicker boats, and to have held so many men, they must have been strong and waterproof too. So you see, Percy's basket is only an ancient boat, Edward. You are much better off than you thought you were."

"Give me Alfred's wooden walls instead, Emmy; your Picts and Scots were very little better than savages — Alfred is my man; he deserves to be called great, if it were only for forming the first English navy. But neither my aunt nor Ellen have wished me joy. I think I shall be offended."

Mrs. Hamilton could not speak at the first moment, for the joy, the animation of her nephew so recalled the day when her own much-loved brother, her darling Charles, had rushed into her room, to tell her all his glee, for no one ever listened to and shared in his joys and troubles as she did. He was then scarcely older than Edward, as full of hope and joy and buoyancy — where was he? Would his fate be that of the bright, beautiful boy before her? And as Edward threw his arms round her neck, and kissed her again and again, telling her he could not be quite sure it was not all a dream, unless she wished him joy too, it was the utmost effort to prevent the fast gathering tears, and so command her voice, that he should not hear her tremble. Poor Ellen looked and felt bewildered. She had always tried to realize that Edward, to be a sailor, must leave her; and in fact aware that his summons would soon come, her aunt and uncle had often alluded to his departure before her, but still she had never thought it near; and now the news was so sudden, and Edward was so wild with joy, she fancied she ought to rejoice too, but she could not; and Percy was obliged to ask her merrily, what ailed her, and if she could not trust to his being a much more worthy brother than such a water-rat who had no business whatever on land, before she could take her place at the breakfast table and try to smile. But her eyes would rest on Edward even then, and she felt as if there were something across her throat and she could not swallow the nice roll which Herbert had so kindly buttered and cut, and so quietly placed in her plate; and when Edward said something very funny, as he was in the habit of doing, and made them all laugh, she tried to laugh too, but instead of a laugh it was a sob that startled herself, for she was quite sure she did not mean to be so foolish; but instead of being reproved, as she was afraid she should be, she felt her aunt's arm thrown gently round her, till she could hide her face on her shoulder, and cry quite quietly for a few minutes, for they went on talking and laughing round the breakfast-table, and nobody took any notice of her, which she was quite glad of, for she could not bear Edward to think she was unhappy when he was so pleased. And after breakfast, though he was in such a desperate hurry to tell Mr. Howard the good news, that when he did set off he left even Percy far behind him, he found time to give her a hearty kiss, and to tell her that he loved her very much, though he could not help being so glad he was going to sea; and that he was quite proud of her, because though he knew she was very sorry he was going, she did not cry and make a fuss as some selfish people would; and then she really did smile.

"It is Monday morning, my dears, and I find Ellis and Morris require my attention for a longer time than I expected," Mrs. Hamilton said, as she entered the school-room, and found the three girls preparing their books, "so I must set you all to work, and see how well you can get on without me till eleven, when I will rejoin you. I shall order the carriage at half-past twelve, and if all I require is completed, we will pay your favorite old ruin a visit, Emmy; the morning is so lovely, that I think we may venture to take our sketch-books, and see what other part of Berry Pomeroy we can take pencil possession of."

Such an anticipation was quite enough for Emmeline. Her dance about the room was only checked by the idea that her lessons would never be ready, nor her exercises and sums done, unless she sat quietly down; and so, with a great effort, she gave all her attention to her various tasks, and mastered them even before her mother returned. Ellen, though she tried quite as much, was not so successful. The Prince William would sail in miniature on her slate, over all her figures. The recollection of the awful storm they had encountered on their voyage to

England would return so vividly, that the very room seemed to heave. And then — but she could not make out why she should think about that then — her mother's death-bed came before her and her promise, and it seemed harder still to part with Edward, from a vague dread that came over her, but still she tried to attend to what she had to do, and congratulated herself on its completion before her aunt appeared.

Caroline, alone, was determined not to work. Because she had not made herself miserable enough already, the most unfounded jealousy entered her head from seeing her mother's caressing kindness toward Ellen at breakfast; why was not her manner as kind to her! She was quite as unhappy, and her mother must see it, but she took no notice of her — only of Ellen. She might be cross sometimes, but she never told stories or tried to hide her faults, and it was very hard and unjust that she should be treated so like a child, and Ellen made so much of; and so she thought and thought, not attempting to do a single thing till she actually made herself believe, for the time, that her kind, indulgent mother had no love for her; and every thing looked blacker than before.

She made no effort to rouse herself even in Mrs. Hamilton's presence, but listened to her remonstrances with such extreme carelessness, almost insolence, that her mother felt her patience failing. The self-control, however, for which she had successfully striven, enabled her so to overcome the irritation, as to retain her own quiet dignity, and simply to desire Caroline to give her attention at once to her studies, and conquer her ill-temper, or not to think of accompanying them on their excursion, as idleness and peevishness were better left to themselves. An insolent and haughty reply rose to Caroline's lips; but with an effort she remained silent, her flushed forehead alone denoting the internal agitation. Emmeline's diligence and the approbation she received irritated her still more; but she rejoiced when she heard her mother tell Ellen there was not a correct line in her French exercise, and her sum, a compound long division, wrong from the very first figure. But the pleasure soon gave place to indignant anger, when, instead of the reproof which she believed would follow, Mrs. Hamilton said very kindly —

"I should very much like these done correctly, Ellen, before we go out; suppose you ensconce yourself in that bay-window, there are a table and chair all ready for you, and we shall not interrupt you as we should if you remain at this table. I know they are both very difficult, to-day especially, but the more merit in their accomplishment, you know the more pleased I shall be.

Ellen obeyed directly; a little care, and with the assistance of her grammar, which her aunt permitted her to refer to, instead of depending entirely on her memory that morning, enabled her to succeed with her French; but four times was that tormenting sum returned to, till at last her tears effaced the figures as fast as they were written. Still, patience and resolution in both teacher and pupil conquered, and the fifth time there was not a figure wrong; and Mrs. Hamilton, fondly putting back the heavy ringlets which in Ellen's absorbed attention had fallen over her tearful cheeks, said, playfully —

"Shall I tell you a secret, my little Ellen? I was quite as disinclined to be firm this morning as you were to be patient; so you see we have both gained a great victory. My conjuring propensities, as Emmy thinks them, told me that you had real cause for some little inattention, and, therefore that it was very cruel in me to be so determined; but my *judgment* would tell me that my *feeling* was wrong, and that to conquer disinclination and overcome a difficulty, was a much better way of lessening even natural sorrow than to give up. I do not expect you to think so just now, but I fancy you are not very sorry this disagreeable, terrible tiresome sum has not to be done to-morrow, which it must have been, had you left it to-day."

Ellen was so glad, that she felt almost happy, and her few other duties were done quite briskly, for Mrs. Hamilton had been so kind as to countermand the carriage till one, that she and Caroline might have time to finish. But Caroline, if she had not tried before, was now still less capable of doing so. Every word of kindness addressed to Ellen increased the storm raging within, and the difficulty of restraining it in Mrs. Hamilton's presence caused it to burst forth with unmitigated violence the moment she quitted the apartment, desiring Emmeline and Ellen to make haste, and put away their books, but still without taking the least notice of her. Invective, reproach, almost abuse, were poured against Ellen, who stood actually frightened at the violence she had so very innocently excited, and at the fearful and deforming passion which inflamed her cousin's every feature. Caroline's anger had miscounted time, or she must have known that her mother could not have gone far enough, for such unusual tones of excitement to escape her quick hearing. Mrs. Hamilton, startled and alarmed, returned directly, and so vividly did her child's appearance and words recall her own misguided sister in those uncontrolled fits of fury, under which she had so often trembled, that present disappointment and dread for the future, took possession of her, and for the moment rendered her powerless. Caroline was too much engrossed to perceive her at first, and she had, therefore, time to rally from the momentary weakness.

"What does this mean?" she exclaimed, fixing her eyes on Caroline, with that expression of quiet but stern reproof, which when she did use it — and it was very seldom — had the power of subduing even the wildest excitement. "What has Ellen done, that you should abuse her with this unjust and cruel and most unfeminine violence? You have indulged your ill-temper till you do not know what you say or do, and you are venting on another the anger which my displeasure has caused you to feel toward me and toward yourself. I desire that you will control it directly, or retire to your own room, till you can behave with some degree of propriety, and not disturb the comfort and happiness of others in this most uncalled-for manner."

"I will not go," answered Caroline, bursting into violent tears, and scarcely aware of what she was saying, "I know I dislike Ellen, and I have reason to dislike her, for before she came, you were never so often displeased with me; you are always kind and indulgent to her, always treat her as a reasonable being, not as the child, the infant you think me. I know you have lost all love for me, or you must have seen I was unhappy, and spoken kindly to me, as you did to Ellen; I have every reason to dislike her, stealing your affection from me as she has, and I do with all my heart!"

"Go, and prepare for our drive, my dear children," Mrs. Hamilton said, as she calmly turned for a moment to Emmeline and Ellen, who both stood bewildered, the former from actual terror that her sister should dare so to address her mother, and the latter from pain at the violent avowal of a dislike which she had intuitively felt, but had always tried to disbelieve. "The beauty of the day will be gone if we linger much longer, and I do not intend to be disappointed of our promised ramble. Do not think any thing of what this unhappy girl is saying; at present she scarcely knows herself, and will by and by wish it recalled, far more intensely than ever we can."

Emmeline longed to throw her arms round her mother, and with tears beseech her to forget what Caroline had said; but, though Mrs. Hamilton had spoken cheerfully, and in quite her usual tone of voice to them, there was something in her countenance, that checked any display of softness even in her affectionate child; something that almost awed her, and she left the room with Ellen to prepare for the promised excursion, which had, however, lost all its anticipated enjoyment from the uncontrolled temper of another.

"Now, Caroline, I will answer you," said Mrs. Hamilton, as soon as they were alone, and again regarding Caroline, who was sobbing violently, with that same searching look. "Your charges are such very heavy ones, that I really must request you during my absence to arrange and define them in some order. I am so perfectly ignorant of having given you any foundation for them, that, before I can attempt defence, you must inform me exactly and definitely of what you complain. That this morning my manner was kinder to Ellen than to you I quite acknowledge. Her inattention and depression had a cause, yours had none; for if you were unhappy, it was from your own fearful temper, which, by encouragement, has blackened every thing around you. You may employ your time till dinner as you choose; but at five o'clock come to me in my dressing-room, prepared to define and inform me of every charge you can bring against me. You will consider this a command, Caroline, disregard or evasion of which will be disobedience."

She left the room, and in a very short time afterward Caroline heard the carriage drive off; but for nearly three long hours she never moved from her seat, so utterly miserable, as scarcely even to change her position. Never in her life before, not in her most angry moments, had she so spoken to her mother, and her remorse was almost intolerable. Again and again she remembered what Mrs. Hamilton had told her so often, that, if she did not strive and pray against the dominion of ill-temper while young, it would become more and more uncontrollable, and the older she became, the more difficult to subdue, even in a moderate degree; and her words were indeed true. It had been many months since temper had gained such an ascendency, and its effects were far, far more violent, and its power over her more determined, and if, as she grew older, it should be still worse, what would become of her? how insufferably wretched! what would she not have given to have recalled her words? The jealousy which had arisen, now she knew not how, had sunk into air before those few calm inquiring sentences from her mother, and in her excessive misery every kind deed and word and look, every fond indulgence and forbearance, in fact, all the love her mother had so lavished on her from her infancy, rushed back upon her, till she actually hated herself, and longed the more intensely for the comfort of that soothing affection, which, in real pain or childish sorrow, had never been refused her.

"Why, why did Annie tell me any thing about that hatefu ball?" she exclaimed, at length, as the sound of many joyous voices and the dressing-bell proclaimed the return of the various members of her family only in time to prepare for dinner. "It was all, all from that; I know now, only from that one thought — one wish. Why was I such a fool, as not to tell mamma at once that I knew I was to be asked, and wished so much to go? — if she had refused me, it would not have been half the pain I have made for myself. And how can I meet papa's eye and Percy's unkind jokes with eyes like these?" she added, as on rising to go to her own room, she caught sight of her own face in a mirror, and actually started at the disfigurement which the violence of her emotion had wrought. "Oh, how I wish mamma had not desired me to go to her; that I could but hide myself from everybody — or get rid of this horrible black cloud."

From every eye but her mother's she could and did hide herself; for saying that her head ached, which was the truth, and she did not wish any thing to take, she refused to go down to dinner. Mrs. Hamilton had successfully exerted herself during their excursion, and Emmeline and Ellen enjoyed themselves so thoroughly as almost to forget the alloy of the morning; and even when Caroline's message recalled it, the boys were all so merry, that it did not disturb them. Percy always declared that Caroline's headache was only another term for temper-ache, and he would certainly have sent her some message of mock pity, if his quick eye had not discovered or fancied that his mother did not look quite as well as usual, and so he contented himself by trying still more to be the life of the dinner-table. Mr. Hamilton had seen at a single glance that all was not quite right, and Caroline's non-appearance and message explained it, to his extreme regret, for he had begun to hope and believe that his wife's extreme solicitude, on her account, was beginning to decrease.

Mrs. Hamilton had not much doubt that silence and solitude had so far had effect on Caroline as to subdue passion, and bring her to a sense of her misconduct; but that had scarcely power to lessen the anxiety and the pain which Caroline's words had so wantonly inflicted. Had she indeed evinced any thing like undue partiality? the idea alone almost brought a smile; fondly, and almost as her own child, as she loved her little niece. The very anxiety Caroline occasioned her, deep ened her affection; the very control she was obliged to exercise in her mode of guiding her, strengthened every feeling toward her. She was so enwrapped in these painfully engrossing thoughts, in the strict examination of her own heart, that she was not aware the time she had appointed had passed by full ten minutes, till she was roused by the handle of her door being softly turned, and left again, as if some one had wished to enter, but hesitated. The very hesitation gave her hope, for she really did not know that the utmost penalty she could have inflicted on Caroline, in the moment of natural indignation, would have failed in producing such an effect as the simple command to seek her, and define her charges against her, when that angry excitement had so calmed, that Caroline would have given worlds, if she might but have not referred to it again. She knew she dared not disobey, but her daring had left her so powerless that she had stood at her mother's door full ten minutes before she could command courage sufficient to open it and enter.

Mrs. Hamilton looked at her changed aspect, the bitter humiliation expressed in every feature, with such pity, that it required even more than her usual exercise of control, to retain the grave, and apparently unmoved tone with which she said —

"You have had a long time in which to reflect on your charges against me, Caroline. I hope they are now sufficiently defined for me to understand and answer them. You may sit down, for you do not seem very capable of standing."

Caroline gladly obeyed, by sitting down on a low ottoman, some little distance from her mother, on whose neck she absolutely longed to throw herself and beseech forgiveness; but Mrs. Hamilton's tone was not such as to give her courage to do so. She remained silent, burying her face in her hands.

"I am waiting your pleasure, Caroline; I should have thought that you had had plenty of time to think during my absence. Of what do you accuse me?"

"Oh, nothing, nothing! mamma, dear mamma, do not speak to me in that tone, I cannot bear it; indeed, indeed, I am miserable enough already; condemn me to any punishment, the severest you can, I know I deserve it — but do not, do not speak so."

"No, Caroline; were I to condemn you to any punishment, it would seem more like vengeance for the pain you have inflicted on me by your accusation of partiality and injustice than from the hope of producing any good end. You are no longer a child, who must be taught the line of duty to a parent

You know it now as well as I can teach it, and if you fail, must be answerable only to yourself. I cannot help you any further, than by requesting you to explain clearly the origin of your complaint against me. Its main ground of offence is, I believe, that since Ellen has become an inmate of my family I have treated you with more harshness and unkindness than I ever did before. Can you look back on the last eighteen months and recall one instance in which this has been the case? I must have an answer, Caroline; you may now think explanation is not necessary, and that you meant nothing when you spoke, but that will not satisfy me nor you, when ill-temper regains ascendency. You need not refrain from answering for fear of wounding me. You can scarcely do that more than you have done already."

Caroline tried to speak, but she could only sob forth, that she could not recall one instance, in which her mother had been more displeased with her than her conduct merited. Acknowledging, but almost inarticulately, that she had sometimes fancied that she had remained longer cold with her than with Ellen, after the committal of a fault — and that — (she stopped.)

"Go on, Caroline."

"I could not feel my faults such heavy ones as Ellen's."

"They are of equal if not greater weight than your cousin's, Caroline. You have been, from your earliest infancy, the object of the most tender and devoted care to your father and myself. Miss Harcourt has followed out our plans; you have never been exposed to any temptation, not even that of casual bad example. Ellen, till she became mine, encountered neglect, harshness, all that could not fail in such a character to engender the faults she has. You cannot compare yourself with her, for, had you been situated as she was, I fear you would have had still heavier failings."

"I should never have told untruths," exclaimed Caroline with returning temper.

"Perhaps not, for some persons are so physically constituted that they do not know what fear is; and harshness would harden, not terrify and crush, as with such dispositions as Ellen's. But Caroline, when temper gains dominion over you, as it has done to-day, do you always think and utter nothing but the truth?"

Caroline turned from that penetrating look and burst into tears. Few as the words were, they seemed to flash light into the very inmost recesses of her heart, and tell her that in moments of uncontrolled temper, in her brooding fancies, she eally did forfeit the truth, on adherence to which she so prided nerself; and that there was no excuse for her in the idea that she did not know what she said or did — for why had religion and reason been so carefully implanted within her, but to enable her to subdue the evil temper, ere it acquired such fearful dominion.

"Perhaps you have never thought of this before, Caroline," resumed Mrs. Hamilton, and her tone was not quite so cold "but think of it in future, and it may help you to conquer yourself. Remember, words can never be recalled, and that, though you may have lost such command over yourself, as scarcely to know the exact sense of what you say, yet those to whom they are addressed, or those who may have only heard them, must believe, and so receive, and perhaps act on false impressions, which no after effort will remove. Now to your next charge, that I treat Ellen as a reasonable being, and you as a child — if you have the least foundation for this supposition, speak it without hesitation — whence has it arisen?"

For one minute Caroline hesitated, but then resolved she would atone for her fault at least by a full confession. She told all the wishes, the hopes Annie's information of Lady Helen's promise had imparted, and the pain it was to feel that her mother thought her such a child as not to speak to her on the subject.

"And if you did think so, Caroline, why did you not, from the first moment that Annie told you of it, come to me, and tell me how very much you wished it? I could not, indeed, have granted your wishes, but your confidence would have been met with such indulgence as would at least have saved you some degree of pain. Believing, as I did, and as Lady Helen assured me I might with safety, that you knew nothing about it — would you have thought it kind or judicious in me, had I said, 'Lady Helen has persuaded me to take you to her ball, but I have refused her.' I was silent to spare you pain, as, had you permitted yourself calmly to think, you would have believed. However, as appearances were, I grant that I have not treated you, in this instance, with the consideration that your age might perhaps have demanded; and from Annie not obeying Lady Helen's desire, that she should not mention the subject to you, have failed in sparing you the pain of disappointment, as I had hoped. But another time, instead of brooding over that which seems want of consideration on my part, come to me at once, and spare yourself and me the pain you have caused me to-day. I do not think you can accuse me of ever meeting your confidence with so much harshness as to check such openness on your part."

Caroline looked hastily up; her mother's tone was almost as fond as usual, and, unable to restrain the impulse any longer, she started from her low seat, and kneeling down close by her, clung round her, passionately exclaiming —

"Mamma! mamma! pray, forgive me; I am so very miser able — I cannot bear myself — I do not know when I shall be happy again; for even if you forgive me, I know — I know — I never can forgive myself."

"I do not wish you to forgive yourself just yet, my dear child," replied her mother, not refusing the kiss Caroline's eyes so earnestly besought. "Your fault has been such an aggravated one, that I fear it must cause you many days of remorse, the most painful kind of suffering which error can bring; but do not try to shake it off; I would rather see you endure it, and not expect happiness for a few days. You know where to seek the only source which can bring peace and comfort, and you must endeavor, by earnest prayer, to strengthen yourself for the conflict you have so often to encounter. You have a very difficult task, my poor child, that I know; and, therefore, do I so try to provide you with a guard and help."

"If I could but conquer it at first," answered Caroline, whose violent excitement had given way to tears of real repentance; "but at first it seems almost a pleasure to me to be cross to everybody, and answer pettishly, and as if it were pleasanter to encourage disagreeable thoughts than to read or do any thing that would remove them. And then, when I would give any thing to escape from them, it seems everybody's fault but my own, and I cannot."

"If you accustomed yourself constantly to pray against this great fault, my dear child, you would find, that its very first approach would so startle you, that you would use every energy to subdue it. But I fear it is only when temper has made you miserable, as it has to-day, that you are quite aware of its enormity. You do not think the fault great enough to demand the watchfulness and care without which it never will be subdued."

"I am afraid I do not, indeed, mamma. I know I do not make it a subject of prayer, as you have so often advised me, except when every thing looks so black, and I am so miserable; and then, I fear, I ask more to be happy again, than for forgiveness of my sin, and for grace and strength to overcome it

I never felt this to be the case so strongly as to-day, but your coldness seems to have shown me my whole self, and I never thought I was so wicked, and so I must be miserable."

Mrs. Hamilton involuntarily drew her child more closely to her. The humility, the bitterness of self-reproach, was so unlike Caroline's usual haughtiness — so very much deeper than they had ever been before, that she hoped, in spite of her anxiety, and her voice audibly trembled as she answered —

"If you really feel this, my Caroline, you will not hesitate to follow my advice, and really pray and watch against this unhappy temper, even when every thing is so smooth and happy, that you cannot imagine why you need. Sin always gains ascendency by using pleasure as his covering. Do not let a single cross word, or momentary unkind thought, pass unnoticed; never cease in your petition for grace and strength, but do not be content with only prayer; you must use effort as well, and if your thoughts will be black, and you feel as if you could not conquer them by yourself, nor banish them even by your favorite employments, come to me, confess them without fear or hesitation to me, and let us try if we cannot conquer them together. Will you promise me to try this plan, Caroline?"

Caroline could not reply, for every kind word her mother spoke, seemed to heighten self-reproach, and make her still more wretched. Mrs. Hamilton felt that there was no refusal in her silence, and continued talking to her in that same gentle strain a little while longer, and then rose to leave her — but Caroline looked so sorrowful that she hesitated.

"No, mamma, I do not deserve that you should stay with me, and so deprive Emmeline and Ellen, and the boys of their favorite hour," she said, though the tears started again to her eyes, for she felt as if it would be an indescribable comfort still to be alone with her mother. "I am too unhappy and too ashamed to join them, if I may remain away?" Mrs. Hamilton answered in the affirmative. "I have not a thing prepared for to-morrow, and — and I do not — indeed, I do not mean to give you any more trouble with my studies. I hate myself for that too."

"Do not attempt to study to-night, my dear Caroline; get up a little earlier to-morrow, to be ready for me, if you like; but though it will be much more painful to you to remain idle the remainder of this evening than to employ yourself, even with the most disagreeable task, I would much rather you should do so. Once let temper be quite subdued, and your heart receive its necessary government, and I have no fear but that you will very quickly make up for lost time; and even if you did not, believe me, my dear child, the graces of the mind, precious as in generally they are considered, and as they are, still are to me actually nothing worth, if unaccompanied by a gentle temper and womanly heart. Do not shrink from the suffering which it will be to sit alone and think on all that has passed to-day; but let your remorse be accompanied by a resolution (which you are quite capable of not only forming, but of keeping) not to rest till by prayer and effort you have sought God's blessing on your difficult task, and so feel strengthened for its fulfilment; and also for persevering in it, for you must not hope to succeed in subduing yourself all at once. Do this, and I shall be better pleased than if to-morrow morning you brought me a treble quantity of mental work."

She embraced and left her — to meditations, from whose bitter, though salutary pain, Caroline made no attempt to escape; though, had it not been for her mother's advice, she would gladly have flown to her studies, and worked with double assiduity, believing that she was, by doing so, atoning for her fault, instead of merely shrinking from its remembrance. It was a trial to join her family even for prayers; for she felt so self-convicted, so humbled, that she fancied every one must despise her; and when, after the service, Percy approached, and, with mock sympathy, inquired how her headache was, and if she had recovered her appetite, and begged her not to be ill at such a critical time, as he most particularly wished to go to Lady Helen's ball, and he could not be so cruel, if she were not well, her spirit was so broken that the large tears rolled down her cheeks, and she turned away without uttering a single word.

"If you had taken the trouble to look in your sister's face, Percy, you would not have spoken so unkindly," said Mrs. Hamilton, more hastily than she was in the habit of interfering; and as Caroline came to her, she whispered some few fond words, that enabled her to wish her father good-night and leave the room, without any farther display of emotion.

"Do you wish your sister to dislike you, Percy?" she said, gently detaining him, as he was following Caroline.

"Dislike me, mother? No! how can you think so?"

"Because you act as if you wished it; you never see her uncomfortable, without trying to make her more so, and is that kind? How can she ever look up to and love you, while such is the case?"

"I only mean it for fun, mother. It is such glorious enjoyment to me to torment, when I see people cross and miserable for nothing."

"And in the enjoyment of your fun, my dear boy, you forget other people's feelings. I must beg you, as an especial favor to myself, that you will do all you can to soothe rather than irritate Caroline, in the short time that intervenes before you go to London. She will have a hard struggle with herself, so do not you make her trial more difficult."

"Do you wish it, mother, dear? you know I would refrain from teasing even for a whole year, if it would please you, and give me the privilege of a kiss whenever I like," he laughingly answered, looking up in her face so archly and yet so fondly that his mother could not help smiling; promising she would not sentence him to any thing so terrible as not to tease for a whole year, as she was quite sure he would fall into his old propensities before a quarter of the time had expired.

CHAPTER XIII.

SUSPICION.—A PARTING, A DOUBLE GRIEF.—INNOCENCE PROVED.—WRONG DONE AND EVIL CONFIRMED BY DOUBT.

Lady Helen's ball took place; and Caroline had so conquered herself, that she could listen to Percy's flowing account of its delights with actual cheerfulness. It was so associated with self-reproach, that she could scarcely think of it without pain; but she was so convinced of her folly in permitting such a very little thing so to affect her temper as to cause all the misery she had endured, that she had resolved to punish herself, not only by listening to Percy, but by herself inquiring the details. She was a girl of really a strong mind, and once convinced of error, once released from the fell dominion of temper, she did not care what pain she endured, or what difficulty she encountered, so that she could but convince her mother how truly she regretted, and tried to atone for past misconduct. It was very easy, as Mrs. Hamilton had told her, to regain lost time in her studies, but not quite so easy to check the cross word or unkind thought, and to break from the black cloud that still at times would envelop her. But she did not give way, constantly even making opportunities for self-denial, and doing little kindnesses for Ellen, though she was too truthful to profess an affection which as yet she could not feel.

Early in the following week Mr. Grahame came over to Oakwood with a petition. Annie having taken cold at the party had been obliged to enact the invalid, much against her inclination, and so entreated her mother to invite Caroline to spend a few days with her; and, to her astonishment, her cold, harsh father volunteered to go himself for her. Mr. Hamilton at once acceded; his wife hesitated; but she went at once to Caroline, who chanced to be reading alone in the school-room, for it was the time of recreation, and told her. For a moment her countenance was actually radiant with delight, the next it clouded over.

"You would like it very much, but you are afraid I shall not permit you to go — is that the meaning of your change of countenance?" asked her mother, half smiling.

"I am afraid of myself, mamma; for I fear I am always more ill-tempered and proud after any such pleasure as going to Moorlands would be."

"Would you rather not go, then?"

"I cannot say quite that, mamma; I should like it very much, if I could but be sure of myself afterward."

"Did you ever feel such a doubt of yourself before, Caroline, when going to stay with Annie?"

"No, mamma; I seem to have thought a great deal more the last few days, and not to feel half so sure of myself."

"Then I think there is less danger for you, that is, of course, if you are willing to risk the temptation of Lady Helen's too kind consideration and lavish praises, which make mine so very tame."

"Oh, mamma, pray do not say so," interrupted Caroline, very eagerly. "Indeed, I would rather hear you speak and see you smile as you do now, than listen to all that Lady Helen is so kind as to say. I know I did like it very much, and that it did sometimes make me fancy when I came home, that you were almost cold. But, indeed, indeed, I hope I am learning to know you better."

"I hope so, too, dearest. But Mr. Grahame is waiting for you; and, by-the-by, begged me to ask you for some lines you promised to copy out for a print in Lady Helen's album. You may do just as you like about going, because you are quite old and wise enough to decide for yourself. Ill-temper always brings such suffering with it, that if pleasure must recall it, you will be wiser not to go; but if you can resist it — if you think you can return to your quiet daily routine as forbearing and gentle and happy as you are now, go, my love, and enjoy yourself as much as you can."

"I will try and remember all you said about prayer when we think we are most secure, dear mamma," answered Caroline, in a very earnest and somewhat lowered voice. "I know whenever I have been to Moorlands before, I have felt so elated, so sure I should never be in an ill-temper, so proud from being made so much of, that I fear I have very often relaxed even in my daily prayers, and never thought it necessary to pray against ill-temper. Do you think if I watch myself, and still pray against it, it will save me from being cross and unkind on my return?"

"It will undoubtedly help you, my dear child, very considerably, and render your trial very much easier, but I cannot promise you that it will entirely prevent the *inclination* to feel pettish and unhappy. I have no doubt that in time it will prevent even that; but now, you know, it is very early days, and you have not yet forgotten the bitter pain of last week; still I think you may venture to go, love, and if I do see you happy and gentle on your return, it will do much toward convincing me you are striving in earnest. Make haste and get ready, and do not forget the poem. I will send over your things. Tell Lady Helen I shall expect all her family next Monday evening, to join Edward's little farewell-party, and you can return with them."

With the most delighted alacrity Caroline hastened to get ready, and in her hurry forgot the poem till she reëntered the school-room, which was still untenanted.

"What shall I do for some writing-paper?" she thought; "the desks are all put away, and it will detain me so long to go up again for the keys, and the volume is too large to carry — oh, I will tear out a blank page from this book, it will not be very elegant, but I can recopy it at Moorlands."

And she hastily tore out a page from an exercise-book which lay open on the table; not perceiving that by doing so, a fellow-leaf, which was written on, was loosened, and fell to the ground, mingling with some torn papers which had been put in a heap to be cleared away. She had just finished it, when Fanny came to tell her Mr. Grahame could not wait any longer, and asking if all the papers on the ground were to be removed, Caroline hastily answered in the affirmative, without looking at them, and the girl bore them off in her apron, the written leaf among them.

Now it so happened that this written leaf had already occasioned trouble. Miss Harcourt had been so displeased with Ellen's careless performance of a French exercise that morning, that she had desired her to write it again. It was very difficult, and had materially shortened the time which she had promised to devote to Edward, who was this week released from his attendance on Mr. Howard, to permit him and Ellen to be as much together as possible. Hurried by him, she left her book open on the table to dry, and finding it closed on her return, put it away, without looking at it. The following day Miss Harcourt, of course, requested to see it, and, to Ellen's utter astonishment, her exercise was not there; only the faulty and blotted theme, with no sign to explain its disappearance. Now we know Miss Harcourt was rather prejudiced against Ellen, and, as she had unhappily failed in truth more than once, (perhaps she was not so unjust and harsh as poor Ellen felt her to be,) she refused to believe her assurance that she had written it. No one had been in the school-room at the time to whom she could refer; if Ellen had never disobeyed or deceived, of course her word would be sufficient, as her brother's and cousins' would.

"That you have failed again, both in obedience and truth, Ellen, I cannot for a moment doubt, and it certainly would be my duty to inform your aunt directly; but as I know it would cause her real suffering to be compelled to punish you just this last week that Edward will be with us for some time, I shall say nothing about it to her, nor inflict any penalty on you to attract her notice, but it is entirely for her sake I forbear. One so hardened in falsehood as you must be, so soon to forget her kind indulgence after your fault only a few weeks ago, can deserve nothing but harshness and contempt. I shall certainly, after this week, warn her not to trust too implicitly in your artful professions of repentance."

Poor Ellen felt too bewildered and too miserable even to cry. That she had written her exercise, she was as positive as that she had been told to do so; but if she had — what had become of it? Harsh as Miss Harcourt seemed, appearances were certainly very much against her. She had not a single proof that she had obeyed, and her word was nothing; even Emmeline looked at her doubtingly, and as if she could scarcely even pity her. It was very little comfort to think her aunt was not to be told. Her own impulse was to go to her, and tell her at once; but how could she be believed? and Mrs. Hamilton's word — "If I ever discover another untruth you will compel me to adopt still severer measures, pain as it will be to myself," the remembrance of all she had suffered, the disappointment it would be to her aunt to think all she had said and read to her were forgotten, when in reality she was constantly thinking of and trying to act on them, all checked the impulse, and terrified her into silence.

Miss Harcourt was not an acute physiognomist; she could only read in Ellen's face hardihood and recklessness. We rather think Mrs. Hamilton would have read something very different; but she was very much engaged with Edward, and if she did think Ellen looked much more out of spirits, she attributed it to natural feeling at the rapid approach of the day of separation. For her brother's sake, to prove to him she could enter into his joy, she tried very hard not to evince the least symptom of depression, and never to cry before him at least; though every night that told her another day had gone, and brought before her all sorts of vague feelings and fancies of dread, she either cried herself to sleep, or laid awake, still more unhappy. The suspicion attached to her seemed to double the severity of the trial of parting. Edward was her own; Edward must love her, with all her faults; but even her aunt, her kind, dear, good aunt, must cease to have any affection for her, if so constantly believed guilty of a sin so terrible as falsehood. And she seemed to love her brother still more than ever, every day that brought the hour of parting nearer — sometimes as if she *could not* bear the pain of not being able to look at his bright face, and listen to his glad laugh and dear voice for three, perhaps six long years. Her aunt's gentle kindness seemed to increase her unhappiness, for though she knew she was innocent, still she felt, if Miss Harcourt had told Mrs. Hamilton, she could not be so caressed and cared for, and she was receiving that which she was believed to have forfeited. Miss Harcourt's face certainly seemed to ask her as distinctly as words, how she could be so artful — so deceitful — as to permit her aunt to take such notice of her; and so she often shrunk away, when she most longed to sit by and listen to her.

Edward's spirits never sobered, except now and then, when he thought of leaving Mrs. Hamilton, to whom he had given the same love he had lavished on his mother, perhaps to a still greater extent, for reverence was largely mingled with it. Mr. Howard, too, was another whom he grieved to leave, and Mrs. Hamilton so trusted in these apparently strong affections and his good disposition, as to feel but little anxiety; merely sorrow that she was to lose him for a profession of danger. She did not know, nor did Mr. Howard, nor Edward himself, that he was one who would be guided more by the influence of those with whom he was intimately thrown, than by any memory of the absent, or judgment of his own.

Ellen's manner on Monday evening annoyed and prejudiced Miss Harcourt still more; Mrs. Greville and Mary, Lady Helen and all her family, bringing Caroline home with them, Mr. Howard, and some of Edward's favorite companions, all assembled at Oakwood, and every one was determined to be gay and cheerful, and Edward's voice was the merriest, and his laugh the happiest there; and Ellen, though her head ached with the effort, and the constant struggle of the preceding week, was quite cheerful too, and talked to Mary Greville, and Lilla and Cecil Grahame, and even to Mr. Howard, as Miss Harcourt felt she had no right to do; and as must prove her to be that which she had always fancied her. Mrs. Hamilton, on the contrary, saw that in the very midst of a laugh, or of speaking, her niece's eye would rest upon Edward, and the lip quite quiver, and her smile become for the moment so strained, that she was satisfied Ellen's cheerfulness proceeded from no want of feeling; she wondered, indeed, at so much control at such an early age, but she loved her for it, notwithstanding. Once only Ellen was nearly conquered. Mary had begged her to sing a little Hindoo air, of which she was particularly fond, and Edward, hearing the request, said eagerly —

"Do sing it, dear Ellen; I am quite as fond of it as Mary is, for it seems to make me think of India and poor mamma, and it will be such a long time before I hear it again."

She had never in her whole life felt so disinclined to sing, so as if it were quite impossible — as if she must cry if she did; but Edward would think it so unkind if she refused, for she did not know herself why his very words should have increased the difficulty, and what reasons could she give him? Mary went and asked Mrs. Hamilton to accompany her; and Ellen did her very best, but her voice would tremble, and just before the end of the second verse it failed entirely; but still she was glad she had tried, for on Mrs. Hamilton saying, very kindly, and in a voice that only she and Mary could hear, "I was half afraid you would not succeed to-night, my dear Ellen; but you were quite right to try," Mary seemed to understand at once why it had been so difficult for her to oblige her, and to be quite sorry she had pressed it so much, and Edward had thanked her, and told her he should sing it in idea very often. She tried to be merry again, but she could not succeed as before, and so she kept as near her aunt as she could, all the remainder of the evening, as if she were only safe there.

Edward, too, had a hard battle with himself, as one by one his favorite companions took leave of him with a hearty shake of the hand, and eager, but in some, half-choked wishes, for his health and prosperity; and when all had gone, and Mr. Howard, who had remained for prayers, took him in his arms, and solemnly prayed God to bless him, and save him from danger and temptation, and permit him to return to his family, improved in all things that would make him an affectionate guardian to his orphan sister, and repay all the love and care of his aunt and uncle, it was a desperate effort that prevented him from sobbing like a child; but he had his midshipman's uniform on for the first time, and he was quite resolved he would not disgrace it; therefore he only returned Mr. Howard's embrace very warmly, and ran out of the room. But when his aunt went into his room an hour afterward, it appeared as if he had put off his pride and his uniform together, for, though he was fast asleep, his pillow was quite wet with tears.

The next morning was a very sad one, though Percy and his father did all they could to make it cheerful: (we ought to have said before that Percy and Herbert were both going with Mr. Hamilton and Edward.) No one liked the idea of losing Edward for so long a time. He had made himself a favorite with all, even with every one of the servants, who, when the carriage was ready at eleven o'clock, thronged into the hall to take a last look at him. He was so altered, that he had that morning, actually of his own accord, shaken hands with every one of them who had ever done any thing for him, especially Ellis and Morris, and Robert, to whom he had given a very handsome present, and thanked him for all his attention.

He kept up very manfully till he came to his aunt, whose emotion, as she held him in a close embrace, was so unusually visible, and for the moment he seemed so to love her, that the idea of the sea lost half its delight, and he felt as if he could almost have liked to remain with her. But Percy's joyous voice —

"Come, Master Edward, I thought you were a sailor, not a schoolboy; off with you; you will not give me time or room for one kiss from mamma before we go," — roused him, and he tried to laugh in the midst of his tears, gave Ellen another kiss, and ran into the carriage, where he was quickly followed by his uncle and cousins, and in a very few minutes Oakwood, dear, happy Oakwood, as his whole heart felt it at that moment was hidden from his sight.

Ellen remained by the window, looking after the carriage long after it was impossible to see or hear it, very pale, and her eyes very heavy, but not in tears; and as her aunt went to her, and put her arm round her, and began talking to her very cheerfully of all Edward would have to write to her about, and how soon they might hear from him, and that Ellen should answer him as often and as fully as she liked, and that she would not even ask to see her letters to him, or all his to her, as they might have many little affectionate things to say to each other that they might not care about any one else seeing, and she would trust them both — Ellen seemed as if one pain was soothed, and if indeed she heard often from him, she might bear his departure. But there was still the other source of unhappiness, recalled every time she met Miss Harcourt's cold, suspicious look, which had not changed even then. Still she tried to join her cousins, and get her work, for there were no studies that morning, and so some little time passed, by Mrs. Hamilton's exertions, almost cheerfully; but then Ellen left the room to get something she wanted, and, in seeking her own, passed Edward's room, the door of which stood half open. She could not resist entering, and every thing spoke of him so vividly, and yet seemed so to tell her he had gone, really gone, and she was quite alone, that all the pain came back again worse than ever, and she laid her head on his pillow, and her long-checked tears flowed with almost passionate violence.

"My dear Ellen, I have been looking for you everywhere," said her aunt's kind voice, full an hour afterward; "Emmeline went into your room and could not find you, and I could not imagine what had become of you. It was not wise of you to come here just this morning, love. You have been so brave, so unselfish all this week, that I must not let you give way now. Try and think only that Edward will be happier as a sailor than he would be remaining with you; and though I know you must miss him very, very painfully, you will be able to bear it better. Poor Alice Seaton, of whom you have heard me speak, has no such comfort; her brother could not bear the idea of a sea life, and is scarcely strong enough for it; and yet, poor fellow, it is the only opening his uncle has for him, and his poor sister has not only that pain to bear — for you can fancy how dreadful it would be, if Edward had left us for a life in which he thought he should be miserable — but is obliged to leave the aunt she loves, as much, I think, as you love me, Ellen, and go as a teacher in a school, to bear her accumulated sorrow quite alone. Sad as your trial is, you have still many things to bless

God for, dearest, as I am sure you will acknowledge, if, when the pain of the present moment has subsided, you think of Alice, and try to put yourself in her place."

"It is not only parting from Edward," answered, Ellen trying to check her tears, but clasping her arms still closer round her aunt as if dreading that her own words should send her from her.

"Not only parting from Edward, Ellen, love! what is it then? tell me," replied Mrs. Hamilton, surprised and almost alarmed. But Ellen could not go on, much as she wished it, for her momentary courage had deserted her, and she coul only cry more bitterly than before. "Have you done any thing wrong, Ellen? and have you forgotten my promise?" inquired her aunt, after waiting several minutes, and speaking very sorrowfully.

"Miss Harcourt thinks I have, aunt; but indeed, indeed, I have not; I have not been so very wicked as to tell another falsehood. I know no one can believe me, but I would rather you should know it, even if—if you punish me again."

"You must try to be more calm, my dear Ellen, and tell me clearly what is causing you so much additional suffering; for I cannot quite understand you. I certainly shall not punish you, unless *quite* convinced you have failed in truth again, which I do not think you have. Tell me exactly what it is, and look at me while you are speaking."

Ellen tried to obey, but her grief had gained such an ascendency, that it was very difficult. Mrs. Hamilton looked very thoughtful when she ceased, for she really was more perplexed than she allowed Ellen to perceive; and the poor child fancying her silence could only mean disbelief and condemnation, remained quiet and trembling by her side.

"I promised you that I would not doubt you, Ellen, and I will not now, though appearances are so strong against you," she said, after several minutes' thought. "Come with me to the school-room, and show me your exercise-book; I may find some clew to explain this mystery."

Ellen thought that was quite impossible; but, inexpressibly comforted by her aunt's trust, she went with her directly.

"Ellen has been telling me that you have been very much displeased with her, my dear Lucy," Mrs. Hamilton said, directly she entered, addressing Miss Harcourt, who was sitting reading with Caroline and Emmeline, "and certainly with great apparent justice; but she is so unhappy about it, that I can scarcely believe that she has forgotten all which passed between us a short time ago, and I am going, therefore, with your permission, to try if I cannot discover something that may throw a light on the subject."

"I am afraid that scarcely will be possible," replied Miss Harcourt; "however, I am glad she has had the candor to tell you, instead of continuing to receive your notice, as she has done the last week." Ellen had brought her book while Miss Harcourt was speaking, and Mrs. Hamilton attentively examined it."

"Did you not begin one like this the same day, Caroline?"

"Yes, mamma; don't you remember we were obliged to send to Harris for them? as the parcel with the stationery did not come from Exeter as soon as we expected. And we noticed how much thinner they were, though they were the same sized books."

"And did I not hear you say something about their having the same number of leaves, and therefore it must have been only the quality of the paper which made the difference?"

"What a memory you have, mamma," answered Caroline, smiling. "I did not think you were taking the least notice of us, but I do remember saying so now, and, indeed, I very often wish the quality had been the same, for our writing looks horrid."

"Do you happen to remember the number of leaves they contained, and if they were both alike?"

"I know they had both the same number, and I think it was two-and-twenty, but I can tell you in a moment." And with her usual quickness of movement, Caroline unlocked her desk, drew forth her book, and ran over the leaves.

"I am right — two-and-twenty."

"And you are quite sure they had both the same number?"

"Perfectly certain, mamma."

"Then, by some incomprehensible means, two leaves have disappeared from Ellen's — here are only twenty. Have you ever torn a leaf out, Ellen?"

"No, aunt, indeed I have not.'

"When did Miss Harcourt tell you to write this missing exercise?"

"Last Monday week — I mean yesterday week."

"Where did you write it, and what did you do with your book afterward?"

"I wrote it at this table, aunt: I was so sorry I had to do it, when Edward depended so much on my going out with him, that I thought it would save time not to get my desk; and as soon as it was done, I left it open to dry. When I came home it was closed, and I put it away without looking at it, and the next morning the exercise was not there."

"Who was in this room after you left it? by-the-by, it was the morning you went to Lady Helen's, Caroline; did you notice Ellen's book open, as she said? Why, what is the matter, my dear?" she added, observing that Caroline looked as if some sudden light had flashed upon her, and then, really grieved.

"I am so very, *very* sorry, mamma; I do believe it has been all my haste and carelessness that has caused Ellen all this unhappiness. I was in such a hurry to copy the poem for Lady Helen, that I tore a blank leaf out of an open book on the table, without thinking whose it was. In my haste the book fell to the ground, I picked it up to write on it, but never noticed if the fellow-leaf fell out, which it must have done, and no doubt Fanny carried it away with some other torn papers, which she asked me if she were to destroy. I am more sorry than I can tell you, Ellen; pray believe that I did not do it purposely."

"I am sure she will, if it be only for the comfort of our knowing the truth," said Mrs. Hamilton, truly relieved, not only from the explanation, but perceiving Caroline's voluntarily offered kiss was willingly and heartily returned by Ellen. It was almost the first she had ever seen exchanged between them.

"I must believe you, dear Caroline, for you never say what you do not mean," said Ellen, earnestly; "but I do so wish Miss Harcourt could see my exercise; she would quite believe me then."

"And we should all be more satisfied," replied Mrs. Hamilton, perceiving in a moment that Miss Harcourt still doubted, and ringing the bell, she desired the footman to send Fanny to her.

"Do you remember taking some torn papers from this room the morning you went to tell Miss Hamilton that Mr. Grahame was waiting?" she asked.

"Yes, madam."

"And were they all torn up in small pieces?"

"No, madam; there was one like the page out of a book, which made me ask Miss Hamilton if they were all to be destroyed. It was such a nice clean piece, only being written on one side, that I wrapped up some lace in it — Mrs. Ellis having only half an hour before scolded me for not keeping it more carefully."

"Bring me the leaf, my good girl, and Miss Ellen will give you a still better piece for the purpose," replied her mistress, quite unable to suppress a smile, and Ellen hastily took out a large sheet of writing paper, and the moment Fanny returned (she seemed gone an age) gave it to her, and seized her own, which she placed in her aunt's hand, without being able to speak a single word.

"I think that is the very theme, and certainly Ellen's writing, my dear, Lucy; we can have no more doubt now," said Mrs. Hamilton, the moment Fanny had left the room, delighted with the exchange, and drawing Ellen close to her, for the poor child could really scarcely stand.

"I have done you injustice, Ellen, and I beg your pardon," replied Miss Harcourt directly, and Mrs. Hamilton would have been better pleased had she stopped there, but she could not help adding, "You know I should never have doubted you, if you had not so often forfeited truth."

Ellen's first impulse had been to go to her, but her last words caused her to bury her face on her aunt's shoulder.

"I really think, Ellen, you ought to thank Ellis for giving Fanny a scolding, as it has done you such excellent service," resumed Mrs. Hamilton, playfully; "and what fee are you going to give me for taking upon myself to prove your innocence in open court? I think myself so very clever, that I shall tell Percy I am a better lawyer without study, than he can hope to be with. You don't seem to be very capable of doing anything but kissing me now, and so I will not be very exacting. You have cried yourself almost ill, and so must bear the penalty. Go and lie down in my dressing-room for an hour or two; Emmeline, go with your cousin, and see what a kind, affectionate nurse you can be till I come. It is never too early to practise such a complete woman's office."

Emmeline, quite proud of the charge, and more grieved than she very well knew how to express, till she was quite alone with Ellen, that she, too, had suspected and been cold to her the last week, left the room with her cousin. Caroline seemed to hesitate for a moment, but she was quite certain by her mother's face that she wished to speak with Miss Harcourt, and so, without being told, took up her book, and went into the library.

"And now, Lucy, I am going to ask you a personal favor," began Mrs. Hamilton, the moment they were alone.

"That I will try and not judge Ellen so harshly again," was her instant reply; "you have every right to *desire* it, my dear friend, not to ask it as a favor; I *was* too prejudiced and too hasty; but your own dear children are so truthful, so open, that I fear they have quite spoiled me for the necessary patience and forbearance with others."

"You have not quite guessed it, Lucy. Appearances were so very strongly against that poor child, that I am not at all astonished you should have disbelieved her assertion. In the moment of irritation, it is not unlikely I should have done so myself; but the favor I am going to ask you, is merely that you will try and *never show* that you doubt her word, or refer to her past failures. I am quite convinced that untruth is not Ellen's natural disposition, but that it has been caused by the same circumstances which have made her such a painfully timid, too humble character. If, with all her efforts to conquer herself, she still finds her word doubted, and the past brought forward, she never will be able to succeed. Examine as strictly and carefully as you please, and as I am sure she will desire, if necessary — as she did to-day — but oblige me, and *never doubt her*. If she finds we never do, it will raise her self-esteem, and give her a still further incentive to adhere as strictly to the truth, as she sees we believe she does. I am certain the habit of falsehood has often been strengthened by the injudicious and cruel references to one or two childish failures. If I am never to be believed, what is the use of trying to tell the truth? is the very natural question; and the present pain of carefulness being greater than the visible amount of evil, the habit is confirmed. Will you oblige me?"

"Of course I will, dearest Mrs. Hamilton; how can you talk so! Have you not a right to desire what you think proper, in my guidance of your children, instead of so appealing to me as an equal?"

"And are you not? My dear Lucy, have I ever, in act or word, considered you otherwise? In the very intrusting my children to your care, do I not prove that I must think you so? Have you lived with me all these years, and not yet discovered that I have some few notions peculiar perhaps to myself, but that one among them is, that we can never consider too much, or be too grateful to those invaluable friends who help us in the training of our children?"

"I have lived long enough with you to know that there never was, never can be, any woman like you, either as wife, mother, mistress, or friend!" exclaimed Miss Harcourt, with most unusual fervor.

"You did not know your own mother, dearest Lucy, as how

I wish you had, or you would not think so. Every firm, truthful, estimable quality I may possess, under God's blessing, I owe to her. As a young child, before she came to me, and some years afterward, I was more like Ellen than either of my own darlings; and that perhaps explains the secret of my love for, and forbearance with her."

"Like Ellen!" repeated Miss Harcourt, much surprised; "forgive me, but, indeed, I can scarcely believe it."

"It is truth, notwithstanding; my poor father's great preference for Eleanor, when we were children, her very superior beauty and quickness, threw me back into myself; and I am quite certain if it had not been for your excellent mother, who came to live with us when I was only seven, my character would have suffered as much from neglect on the one side, and too painful humility on my own, as Ellen's has done. I can understand her feelings of loneliness, misappreciation, shrinking into herself, better even than she does herself."

"But your affection and kindness ought to have altered her character by this time."

"Hardly — eighteen months is not long enough to remove the painful impressions and influences of eleven sorrowful years. Besides, I scarcely know all these influences; I fear sometimes that she has endured more than I am aware of. So you must think charitably of my fancy, dearest Lucy," she added, smiling, "and help me to make Ellen as much like me as a woman, as I believe she is to me as a child; and to do so, try and think a little, a very little, more kindly and hopefully of her than you do."

"I really do wish you were not quite so penetrating, dearest Mrs. Hamilton; there is no hiding a single feeling or fancy from you," answered Miss Harcourt, slightly confused, but laughing at the same time. "What with your memory, and your quick observation, and your determined notice of little things, you really are a most dangerous person to live with; and if you were not more kind, and indulgent, and true than anybody else, we should all be frightened to come near you."

"I am glad I have some saving qualities," replied Mrs. Hamilton, laughing also; "it would be rather hard to be isolated because I can read other people's thoughts. However, we have entered into a compact," she continued, rather more seriously; "you will never show that you doubt Ellen, and in any difficult matter, come at once to me," and Miss Harcourt willingly assented.

The day passed much more happily than the morning could

have anticipated. Emmeline's nursing was so affectionate and successful, that Ellen was quite able to join them at dinner and her aunt had selected such a very interesting story to read aloud, in which one character was a young sailor, that the hours seemed to fly; and then they had a long talk about poor Alice Seaton and her brother, whether it would be possible for Mr. Hamilton to place young Seaton in a situation that he liked better, and that his health was more fitted for. Ellen said she should like to see and know Alice so much, for her trial must be such a very hard one, that her aunt promised her she should in the midsummer holidays, for Alice should then come and spend a week with them. It seemed as if not to be able to wish Edward good-night, and kiss him, brought back some of the pain again; but she found that thinking about poor Alice, and fancying how miserable she must be, if she loved her aunt as dearly as she did Mrs. Hamilton, to be obliged to part from her as well as her brother, and live at a school, made her pain seem less absorbing; as if to help Alice would do more toward curing it than any thing. And though, of course, every day, for a little while, she seemed to miss Edward more and more, still her aunt's affection and her own efforts, prepared her to see her uncle and cousins return, and listen to all they could tell her about him, without any increase of pain.

PART III.

SIN AND SUFFERING.

CHAPTER I.

ADVANCE AND RETROSPECT.

Our readers must imagine that two years and four months have elapsed since our last visit to the inmates of Oakwood. It was the first week in March that Edward Fortescue (only wanting ten days for the completion of his fourteenth year) quitted a home which was happier than any he had ever known, to enter the world as a sailor; and it is the 7th of June, two years later, the day on which Ellen Fortescue completes her fifteenth year, that we recommence our narrative.

Over this interval, however, much as we are anxious to proceed, we must take a brief glance, clearly to understand the aspect of the Oakwood home affairs, which, from the increasing age of the younger members, had undergone some slight change. The greatest and most keenly felt was the departure of Percy and Herbert for college, the October twelvemonth after Edward had gone; the house seemed actually desolate without them. Percy's wild jokes and inexhaustible spirits, and Herbert's quiet, unobtrusive kindness, much as they had always been truly appreciated by their home circle, still scarcely seemed to have been fully felt till the young men were gone; and the old house actually seemed enwrapped in a silence, which it required very determined effort on the part of all who remained in the least degree to dispel.

Our readers who are mothers, and earnest ones, will easily understand the anxious tremblings of Mrs. Hamilton's heart, when she parted from her boys for the world: for such, to spirits fresh, boyish, unsophisticated, as they still were, Oxford could not fail to be. For Herbert, indeed, she had neither fear nor doubt: no sneer, no temptation, no bad example, would affect him, in whom every passing year seemed to increase and deepen those exalted feelings which, in his earliest childhood, had "less in them of earth than heaven." His piety was so real, his faith so fervent, his affections so concentrated in his home and in one other individual, his love and pursuit of study so ardent and unceasing, his one aim, to become worthy in heart and mind to serve God as his minister, so ever present, that he was effectually guarded even from the world. Percy had none of these feelings to the same extent, save his ardent love for home and its inmates — his mother, above all. He did, indeed, give every promise that the principles so carefully instilled had taken firm root, and would guide his conduct in the world; but Mrs. Hamilton was too humble-minded — too convinced that every human effort is imperfect, without the sustaining and vitalizing grace of God, to rest in security, as many might have done, that *because* she had so worked, so prayed, she *must* succeed. She was hopeful, indeed, very hopeful — how could she be otherwise when she beheld his deep, though silent, reverence for sacred things — his constant and increasing respect and love for his father — his devoted affection for herself — his attachment to Herbert, which seemed so strangely yet so beautifully to combine almost reverence for his superior mind and holier spirit, with the caressing protectiveness of an elder for a younger — a stronger for a weaker? There was much in all this to banish anxiety altogether, but not from such a heart as Mrs. Hamilton's, whose very multiplicity of blessings made her often tremble, and led her to the footstool of her God, with a piety as humble, as constant, as fervent, as many believe is the fruit of adversity alone.

Caroline had sufficiently improved as greatly to decrease solicitude on her account: though there was still a want of sufficient humility, a too great proneness to trust implicitly in her own strength, an inclination to prejudice, and a love of admiration, which all made Mrs. Hamilton fear would expose her to some personal sorrow ere they were entirely overcome. To produce eternal good, she might not murmur at temporal suffering; but her fond heart, though it could anticipate it calmly for herself, so shrunk from it, as touching her child, that the nearer approached the period of Caroline's introduction to the gay world, the more painfully anxious she became, and the more gladly would she have retained her in the retirement of Oakwood, where all her better and higher qualities alone had play. But she knew this could not be; and she could only *trust* that her anxiety would be proved as groundless with Caroline, as every letter from Oxford proved it to be with Percy, and *endeavor* to avert it by never wavering in her watchful and guiding love.

Emmeline, at fifteen, was just the same sportive, happy, innocent child as she had been at twelve. Her feelings were, indeed, still deeper, her imagination more vivid, her religion more fervid. To her every thing was touched with poetry — it mattered not how dull and commonplace it might seem to other people; but Mrs. Hamilton's judicious care had so taught that *Truth* alone was poetry and beauty — the Ideal only lovable when its basis was the Real — that she was neither romantic nor visionary. Keen as her sensibilities were, even over a work of fiction, they prompted the *deed* and *act* of kindness, not the tear alone. For miles round her father's large domain she was known, loved, so felt as a guardian spirit, that the very sound of her step seemed to promise joy. She actually seemed to live for others — making their pleasures hers; and, withal, so joyous, especially in her own home and at Greville Manor, that even anxiety seemed exorcised when she was near. Before strangers, indeed, she would be as shy as a young fawn; though even then natural kindliness of heart prompted such kindness of word and manner, as always to excite the wish to see her again.

Edward, in the two years and a quarter which he had been away, had only once occasioned anxiety. Two or three months after he had sailed, he wrote home in the highest terms of a certain Gilbert Harding, one of the senior midshipmen of his ship, from whom he had received kindness upon kindness; and who, being six or seven years older than himself, he jestingly wrote to his aunt and uncle, must certainly be the very best friend he could have chosen, as he was much too old to lead him into mischief. Why he (Harding) had taken such a fancy to him, Edward could not tell; but he was so excessively kind, so taught him his duty, and smoothed all the difficulties and disagreeables which, he owned, had at first seemed overwhelming, that he never could be grateful enough. He added, that, though not a general favorite with his immediate messmates, he was very highly esteemed by Sir Edward Manly and his other superior officers, and that the former had much commended him for his kindness to the youngest boy on board, which Edward was. It was very easy to perceive that young Fortescue's susceptible affections had all been not only attracted, but already riveted by this new friend. All the young party of Oakwood rejoiced at it; Mrs. Hamilton would have done so also, had she not perceived an anxious expression on her husband's face, which alarmed her. He did not, however, make any remark tell he had spoken to Mr. Howard, and then imparted to his wife alone (not choosing to create suspicion in the open hearts of his children) that this Gilbert Harding, though very young at the time, had been one of the principal actors in the affair which had caused Mr. Howard to dismiss his pupils, as we related in a former page; that his very youth, for he could scarcely have been more than eleven or twelve, and determined hardihood, so marked natural depravity, that Mr. Howard had had less hope for him than for any of the others. This opinion had been borne out by his after conduct at home; but the affair had been successfully hushed up by his family; and by immense interest he had been permitted to enter the navy, where, it was said, his youthful errors had been so redeemed, and his courage and conduct altogether had so won him applause, that no farther fears were entertained for him. Mr. Howard alone retained his opinion, that the disposition was naturally bad, and doubted the *internal* response to the seeming *outward good;* and he was grieved and anxious beyond measure, when he heard that he was not only on board the same ship as Edward, but already his favorite companion and most trusted friend. His anxiety, of course, extended itself to Mr. and Mrs. Hamilton to such a degree, that at the first moment they would gladly have endeavored to exchange his ship; but this would have seemed very strange to Sir Edward Manly, who was one of Mr. Hamilton's most valued friends. He had, in fact, actually delayed Edward's becoming a midshipman till Sir Edward could take him in his own ship, and now to place him elsewhere was really impossible; and, after all, though he might be removed from Harding's influence, how could his anxious guardians know all with whom he might be thrown? They were obliged to content themselves with writing earnestly and affectionately to Edward; and, painful as it was, to throw a doubt and shade over such youthful confidence and affection, implored him not to trust too implicitly in Harding; that his character had not always been free from stain; that he (Edward) was still so young and so susceptible, he might find that he had imbibed principles, and been tempted to wrong almost unconsciously, and suffer from its effects when too late to escape. They wrote as affectionately and indulgently as they could — Mr. Howard, as well as his aunt and uncle; but still they felt that it certainly did appear cruel to warn a young, warm heart to break off the first friendship it had formed; especially as he beheld that friend approved of by his captain, and looked up to by the crew. And that Edward's reply was somewhat cold, though he did promise caution, and assure them he had not so forgotten the influences and principles of Oakwood as to allow any one to lead him into error, did not surprise them. He never referred to Harding again, except sometimes casually to mention his companionship, or some act which had won him approval; and they really hoped their letters had had at least the effect of putting him on his guard. Sir Edward Manly's own reply to Mr. Hamilton's anxious appeal to him, however, succeeded in quieting their fears; he assured them he had seen nothing in Harding's conduct, since he had been at sea, to render him an unfit companion for any boy; that he had heard of some boyish faults, but it was rather hard he was to suffer from them as a man; and he assured his friends that he would keep a strict look-out after young Fortescue, and the first appearance of a change in a character which, young as he was, he could not help loving, should be inquired into, and the friendship ended by sending Harding to some other ship. So wrote Sir Edward Manly, with the fullest possible intention to perform; and Edward's anxious friends were happy, more especially as letter after letter brought praises of the young sailor from captain, officers, and crew, and his own epistles, though brief, were affectionate and satisfactory.

It was happy for Mr. and Mrs. Hamilton, and Mr. Howard, too, that they were ignorant of the multiplicity of great and little things which could not fail to engross the mind of Sir Edward Manly, who was not only captain of the Prince William, a gallant seventy-four, but commander of the little flotilla which accompanied him, or they could not have rested so secure Happy for them, too, during those years of separation, that they were not perfectly acquainted with Edward's real weakness of character, or of the fearful extent of mischief which the influences of his first twelve years had engendered. Had he remained at Oakwood till nineteen or twenty, it *is* probable they would have been insensibly conquered, and the impressions of good, which he had appeared so readily to receive, really taken root and guided his after life, but eighteen months could not do this, as Mrs. Hamilton would have felt, had she known *all* the effect of her sister's ill-judged partiality and indulgence; but this, as we have already mentioned, was concealed from her by the bright, lovable, winning qualities, which alone were upper most. Our readers, in fact, know more of Edward (if they have at all thought of his conduct in so frequently allowing his sister to suffer for him) than his aunt, penetrative as she was; and, therefore, in the events we shall have occasion to relate, we trust that Mrs. Hamilton will not appear an inconsistent character, inasmuch that one in general so successfully observant, should fail in penetration when most needed.

Edward's life at Oakwood had been so very happy, its pleasures and indulgences so innocent, so numerous, that he did not himself know his liability to temptation, from the excessive love of pleasure which his mother's indiscreet indulgence had originally infused. The control which his uncle and Mr. Howard exercised over him had been so very gentle and forbearing, that he had scarcely ever felt the inclination to exert self-will, and when it so chanced that he had, Ellen had covered his fault, or borne its penalty for him. He thought he had guided himself, when, in fact, he was guided; but this could no longer be the case when one of the little world which thronged a first-rate man-of-war. Outward actions were, indeed, under control; but what captain, the most earnest, most able in the world, could look into and guide the *hearts* of all those committed to his care? And almost the first action of Edward's unbiased will was indignantly to tear into shreds, and scatter to the winds and the waves, those affectionate and warning letters, and cling the more closely to, rest the more confidingly on, Harding, for the wrong that he thought he had done him, by allowing his eye even to rest for a moment on such base, unfounded aspersions on his name.

When Mrs. Hamilton told Ellen that her letters to her brother, and his to her, should never be subjected to any scrutiny but their own, she acted on a principle which many parents and guardians would consider as high-flown and romantic, and which she herself had most painful reason to regret — the effects, at least, but not the principle itself, for that was based on too refined a feeling to waver, even though she suffered from it. She could not bear, nor could her husband, the system which prevailed in some families of their acquaintance, that their children could neither receive nor write letters to each other, or their intimate friends, without being shown to their seniors. As for opening and reading a letter directed to one of them, before its possessor saw it, as they had seen done, it was, in their estimation, as much dishonor and as mean, as if such a thing had been done to an adult. Perfect confidence in their home they had indeed instilled, and that confidence was never withheld. There was a degree of suspicion attached to a demand always to see what a child had written or received, from which Mrs. Hamilton's pure mind actually shrunk in loathing. In the many months the Grahame family passed in London, Annie and Caroline corresponded without the least restraint; no doubt many would pronounce Mrs. Hamilton very unwise, knowing Annie so well, and trembling for Caroline as she did; but, as she told Miss Harcourt, she had some notions peculiar to herself, (they always had the sanction and sympathy of her husband, however,) and this was one of them. She was always pleased and interested in all that her children read to her, either from their own epistles or those they received, and if they wished it, read them herself, but she never asked to do so, and the consequence was, that the most perfect confidence was given.

When Ellen and Edward parted, they were both so young, that Mr. Hamilton had hesitated as to whether his wife was quite justified in the perfect trust with which she treated them, and whether it would not be wiser to overlook their correspondence; but Mrs. Hamilton so argued that their very youth was their safeguard, that they were all in all to each other, and as such she wished them to feel they were bound by even a closer and a fonder tie than that of brother and sister under other circumstances, so won over her husband that he yielded; and from the long extracts that Ellen would read of Edward's letters to the family in general, and of her own to her aunt, he was quite satisfied as to the wisdom of his wife's judgment.

For full a year after Edward's departure, Ellen's conduct and general improvement had given her aunt nothing but pleasure; even Miss Harcourt's and Caroline's prejudice was nearly removed, though, at times, the fancy would steal over both that she was not exactly what she seemed, and that that which was hidden was not exactly that which Mrs. Hamilton believed it; and this fancy, strengthened by a certain indefinable yet *felt* change in Ellen, commencing about thirteen months after she had parted from her brother. Mrs. Hamilton herself, for some time strove against belief, but at length she could no longer conceal from herself that Ellen *was* becoming reserved again, and fearful, at times almost shrinking, and sad, as in her childhood. The openness, and almost light-heartedness, which for one brief year had so characterized her, seemed completely but so insensibly to have gone, that Mrs. Hamilton could not satisfy herself as to the time of the commencement, or reason of the change. Her temper, too, became fitful, and altogether her aunt's anxiety and bewilderment as to her real character returned in full force. Once, when gently questioned as to why her temper was so altered, Ellen confessed with tears, that she knew it was, but she could not help it, she believed she was not well; and Mrs. Hamilton called in Mr. Maitland, who said that she really was in a highly nervous state, and required care and quietness, and the less notice that was taken of her momentary irritability or depression the better. Little did the worthy man imagine how his young patent blessed him for these words; giving a reason for and so allowing the trepidation which paled her cheek, parched her lips, and made her hand so tremble, when she received a letter from her brother, to pass unnoticed.

But change in manner was not all; almost every second or third month Ellen's allowance of pocket-money (which was unusually liberal, as Mrs. Hamilton wished to accustom her girls, from an early age, to purchase some few articles of dress for themselves, and so learn the value of money) most strangely and mysteriously disappeared. Ellen either could not or would not give any account of it; and, of course, it not only exposed her to her aunt's most serious displeasure, but inexpressibly heightened not only Mrs. Hamilton's bewilderment and anxiety, but Miss Harcourt's and Caroline's unspoken prejudice. From the time of Edward's departure, Ellen had never been discovered in or suspected of either uttering or acting an untruth; but her silence, her apparent determined ignorance of, or resolution not to confess the cause of the incomprehensible disappearance of her allowance, naturally compelled Mrs. Hamilton to revert to the propensity of her childhood, and fear that truthfulness was again deserting her. Her displeasure lasting, of course, the longer from Ellen's want of openness, and the air of what almost appeared to her anxious yet still affectionate aunt like sullen defiance (in reality, it was almost despair,) when spoken to, caused a painful degree of estrangement between them, always, however, giving place to Mrs. Hamilton's usual caressing manner, the moment Ellen seemed really repentant, and her month's expenditure could be properly explained.

For six or eight months before the day on which we recommence our narrative, there had been, however, nothing to complain of in Ellen, except still that unnatural reserve and frequent depression, as if dreading something she knew not what, which, as every other part of her conduct was satisfactory, Mrs. Hamilton tried to comfort herself was physical alone. No reference to the past was ever made: her manner to her niece became the same as usual; but she could not feel secure as to her character, and, what was most painful, there were times when she was compelled to doubt even Ellen's affection for herself, a thing she had never had the slightest cause to do even when she was a little inanimate child.

But very few changes had taken place in the Greville and Grahame families. Mrs. Greville's trial continued in unmitigated, if not hightened bitterness: the example, the companionship of his father had appeared to have blighted every good seed which she had strenuously endeavored to plant in the bosom of her son. At sixteen he was already an accomplished man of the world, in its most painful sense: he had his own companions, his own haunts; scarcely ever visiting his home, for a reason which, could his poor mother have known it, would have given her some slight gleam of comfort. He could not associate either with her or his sister, without feeling a sort of loathing of himself, a longing to be to them as Percy and Herbert Hamilton were at Oakwood; and not having the moral courage sufficient to break from the control of his father, and the exciting pleasures in which that control initiated him, he shrunk more and more from the only spot in which better feelings were so awakened within him as to give him pain. To deaden this unacknowledged remorse, his manner was rude and unfeeling, so that his very visits, though inexpressibly longed for by his mother, brought only increase of grief.

Mrs. Greville seemed herself so inured to suffering, that she bore up against it without any visible failing of health; struggling against its enervating effects, more, perhaps, than she was aware of herself, for the sake of one treasure still granted her — her own almost angel Mary, — who, she knew, without her love and constant cheerfulness, must sink beneath such a constant aggravated trial. Yet that very love brought increase of anxiety from more than one cause. As yet there was no change in their manner of living, but Mrs. Greville knew that, from the excesses of her husband and son, there very soon must be. Ruin, poverty, all its fearful ills, stood before her in perspective, and how could Mary's fragile frame and gentle spirit bear up against them? Again and again the question pressed upon her — Did Herbert Hamilton indeed love her child, as every passing year seemed to confirm? and if he did, would — could his parents consent to his union with the child of such a father, the sister of such a brother? There were always long messages to Mary in Herbert's letters to his mother which Mrs. Hamilton not only delivered herself, but sometimes even put the whole letter into Mary's hand, and at last laughingly said, she really thought they had much better write to each other, as then she should chance to get a letter all to herself, not merely be the medium of a communication between them; and Mary, though she did slightly blush, which she was in the habit of doing for scarcely any thing, seemed to think it so perfectly natural, that she merely said, if Herbert had time to write to her, she should like it very much, and would certainly answer him.

"My dear Emmeline, what are you about?" was Mrs. Greville's anxious appeal, the moment they were alone.

"Giving pleasure to two young folks, of whom I am most excessively fond," was Mrs. Hamilton's laughing reply. "Don't look so terrified, my dear Jessie. They love each other as boy and girl now, and if the love should deepen into that of man and woman, why, all I can say is — I would rather have your Mary for my Herbert than any one else I know."

"She is not only *my* Mary!" answered the poor mother, with such a quivering of eye and lip, that it checked Mrs. Hamilton's joyousness at once.

"She is *your* Mary, in all that can make such a character as my Herbert happy," was her instant reply, with a pressure of Mrs. Greville's hand, that said far more than her words. "I am not one of those who like to make matches in anticipation, for man's best laid schemes are so often overthrown by the most trifling but unforeseen chances, that display a much wiser providence than our greatest wisdom, that I should consider it almost sinful so to do; but never let a thought of suffering cross your mind, dearest Jessie, as to what my husband's and my own answer will be, if our Herbert should indeed ever wish to choose your Mary as his wife, and, certainly a most important addition, should she wish it too. Our best plan now is to let them follow their own inclinations regarding correspondence. We can, I am sure, trust them both, for what can be a greater proof of my boy's perfect confidence in my sympathy with his feelings toward her, than to make me his messenger, as he has done, and as he, no doubt, will continue to do, even if he write. I have not the smallest doubt, that he will inclose me his letters to her unsealed, and I rather think your Mary will send me her replies in the same unreserved manner."

And she was right, Nor, we think, did the purity and innocence of those letters, so intensely interesting to each other give place to any other style, even when they chanced to dis cover that Mrs. Hamilton was utterly ignorant of their contents, except that which they chose to read or impart to her themselves.

But even this assurance on the part of one so loved and trusted as Mrs. Hamilton, could not entirely remove Mrs. Greville's vague anticipations of evil. Mr. Greville always shunned, and declared he hated the Hamilton family; but as he seemed to entertain the same feeling toward herself and her poor Mary, she tried to comfort herself by the idea that he would never trouble his head about his daughter; or be glad to get her out of his way, especially if she married well. Still anxiety for the future would press upon her; only calmed by her firm, unchanging faith in that gracious, ever-watchful Providence, who, if in spite of her heavy troubles she still tried to trust and serve, would order all things for the best; and it was this, this faith alone, which so supported her, as to permit her to make her child's home and heart almost as happy as if her path had all been smooth.

In the Grahame family a change had taken place, in Master Cecil's being sent to Eton some time before his father had intended; but so many cases of Lady Helen's faulty indolence and ruinous indulgence had come under his notice, that he felt to remove the boy from her influence must be accomplished at any cost. Cecil was quite delighted, but his mother was so indignant, that she overcame her habitual awe of her husband sufficiently to vow that she would not live so far from her son, and if he must go to school, she must leave Moorlands. Grahame, with equal positiveness, declared that he would not give up a home endeared to him so long, nor so entirely break off his companionship with his dearest friends. A very stormy dialogue of course took place, and ended by both parties being more resolved to entertain their own opinion. The interposition of Mr. and Mrs. Hamilton, however, obtained some concession on Grahame's part, and he promised that if Lady Helen would make Moorlands her home from the middle of July till the end of October, November and December should be spent in the vicinity of Eton, and she should then have six months for London and its attractions. This concession brought back all Lady Helen's smiles, and charmed Annie, though it was a source of real regret to Caroline, who could not help feeling a little pained at her friend's small concern at this long separation from her. But still she loved her; and, as Annie wrote frequently, and when she was at Moorlands never tired of her society, (the eight months of absence giving her so much interesting matter to impart,) Caroline was not only satisfied, but insensible to the utter want of sympathy which Annie manifested in *her* pursuits, *her* pleasures. Mrs. Hamilton often wished that Caroline had chosen one more deserving of her friendship, but she trusted that time and experience would teach her Annie's real character, and so did not feel any anxiety on that score.

There was only one member in Grahame's family, that Mr. and Mrs. Hamilton hoped might bring joy and comfort to their friend, and that was his little Lilla. She was five years younger than Annie, and being much less attractive, seemed almost forgotten, and so was spared the dangerous ordeal of flattery and indulgence to which Annie had been subject; and from being more violent and less agreeable than Cecil, was not so frequently spoiled by her mother. They feared the poor child would have much to endure from her own temper, Annie's overbearing insolence, and Lady Helen's culpable indolence; but Mrs. Hamilton hoped, when she resided part of the year in London, as she felt she would very soon be called upon to do, to be enabled to rouse Grahame's attention toward his youngest child, and prevail on him to relax in his sternness toward her; and by taking notice of her continually herself, instil such feelings in her as would attract her toward her father, and so increase the happiness of both. Every visit of the Grahame family to Moorlands, she resolved to study Lilla well, and try all she could to make one in reality so estimable, as her husband's friend, happy, in one child at least.

It had been Mr. and Mrs. Hamilton's intention to go to London the January after Caroline was seventeen, and give her the advantage of finishing masters, and a partial introduction to the world, by having the best society at home, before she launched into all its exciting pleasures; to return to Oakwood in July or August, and revisit the metropolis the following February or March, for the season, when, as she would be eighteen and a half, she should be fully introduced. Caroline, of course, anticipated this period with intense delight. She was quite satisfied that in her first visit she should study as much as, if not more than before; and content and thankful that her mother would allow her to enter so far into society, as always to join dinner or evening parties at home, and go to some of her most intimate friends, when their coteries were very small and friendly; and another eagerly anticipated delight, sometimes go to the opera and the best concerts, and visit all the galleries of art.

To poor Emmeline these anticipations gave no pleasure whatever; she hated the very thought of leaving Oakwood, firmly convinced that not the most highly intellectual, nor the most delightful social enjoyment in London, could equal the pure delights of Devonshire and home. Ellen seemed too engrossed with her own thoughts to evince a feeling either way, much to her aunt's regret, as her constant quietness and seeming deter mined repression of her sentiments, rendered her character still more difficult to read.

But a heavy disappointment was preparing for Caroline, in the compelled postponement of her bright anticipations; to understand the causes of which, we must glance back on an event in the Hamilton family, which had occurred some years before its present head was born. In the early part of the reign of George the Third, Arthur Hamilton, the grandfather of our friend of the same name, had been sent by government to the coast of Denmark: his estimable character so won him the regard of the reigning sovereign, Christian VII., that, on his departure, the royal wish was expressed for his speedy return. On his voyage home, he was wrecked off the Feroe Islands, and rescued from danger and death by the strenuous exertions of the islanders, who entertained him and the crew with the utmost hospitality, till their ship was again seaworthy. During his involuntary detention, Mr. Hamilton became deeply interested in the Feroese, a people living, it seemed, in the midst of desolation, a cluster of small rocky islets, divided by some hundred miles of stormy sea from their fellows. He made the tour of the islands, and found almost all their inhabitants possessing the same characteristics as those of Samboe, the island off which he had been wrecked; kind, hospitable, honest, temperate, inclined to natural piety, but so perfectly indifferent to the various privations and annoyances of their lot, as to make no effort toward removing them. Travelling either by land or sea was so dangerous and difficult, that in some parishes the clergyman could only perform service twice a year,* or once every one, two, or three months. The islands in which the clergyman resided were, Mr. Hamilton observed, in a much higher state of civilization and morality than Samboe and some others, and an earnest desire took possession of him, to do some real service for those who had saved him from danger and treated him so hospitably. He very speedly acquired their language, which gave him still more influence. He found, also, that if their

* For this account of Feroe and the Feroese the author is indebted to a "History of the Islands, by a Resident."

ancient customs and traditions were left undisturbed, they were very easily led, and this discovery strengthened his purpose. — His departure was universally regretted; and his promise to return imagined too great a privilege to be believed.

As soon as his political duties in England permitted, Mr Hamilton revisited Denmark, and was received with such cordiality as to encourage him to make his petition for the improvement of his majesty's poor subjects of Samboe. It was granted directly; the little island so far made over to him, that he was at liberty to introduce and erect whatever he pleased within it; and Mr. Hamilton, all eagerness for the perfection of his plans, returned with speed to England; obtained the valuable aid of a poor though worthy clergyman, who, with his wife, voluntarily offered to make Samboe their home, and assist their benefactor (for such Mr. Hamilton had long been) to the very best of their ability. A strong-built vessel was easily procured, and a favorable voyage soon transported them to Feroe. The delight of the Samboese at beholding their former guest again, prepossessed Mr. and Mrs. Wilson in their favor, and Mr. Hamilton, before his six months' sojourn with them was over, beheld the island in a fair way of religious and moral improvement — Schools were formed and masters appointed — houses were made more comfortable — women and young children more cared for, and employments found, and sufficiently rewarded to encourage persevering labor. Three or four times Mr. Hamilton visited the island again before his death, and each time he had more reason to be satisfied with the effect of his schemes. Mr. and Mrs. Wilson were perfectly happy. Their son was united to the pretty and excellent daughter of one of the Danish clergymen, and a young family was blooming round them, so that there seemed a fair promise of the ministry of Samboe continuing long in charge of the same family.

Mr. Hamilton, on his death-bed, exacted a promise from his son that he would not permit the island to fall back into its old habits; but that, if required, he would visit it himself. The visit was not required, but Percy Hamilton, (the father of the present possessor of Oakwood,) from respect to his father's memory, made a voyage to Samboe on the demise of the elder Wilson. He found every thing flourishing and happy; Frederic Wilson had been received as their pastor and head, with as much joy as their regret for his father would permit; and Mr. Hamilton returned to England, satisfied with himself, and inexpressibly touched by the veneration still entertained in that distant island for his father. The same promise was demanded by him from his son, and Arthur Hamilton had visited Feroe directly after the loss of his parent, and before his engagement with Miss Manvers. He found it in the same satisfactory condition as his predecessors had done, and the letters he regularly received confirmed it; but for the last year and a half he had received no tidings. Frederic Wilson, he knew, was dead, but his last account had told him his eldest son, who had been educated in Denmark, had been gladly received by the simple people, and promised fair to be as much loved, and do the same good as his father and grandfather. The silence then was incomprehensible, and Mr. Hamilton had resolved, if another year passed without intelligence, it would be a positive duty to visit it himself.

CHAPTER II.

A LETTER, AND ITS CONSEQUENCES.

It was the seventh of June, and one of those glorious mornings, when nature looks lovelier than ever. The windows of the breakfast-room were thrown widely open, and never did the superb trees of Oakwood Park look richer or display a greater variety of green. The flower-garden, on part of which the breakfast-room opened, was actually dazzling with its profusion of brilliant flowers, on which the sun looked down so gloriously; a smooth lawn, whose green was a perfect emerald, stretched down from the parterre, till it was lost in woody openings, which disclosed the winding river, that, lying as a lake on one side, appeared to sweep round some exquisite scenery on the opposite side, and form another lake, about a mile further. It was Emmeline's favorite view, and she always declared, that it so varied its aspects of loveliness, she was sure it never looked two mornings exactly alike, and so long would she stand and admire, that her mother often threatened to send her her breakfast in her own room, where the view, though picturesque, would not so completely turn her attention from the dull realities of life. There were some letters on the table this morning, so she had a longer time to drink in poetry than usual.

"Who can offer Ellen a more precious birthday-gift than mine?" exclaimed Mrs. Hamilton, playfully holding up a letter as her niece entered. "I wonder if Edward remembered how near his sister was to fifteen, and so wrote on the chance of your receiving it on the day itself?"

"Why, Ellen, what a queer effect pleasure has on you! I always notice you turn quite pale whenever Edward's letters are given to you," interposed Emmeline, looking at her cousin, and laughing. "I am sure, the very hurry I am in to open Percy's and Herbert's, must give me a color, and you are as deliberate as if you did not care about it. I do wish you would not be so cold and quiet."

"One giddy brain is quite enough in a house," rejoined her father, in the same mirthful tone, and looking up from his letter, he called Ellen to him, and kissed her. "I forgot the day of the month, my little girl, but I am not too late, I hope, to say, God bless you, and wish that every year may pass more happily, more usefully, and more prepared for eternity than the last!"

"I do not think you have forgotten it, my dear uncle," replied Ellen, gratefully (she had not yet opened her brother's letter); "for my aunt says, I am to thank you as well as her for this beautiful birth-day gift," and she displayed an elegant little gold watch; "indeed, I do not know how to thank you for all your kindness!" she added, so earnestly that tears came to her eyes.

"I will say, as I have heard your aunt often say — by trying to be a little more lively and unreserved, my dear Ellen; that would prove our kindness and affection made you happy, better than any thing; but I am not going to lecture you on your birthday, and with a letter from Edward in your hand," he continued smiling. "Open it, my dear, I want to know its date; I rather think my friend Manly's must be written later."

"Nothing in it for me, Ellen?" asked her aunt. "What a lazy boy he has grown!"

"An inclosure for you, Ellen; why, that is as queer as your paleness!" said Emmeline.

"Do let your cousin's paleness alone," interposed Mrs. Hamilton, gayly. "I really cannot perceive she has any less color than usual, and as for the inclosure, Edward often has something to add at the last moment, and no room to insert it, and so there is nothing remarkable in his using another half sheet."

"Emmeline always creates wonders out of shadows," said Caroline, dryly.

"And you never see any thing but dull, coarse, heavy reali

ties," laughed her sister in reply. "Come, Ellen, tell us something of this idle brother of yours, who promised to write to me every packet, and never does."

Ellen read nearly the whole letter aloud, and it was unusually entertaining, for the ship had been cruising about the last month, and Edward described the various scenes and new places he had visited more lengthily than usual. He anticipated with great glee an engagement with some desperate pirates, whose track they were pursuing.

"Does he mention an engagement?" inquired Mr. Hamilton.

"No, uncle; he concludes quite abruptly, saying they have just piped all hands, and he must be off. The direction does not seem his writing."

"Nor is it; Sir Edward sealed, directed, and put it up for him in his own to me. They had piped all hands, as he calls it, because the pirate ship was in sight, and an engagement did take place."

"And Edward — oh, uncle, is he hurt? I am sure, he is, by your face," exclaimed Ellen, trembling; and all the little circle looked alarmed.

"Then my face is a deceiver," replied Mr. Hamilton, quite cheerfully. "He only received a slight flesh wound in his right arm, which prevented his using it to complete his letter, and I rather think he would have willingly been hurt still more, to receive such praises as Sir Edward lavishes on him. Listen to what he says — 'Not a boy or man on board distinguished himself more than your nephew: in fact, I am only astonished he escaped as he did, for those pirates are desperate fighters, and when we boarded them, Fortescue was in the midst of them, fighting like a young lion. Courage and gallantry are such dazzling qualities in a young lad, that we think more of them perhaps than we ought, but I cannot say too much for your nephew; I have not a lad more devoted to his duty. I was glad to show him my approbation by giving him some days' liberty, when we were off New York; but I have since told him the air of land certainly did not agree with him, for he has looked paler and thinner ever since. He is growing very fast; and altogether, if I have occasion to send another prize schooner home, I think it not improbable I shall nominate him as one of the officers, that he may have the benefit of the healtful breezes of Old England, to bring back his full strength.' There, Ellen, I think that is a still better birthday-present than even Edward's own letter. I am as proud of my nephew as Sir Edward is."

"And do you think he really will come?" asked Ellen, trying to conquer her emotion.

"We will hope it, dearest," replied her aunt, kindly. "But do not think too much about it, even if Sir Edward be not able to do as he says. His own ship will be coming home in a year or two, and you owned to me yourself this morning, it did not seem as long as it really is, since our dear sailor left us; so the remaining time will soon pass. Finish your breakfast, and go, love, and enjoy his letter again to yourself."

And Ellen gladly obeyed; for it was from no imaginary cause that the receipt of Edward's letters so often paled her cheek, and parched her lip with terror. She knew that concerning him which none else but Harding did; and even when those letters imparted nothing but that which she could read to her family, the dread was quite enough to banish any thing like the elastic happiness, natural to her age, and called for by the kindness of those she loved. His letter this time, however, had not a word to call for that sickness of the heart, with which she had received it; and she read it again and again, with a thankfulness too intense for words.

"You dropped this, Ellen dear," said the voice of her cousin Emmeline at her door, ten minutes after she left the breakfast-room. "It was under the table, and I do not think you have read it; it is the inclosure I was so amused at."

"I dare say it is a letter written for some other opportunity, and forgotten to be sent; it is only a few words," replied Ellen, as she looked at its length, not at its meaning, for the fearful lesson of quiet unconcern when the heart is bursting had been too early learned.

"Then I will leave you in peace: by-the-by, cousin mine, papa told me to tell you, that as the Prince William is soon going to cruise again, your answer to Edward must be ready this day week, the latest, and mamma says, if you like to write part of it now that all Edward's little love-speeches are fresh in your mind, you can do so; it is your birthday, and you may spend it as you like. How I shall enjoy making a lion of my cousin, when he comes!" — and away tripped the happy girl, singing some wild snatch of an old ballad about sailors.

Ellen shut the door, secured it, and with a lip and cheek colorless as her robe, an eye strained and bloodshot, read the following words — few indeed!

"Ellen! I am again in that villain's power, and for a sum so trifling, that it maddens me to think I cannot discharge it without again appealing to you. I had resolved never to play again — and again some demon lured me to those Hells! If I do not pay him by my next receipts from home, he will expose me, and what then — disgrace, expulsion, *death!* for I will not survive it; there are easy means of self-destruction to a sailor, and who shall know but that he is accidentally drowned? You promised me to save part of every allowance, in case I needed it. If you would indeed save me, send me five-and-thirty pounds. Ellen! by some means, I *must* have it; but breathe it to my uncle or aunt — for if *she* knows it, *he* will — and you will never see me more!"

For one long hour Ellen never moved. Her brain felt scorched, her limbs utterly powerless. Every word seemed to write itself in letters of fire on her heart and brain, till she could almost have screamed, from the dread agony; and then came the heavy weight, so often felt before, but never crushing every thought and energy as now, the seeming utter impossibility to comply with that fearfully urged demand. *He* called it a sum so trifling, and *she* felt a hundred, ay, a thousand pounds were not more difficult to obtain. She had saved, indeed, denying herself every little indulgence, every personal gratification, spending only what she was obliged, and yet compelled to let her aunt believe she had properly expended all, that she might have the means of sending him money when he demanded it, without exposing herself to doubt and displeasure as before; but in the eight months since his last call, she had only been enabled to put by fifteen pounds, not half the sum he needed. How was she to get the rest? and she had so buoyed herself with the fond hope, that even if he did write for help again, she could send it to him so easily — and now — her mind seemed actually to reel beneath the intense agony of these desperate words. She was too young, too believing, and too terror-stricken to doubt for a moment the alternative he placed before her, with a vividness, a desperation, of which he was unconscious himself. Those words spoken, would have been terrible, almost awful in one so young — though a brief interval would have sufficiently calmed both the hearer and the speaker, to satisfy that they were *but words*, and that self-destruction is never breathed, if really intended: but *written*, the writer at a distance, imagination at liberty to heighten every terror, every reality; their reader, a young loving girl, utterly ignorant of the world's ways and temptations, and the many errors to which youth is subject, but from which manhood may spring up unsullied; and so believing, almost crushed by the belief, that her brother, the only one, her own — respected, beloved, as he was said to be — had yet committed such faults, as would hurl him from his present position to the lowest depth of degradation, for what else could tempt him, to swear not to survive it? Was it marvel, that poor Ellen was only conscious that she must save him? Again did her dying mother stand before her — again did her well-remembered voice beseech her to save him, her darling, beautiful Edward, from disgrace and punishment — reiterate that her word was pledged, and she *must* do it, and if she suffered — had she not done so from infancy — and what was her happiness to his? Define why it should be of less moment, indeed, she could not. It was the fatal influences of her childhood working alone.

How that day passed, Ellen never knew. She had been too long accustomed to control, to betray her internal suffering, (terror for Edward seemed to endow her with additional self command,) except by a deadly paleness, which even her aunt at length remarked. It was quite evening, and the party were all scattered, when Mrs. Hamilton discovered Ellen sitting in one of the deep recesses of the windows; her work in her lap, her hands clasped tightly together, and her eyes fixed on the beautiful scenery of the park, but not seeing a single object.

"My dear Ellen, I am going to scold you, so prepare," was her aunt's lively address, as she approached and stood by her. "You need not start so guiltily and look so very terrified, but confess that you are thinking about Edward, and worrying yourself that he is not quite so strong as he was, and magnifying his wound, till you fancy it something very dreadful, when, I dare say, if the truth were told, he himself is quite proud of it; come confess, and I will only give you a very little lecture, for your excessive silliness."

Ellen looked up in her face; that kind voice, that affectionate smile, that caressing, constantly forgiving love, would they again all be forfeited, again give way to coldness, loss of confidence, heightened displeasure? How indeed she was to act, she knew not; she only knew there must be concealment, the very anticipation of which, seemed too terrible to bear, and she burst into an agony of tears.

"Why, Ellen — my dear child — you cannot be well, to let either the accounts of your brother, or my threatened scolding, so affect you, and on your birthday, too! Why, all the old women would say it was such a bad omen, that you would be unhappy all the year round. Come, this will never do, I must lecture, in earnest, if you do not try to conquer this unusual weakness. We have much more to be thankful for, in Sir

Edward's account of our dear sailor, than to cry about; he might have been seriously wounded or maimed, and what would you have felt then? I wonder if he will find as much change in you as we shall in him. If you are not quite strong and quite well, and quite happy to greet him when he comes, I shall consider my care insulted, and punish you accordingly. Still no smile. What is the matter, dearest? Are you really not well again?"

Ellen made a desperate effort, conquered her tears, and tried to converse cheerfully. It was absolute agony to hear Edward's name, but she nerved herself to do so, to acknowledge she was thinking of him; and that it *was* very silly to worry about such a slight wound: and when Mrs. Hamilton proposed that they should walk over to Greville Manor, and tell the good news to Mrs. Greville and Mary, acquiesced with apparent pleasure.

"Ah do, mamma: you have not asked me, but I shall go notwithstanding," exclaimed Emmeline, springing through the open window, with her usual airy step.

"Why Emmeline, I thought you were going to the village with your sister!"

"No; she and Miss Harcourt were talking much too soberly to suit me this evening. Then I went to tease papa, but he let me do just what I pleased, being too engrossed with some disagreeable farmers, to notice me; so in despair, I came here. Why, Ellen, you look as if this were any day but what it is; unless you cry because you are getting old, which I am very often inclined to do — only think, I am sixteen next December — how dreadful! I do wish my birthday were in June."

"And what difference would that make?"

"A great deal, mamma; only look how lovely every thing is now; nature is quite juvenile, and has dressed herself in so many colors, and seems to promise so many more beauties, that, whether we will or no, we must feel gay and young; but in December, though it is very delightful in the house, it is so drear and withered without, that if born in such a season, one must feel withered too."

"When do you intend to speak in prose, Emmeline?"

"Never, if I can help it, mamma; but I must learn the lesson before I go to London, I suppose; that horrid London! that is one reason why I regret the years going so fast; I know I shall leave all my happiness here."

"You will be more ungrateful, than I believe you, if you do," replied her mother. So pray banish such foolish fancies as fast as you can; for if you encourage them, I shall certainly suppose that it is only Oakwood you love; and that neither your father nor myself, nor any member of your family, has any part in your affections, for we shall be with you, wherever you are."

"Dear mamma, I spoke at random, forgive me," replied Emmeline, instantly self-reproached. "I am indeed the giddy brain papa calls me; but you cannot tell how I love this dear old home."

"Indeed I think I can, my dear child, loving it as I do myself; but come, we shall have no time for our visit, if we do not go at once."

Days passed, and were each followed by such sleepless feverish nights, that Ellen felt it almost a miracle that she could so seem, so act, as to excite no notice. The image of her dying mother never left her, night or day, mingled with the horrid scene of her father's death, and Edward disgraced, expelled, and seeking death by his own hand. There was only one plan that seemed in the least feasible, and that was to send to him, or sell herself the watch she had received on her birthday, and if that was not enough, some few trinkets, which had been her mother's and which the last six months her aunt had given into her own care. She ventured casually to inquire if there were any opportunity of sending a parcel to Edward; but the answer was in the negative, and increased her difficulty. The only person she dared even to think of so far intrusting with her deep distress and anxiety for money, but not its cause, was widow Langford, the mother of Robert (the young gentlemen's attendant, whom we have had occasion more than once to mention, and the former nurse of all Mr. and Mrs. Hamilton's children.) She occupied a cottage on the outskirts of the park, and was not only a favorite with all the young party, Ellen included, (for she generally came to nurse her in her many illnesses,) but was regarded with the greatest confidence and affection by Mr. and Mrs. Hamilton themselves. They had endeavored to return her unwavering fidelity and active service, by taking her only child Robert into their family, when only seven; placing him under the immediate charge of Morris, the steward, and of course living in the same house, of his mother also; and when fifteen, making him personal attendant to Percy and Herbert, who were then about ten and eleven years old. An older and more experienced domestic had, however, accompanied the young men to college, and Robert remained employed in many little confidential services for his master at Oakwood.

To widow Langford, Ellen tried to resolve that she would

apply, but her fearful state of mental agony had not marked the lapse of time, or had caused her to forget that her letter must be ready in a week. The party were all going a delightful excursion, and to drink tea at Greville Manor, so that they would not be home till quite late; but in the morning, Ellen, though she had dressed for going out, appeared to have every symptom of such a violent headache, that her aunt advised her remaining quietly at home, and she assented with eagerness, refusing every offer of companionship, saying if the pain went off, she could quite amuse herself, and if it continued, quietness and Ellis's nursing were the best things for her.

"But give me your letter before we go out, Ellen, I am only waiting for it, to close mine to Sir Edward. Why, my dear have you forgotten I told you it must be ready by to-day?" her uncle added, surprised at her exclamation that she had not finished it. "It must be done and sent to T—, before four to-day, so I do hope your head will allow you to write, for Edward will be wofully disappointed if there be not a line from you, especially as, from his ship cruising about, it may be several weeks before he can hear again. I must leave my letter with you, to inclose Edward's and seal up, and pray see that it goes in time."

Ellen tried to promise that it should, but her tongue actually clove to the roof of her mouth; but all the party dispersing at the moment, her silence was unnoticed. Mr. Hamilton gave her his letter, and in half an hour afterward she was alone. She sat for nearly an hour in her own room, with her desk before her, her face buried in her hands, and her whole frame shaking as with an ague.

"It must be," she said at length, and unlocking a drawer, took thence a small cross, and one or two other trinkets, put them up, and taking off her watch, looked at it with such an expression of suffering, that it seemed as if she could not go on, carefully folded it up with the other trinkets, and murmuring, "If nurse Langdon will but take these, and lend me the twenty pounds till she can dispose of them, I may save him yet — and if she betray me — if she tell my aunt afterward, at least only I shall suffer; they will not suspect him. But oh — to lose — to be doubted, hated, which I must be at last. Oh, mother mother! Why may I not tell my aunt? she would not disgrace him." And again she crouched down, cowed by that fearful struggle to the very earth. After a few minutes, it passed, and deliberately putting on her bonnet and shawl, she took up her trinkets, and set off to the widow's cottage, her limbs so trembling, that she knew not how she should accomplish even that short walk.

The wind was unusually high, although the day was otherwise lovely, and she was scarcely able to stand against the strong breeze, especially as every breath seemed to increase the pain in her temples; but she persisted. The nearest path lay through a thick shrubbery, almost a wood, which the family never used, and, in fact, the younger members were prohibited from taking, but secrecy and haste were all which at that moment entered Ellen's mind. She felt so exhausted by the wind blowing the branches and leaves noisily and confusedly around, that on reaching a sort of grassy glade, more open than her previous path, she sat down a minute on a mossy stone. The wind blew some withered sticks and leaves toward her, and, among them, two or three soiled pieces of thin paper, stained with damp, one of which she raised mechanically, and started up with a wild cry, and seized the others almost unconsciously. She pressed her hands over her eyes, and her lips moved in the utterance of thanksgiving. "Saved! — Edward and myself, too! — some guardian angel must have sent them!" if not actually spoken, were so distinctly uttered in her heart, that she thought she heard them; and she retraced her steps, so swiftly — so gladly, the very pain and exhaustion were unfelt. She wrote for half an hour intently — eagerly; though that which she wrote she knew not herself, and never could recall. She took from the secret drawer of her desk (that secret drawer which, when Percy had so laughingly showed her the secret of its spring, telling her nobody but himself knew it, she little thought she should have occasion so to use,) some bank notes, of two, three, and five pounds each, making the fifteen she had so carefully hoarded, and placed with them the two she had found. As she did so, she discovered that two had clung so closely together that the sum was five pounds more than she wanted. Still, as acting under the influence of some spell, she carelessly put one aside, sealed up the packet to Edward, inclosed it in her uncle's to Sir Edward Manly, and despatched it full four hours before the hour Mr. Hamilton had named. It was gone; and she sat down to breathe. Some impulse, never experienced before, urged her, instead of destroying Edward's desperate letter, as she had done similar appeals, to retain it in a blank envelop in that same secret drawer. As she tried to rouse herself from a sort of stupor which was strangely creeping over her, her eye caught the five pound note which she had not had occasion to use, and a thought of such overwhelming wretchedness rushed upon her, as effectually, for the moment, to disperse that stupor, and prostrate her in an agony of supplication before her God.

"What have I done?" — if her almost maddening thoughts could have found words, such they would have been — "How dared I appropriate that money, without one question — one thought — as to whom it could belong? Sent me? No, no! Who could have sent it? Great God of Mercy! Oh, if Thy wrath must fall on a guilty one, pour it on me, but spare, spare my brother! I have sinned, but I meant it not — thought not of it — knew not what I did! Thou knowest, Thou alone canst know, the only thought of that moment — the agony of this. No suffering, no wrath, can be too great for me; but, oh! spare him!"

How long that withering agony lasted, Ellen knew not, nor whether her tears fell, or lay scorching her eyes and heart. The note lay before her like some hideous spectre, from which she vainly tried to turn. What could she do with it? Take it back to the spot where the others had been blown to her? She tried to rise to do so; but, to her own terror, she found she was so powerless, that she actually could not walk. With desperate calmness she placed it in the little secret drawer, put up the remainder of her papers, closed and locked her desk, and laid down upon her bed, for she could sit up no longer. Ellis came to her with an inquiry after her head, and if she could take her dinner. Ellen asked for a cup of coffee, and to be left quite quiet instead, as writing had not decreased the pain; and the housekeeper, accustomed to such casual attacks, did as she was requested, and came frequently to see her in the course of the afternoon and evening; still without perceiving any thing unusual, and, therefore, not tormenting her with any expression of surprise or anxiety.

Thought after thought congregated in the poor girl's mind, as she thus lay; so fraught with agony that the physical suffering, which was far more than usual, was unfelt, save in its paralyzing effect on every limb. Her impulse was to confess exactly what she had done to her aunt, the moment she could see her, and conjure her to sentence her to some heavy chastisement, that must deaden her present agony; but this was impossible without betraying Edward, and nullifying for him the relief she had sent. How could she confess the sin, without the full confession of the use to which that money had been applied? Whose were the notes? They were stained with damp, as if they must have lain among those withered leaves some time;

and yet she had heard no inquiry made about them, as the loss of so large a sum would surely have demanded. The only plan she could think of, as bringing the least hope of returning peace, was still to beseech Mrs. Langford to dispose of her watch and trinkets, and the very first mention she heard made of the loss to return the full sum to the real possessor, if possible, so secretly as for it not to be traced to herself. She thought, too, that if she gave her trinkets, one by one, not all together, to Mrs. Langford, it would be less suspicious, and, perhaps, more easily prevail on her to grant her secrecy and assistance; and if she positively refused, unless Ellen revealed the reason of her desiring their disposal, and would solemnly promise secrecy, she would tell her so much of her intense misery, as might perhaps induce her to give her aid. If she did not demand the reason and betrayed her, she must endure the doubt and serious displeasure such a course of acting on her part would inevitably produce; but two things alone stood clear before her; she *must* replace that money — she *must* keep Edward's secret. She would have gone that very day to Mrs. Langford, but she could not move, and Ellis, at seven o'clock, prevailed on her to undress and go to bed.

"Not better, my Ellen? I hoped to-day's perfect quietness would have removed your headache, and am quite disappointed," was Mrs. Hamilton's affectionate address, as she softly entered her niece's room, on the return of the happy party at eleven at night, and placing the lamp so that the bed remained in shade she could not see any expression in Ellen's face, except that of suffering, which she naturally attributed to physical pain. "How hot your hands and face are, love; I wish you had not left Edward's letter to write to-day. I am afraid we shall be obliged to see Mr. Maitland's face again to-morrow; if he were not as kind a friend as he is a skilful doctor, I am sure you would get quite tired of him, Ellen. Shall I stay with you? I cannot bear leaving you in pain and alone!" But Ellen would not hear of it; the pain was not more than she was often accustomed to, she said, and, indeed, she did not mind being alone — though the unusual, almost passionate, warmth with which she returned Mrs. Hamilton's fond kiss, betrayed it was no indifference to the affectionate offer which dictated her refusal. It was well Mrs. Hamilton, though anxious enough to feel the inclination to do so, did not visit her niece again, or the convulsive agony she would have witnessed, the choking sobs which burst forth, a few minutes after she disappeared from Ellen's sight, would have bewildered and terrified her yet more.

CHAPTER III.

A SUMMONS AND A LOSS.

Mr. Maitland declared Ellen to be ill of a nervous fever, which for three days confined her to her bed, and left her very weak for some little time, and so nervous that the least thing seemed to startle her; but, as he said it was no consequence, and she would soon recover, Mrs. Hamilton adopted his advice, took no notice of it, and only endeavored to make her niece's daily routine as varied in employment, though regular in hours and undisturbed in quiet, as she could. Perhaps she would have felt more anxious, and discovered something not quite usual in Ellen's manner, if her thoughts had not been painfully preoccupied. About a week after their excursion she entered the library earlier than usual, and found her husband intently engaged with some despatches just received. She saw he was more than ordinarily disturbed, and hesitated a moment whether to address him; but he was seldom so engrossed as to be unconscious of the presence of his wife.

"I am really glad you are here at this moment, Emmeline, for I actually was weak enough to shrink from seeking you with unpleasant news. Letters from Feroe have at length arrived, and my personal presence is so imperatively needed, that I am self-reproached at not going before; the long silence ought to have convinced me that all was not as it should be."

"But what has occurred, Arthur? I had no idea you contemplated the necessity of going," replied his wife very quietly, as she sat down close by him; but the fiat of separation, the thoughts of a perilous voyage, a visit to an almost desolate island, and the impossibility of receiving regular letters, so crowded upon her all at once, that it was a strong effort to speak at all.

"No, dearest; for what was the use of tormenting you with disagreeable anticipations, when there really might have been no foundation for them. The last accounts from Samboe, were, as you know, received nearly two years ago, telling me that Frederic Wilson was dead, but that his son had been received as his successor in the ministry, and as civil guardian of the island, with, if possible, a still greater degree of popularity than his predecessors, from his having been educated in Denmark. His parents had lived on straitened means to give him superior advantages, which, as it proves, he would have been much better without. The vices he has acquired have far outrun the advantages. His example, and that of a band of idle, irregular spirits who have joined him, has not only scandalized the simple people but disturbed their homesteads, brought contention and misery, and in some cases bloodshed; so that in point of social and domestic position, I fear they have sunk lower than when my grandfather first sought the island. The mother of this unhappy young man has, naturally, perhaps, but weakly, shrunk from informing against him; but her brother, the clergyman of Osteroe, has at length taken upon himself to do so, clearly stating that nothing but personal interference and some months' residence among them will effect a reformation; and that the ruin is more to be regretted, as the little island has been for more than half a century the admiration not only of its immediate neighbors, but of all who have chanced to harbor off its coast. He states, too, that if properly directed and not exposed to the contagion of large cities, as his brother has been, poor Wilson's younger son, now a boy of eleven, may become as worthy and judicious a pastor as his father and grandfather, and so keep the office in his family, as my grandfather was so desirous of doing. The question is, how is this boy to be educated on the island, and whom can I find to take the ministry meanwhile?"

"And must your own residence there be very long?" inquired Mrs. Hamilton, still in that quiet tone, but her lip quivered.

"It depends entirely on whom I can get to accompany me, dearest. I must set Mr. Howard and Morton to work to find me some simple-minded, single-hearted individual, who will regard this undertaking in the same missionary spirit as the elder Wilson did. If I am happy enough to succeed in this, I hope a year, or somewhat less, will be the farthest limit of our separation."

"A year! a whole long year — dearest Arthur, must it be so very, very long?"

"Who tried to persuade Ellen, a fortnight ago, that a year, even two years, would pass so very quickly?" replied Mr. Hamilton, trying to smile, and folding his arm fondly round his wife, he kissed the cheek which had become pale from the effort to restrain her feelings. "It is indeed an unexpected and a painful trial, and, as is generally the case with our rebellious spirits, I feel as if it would have been better borne at any other period than the present. We had so portioned out this year, had so anticipated gratifying Caroline by introducing her to the so long and so eagerly anticipated pleasures of London next January, that I cannot bear to think of her disappcint ment."

"And our boys, too, they say it is so strange to be without their father, even in college term; what will it be when they come home for the long vacation, to which we have all so looked forward? But this is all weakness, my own dear husband; forgive me, I am only rendering your duty more difficult," she added, raising her head from his shoulder, and smiling cheerfully, even while the tears glistened in her eyes. "I must try and practise my own lesson, and believe the term of separation will really pass quickly, interminable as it now seems. We have been so blessed, so guarded from the bitter pang of even partial separation for twenty years, that how dare I murmur now the trial has come? It is God's pleasure, dearest Arthur, though it seems like the work of man, and as HIS we can endure it."

"Bless you, my beloved! you have indeed put a new spirit in me by those words," replied her husband, with a fondness, the more intense from the actual veneration that so largely mingled with it. "And bitter disappointment as it is to me to be from home when our sons return, it is better so, perhaps, for their company will wile away at least nearly three months of my absence."

Mr. and Mrs. Hamilton remained some hours together that morning in earnest conversation. All of individual regret was conquered for the sake of the other: its expression, at least, not its feeling; but they understood each other too well, too fondly, to need words or complaints to prove to either how intensely painful was the very thought of separation. To elude the performance of a duty which many persons, unable to enter into the hope of effecting good, would, no doubt, pronounce Quixotic — for what could the poor inhabitants of Samboe be to him? — never entered either Mr. or Mrs. Hamilton's mind. He was not one to neglect his immediate duties for distant ones; but believed and acted on the belief, that both could be united. His own large estate, its various farms, parishes, and villages, were so admirably ordered, that he could leave it without the smallest scruple in the hands of his wife and steward. Though interested in, and actually assisting in the political movements of his country, he was still, as from his youth he had firmly resolved to be, a free, independent Englishman; bound to no party, but respected by all; retaining his own principles unshaken as a rock, though often and often his integrity had been tried by court bribes and dazzling offers. And yet, rare blending with such individual feelings, Arthur Hamilton looked with candor and kindness on the conduct and principles of others, however they might differ from his own, and found excuses for them, which none others could. That he should give up all the comforts, the luxuries, the delights of his peculiarly happy home, to encounter several months' sojourn in a bleak, half-civilized island, only in the hope of restoring and insuring moral and religious improvement to a small colony of human beings, whose sole claim upon him was, that they were immortal as himself, and that they had done a kindness to his grandfather more than half a century back, was likely to, and no doubt did, excite the utmost astonishment in very many circles; but not a sneer, not a word seeming to whisper good should be done at home before sought abroad, could find a moment's resting-place near Arthur Hamilton's name.

For half an hour after Mrs. Hamilton quitted her husband she remained alone, and when she rejoined her family, though she might have been a shade paler than her wont, she was as cheerful in conversation and earnest in manner as usual. That evening Mr. Hamilton informed his children and Miss Harcourt of his intended departure, and consequent compelled change of plan. Emmeline's burst of sorrow was violent and uncontrolled. Caroline looked for a minute quite bewildered, and then hastening to her father threw one arm round his neck, exclaiming, in a voice of the most affectionate sincerity, "Dear papa, what shall we do without you for such a long time?"

"My dear child! I thank you for such an affectionate thought; believe me, the idea of your wishes being postponed has pained me as much as any thing else in this unpleasant duty."

"My wishes postponed, papa — what do you mean?"

"Have you quite forgotten our intended plans for next January, my love? My absence must alter them."

For a moment an expression of bitter disappointment clouded Caroline's open countenance.

"Indeed, papa, I had forgotten it; I only thought of your going away for so many months. It is a great disappointment, I own, and I dare say I shall feel it still more when January comes; but I am sure parting from you must be a still greater trial to mamma, than any such disappointment ought to be to me; and, indeed, I will try and bear it as uncomplainingly and cheerfully as she does."

Her father almost involuntarily drew her to his heart, and kissed her two or three times, without speaking; and Caroline was very glad he did so, for when she looked up again, the tears that would come at the first thought of her disappointment were bravely sent back again; and she tried to cheer Emmeline, by assuring her she never could be like her favorite heroines of romance, if she behaved so very much like a child; taking the opportunity when they retired for the night, to say more seriously —

"Dear Emmeline, do try and be as lively as you always are. I am sure poor mamma is suffering very much at the idea of papa's leaving us, though she will not let us see that she does, and if you give way so, it will make her more uncomfortable still."

Emmeline promised to try; but her disposition, quite as susceptible to sorrow as to joy, and not nearly as firm as her sister's, rendered the promise very difficult to fulfil. It was her first sorrow; and Mrs. Hamilton watched her with some anxiety, half fearful that she had been wrong to shield her so carefully from any thing like grief, if, when it came, she should prove unequal to its firm and uncomplaining endurance. Ellen had been out of the room when Mr. Hamilton had first spoken; and engaged in soothing Emmeline; when she reëntered and the news was communicated to her, he did not observe any thing particular in her mode of receiving it. But Mrs. Hamilton was so struck with the expression of her countenance, which, as she tried somewhat incoherently to utter regrets, took the place of its usual calm, that she looked at her several minutes in bewilderment; but it passed again, so completely, that she was angry with herself for fancying any thing uncommon. Caroline, however, had remarked it too, and she could not help observing to Miss Harcourt, the first time they were alone —

"You will say I am always fancying something extraordinary, Miss Harcourt; but Ellen certainly did look pleased last night, when mamma told her of papa's intended departure."

"The expression must have been something extraordinary for you to remark it at all," replied Miss Harcourt; nobody but Mrs. Hamilton, whose penetration is out of the common, can ever read any thing on Ellen's face."

"And it was for that very reason I looked again; and mamma noticed it too, and was surprised, though she did not say any thing. If she really be pleased she is most ungrateful, and all her profession of feeling mamma and papa's constant kindness sheer deceit. I never shall understand Ellen, I believe; but I do hope mamma will never discover that she is not exactly that which her affection believes her."

"Pray do not talk so, my dear Caroline, or I shall be tempted to confess that you are giving words to my own feelings. Her conduct with regard to the disappearance of her allowance, the wholly unsatisfactory account of its expenditure, even every month, for she seems to me to mention many things she has never had, banish every hopeful feeling, and I dread more than I can tell you, the very thing you have expressed. But all this is very wrong; we have relieved each other by a mutual acknowledgment, and now let us never revert, even in thought, if possible, to the subject."

Caroline willingly acquiesced, for it was far from agreeable. Mr. Hamilton's preparations, meanwhile, rapidly progressed. He imparted his wishes for a companion willing to remain in the island, till young Wilson should be prepared for the ministry, both to Mr. Howard and Mr. Morton, (the latter still remained in his desolate parish, still more isolated in feeling from the loss of both his parents, and Percy's absence,) and both, especially Morton, gave him every hope of obtaining the character he wanted. His next inquiry was at Dartmouth for strong, well-built vessel, fitted to encounter the stormy seas between Scotland and Feroe, determining to do all in his power to provide some means of regular communication between himself and the beloved inmates of his home. Wick, in Caithness, was the farthest post town to which letters could be addressed. Every ten days or fortnight communications were to be sent there, and the Siren, after conveying him to Feroe, was regularly to ply between Samboe and Wick, bringing from the latter place to Mr. Hamilton the various letters that had accumulated there, should unfavorable winds have lengthened the voyage, and forwarding his through that post to his home. By this means, he hoped to hear and be heard of regularly; an intense relief, if it really could be so accomplished, to his wife.

As soon as a ship, a competent captain, mate, and crew were obtained, Mr. Hamilton set off for Oxford and London, wishing in the latter place to see his friend Grahame, and in the former to pass a few days with his sons, who, knowing nothing of his summons, received him with unbounded delight. Their regret, when they heard the cause of his visit, was as great as their joy had been. Percy, in a desperate fit of impatience, wished the little island and all its concerns at the botton of the sea, the best place for such unruly, disagreeable people; and he was only sobered when his father put before him that, though it must be a very heightened individual disappointment, it was the greatest comfort to him, to think that they would both be with their mother and sisters the first few months of his absence. Percy instantly altered his tone.

"You are quite right, my dear father; I was very selfish not to think of it. Trust me for making my dearest mother as cheerful and has happy as I can. You don't know what a guardian angel the thought of her love has been to me in temptation; and as for Bertie, if ever I thought he was studying himself ill, and not taking the care of himself he ought, or wanted him to take exercise and recreation, when he thought me a great bore, the word mother, made him yield at once."

And Herbert's kindling eye and cheek bore testimony to the truth of his brother's words. His only feeling and exclamation had been, if he might but accompany his father, and save him all the trouble he could; allowing, however, its impossibility, when the circumstances of his still delicate health and the necessity for uninterrupted study, were placed before him.

That visit to Oxford was a proud one for Mr. Hamilton. His sons held that place in the estimation of the professors, superiors, and their fellow-collegians, which their early influences had promised, and which, as the sons of Arthur Hamilton, seemed naturally their own. Percy could so combine firmness in principle, unbending rectitude in conduct, with such a spirit of fun and enjoyment, as rendered him the prime mover of all sports at Oxford, as he had been at Oakwood; and Herbert, though so gentle and retiring as (until Percy's spirit was roused to shield him) gained him many nicknames and many petty annoyances, silently and insensibly won his way, and so bore with the thoughtless, the mirthful, and even the faulty, as at length to gain him the privilege of being allowed to do just as he liked, and win, by his extraordinary talents, the admiration and love of all the professors with whom he was thrown.

Morton had promised to introduce a person to Mr. Hamilton on his return from Oxford, who, if approved of, would be his willing, his eager assistant, and gladly remain in the island, attending to all that was required in its superintendence, and in the education of young Wilson, till he was old enough and properly fitted to take his father's place. Great, then, was Mr. Hamilton's disappointment, when Morton entered his library, according to appointment, but quite alone. Still greater was his astonishment, when he found it was Morton himself, thus eagerly desirous to become his companion, urging his wishes, his motives, Mr. Howard's sanction, with such earnestness, such single-mindedness of purpose, that every objection which, for Morton's own sake, Mr. Hamilton so strenuously brought forward, was overruled; and after a lengthened interview, matters were arranged to the entire satisfaction of both parties. The idea of the companionship and aid of such a friend as Morton bringing as great a relief to both Mr. and Mrs. Hamilton, as their acquiescence filled the whole heart of the young missionary with the most unbounded gratitude and joy. He suggested many little things, which, in the agitation of his hasty summons, had escaped his friends, and his whole being seemed transformed from despondency and listlessness to energy and hope. Engrossed as he was, Mr. Hamilton's usual thought for others had not deserted him, and he remarked that one of his household, Robert Langford, so often mentioned, appeared to linger in the library after morning and evening service, as if anxious to speak to him, but failing in courage so to do. He thought, too, that the young man seemed quite altered, dispirited, gloomy, almost wretched at times, instead of the mirthful, happy being he had been before. Determining to give him an opportunity of speaking before his departure, if he wished it, Mr. Hamilton summoned him to arrange, write a list, and pack some books, which Morton had selected to take with him. For some time Robert pursued his work in persevering silence, but at length fixed his eyes on his master with such beseeching earnestness, that Mr. Hamilton inquired the matter at oncc. It was some sime before the young man could sufficiently compose himself to speak with any coherency, but at last Mr. Hamilton gathered the following details.

About five weeks previous (the first day of June) he had been intrusted, as he had very often before been, by his master, with certain papers and law articles to convey to Plymouth, and with a pocket-book containing thirty pounds, in two ten and two five pound notes, which he had orders to leave at some poor though respectable families, whom Mr. Hamilton was in the habit of occasionally assisting, though they were out of his own domains. The morning he was to have started on this expedition a cousin, whom he had always regarded as a brother, came unexpectedly to see him. He had just arrived at Plymouth from a four years' residence with his regiment in Ireland: and Robert's glee was so great as to require reiterated commands from the steward to take care of the papers, and not stay at his mother's cottage, where he was to take his cousin, later than the afternoon. He lingered sc long before he set off from Oakwood, that he gathered up all the papers as quickly as he could, forgot his principal charge, so far at least as not to look to the secure fastening of the pocket-book, and hastened with his cousin through the brushwood and glade we have before mentioned, to his mother's cottage. It was very hot, and the young men, heated and in eager conversation, took off their coats, threw them loosely over their arms, and proceeded on their walk without them, much too engrossed with each other to be aware that, as they carried their coats, it was the easiest and most natural thing possible for all the smaller contents of their pockets to fall out, and if not missed directly, from the winding and rugged wood path, not likely to be found again.

A draught of cider and half an hour's rest at Mrs. Langford's cottage sufficiently revived Robert to resume his coat; he satisfied himself that his packet of papers was secure, and, as he imagined from the feel of another pocket, the pocket-book also.

What, then, was his consternation, when he approached the first house at which he was to leave ten pounds of the money, about twenty miles from Oakwood, to discover that the pocket-book was gone! and that which, by its feel, he believed to have been it, an old card-case, that his young master Percy had laughingly thrown at him one day after failing in his endeavor to emblazon it, the sticky materials he had used causing it to adhere to whatever it touched, and so preserving it in Robert's pocket, when almost all the other things had fallen out. He racked his memory in vain as to what could have become of it, convinced that he had not left it at Oakwood, as he first sincerely wished that he had. Two or three other things had also disappeared, and it suddenly flashed upon him, that when carrying his coat over his arm they must have fallen out. He cursed his thoughtlessness again and again, and would have retraced his steps immediately, but the papers with which he was intrusted had to be delivered at Plymouth by a certain hour, and he could not do it. The intense heat of the day gave place in the evening to a tremendous storm of thunder and lightning, wind, and very heavy rain, which last continued unabated through the night. He returned home, or rather to his mother's cottage, the next day, in a state of mind little removed from distraction; searching the path he had traversed with his cousin in every direction, but only succeeded in finding some worthless trifles, and the pocket-book itself, but open and empty; but at a little distance from it one five pound note. In an instant he remembered that in his hurry he had failed to see to its proper fastening; if he had, all would have been right, for the wind and rain would hardly have had power to open it, and disperse its contents. Hour after hour he passed in the vain search for the remainder; the storm had rendered the path more intricate; the ground was slimy, and quantities of dried sticks and broken branches and leaves almost covered it. He told his tale to his mother in the deepest distress; what was he to do? She advised him to tell the steward the whole story, and to request him to keep back the sum she was in the habit of receiving quarterly, till the whole amount could be repaid. Robert obeyed her, but with most painful reluctance, though even then he did not imagine all the misery his carelessness would entail upon him. Morris, as was natural, was exceedingly displeased, and not only reproved him very severely, but let fall suspicions as to the truth of his story; he knew nothing of his cousin, he said, and could not say what company he might have been led into. If the notes had fallen out of his pocket during his walk, they must be found; it was all nonsense that the wind and rain could so have scattered and annihilated them, as to remove all trace of them. He would not say any thing to his master, because it would only annoy him, and the charities he would give himself, not from Mrs. Langford's allowance, but from Robert's own wages, which he should certainly stop till the whole sum was paid; he should take care how he intrusted such a responsible office to him again.

Robert was at first indignant, and violent in his protestations of the truth of his story; but as it got wind in the servants' hall, as he found himself suspected and shunned by almost all, as days merged into weeks, and there was no trace of the notes, and Morris and Ellis both united in declaring that, as no strangers passed through that part of the park, if found they must have been heard of, the young man sunk into a state of the most gloomy despondency, longing to tell his kind master the whole tale, and yet, naturally enough, shrinking from the dread of his suspicion of his honesty, as more terrible than all the rest.

But Mr. Hamilton did not suspect him, and so assured him of his firm belief in his truth and innocence, that it was with great difficulty poor Robert refrained from throwing himself at his feet to pour forth his gratitude. He was so severely punished from his heedlessness, that his master would not say much about it, and soon after dismissing him, summoned Morris, and talked with him some time on the subject, declaring he would as soon suspect his own son of dishonesty as the boy who had grown up under his own eye from infancy, and the son of such a mother. It *was* very distressing for Mrs. Langford certainly, the old steward allowed, and she looked sad enough; but it was no use, he had tried hard enough to prevent his suspicions, but they would come. None but the servants and the woodmen and gardeners went that path, and if the notes had been dropped there, they must have been found; and it was a very hard thing for the other servants, as none knew who might be suspected of appropriating them. His master was much too kind in his opinions, but he must forgive him if he continued to keep a sharp look out after the young man. Morris was very old, and somewhat opinionated; so all that his master could succeed in, was to insist that he should only keep back half of Robert's wages, till the sum was paid.

"Take away the whole, and if he have been unfortunately led into temptation, which I do not believe he has, you expose him to it again," was his judicious command. "It is all right he should return it, even though lost only by carelessness; but I will not have him put to such straits for want of a little money, as must be the case if you deprive him of all his wages; and now, my good Morris, if you cannot in conscience repeat my firm opinion of this lad's innocence to the servants, I must do it myself."

And that very evening after prayers, when the whole household were assembled in the library, Mr. Hamilton addressed them simply and briefly, mentioning that Robert Langford had himself told his tale to him, and that it was his own opinion, and that of their mistress, that he did not deserve the suspicions attached to him, and that his fellow-servants would all be acting more charitably and religiously if they believed his story, until they had had some strong proof to the contrary; he could not, of course, interfere with private opinion; he could only tell them his own and their lady's. He acknowledged it was a very unpleasant occurrence, but he begged them all to dismiss the idea that suspicion could be attached to either of them; he felt too convinced that had any one of his household chanced to find the missing notes, they would at once have mentioned it to the steward or housekeeper, more especially since Robert's loss had been known among them only a few days after it had occurred. Appropriation, he need not tell them, in such a case was theft, and of that sin, he was perfectly certain, not one present would be guilty. He allowed that it would be much more satisfactory to have the tangible proof of Robert's innocence by discovering some trace of them, but it was not unlikely the heavy wind and rain had destroyed the thin material of the notes or borne them into the brambly brushwood, where it was scarcely possible they could be found.

If the attention of Mrs. Hamilton, her daughters, and Miss Harcourt had not been naturally riveted on Mr. Hamilton's address, and its effect on the servants, especially Robert, whose emotion was almost overpowering, they must have remarked that Ellen had shrunk into the shade of the heavy curtains falling by one of the windows, and had unconsciously grasped the oaken back of one of the massive chairs; lips, cheek, and brow, white and rigid as sculptured marble. An almost supernatural effort alone enabled her to master the crushing agony, sending the blood up to her cheeks with such returning violence, that when she wished her aunt and uncle good night, she might have been thought more flushed than pale; but it passed unnoticed Mrs. Hamilton too much annoyed on Mrs. Langford's account to think at that moment of any thing but how she could best set the poor mother's heart at rest. It was very evident that though some of the domestics, after their master's address, came up to Robert, shook hands with him and begged his pardon, the greater number still sided with Morris, and retained their own less favorable opinion, and she could well imagine what Mrs. Langford's sufferings must be. It only wanted five days to that fixed for Mr. Hamilton's departure, wind permitting; and there were so many things to think of and do for him, that his family could have little thought of any thing else; but Mrs. Hamilton assured her husband she would leave no means untried to prove Robert's innocence.

For nearly an hour that same night did Ellen, after her attendant had left her, sit crouched by the side of her bed as if some bolt had struck and withered her as she sat. One word alone sounded and resounded in her ears; she had known it, pronounced it to be such to herself numbers of times, but it had never mocked and maddened her as when spoken in her uncle's voice, and in his deepest, most expressive tone — "theft!" And she was the guilty one — and she must see the innocent bearing the penalty of her crime, suspicion, dislike, avoidance, for she dared not breathe the truth. Again came the wild, almost desperate, resolve to seek Mrs. Hamilton that very moment, avow herself the criminal, implore her to take back every trinket belonging to her, to replace it, and do with her what she would. But if she did confess, and so draw attention to her, how could she keep her brother's secret? Could she have firmness to bear all, rather than betray it? What proof of her inward wretchedness and remorse could there be in the mere confession of appropriation, when the use to which she had applied that money and all concerning it, even to the day it was found, must be withheld, lest it should in any way be connected with her letter to her brother. She must be silent; and the only prayer which, night and morning, ay, almost every hour, rose from that young heart, was for death, ere it was too late for God's forgiveness.

CHAPTER IV.

THE BROKEN DESK.

THE many secret wishes for an unfavorable wind, that Mr. Hamilton might stay at Oakwood still a little longer, were not granted, and he left his family the very day he had fixed, the 14th of July, just three weeks after his summons, and about ten days before his sons were expected home. Without him Oakwood was strange indeed, but with the exception of Emmeline, all seemed determined to conquer the sadness and anxiety, which the departure of one so beloved, naturally occasioned. Emmeline was so unused to any thing like personal sorrow, that she rather seemed to luxuriate in its indulgence.

"Do you wish to both disappoint and displease me, my dear Emmeline?" her mother said, one day, about a week after her husband had gone, as she entered the music-room, expecting to find her daughter at the harp, but perceiving her instead, listless and dispirited, on the sofa. "Indeed, you will do both, if you give way to this most uncalled-for gloom."

"Uncalled for," replied Emmeline, almost pettishly.

"Quite uncalled for, to the extent in which you are indulging it; and even if called for, do you not think you would be acting more correctly, if you thought more of others than yourself, and tried to become your own cheerful self for their sakes? It is the first time you have ever given me cause to suspect you of selfishness; and I am disappointed."

"Selfishness, mamma; and I do hate the thought of it so Am I selfish?" she repeated, her voice faltering, and her eyes filling fast with tears.

"I hope not, my love: but if you do not try to shake off

this depression, we must believe you to be so. Your father's absence is a still greater trial to Caroline than it is to you, for it compels a very bitter disappointment, as well as the loss of his society; and yet, though she feels both deeply, she has exerted herself more than I ever saw her do before, and so proves, more than any words or tears could do, how much she loves both him and me."

"And do you think I love you both, less than she does?" replied Emmeline, now fairly sobbing.

"No, dearest; but I want you to prove it in the same admirable manner. Do you think I do not feel your father's absence, Emmeline? but would you like to see me as sad and changed as you are?"

Emmeline looked up in her face, for there was something in the tone that appealed to her better feelings at once. Throwing her arms round her, she sobbed—

"Dear mamma, do forgive me. I see now I have been very selfish and very weak, but I never, never can be as firm and self-controlled as you and Caroline are."

"Do not say never, love, or you will never try to be so. I am quite sure you would not like to be one of those weak, selfish characters, who lay all their faults, and all the mischief their faults produce, on a supposed impossibility to become like others. I know your disposition is naturally less strong and firm than your sister's, but it is more elastic, and still more joyous; and so had you not too weakly encouraged your very natural sorrow, you would have been enabled to throw it off, and in the comfort such an exertion would have brought to us, fully recompensed yourself."

"And if I do try now?"

"I shall be quite satisfied, dearest; though I fear you will find it more difficult than had you tried a few days ago. Confess that I am right. Did you not, after the first two or three days, feel that you could have been cheerful again, at least at times, but that you fancied you had not felt sorry enough, and so increased both sorrow and anxiety by determinedly dwelling on them, instead of seeking some pursuit?"

"Dear mamma, shall I never be able to hide a feeling from you?" answered Emmeline, so astonished, that her tears half dried. "I did not know I felt so myself till you put it before me, and now I know that I really did. Was it very wrong?"

"I will answer your question by another, love. Did you find such pertinacious indulgence of gloom help you to bring the object of your regret and anxiety, and of your own grief, before your Heavenly Father?"

Emmeline hesitated, but only for a minute, then answered, with a crimson blush —

"No, mamma; I could not pray to God to protect dear papa, or to give me His blessing, half as earnestly and believingly as when I was happier; the more I indulged in gloomy thoughts, the more difficulty I had to turn them to prayer, and the last few days, I fear, I have not even tried."

"Then, dearest, is it necessary for me to answer your former question? I see by that conscious look that it is not. You have always trusted my experience and affection, my Emmeline, trust them now, and try my plan. Think of your dear father, whom you cannot love too well, or whose compelled absence really regret too much; but so think of him, as to pray continually in spirit to your gracious God, to have him always in His holy keeping, either on sea or land, in storm or calm, and so prosper his undertaking, as to permit his return to us still sooner than we at present expect. The very constant prayer for this, will make you rest secure and happy in the belief that our God is with him wherever he is, as He is with us, and so give you cheerfulness and courage to attend to your daily duties, and conquer any thing like too selfish sorrow. Will you try this, love, even if it be more difficult now than it would have been a few days ago?"

"I will indeed, mamma," and she raised her head from her mother's shoulder, and tried to smile. "When you first addressed me to-day, I thought you were almost harsh, and so cold — so you see even there I was thinking wrong — and now I am glad, oh, so glad, you did speak to me!"

"And I know who will be glad too, if I have prevented his having a Niobe for his Tiny, instead of the Euphrosyne, which I believe he sometimes calls you. I thought there was one particular duet that Percy is to be so charmed with, Emmy. Suppose you try it now." And, her tears all checked, her most unusual gloom dispersed, Emmeline obeyed with alacrity, and finding, when she had once begun, so many things to get perfect for the gratification of her brothers, that nearly three hours slipped away quite unconsciously; and when Caroline returned from a walk, she was astonished at the change in her sister, and touched by the affectionate self-reproach with which Emmeline, looking up in her face, exclaimed —

"Dear Caroline, I have been so pettish and so cross to you since papa left, that I am sure you must be quite tired of me; but I am going to be really a heroine now, and not a sham sentimental one; and bear the pain of papa's absence as bravely as you do."

And she did so; though at first it was, as her mother had warned her, very difficult to compel the requisite exertion, which for employment and cheerfulness, was now needed; but when the *will* is right, there is little fear of failure.

As each day passed, so quickly merging into weeks, that five had now slipped away since that fatal letter had been sent to Edward, the difficulty to do as she had intended, entreat Mrs. Langford to dispose of her trinkets and watch, became to Ellen, either in reality or seeming, more and more difficult. Her illness had confined her to her room for nearly a week, and when she was allowed to take the air, the state of nervous debility to which it had reduced her, of course prevented her ever being left alone. The day after Mr. Hamilton's appeal to his domestics, she had made a desperate attempt, by asking permission to be the bearer of a message from her aunt to the widow; and as the girls were often allowed and encouraged to visit their nurse, the request was granted without any surprise, though to the very last moment she feared one of her cousins or Miss Harcourt would offer to accompany her. They were all, however, too occupied with and for Mr. Hamilton, and she sought the cottage, and there, with such very evident mental agony, besought Mrs. Langford to promise her secrecy and aid, that the widow, very much against her conscience, was won over to accede. She was in most pressing want of money, she urged, and dared not appeal to her aunt. Not daring to say the whole amount which she so urgently required at once, she had only brought with her the antique gold cross and two or three smaller ornaments, which had been among her mother's trinkets, and a gold locket Percy had given her. Mrs. Langford was painfully startled. She had no idea her promise comprised acquiescence and assistance in any matter so very wrong and mysterious as this; and she tried every argument, every persuasion, to prevail on Ellen to confide all her difficulties to Mrs. Hamilton, urging that if even she had done wrong, it could only call for temporary displeasure, whereas the mischief of her present proceeding might never come to an end, and must be discovered at last; but Ellen was inexorable, though evidently quite as miserable as she was firm, and Mrs. Langford had too high an idea of the solemn nature of a pledged word to draw back, or think of betraying her. She said that, of course, it might be some weeks before she could succeed in disposing of them all; as to offer them all together, or even at one place, would be exposing herself to the most unpleasant suspicions.

One step was thus gained, but nearly a fortnight had passed, and she heard nothing from the widow.

"Will they never come?" exclaimed Emmeline, in mirthful impatience, one evening, about four days after her conversation with her mother; "it *must be* past the hour Percy named."

"It still wants half an hour," replied Mrs. Hamilton; adding, "that unfortunate drawing, when will it succeed in obtaining your undivided attention?"

"Certainly not this evening, mamma; the only drawing I feel inclined for, is a sketch of my two brothers, if they would only have the kindness to sit by me."

"Poor Percy," observed Caroline, dryly; "if you are to be as restless as you have been the last hour, Emmeline, he would not be very much flattered by his portrait."

"Now that is very spiteful of you, Caroline, and all because I do not happen to be so quiet and sober as you are; though I am sure all this morning, that mamma thought by your unusually long absence that you were having a most persevering practice, you were only collecting all Percy's and Herbert's favorite songs and pieces, and playing them over, instead of your new music."

"And what if I did, Emmeline?"

"Why, it only proves that your thoughts are quite as much occupied by them as mine are, though you have so disagreeably read, studied, worked, just as usual, to make one believe you neither thought nor cared any thing about them."

"And so, because Caroline can control even joyous anticipation, she is to be thought void of feeling, Emmy. I really can pronounce no such judgment; so, though she may have settled to her usual pursuits, and you have literally done nothing at all to-day, I will not condemn her as loving her brothers less."

"But you will condemn me as an idle, unsteady, hair-brained girl," replied Emmeline, kneeling on the ottoman at her mother's feet, and looking archly and fondly in her face. Then do let me have a fellow-sufferer, for I cannot stand condemnation alone. Ellen, do put away that everlasting sketch, and be idle and unsteady, too!"

"It won't do, Emmy; Ellen has been so perseveringly industrious since her illness, that I should rather condemn her for too much application than too great idleness. But you really have been stooping too long this warm evening, my love," she added, observing, as Ellen, it seemed almost involuntarily, looked up at her cousin's words, that her cheeks were flushed almost painfully. "Oblige Emmeline this once, and be as idle as she is: come and talk to me, I have scarcely heard a word from you to-day; you have been more silent than ever, I think, since your uncle left us; but I must have no gloom to greet your cousins, Ellen."

There was no rejoinder to these kind and playful words. Ellen did indeed put aside her drawing, but instead of taking a seat near her aunt, which in former days she would have been only too happy to do, she walked to the farthest window, and ensconcing herself in its deep recess, seemed determined to hold communion with no one. Miss Harcourt was so indignant as scarcely to be able to contain its expression. Caroline looked astonished and provoked. Emmeline was much too busy in flying from window to window, to think of any thing else but her brothers. Mrs. Hamilton was more grieved and hurt than Ellen had scarcely ever made her feel. Several times before, in the last month, she had fancied there was something unusual in her manner; but the many anxieties and thoughts which had engrossed her since her husband's summons and his departure, had prevented any thing, till that evening, but momentary surprise. Emmeline's exclamation that she was quite sure she heard the trampling of horses, and that it must be Percy, by the headlong way he rode, prevented any remark, and brought them all to the window; and she was right, for in a few minutes a horseman emerged from some distant trees, urging his horse to its utmost speed, waving his cap in all sorts of mirthful gesticulation over his head, long before he could be quite sure that there was anybody to see him. Another minute, and he had flung the reins to Robert, with a laughing greeting, and springing up the long flight of steps in two bounds, was in the sitting-room and in the arms of his mother, before either of his family imagined he could have had even time to dismount.

"Herbert?" was the first word Mrs. Hamilton's quivering lip could speak.

"Is quite well, my dearest mother, and not five minutes' ride behind me. The villagers would flock round us, with such an hurrah, I thought you must have heard it here; so I left Bertie to play the agreeable, and promised to see them to-morrow, and galloped on here, for you know the day we left, I vowed that the first-born of my mother should have her first kiss."

"Still the same, Percy — not sobered yet, my boy?" said his mother, looking at him with a proud smile; for while the tone and manner were still the eager, fresh-feeling boy, the face and figure were that of the fine-growing, noble-looking man.

"Sobered! why, mother, I never interd to be," he answered.

joyously as he alternately embraced his sisters, Miss Harcourt, and Ellen, who, fearing to attract notice, had emerged from her hiding-place; "if the venerable towers of that most wise and learned town, Oxford, and all the grave lectures and long faces of sage professors have failed to tame me, there can be no hope for my sobriety; but here comes Herbert, actually going it almost as fast as I did. Well done, my boy! Mother, that is all your doing; he feels your influence at this distance. Why, all the Oxonians would fancy the colleges must be tumbling about their ears, if they saw the gentle, studious, steady Herbert Hamilton riding at such a rate." He entered almost as his brother spoke; and though less boisterous, the intense delight it was to him to look in his mother's face again, to be surrounded by all he loved, was as visible as Percy's; and deep was the thankfulness of Mrs. Hamilton's ever anxious heart, as she saw him looking so well — so much stronger than in his boyhood. The joy of that evening, and of very many succeeding days, was, indeed, great; though many to whom the sanctity and bliss of domestic affection are unknown, might fancy there was little to call for it; but to the inmates of Oakwood it was real happiness to hear Percy's wild laugh and his inexhaustible stories, calling forth the same mirth from his hearers — the very sound of his ever-bounding step, and his boisterous career from room to room, to visit, he declared, and rouse all the bogies and spirits that must have slept while he was away: Herbert's quieter but equal interest in all that had been done, studied, read, even thought and felt, in his absence: the pride and delight of both in the accounts of Edward, Percy insisting that to have such a gallant fellow of a brother ought to make Ellen as lively and happy as Emmeline, who was blessed nearly in the same measure — looking so excessively mischievous as he spoke, that, though his sister did not at first understand the inference, it was speedily discovered, and called for a laughing attack on his outrageous self-conceit. Herbert more earnestly regretted to see Ellen looking as sad and pale as when she was quite a little girl, and took upon himself gently to reproach her for not being, or, at least, trying to make herself more cheerful, when she had so many blessings around her, and was so superlatively happy in having such a brave and noble-hearted brother. If he did not understand her manner as he spoke, both he and the less observant Percy were destined to be still more puzzled and grieved as a few weeks passed, and they at first fancied and then were quite sure that she was completely altered, even in her manner to their mother

Instead of being so gentle, so submissive, so quietly happy to deserve the smallest sign of approval from Mrs. Hamilton, she now seemed completely to shrink from her, either in fear, or that she no longer cared either to please or to obey her. By imperceptible, but sure degrees, this painful conviction pressed itself on the minds of the whole party, even to the light-hearted, unsuspicious Emmeline, to whom it was so utterly incomprehensible, that she declared it must be all fancy, and that they were all so happy that their heads must be a little turned.

"Even mamma's!" observed Caroline, dryly.

"No; but she is the only sensible person among us, for she has not said any thing about it, and, therefore, I dare say does not even see that which we are making such a wonder about."

"I do not agree with you, for I rather think she has both seen and felt it before either of us, and that because it so grieves and perplexes her, she cannot speculate or even speak about it as we do. Time will explain it, I suppose, but it is very disagreeable."

It was, indeed, no fancy; but little could these young observers, or even Mrs. Hamilton, suspect that which was matter of speculation or grief to them, was almost madness in its agony of torture to Ellen; who, as weeks passed, and but very trifling returns for her trinkets were made her by Mrs. Langford, felt as if her brain must fail before she could indeed accomplish her still ardently desired plan, and give back the missing sum to Robert, without calling suspicion on herself. She felt to herself as changed as she appeared to those that observed her; a black impenetrable pall seemed to have enveloped her heart and mind, closing up both, even from those affections, those pursuits, so dear to her before. She longed for some change from the dense impenetrable fog, even if it were some heavy blow — tangible suffering of the fiercest kind was prayed for, rather than the stagnation which caused her to move, act, and speak as if under some fatal spell, and look with such terror on the relation she had so loved, that even to be banished from her presence she imagined would be less agony, than to associate with her, as the miserable, guilty being she had become.

Mrs. Hamilton watched and was anxious, but she kept both her observations and anxiety to herself, for she would not throw even a temporary cloud over the happiness of her children. A fortnight after the young men's arrival, letters came most unexpectedly from Mr. Hamilton, dated twelve days after he had left, and brought by a Scottish trader whom they had encountered near the Shetland Isles, and who had faithfully forwarded then. from Edinburgh, as he had promised. The voyage had been most delightful, and they hoped to reach Feroe in another week. He wrote in the highest terms of Morton; the comfort of such companionship, and the intrinsic worth of his character, which could never be known, until so closely thrown together.

"I may thank our Percy for this excellent friend," he wrote. "He tells me his brave and honest avowal of those verses, which had given him so much pain, attracted him more toward me and mine, than even my own efforts to obtain his friendship. Percy little thought when he so conquered himself the help he would give his father — so little do we know to what hidden good, the straightforward, honest performance of a duty, however painful, may lead."

"My father should thank you, mother, not me," was Percy's rejoinder, with a flushed cheek and eye sparkling with animation, as his mother read the passage to him.

"No such thing, Percy; I will not have you give me all the merit of your good deeds. I did but try to guide you, my boy; neither the disposition to receive, nor the fruit springing from the seeds I planted, is from me."

"They are, mother, more than you are in the least aware of!" replied, he, with even more than his usual impetuosity, for they happened to be quite alone; "I thought I knew all your worth before I went to Oxford, but I have mingled with the world now; I have been a silent listener and observer of such sentiments, such actions, as I know would naturally have been mine, and though in themselves perhaps of little moment, saw they led to irregularity, laxity of principle and conduct, which *now* I cannot feel as other than actual guilt; and what saved me from the same? The *principle* which from my infancy you taught. I have questioned, led on in conversation, these young men to speak of their boyhood and their homes, and there were none guided, loved as I was; none whose parents had so blended firmness with indulgence, as while my wild, free spirits were unchecked, prevented the ascendency of evil. *I could not do* as they did. Mother! love you more, perhaps, I cannot, but every time I join the world, fresh from this home sanctuary, I must bless and venerate you more! To walk through this world with any degree of security, man *must* have principle based on the highest source; and that principle can only be instilled by the constant example of a mother and the associations of a home!" Mrs. Hamilton could not answer, but — a very unusual sign of weakness with her — tears of the most intense happiness poured down on the cheek of her tor, as in his impetuosity he knelt before her, and ended his very unusually grave appeal by the same loving caresses he was wont to lavish on her, in his infancy and boyhood.

The letters from Mr. Hamilton, of course, greatly increased the general hilarity, and the arrival of Mr. Grahame's family about the same time, added fresh zest to youthful enjoyment. In the few months she spent at Moorlands, Annie actually condescended to be agreeeble. Percy, and some of Percy's boyish friends, now young men, as himself, were quite different to her usual society, and as she very well knew the only way to win Percy's even casual notice was to throw off her affectation and superciliousness as much as possible, she would do so, and be pleasing to an extent that surprised Mrs. Hamilton, who, always inclined to judge kindly, hoped more regarding Annie than she had done yet. Little could her pure mind conceive that, in addition to the pleasure of flirting with Percy, Annie acted in this manner actually to throw her off her guard, and so give her a wider field for her machinations when Caroline should enter the London world; a time to which, from her thirteenth year, she had secretly looked as the opportunity to make Caroline so conduct herself, as to cover her mother with shame and misery, and bring her fine plans of education to failure and contempt.

Mrs. Greville and Mary were also constantly at the Hall, or having their friends with them; Herbert and Mary advancing in words or feelings not much farther than they had ever done as boy and girl, but still feeling and acknowledging to their mutual mothers that, *next* to them, they loved each other better than all the world, and enjoyed, each other's society more than any other pleasure which life could offer. Excursions by land or water, sometimes on horseback, sometimes in the carriages, constant little family reunions, either at Oakwood, Moorlands, or Greville Manor, passed days and evenings most delightfully, to all but Ellen, who did not dare stay at home as often as inclination prompted, and whose forced gayety, when in society, did but increase the inward torture when alone. Mrs. Hamilton had as yet refrained from speaking to her — still trying to believe she must be mistaken, and there really was nothing strange about her. One morning, however, about a month after the young men had been at home, her attention was unavoidably arrested by hearing Percy gayly ask his cousin —

"Nelly, Tiny wrote me such a description of your birthday watch, that I quite forgot, I have been dying to see it all the time I have been at home; show it me now, there's a dear; it cannot be much use to you, that's certain, for I have never seen you take it from its hiding-place."

Ellen answered, almost inarticulately, it was not in her power to show it him.

"Not in your power! You must be dreaming, Nell, as I think you are very often now. Why, what do you wear that chain, and seal and key for, if you have not your watch on too?"

"Where is your watch, Ellen? and why, if you are not wearing it, do you make us suppose you are?" interrupted Mrs. Hamilton, startled out of all idea that Ellen was changed only in fancy.

Ellen was silent, and to Percy's imagination, so sullenly and insolently so, that he became indignant.

"Did you hear my mother speak to you, Ellen? Why don't you answer?"

"Because I thought my watch was my own to do what I liked with, to wear or to put away," was the reply; over neither words nor tone of which, had she at that moment any control, for in her agonized terror, she did not in the least know what she said.

"How dare you answer so, Ellen? Leave the room, or ask my mother's pardon at once," replied Percy, his eyes flashing with such unusual anger, that it terrified her still more, and under the same kind of spell she was turning to obey him, without attempting the apology he demanded.

"Stay, Ellen; this extraordinary conduct must not go on any longer without notice on my part. I have borne with it, I fear, too long already. Leave us, my dear Percy; I would rather speak with your cousin alone."

"I fear it will be useless, mother; what has come over Ellen I *cannot* imagine, but I never saw such an incomprehensible change in my life."

He departed, unconscious that Ellen, who was near the door transfixed at her aunt's words, made a rapid movement as to catch hold of his arm, and that the words, "Do not go, Percy, for pity's sake!" trembled on her pale lips, but they emitted no sound.

What passed in the interview, which lasted more than an hour, no one knew; but to the watchful eyes of her affectionate children, there were traces of very unusual disturbance on Mrs. Hamilton's expressive countenance when she rejoined them; and the dark rim round Ellen's eyes, the deadly pallor of her cheeks and lips seemed to denote that it had not been deficient in suffering to her; though not one sign of penitence, one word of acknowledgment that she was, and had been for some weeks in error, by her extraordinary conduct — not even a softening tear could her aunt elicit. She had never before so failed — never, not even when the disappearance of her allowance had caused extreme displeasure, had Ellen evinced such an apparently sullen spirit of determined hardihood. She would not attempt defence or reply to the acted falsehood with which she was charged, of appearing to wear her watch when she did not, or to say what she had done with it. Mrs. Hamilton spoke to her till she was almost exhausted, for her own disappointment was most painful, and she had not a gleam of hope to urge her on. Her concluding words were these —

"That you are under the evil influence of some unconfessed and most heinous fault, Ellen, I am perfectly convinced; what it is time will reveal. I give you one month to decide on your course of action; subdue this sullen spirit, confess whatever error you may have been led into, and so change your conduct as to be again the child I so loved, spite of occasional faults and errors, and I will pardon all that is past. If, at the end of a month, I find you persisting in the same course of rebellion and defiance, regardless alike of your duty to your God and to me, I shall adopt some measures to compel submission. I had hoped to bring up all my children under my own eye, and by my own efforts; but if I am not permitted so to do, I know my duty too well to shrink from the alternative. You will not longer remain under my care; some severer guardian and more rigid discipline may bring you to a sense of your duty. I advise you to think well on this subject, Ellen; you know me too well, I think, to imagine that I speak in mere jest."

She had left the room as she spoke, so, that if Ellen had intended reply, there was no time for it. But she could not have spoken. Go from Oakwood, and in anger! Yet it was but just; it was better, perhaps, than the lingering torture she was then enduring — better to hide her shame and misery among strangers, than remain among the good, the happy — the guilty wretch she was. She sat and thought till feeling itself became utterly exhausted, and again the spell, the stupor of indifference, crept over her. She would have confessed, but she knew that it could never satisfy, as the half confession she would have been compelled to make it, and the dread of herself, that she should betray her brother, sealed her lips.

Robert's story, and the strange disappearance of the notes, had of course been imparted to Percy and Herbert. In fact, the change in the young man, from being as light-hearted as his young master himself, to gravity and almost gloom — for the conviction of his master and mistress, as to his innocence, could not cheer him, while suspicion against him still actuated Morris, and many of the other servants — would have called the young men's attention toward him at once. The various paths and glades between the Hall and Mrs. Langford's cottage had been so searched, that unless the storm had destroyed them or blown the notes very far away, it seemed next to impossible, that they could not be found. Mr. Hamilton knew the number of each note, had told them to his wife, and gave notice at his banker's that though he did not wish them stopped, he should like to know, if possible, when they had passed. No notice of such a thing had been sent to Oakwood, and it seemed curious that, if found and appropriated, they should not yet have been used, for ten weeks had now slipped away since their loss, and nearly nine since the letters had been sent to Edward and his captain, answers to which had not yet been received; but that was nothing remarkable, for Edward seldom wrote above once in three or four months.

It was nearing the end of August, when one afternoon Mrs. Hamilton was prevented joining her children in a sail up the Dart, though it had been a long promise, and Percy was, in consequence, excessively indignant; but certain matters relative to the steward's province demanded a reference to his mistress, and Morris was compelled to request a longer interview than usual. Ellen had chosen to join the aquatic party, a decision now so contrary to her usual habits, that Mrs. Hamilton could not help fancying it was to prevent the chance of being any time alone with her. There had been no change in her manner, except a degree more care to control the disrespectful or pettish answer; but nothing to give hope that the spirit was changing, and that the hidden error, whatever it might be, would be acknowledged and atoned. Mrs. Hamilton was nerving her own mind for the performance of the alternative she had placed before her niece, passing many a sleepless night in painful meditations. If to send her from Oakwood were necessary, would it produce the effect she wished? with whom could she place her? and what satisfactory reason could she assign for doing so? She knew there would be a hundred tongues to cry shame on her for sending her orphan niece from her roof, but that was but one scarcely-tasted bitter drop in the many other sources of anxiety. But still these were but her nightly sorrows; she might have been paler when she rose, but though her children felt quite sure that Ellen was grieving her exceedingly, her cheerful sympathy in their enjoyments and pursuits never waned for a moment.

Morris left her at six o'clock, all his business so satisfactorily accomplished, that the old man was quite happy, declaring to Ellis, he had always thought his mistress unlike any one else before; but such a clear head for reducing difficult accounts and tangled affairs to order, he had never imagined could either be possessed by, or was any business of, a woman. Not in the least aware of the wondering admiration she had excited, Mrs. Hamilton had called Robert and proceeded to the school-room to get a pattern of embroidery and a note, which Caroline had requested might be sent to Annie Grahame that evening; the note was on the table, but the pattern and some silks she had neglected to put up till her brothers were ready, and they so hurried her, that her mother had promised she would see to it for her. The embroidery box was in a panelled closet of the school-room, rather high up, and in taking especial care to bring it safely down, Robert loosened a desk from its equilibrium, and it fell to the ground with such force as to break into several pieces, and scatter all its contents over the floor. It was Ellen's! the pretty rose-wood desk which had been her gift, that memorable New Year's Eve, and was now the repository of her dread secret. It was actually in fragments, especially where the ink-stands and pens had been, and the spring broken, the secret drawer burst open, and all its contents were disclosed. Robert was much too concerned to think of any thing but his own extreme carelessness, and his mistress's reprimand; and he busied himself in hastily picking up the contents, and placing them carefully on the table, preparatory to their arrangement by Mrs. Hamilton in a drawer of the table which she was emptying for the purpose. She laid them carefully in, and was looking over a book of very nicely written French themes, glad there was at least one thing for which she might be satisfied with Ellen, when an exclamation —

"Why, there is one of them! I am so glad," and as sudden a stop and half-checked groan from Robert startled her. She looked inquiringly at him, but he only covered his face with one hand, while the other remained quite unconsciously covering the secret drawer out of which the contents had not fallen, but were merely disclosed.

"What *is* the matter, Robert? what have you found to cause such contradictory exclamations? Speak, for God's sake!" escaped from Mrs. Hamilton's lips, for by that lightning touch of association, memory, thought, whatever it may be, which joins events together, and unites present with past, so that almost a life seems crowded in a moment, such a suspicion flashed upon her as to make her feel sick and giddy, and turn so unusually pale, as effectually to rouse Robert, and make him spring up to get her a chair.

"Nothing, madam, indeed it can be nothing — I must be mistaken — I am acting like a fool this afternoon, doing the most unheard-of mischief, and then frightening you and myself at shadows."

"This evasion will not do, Robert; give me the papers at which you were so startled."

He hesitated, and Mrs. Hamilton extended her hand to take them herself; but her hand and arm so shook, that to hide it from her domestic, she let it quietly drop by her side, and repeated her command in a tone that brooked no farther delay. He placed the little drawer and its contents in her hand, and, without a word withdrew into the farthest window. For full five, it might have been ten minutes, there was silence so deep, a pin-fall might have been loully heard. It was broken by Mrs. Hamilton.

"Robert!"

There was neither change nor tremor in the voice, but the fearful expression of forcibly-controlled suffering on her death-like countenance so awed and terrified him, he besought her, almost inarticulately, to let him fetch a glass of water — wine — something —

"It is not at all necessary, my good boy; I am perfectly well. This is, I believe, the only note that can be identified as one of those you lost; these smaller ones (she pointed to three, of one, two, and four pounds each, which Ellen had received at long intervals from Mrs. Langford) have nothing to do with it?"

"No, madam, and that — that may not —"

"We cannot doubt it, Robert, I have its number; I need not detain you, however, any longer. Take care of these broken fragments, and if they can be repaired, see that it is done. Here is Miss Hamilton's note and parcel. I believe you are to wait for an answer, at all events inquire. I need not ask you to be silent on this discovery, till I have spoken to Miss Fortescue, or to trust my promise to make your innocence fully known."

"Not by the exposure of Miss Ellen! Oh, madam, this is but one of them, the smallest one — it may have come to her by the merest chance — see how stained it is with damp — for the sake of mercy, oh, madam, spare her and yourself too!" and in the earnestness of his supplication Robert caught hold of her dress, hardly knowing himself how he had found courage so to speak. His mistress's lips quivered.

"It is a kind thought, Robert, and if justice to you and mercy to the guilty can, by any extenuating clause unknown to me now, be united, trust me, they shall. Now go."

He obeyed in silence, and still Mrs. Hamilton changed not that outward seeming of rigid calm. She continued to put every paper and letter away, (merely retaining the notes,) locked the drawer, took possession of the key, and then retired to her own room, where for half an hour she remained alone.

It is not ours to lift the veil from that brief interval. We must have performed our task badly indeed, if our readers cannot so enter into the lofty character, the inward strivings and outward conduct of Mrs. Hamilton, as not to imagine more satisfactorily to themselves than we could write it, the heart-crushing agony of that one half hour; and anguish as it was, it did but herald deeper. There was not even partial escape for her, as there would have been, had her husband been at home. Examination of the culprit, whose mysterious conduct was so fatally explained, that she did not even dare hope this was the only missing note she had appropriated — compelled confession of the use to which it had been applied — public acknowledgment of Robert's perfect truth and innocence, all crowded on her mind like fearful spectres of pain and misery, from which there could be no escape; and from whom did they spring? Ellen! the child of her adoption, of her love; whose character she had so tried to mould to good; whose young life she had so sought to make happier than its earliest years; for whom she had so hoped, so prayed, so trusted; had borne with anxiety and care, tended in physical suffering with such untiring gentleness, such exhaustless love — and now!

CHAPTER V.

THE CULPRIT AND THE JUDGE

It was nearly seven when the young party returned, delighted as usual with their afternoon's amusement; and Percy, shouting loudly for his mother, giving vent to an exclamation of impatience at finding she was still invisible.

"I shall wish Morris and all his concerns at the bottom of the Dart, if he is so to engross my mother when I want her," he said, as he flung himself full length on a couch in the music-room, desiring Emmeline to make haste and disrobe, as he must have an air on the harp to soothe his troubled spirit.

Herbert, to look for a poem, the beauty of which he had been discussing with Miss Harcourt during their sail, entered the library, but perceiving his mother, would have retreated, thinking her still engaged; but she looked up as the door opened, and perceiving him, smiled, and asked him if they had had a pleasant afternoon. He looked at her earnestly, without making any reply; then approaching her, took one of her hands in his, and said, fondly —

"Forgive me, dearest mother; I ought not, perhaps, to ask, but I am sure something is wrong. You are ill — anxious — may I not share it? Can I do nothing?"

"Nothing, my Herbert; bless you for your watchful love — it is such comfort." And the long pressure of the hand which so warmly clasped hers, the involuntary tenderness with which these few words were said, betrayed how much she needed such comfort at that moment; but she rallied instantly. "Do not look so anxious, dear boy, I am not ill — not quite happy, perhaps, but we know where to look for strength to bear trial, Herbert. Wait tea for me till eight o'clock; it is probable I may be engaged till then;" and, satisfied that she did not wish to be more explicit, Herbert took his book, and somewhat sorrowfully left her.

Ten minutes more, and the massive door unclosed again, but no step advanced, for the intruder remained rooted where the door had closed. It was a very large and lofty room, with an arched and Gothic roof, of black and fretted oak, the walls and chimney-piece of the same material and most elaborate workmanship. A sort of dais, remnant of olden times, divided the upper part of the room, by two or three steps, from the lower. On this dais was the raised reading-desk of superbly carved oak, at which Mr. Hamilton officiated morning and evening, and two library tables of more modern workmanship stood on each side, but rather lower down. Except the massive oaken chairs and couches, and three or four curious tables scattered about, and the well-filled book-cases, forming, to the height of five feet, the border, as it were, of the fretted wood-work of the walls, and filling up the niches formed by the windows; the lower part of the hall, two-thirds of the length, was comparatively unoccupied, showing its vast space and superb roof to still greater advantage. The magnificently stained windows, one on the dais — a deep oriel — threw such subdued light into the room, as accorded well with its other appointments; but as evening advanced, gave it that sort of soft, holy light, which always impresses the spirit with a species of awe.

We do not think it was that feeling alone which so overpowered the second intruder, as to arrest her, spell-bound, on the threshold. Mrs. Hamilton was seated at one of the tables on the dais nearest the oriel window, the light from which fell full on her, giving her figure, though she was seated naturally enough in one of the large, maroon velvet, oaken chairs, an unusual effect of dignity and command, and impressing the terrified beholder with such a sensation of awe, that, had her life depended on it, she could not for that one minute have gone forward; and even when desired to do so by the words —

"I desired your presence, Ellen, because I wished to speak to you; come here without any more delay:" — how she walked the whole length of that interminable room, and stood facing her aunt, she never knew.

Mrs. Hamilton for a full minute did not speak, but she fixed that searching look, to which we have once before alluded, upon Ellen's face; and then said, in a tone which, though very low and calm, expressed as much as that earnest look —

"Ellen! is it necessary for me to tell you why you are here — necessary to produce the proof that my words are right, and that you *have* been influenced by the fearful effects of some unconfessed and most heinous sin? Little did I dream its nature."

For a moment Ellen stood as turned to stone, as white and rigid — the next she had sunk down, with a wild, bitter cry at Mrs. Hamilton's feet, and buried her face in her hands.

"Is it true — can it be true — that you, offspring of my own sister, dear to me, cherished by me as my own child — you have been the guilty one to appropriate, and conceal the appropriation of money, which has been a source of distress by its loss, and the suspicion thence proceeding, for the last seven weeks? — that you could listen to your uncle's words, absolving his whole household as incapable of a deed which was actual theft, and yet, by neither word nor sign, betray remorse or guilt? — could behold the innocent suffering the fearful misery of suspicion, loss of character, without the power of clearing himself, and stand calmly, heedlessly by — only proving by your hardened and rebellious temper that all was not right within — Ellen, can this be true?"

"Yes!" was the reply, but with such a fearful effort, that her slight frame shook as with an ague; "thank God, that it is known! I dared not bring down the punishment on myself, but I can bear it."

"This is mere mockery, Ellen; how dare I believe even this poor evidence of repentance, with the recollection of your past conduct? What were the notes you found?"

Ellen named them.

"Where are they? — This is but one, and the smallest."

Ellen's answer was scarcely audible.

"Used them — and for what?"

There was no answer, neither then, nor when Mrs. Hamilton sternly reiterated the question. She then demanded —

"How long have they been in your possession?"

"Five or six weeks;" but the reply was so tremulous, it carried no conviction with it.

"Since Robert told his story to your uncle, or before?"

"Before."

"Then your last answer was a falsehood, Ellen; it is full seven weeks since my husband addressed the household on the subject. You could not have so miscounted time, with such a deed to date by. Where did you find them?"

Ellen described the spot.

"And what business had you there? You know that neither you nor your cousins are ever allowed to go that way to Mrs. Langford's cottage, and more especially alone. If you wanted to see her, why did you not go the usual way? And when was this? — you must remember the exact day. Your memory is not in general so treacherous."

Again Ellen was silent.

"Have you forgotten it?"

She crouched lower at her aunt's feet, but the answer was audible —

"No."

"Then answer me, Ellen, this moment, and distinctly; for what purpose were you seeking Mrs. Langford's cottage by that forbidden path, and when?"

"I wanted money, and I went to ask her to take my trinkets — my watch, if it must be — and dispose of them as I had read of others doing, as miserable as I was; and the wind blew the notes to my very hand, and I used them. I was mad then — I have been mad since, I believe; but I would have returned the whole amount to Robert, if I could but have parted with my trinkets in time."

To describe the tone of utter despair, the recklessness as to the effect her words would produce, is impossible. Every word increased Mrs. Hamilton's bewilderment and misery. To suppose that Ellen did not feel was folly. It was the very depth of wretchedness which was crushing her to the earth, but every answered and unanswered question but deepened the mystery, and rendered her judge's task more difficult.

"And when was this, Ellen? I will have no more evasion — tell me the exact day."

But she asked in vain. Ellen remained moveless, and silent as the dead.

After several minutes, Mrs. Hamilton removed her hands from her face, and compelling her to lift up her head, gazed searchingly on her deathlike countenance for some moments in utter silence, and then said, in a tone that Ellen never in her life forgot —

"You cannot imagine, Ellen, that this half-confession will either satisfy me, or in the smallest degree redeem your sin. One and one only path is open to you; for all that you have said and left unsaid but deepens your apparent guilt, and so blackens your conduct, that I can scarcely believe I am addressing the child I so loved — and could still so love, if but one real sign be given of remorse and penitence — one hope of returning truth. But that sign, that hope can only be a full confession. Terrible as is the guilt of appropriating so large a sum, granted it came by the merest chance into your hand; dark as is the additional sin of concealment when an innocent person was suffering — something still darker, more terrible, must be concealed behind it, or you would not, could not, continue thus obdurately silent. I can believe that under some heavy pressure of misery, some strong excitement, the sum might have been used without thought, and that fear might have prevented the confession of any thing so dreadful; but what was this heavy necessity for money, this strong excitement? What fearful and mysterious difficulties have you been led into to call for either? Tell me the truth, Ellen, the whole truth; let me have some hope of saving you and myself the misery of publicly declaring you the guilty one, and so proving Robert's innocence. Tell me what difficulty, what misery so maddened you, as to demand the disposal of your trinkets. If there be the least excuse, the smallest possibility of your obtaining in time forgiveness, I will grant it. I will not believe you so utterly fallen. I will do all I can to remove error, and yet to prevent suffering; but to win this, I *must have* a full confession — every question that I put to you must be clearly and satisfactorily answered, and so bring back the only comfort to yourself, and hope to me. Will you do this, Ellen?"

"Oh, that I could!" was the reply in such bitter anguish, Mrs. Hamilton actually shuddered. "But I cannot — must not — dare not. Aunt Emmeline, hate me, condemn me to the severest, sharpest suffering; I wish for it, pine for it: you cannot loathe me more than I do myself, but do not — do not speak to me in these kind tones — I cannot bear them. It was because I knew what a wretch I am, that I have so shunned you, I was not worthy to be with you; oh, sentence me at once! I dare not answer as you wish."

"Dare not!" repeated Mrs. Hamilton, more and more bewildered, and, to conceal the emotion Ellen's wild words and agonized manner had produced, adopting greater sternness. "You dare commit a sin, from which the lowest of my household would shrink in horror, and yet tell me you dare not make the only atonement, give me the only proof of real penitence I demand. This is a weak and wicked subterfuge, Ellen, and will not pass with me. There can be no reason for this fearful obduracy, not even the consciousness of greater guilt, for I promise forgiveness, if it be possible, on the sole condition of a full confession. Once more, will you speak? Your hardihood will be utterly useless, for you cannot hope to conquer me; and if you permit me to leave you with your conduct still clothed in this impenetrable mystery, you will compel me to adopt measures to subdue that defying spirit, which will expose you and myself to intense suffering, but which *must* force submission at last."

"You cannot inflict more than I have endured the last seven weeks," murmured Ellen, almost inarticulately. "I have borne that, I can bear the rest."

"Then you will not answer? You are resolved not to tell me the day on which you found that money, the use to which it was applied, the reason of your choosing that forbidden path, permitting me to believe you guilty of heavier sins than may be the case in reality. Listen to me, Ellen; it is more than time this interview should cease, but I will give you one chance more. It is how half-past seven" — she took the watch from her neck and laid it on the table — "I will remain here one half-hour longer: by that time this sinful temper may have passed away, and you will consent to give me the confession I demand. I cannot believe you so altered in two months as to choose obduracy and misery, when pardon, and in time con fidence and love, are offered in their stead. Get up from that crouching posture, it can be but mock humility, and so only aggravates your sin."

Ellen rose slowly and painfully, and seating herself at the table, some distance from her aunt, leaned her arms upon it, and buried her face within them. Never before, and never after did half an hour appear so interminable to either Mrs. Hamilton or Ellen. It was well for the firmness of the former, perhaps, that she could not read the heart of that young girl, even if the cause of its anguish had been still concealed. Again and again did the wild longing, turning her actually faint and sick with its agony, come over her to reveal the whole, to ask but rest and mercy for herself, pardon and security for Edward; but then clear, as held before her in letters of fire, she read every word of her brother's desperate letter, particularly "Breathe it to my uncle or aunt, for if she knows it he will, and you will never see me more." Her mother, pallid as death, seemed to stand before her, freezing confession on her heart and lips, looking at her threateningly, as she had so often seen her, as if the very thought were guilt. The rapidly advancing twilight, the large and lonely room, all added to that fearful illusion, and if Ellen did succeed in praying, it was with desperate fervor, for strength not to betray her brother. If ever there were a martyr spirit, it was enshrined in that young, frail form.

But how could Mrs. Hamilton imagine this? How could her wildest fancy bring Edward — the brave, happy, eager Edward, of whom captain, officers, and crew wrote in such terms of praise and admiration, who had never given cause for anxiety, and who was so far distant — as the uniting link to this terrible mystery? Was it not more natural that he should not enter the incongruous and painful thoughts floating through her brain, save as her last resource, by his influence, to obtain the truth from Ellen? The more she thought, the more agonizing her thoughts became; what could induce this determined silence, but a conviction of deeper guilt, and what could that guilt be? The most terrible suspicions crossed her mind; she had heard though she had scarcely believed in them, of entanglements even where the guardianship had been most rigid. Could one so young, seemingly so innocent, have fallen into the power of some desperate character, who was working on her thus? How could she be sure she intended to take her trinkets to Mrs. Langford? Her choosing that forbidden path which was never by any chance trodden by the family or their friends, her constant desire lately not to join them in their excursions, preferring, and often finding some excuse to remain alone — all came to Mrs. Hamilton's mind, with such an overpowering sensation of dread and misery, that the worst guilt Ellen could have avowed would scarcely have been worse than anticipation pictured; and yet every thought was so vague, every fancy so undefined — there was nothing she could grasp at as a saving hope, or in the remotest degree excusing cause; such obdurate silence in one so young, generally so yielding, could and must conceal nothing but still more fearful sin. The darkness which had gathered round them, save the brightening light of the harvest moon, suddenly awakened her to the lapse of time. The moonlight fell full on the face of the watch, which was a repeater. It wanted but three minutes more, and Mrs. Hamilton watched the progress of the hand with such sickening dread, that when it reached the hour, she had scarcely strength to strike it, and so give notice — for words she had none — that the hour of grace had passed. But she conquered the powerlessness, and those soft chimes, which, when Ellen first came to Oakwood, had been such a constant source of childish wonder and delight, now rang in her ears louder, hoarser, more fearfully distinct, than even those of the ancient time-piece in the hall, which at the same moment rang out the hour of eight.

The sound ceased, and with heightened dignity, but in perfect silence, Mrs. Hamilton rose, passed her niece, and had nearly reached the door, when she paused, and turned toward Ellen, as if irresolute. Ellen's eyes had watched her as in fascination, and the pause endowed her with just sufficient power to spring forward, fling herself at her aunt's feet, and clasping her knees with all her little remaining strength, passionately implore —

"Aunt Emmeline, aunt Emmeline, speak to me but one word, only one word of kindness before you go. I do not ask for mercy, there can be none for such a wretch as I am; I will bear without one complaint, one murmur, all you may inflict — you cannot be too severe. Nothing can be such agony as the utter loss of your affection; I thought, the last two months, that I feared you so much that it was all fear, no love, but now, now that you know my sin, it has all, all come back to make me still more wretched." And before Mrs. Hamilton could prevent, or was in the least aware of her intention, Ellen had obtained possession of one of her hands, and was covering it with kisses, while her whole frame shook with those convulsed, but completely tearless sobs.

"Will you confess, Ellen, if I stay? Will you give me the

proof that it *is* such agony to lose my affection, that you *do* love me as you profess, and that it is only one sin which has so changed you? One word, and, tardy as it is, I will listen, and, if I can, forgive."

Ellen made no answer, and Mrs. Hamilton's newly-raised hopes vanished; she waited full two or three minutes, then gently disengaged her hand and dress from Ellen's still convulsive grasp; the door closed, with a sullen, seemingly unwilling sound, and Ellen was alone. She remained in the same posture, the same spot, till a vague, cold terror so took possession of her, that the room seemed filled with ghostly shapes, and all the articles of furniture suddenly transformed to things of life! and springing up, with the wild, fleet step of fear, she paused not till she found herself in her own room, where flinging herself on her bed, she buried her face on her pillow, to shut out every object — oh, how she longed to shut out thought!

It was such a different scene, such a fulness of innocent joy, on which Mrs. Hamilton entered, that though she thought herself nerved to control all visible emotion, the contrast almost overpowered her; knowing, too, that the fatal effects of one person's sin must banish that innocent enjoyment, and would fall on them all as some fearful, joy-destroying blow. The room, one of the least spacious, was cheerfully lighted, the urn hissing upon the table, at which Caroline, as usual, was presiding, only waiting for her mother's appearance, to satisfy Percy, who was loudly declaring he was famished in two senses — for want of his mother's company, and of some restorative for his craving appetite. He was lounging on the sofa, playing with Emmeline's flowing ringlets, as she sat on a low stool by his side, chatting with him, in as discursive a strain as his fancy willed. Herbert and Miss Harcourt were still in earnest discussion on their poem, from which Herbert was occasionally reading aloud such beautiful passages, and with such richness of intonation, and variety of expression, that Caroline, and even Percy and Emmeline, would pause involuntarily to listen.

"At length!" exclaimed Percy, springing up, as did Herbert at the same moment, to get their mother a chair, and place her comfortably as usual in the midst of them. "Mother, I really did begin to think you intended to punish my impatience by not joining us at all to-night."

"I did not know you were impatient, my dear boy, or perhaps I might have done so!" was her quiet, and even smiling reply. "I fear, indeed, waiting for me so long after a water-excusion, must have caused you to be impatient in another sense."

"What! that we must be all famished? I assure you, we are, and the loss of your society sharpened the pangs of hunger. I owe Morris a grudge, and will certainly serve him out one day, for detaining you so long when I wanted you."

"It was not Morris that detained me," answered Mrs. Hamilton, somewhat hurriedly. "I had done with him by six o'clock; but come, tell me something about your excursion," she added, evidently anxious to elude farther remark, and perceiving at once that Miss Harcourt and Herbert both looked at her very anxiously. "How did your boat go, and how did Caroline's voice and your flute sound on the water, Percy? Herbert, I see, has found poetry, as usual, and made Miss Harcourt his companion; you must tell me what verses our beautiful river recalled this afternoon; and you, Emmy, have you any more sketches to fill up?"

Her children eagerly entered on their day's enjoyment — Herbert conquering his anxiety, to emulate his mother's calmness, but Miss Harcourt had been too painfully startled by the unusual expression of forcibly-controlled suffering on her friend's face, to do so with any success. Nearly an hour, however, passed animatedly as usual; each found so much to tell, and Percy was in such wild spirits, that it was utterly impossible for there to be any thing like a pause. Tea had always been a favorite meal at Oakwood, as bringing all the family together after the various business of the day, and it continued to be so. They had lingered over it as usual, when Caroline suddenly exclaimed —

"What has become of Ellen? I had quite forgotten her till this moment; how neglectful she will think us! Do ring the bell, Percy, that we may send and let her know."

"If she has no recollection of meal-time, I really think we need not trouble ourselves about her," was Percy's half-jesting, half-earnest reply, for Ellen's changed manner to his mother had made him more angry with her, and for a longer time together, than he had ever been with anybody, especially a woman, in his life. He stretched out his hand, however, to ring the bell, but Mrs. Hamilton stopped him.

"You need not, Percy; your cousin will not wish to join us, she said; and her tone was now so expressive of almost anguish, that every one of that happy party startled and looked at her with the most unfeigned alarm, and Percy, every thought of jest and joyousness checked, threw his arms round her, exclaiming —

"Mother, dearest! what *has* happened! — that unhappy girl

again! I am sure it is. Why do you not cast her off from your heart at once; she will bring you nothing but sorrow for all your love."

"Percy, how can you be so harsh? — how unlike you!" exclaimed Emmeline, indignantly, as Mrs. Hamilton's head, for a few minutes of natural weakness, sunk on her son's encircling arm. "We have all given mamma trouble and pain enough one time or other, and what would have become of us if she had cast us off? and Ellen has no mother, too — for shame!"

"Hush!" answered Percy, almost sternly, for there were times when he could quite throw off the boy. "This is no light or common matter, to affect my mother thus. Shall we send for Mr. Howard, mother?" he continued, fondly; "in my father's absence he is your ablest friend — we can only feel, not counsel."

But there are times when feeling can aid in bringing back control and strength, when counsel alone would seem so harsh and cold, we can only weep before it; and the fond affection of her children, the unusual assumption of protecting manliness in Percy, so touchingly united with the deep respect that prevented the least intrusive question as to the cause of her distress till she chose to reveal it, gave her power to send back the tears that had escaped at first so hot and fast, and though still holding his hand, as if its very pressure was support, she was enabled calmly to relate the fatal discovery of that evening. Its effect was, in truth, as if a thunderbolt had fallen in the midst of them. An execration, forcibly checked, but passionate as his nature, burst from the lips of Percy, as he clasped his arm close round his mother, as thus to protect her from the misery he felt himself. Herbert, with a low cry of pain, buried his face in his hands. Caroline, shocked and bewildered, but her first thought for her mother, could only look at, and feel for her, quite forgetting that her every prejudice against Ellen did indeed seem fulfilled. Emmeline at first looked stunned, then sinking down at Mrs. Hamilton's feet, hid her face on her lap, and sobbed with such uncontrolled violence, that it might have seemed as if she herself, not Ellen, were the guilty cause of all this misery. Miss Harcourt, like Caroline, could only think and feel for Mrs. Hamilton; for she knew so well all the hope, interest, and love which Ellen had excited, and what must be the bitter suffering of this fearful disappointment.

"Do not weep thus, love," Mrs. Hamilton said, addressing Emmeline, after nearly a quarter of an hour had passed, and the various emotions of each individual had found vent in words well illustrative of their respective characters; all but Emmeline, who continued to sob so painfully, that her mother successfully forgot her own sorrow to comfort her. "Ellen is still very young, and though she is giving us all this misery and disappointment now, she may become all we can wish her, by-and-by. We must not give up all hope, because now all my cares seem so blighted. There is some fatal mystery attached to her conduct; for I am indeed deceived if she is not very wretched, and there is some hope in that."

"Then why does she not speak?" rejoined Percy, impetuously; for when he found his mother resuming control and firmness, he had given vent to his indignation by striding hastily up and down the room. "What but the most determined hardihood and wickedness can keep her silent, when you promise forgiveness if she will but speak? What mystery can there, or ought there, to be about her, when she has such an indulgent friend as yourself to bring all her troubles to? Wretched! I hope she is, for she deserves to be, if it were only for her base ingratitude."

"Percy! dear Percy! do not speak and judge so very harshly," interposed Herbert, with deep feeling; "there does, indeed, seem no excuse for her conduct, but if we ever should find that there is some extenuating cause, how unhappy we shall be for having judged her still more harshly than she deserved."

"It is impossible we can do that," muttered Percy, continuing his angry walk. "Nothing but guilt can be the cause of her keeping any thing from my mother. Ellen knows, as we all know, that even error, when confessed, has always been forgiven, sorrow always soothed, and every difficulty removed. What can her silence spring from, then, but either defying obstinacy or some blacker sin?"

"It does seem like it, unhappily," rejoined Caroline, but very sorrowfully, not at all as if she triumphed in her own previous penetration; "but she cannot persevere in it long. Dear mamma, do not look so distressed: it is impossible she can resist you for any length of time."

"She has resisted every offer of kindness, my dear child, and it is the difficulty as to what course to pursue, to compel submission and confession, that so grieves and perplexes me."

"Let me seek Mr. Howard, dearest mother," answered Herbert; "he is so good, so kind, even in his severest judgments, that I really think Ellen will scarcely be able to persevere in her mistaken silence, if he speak to her."

Mrs. Hamilton paused for some moments in thought.

"I believe you are right, Herbert. If I must have counsel out of my own family, I cannot go to a kinder, wiser, or more silent friend. If the fearful shame which I must inflict on Ellen to-night of proving Robert's innocence before my whole household, by the denouncement of her guilt, have no effect in softening her, I will appeal to him."

"Oh, mamma, must this be — can you not, will you not spare her this?" implored Emmeline, clinging to her mother, in passionate entreaty; "it would kill me, I know it would. Do not — do not expose her to such shame."

"Do you think it is no suffering to my mother to be called upon to do this, Emmeline, that you add to it by this weak interference?" replied Percy, sternly, before his mother could reply. "Shame! she has shamed us all enough. There wants little more to add to it."

But Emmeline's blue eyes never moved from her mother's face, and Miss Harcourt, longing to spare Mrs. Hamilton the suffering of such a proceeding, tried to persuade her to evade it, but she did not succeed.

"One word of confession — one evidence that her sin originated in a momentary temptation, that it conceals nothing darker — one real proof of penitence, and God knows how gladly I would have spared myself and her; but as it is, Lucy, Emmeline, do not make my duty harder."

Few as these words were, the tone that spoke them was enough. No more was said, and Mrs. Hamilton tried, but with very little success, to turn her children's thoughts to other and pleasanter things. Time seemed to lag heavily, and yet when the prayer-bell sounded, it fell on every heart as some fearful knell which must have been struck too soon.

All were assembled in the library, and in their respective places, all but one, and Herbert waited her appearance.

"Tell Miss Fortescue that we are only waiting for her to commence prayers;" and Fanny, the young ladies' attendant, departed to obey, wondering at Miss Ellen's non-appearance, but hearing nothing unusual in her mistress's voice. She returned, but still they waited; again the door unclosed, and Emmeline bent forward in an attitude of agony and shame, unable even to look at her cousin, whose place was close beside her; but the words she dreaded came not then — Herbert, at his mother's sign, commenced the service, and it proceeded as usual. The fearful struggle in Mrs. Hamilton's gentle bosom, who might read, save the all-pitying God, whom she so fervently addressed for strength and guidance? The voice of her son ceased, and the struggle was over.

"Before we part for the night," she said, when all but one had arisen, "it is necessary that the innocent should be so justified before you all, that he should no longer be injured by suspicion and avoidance. It is nearly two months since your master assured you of his own and of my perfect conviction that Robert Langford had told the truth, and that the missing notes had been unfortunately lost by him; not appropriated, as I fear most of you have believed, and are still inclined to do. The complete failure of every search for them has induced a very uncomfortable feeling among you all as to the person on whom suspicion of finding and appropriating them might fall, none but the household frequenting that particular path, and none being able to suppose that the storm could have so dispersed as to lose all trace of them. I acknowledge it was unlikely, but not so unlikely as that Robert Langford should have failed in honesty, or that any of my household should have appropriated or concealed them. All mystery is now, however, at an end; the missing notes have been traced and found; and that all suspicion and discomfort may be removed from among you, it becomes my duty to designate the individual who has thus transgressed every duty to God and man, not by the sin alone; but by so long permitting the innocent to suffer for the guilty, more especially as that individual is one of my own family" — for one moment she paused, whether to gain strength, or to give more force to her concluding words, no one could tell — "ELLEN FORTESCUE!"

CHAPTER VI.

THE SENTENCE, AND ITS EXECUTION.

THE excitement which reigned in the servants' hall, after they had withdrawn, in the most respectful silence, from the library, was extreme. Robert, utterly unable to realize relief in this proof of his own innocence, could only pace the hall in agony, deploring his mad carelessness, which, by exposing to temptation, had caused it all; and Morris and Ellis deepened the remorse by perfectly agreeing with him. Before they sepa-ated, the old steward called them all together; and, his voice trembling with agitation, the tears actually running down his furrowed cheeks, told them that even as their mistress had done her duty to the utmost, ay, more than the utmost by them — for it must have well-nigh broken her heart to do it — a solemn duty was demanded from them to her, and that if either man, woman, or child failed in it, he should know that they had neither feeling, honor, nor gratitude in their hearts, and deserved and should be scouted by them all; and that duty was never to let the event of that night pass their lips, even to each other. It was enough that all mystery and suspicion had been taken from them, and that time would clear up the remainder; he never would believe the grandchild of his mistress's father, one she had so loved and cared for, could wilfully act as appearances seemed to say; that he was sure, one day or other, they would all find there was much more to pity than to blame; and till then, if they had the least spark of generous or grateful feeling, they would forget the whole affair, and only evince their sense of their mistress's conduct, by yet greater respect and attention to their respective duties.

The old man's speech was garrulous, and perhaps often faulty in grammar, but it came from the heart, and so went to the heart at once, and not one held back from the pledge of silence he demanded. There are some who imagine that the refinement of feeling which alone could actuate Morris's speech, and its warm and immediate response, is only to be found among the educated and the rich; how little those who thus suppose understand the human heart! Kindness begets kindness; and if superiors will but think of, and seek the happiness, temporal and eternal, of their inferiors — will but prove that they are considered as children of one common Father — there needs no equality of rank to create equality of happiness, or equality of refined, because *true* feeling.

The next morning, when Mrs. Hamilton had occasion to speak to Morris about some farm receipts, which had not been forthcoming the preceding day, she recalled him as he was departing; but the words she had to say seemed unusually difficult, for her voice audibly faltered, and her face was completely shaded by her hand. It was simply to ask that which Morris's loving reverence had already done; and when the old man, in those earnest accents of heartfelt respect and kindness, which never can be mistaken, related what had passed, his mistress hastily extended her hand to him, saying, in a tone he never forgot —

"God bless you, Morris! I ought to have known your love for your master's house would have urged this, without any request from me. I cannot thank you enough." The kiss he ventured to press upon the delicate hand which pressed his rough palm, was not unaccompanied, though he did force back the tear, and most respectfully, yet very earnestly, beseech his mistress not to take on too much. There must be some cause, some mystery; no one belonging to her could so have acted without some very fearful temptation, some very powerful reason, and it would all come straight one day.

But whatever the future, the present was only suffering; for to obtain a full confession from Ellen, Mrs. Hamilton felt so absolutely incumbent on her, that she steadily refused to listen to either pity or affection, which could shake her firmness; and the opinion and advice of Mr. Howard strengthened the determination. He had a private interview with Ellen, but it was attended with so very little success, that he left her far more bewildered and grieved than he had sought her; but fully convinced it was mere hardihood and obstinacy, which caused her incomprehensible and most guilty silence. Not even allowing, as Mrs. Hamilton had, that there was any evidence of misery and remorse; perhaps she had been more quiet, more resolutely calm, and if it had not been for the strong appearances against her, he surely must have seen it was the strength and quiet of despair, not the defiance he believed.

"This rebellious spirit must be conquered," he said, on rejoining Mrs. Hamilton, who, with her children and Miss Harcourt, had most anxiously and yet hopefully awaited the result of his interference. "We should actually be sharing her sin, if we permit her to conquer us by obduracy and self-will. Solitary confinement and complete idleness may bring her to a better temper, and, in fact, should be persisted in, till a full confession be made. If that fail, my dear Mrs. Hamilton, your niece should be banished from Oakwood. She must not remain here, a continual source of anxiety and misery to you, and of successful hardihood to herself; but of that there will be time enough to think when you have an answer from Mr. Hamilton; his judgment from a distance may be wiser than ours on the spot, and irritated as we are by such unaccountable obstinacy in one we have always thought almost too yielding."

And it was this incomprehensible change of character, in seeming, that still more perplexed Mrs. Hamilton, and so made her believe there must be some worse fault, or dangerous entanglement, demanding such resolute pertinacity in concealment.

Closely connected with Ellis's private apartments, and having neither inlet nor outlet, save through the short passage opening from her sitting-room, were two small but not uncomfortable apartments, opening one into the other, and looking out on a very pretty but quite unfrequented part of the park. They had often been used when any of Ellis's children or grandchildren came to see her, and were in consequence almost sufficiently habitable, without any further preparation, except the turning one into a sitting-room, which Ellis's active care speedily accomplished. Her mistress inspected them, at her desire, suggested one or two additional comforts, and then held a long confidential conversation with her. She had such perfect confidence in her (for Ellis had been from a child — married, and become mother and widow, and married her children — all as an inmate of the Hamilton family, and had held the confidential post of housekeeper for sixteen years) that she did not hesitate one moment to commit Ellen entirely to her care, at least till she could receive an answer about her from her husband. She depended on her to watch over her health, to see that she took daily exercise with her, in those parts of the park where she was not likely to attract notice, as being with her instead of with any member of her family, and that she took her regular meals; to be with her whenever she took them, and at casual times in the day, not so as to remove the impression of solitude and disgrace, but to be enabled to watch her closely, and the least symptom of a softening spirit to report instantly to her.

"She will, of course, join us in the hours of devotion, though not occupying her usual place, for she who has lowered herself, in the sight of God and man, beneath the humblest of my domestics, may no longer kneel above them," she said in conclusion. "But of my determination on the point she is already aware; and she will go with us as usual to church; I will have no remark made, further than I can avoid. Be as kind to her as you can, Ellis, consistent with your character as a wise and watchful guardian. God in mercy grant that her heart may be so softened, that you will not fill that painful position long. And now to see her."

But Percy's watchful care had so quietly interposed, that his mother found herself in their usual sitting-room, and in the midst of them all, before she could seek Ellen: and when, with half reproach, she told him, that she had still a most painful duty to accomplish, therefore he ought not to have prevented it, he answered impetuously —

"Mother, you shall not see Ellen any more alone! she has

made you miserable enough already, and each time that she sees you, her deceitful appearance of remorse and suffering, for they *cannot* be real, or she would speak, but add to it; send for her here, and tell her your decision before us all."

And Mrs. Hamilton complied, for she felt as if her firmness would be less likely to fail, than if Ellen attempted any thing like supplication with her alone. But not a word of supplication came. Ellen had answered the summons, by quietly accompanying Ellis, who had been sent for her, to her aunt's presence, pale, indeed, as marble, but so tearless and still, as to seem unmoved. An expression of actual relief stole over her features as she heard her sentence, undisturbed even when told that this would only be, till Mr. Hamilton's sentence came; as, if she continued silent until then, of course whatever severer measures he might dictate would be instantly obeyed. But when Mrs. Hamilton proceeded to say that she intended writing the whole affair to Edward, that his influence might awaken her to a sense of the fearfully aggravated guilt she was incurring by her silence, an expression of the most intense agony succeeded the previous calm, and sinking down before her, Ellen wildly implored —

"Oh, aunt Emmeline, in mercy spare him! do not, oh, do not throw such shame upon him, he who is so brave, admired, honored! do not, oh, if you have any pity left, do not make him hate me, loathe me too, my own only brother! he must throw me off. How can he bear such shame upon his name! Oh, do, with me more than you have said, any thing, every thing, but that. Spare him!"

"Spare him yourself," interposed Percy, sternly. — (He was standing, with his arms crossed, by a window; Herbert was leaning at the back of Mrs. Hamilton's chair; Caroline and Miss Harcourt trying very steadily to work, and Emmeline bending over a drawing, which her tears were utterly spoiling.) — "If the knowledge of your sin make him miserable, as it must, be yourself the one to save him — you alone can. Speak; break this determined and most guilty silence, and his influence will not be needed, and my mother will be silent to him concerning what has passed, now and forever, as we will all. If you so love him, spare him the shame you have brought on all of us; if not, it is mere words, as must be the love you have professed all these years for my mother."

Ellen turned her face toward him for a single minute, with such an expression of unutterable misery, that he turned hastily away, even his anger in part subdued, and Mrs. Hamilton could scarcely reply.

"I cannot grant your request, Ellen, for to refuse it, appears to me the only means of softening you. It may be a full fortnight before I can write to Edward, for we must receive letters first. If during that interval you choose to give me the only proof of repentance that can satisfy me, or bring the least hope of returning happiness to yourself, I shall now know how to act. I would indeed spare your brother this bitter shame, but if you continue thus obdurate, no entreaties will move me. Rise, and go with Ellis. Punishment and misery, repentance and pardon, are all before you; you alone can choose. I shall interfere no more, till your uncle's sentence comes." And longing to end this painful scene, for her mistress's sake, Ellis led Ellen from the room, and conducted her to the apartments assigned her. She felt much too angry and annoyed at the pain and trouble Ellen was giving her mistress, to evince any thing like kindness toward her at first, but she had not been under her care above a week before her feelings underwent a complete change.

Suffering as she was enduring, more especially from the conviction, that to every one of those she loved (for affection for each one of the family had now returned with almost passionate violence) she must be an object of hate and loathing, yet that her sin was known, was a relief so inexpressibly blessed, she felt strengthened to endure every thing else. She knew, and her God knew, the agonized temptation to the momentary act, and the cause of her determined silence. She felt there was strange comfort in that; though she knew no punishment could be too severe for the sin itself, and she prayed constantly to be enabled to bear it, and still not to betray her brother; and the consequence of these petitions was a calm, gentle, deeply submissive demeanor. Not a murmur ever passed her lips, and Ellis scarcely ever saw the signs of tears, which she longed for; for the quiet, but fearfully intense suffering, Ellen's very evident daily portion, alarmed her for its effect upon her always delicate health. As yet, however, there was no outward appearance of its failing, it rather bore up, from the cessation of the nervous dread and constant terror, which she had endured before; and before Mr. Hamilton's letter arrived, a month after the fatal discovery, Ellis had drawn her own conclusions, and her manner, instead of being distant and cold, had become so excessively kind and feeling, that the poor girl felt some heavy change must be impending, she dared not look to the continuance of such comfort.

But Mrs. Hamilton never saw her niece, save when no words

could pass between them; and she could not judge as Ellis did. She could only feel, as each day passed, without bringing the desired proof of sorrow and amendment, more and more bewildered, and very wretched. Though, for her children's sake, she so conquered the feeling as, after the first week, to restore cheerfulness, and promote the various amusements they had all so enjoyed. Ellen's disappearance had of course to be accounted for, to the intimate friends with whom they so constantly were; but her acknowledgment that she had been disappointed in her, and that her conduct would not allow her any social or domestic indulgence, at least for a time, satisfied the elder members. Annie, for the first time, discovered that Caroline was her match in cleverness, merely from her excessive truth and simplicity, and that, manœuvre as she might, she could not discover the smallest clew to this sudden mystery. And Mary, for the first time, and on this one subject alone, found Herbert and Emmeline impenetrably reserved.

As soon as Mrs. Langford had been informed by her son, at his mistress's desire, of the unanswerable proof of his innocence, she hastened to the Hall, and requesting a private interview with Mrs. Hamilton, placed at once in her hands all the trinkets and watch, with which she had been at different times intrusted; related all that had passed between her and Miss Fortescue, the excessive misery she seemed to be enduring; and confessed that the few pounds she had given her, as the sums obtained by the sale of the trinkets, she had advanced herself, having resolved that nothing should induce her to dispose of them; and that of course it was the difficulty she had in advancing their right value, which had occasioned the length of time that had elapsed since Ellen had first sought her.

"Would it not go far to prove she really did wish to return the money?" Mrs. Hamilton thought, long after the widow had left her, and the sums she had advanced returned with interest. "Was it to return the fatally appropriated sum, or because she needed more? Ellen had so positively, and with such agony asserted the first, that it was scarcely possible to disbelieve her; but what was this fearful difficulty, this pressing demand by one so young for so much money? Why, if it were comparatively innocent, would she not speak?" The more she thought, the more perplexed and anxious she seemed to become. The act itself of endeavoring to dispose of the trinkets, especially those that had been given and received, as doubly valuable because they had been worn by her mother, would have been sufficiently faulty to have occasioned natural displeasure, but compared with other known and unknown faults, it sunk into almost nothing. Mrs. Hamilton collected them all together, those Mrs. Langford had returned, and the few remaining in her niece's drawer, and carefully put them away, till circumstances might authorize her returning them to Ellen, and determined on saying nothing more on the subject either to Ellen or her own family.

One thing Ellis reported to her regarding Ellen, which certainly seemed like a consciousness of the wrong she had done Robert, and a wish to atone for it. She begged Ellis so earnestly that she might see him, if it were only for five minutes, that she could not resist her; and when he came, she implored him so touchingly, so pleadingly to forgive her long silence himself, and entreat his mother to do so too—assuring him, that it was the hope of being able to restore the notes to him, without revealing her identity, which had caused the silence—that it was scarcely possible to listen to her unmoved. It was no false humility, but the deepest, most unfeigned contrition for having been the cause of injury.

Ten days after Ellen's imprisonment, the letter arrived from Sir Edward Manly, which Mrs. Hamilton had alluded to as necessary to be received, before she could write to her nephew, and the news it brought, though somewhat alloyed, would at another time have been received with the greatest delight. Edward was returning. In three weeks, or a month at the utmost, after the receipt of his commander's letter, he might be with them all; invalided home for a three or four months' leave. There had been another, and rather severe engagement, in which young Fortescue had still more distinguished himself; but from his headlong courage had been severely, but not at all seriously hurt. Sir Edward intended sending the pirate frigate which they had taken to England, as she was a tight-built, well looking craft enough, he wrote, if manned with honorable men instead of desperate villains; and had nominated Harding and Fortescue to accompany the second lieutenant, as her officers.

The name of Harding produced no disagreeable reminiscences in Mrs. Hamilton's mind. It had been so very long since Edward had even mentioned him, that she had almost forgotten his early fancy for him. Her only thought now was thankfulness that her gallant nephew had been preserved, and that he was coming home. It could scarcely be pleasure she felt, though all the young party did, for there was such an excitement in Edward's courage, and in his having been in two desperate engagements, and seen so much, that, with the buoyancy happily natural to well-disposed youth, they could only think and talk of his return, forgetting the alloy that must cloud it. Percy and Herbert hoped he would arrive within the three weeks, as then they should be with him at least a week or ten days. If delayed, he would very provokingly just arrive as they would be returning to college.

After much painful deliberation, Mrs. Hamilton determined on making Herbert her messenger with these unexpected tidings to Ellen; hoping more than she expressed that his gentle eloquence in bringing before her the misery to which she must condemn her brother if she would persist in this silence, and so compel an appeal to him, would have some effect; especially as she charged him to impress upon her that even now confession should bring pardon, and concealment of all from Edward. Herbert gladly undertook the mission, and so feelingly, so earnestly discharged it, that poor Ellen felt more heart-broken than she had done yet, and almost incapable of retaining her firmness. But she did; for danger to Edward seemed more imminent now that he was coming home, to the very vicinity of his dreaded uncle, than when he was at a distance. She could only feel thankful — if concealment were indeed so absolutely necessary as he had declared it to be — that Mr. Hamilton was still from home, and might continue to be so during Edward's visit. It was difficult to repress the sickening shudder, when Herbert chanced to mention that Harding was her brother's companion in his voyage home, and difficult, not to express more disappointment than the occasion warranted, that Edward had not answered her last letter. He must have received it, Herbert said, for Sir Edward acknowledged his father's in which hers to Edward had been inclosed. He left her, after a very long interview, deeply grieved at the failure of all his persuasions, all his remonstrances, but compelled, he could not satisfactorily explain why, either to himself or to his family, to pity far more than blame. Percy declared, as did Caroline and Miss Harcourt, that it must be only his own too kind and gentle disposition, which never could blame anybody or any thing. Mrs. Hamilton was bitterly disappointed; Mr. Howard insisted that such obduracy demanded nothing but the sternest treatment, and he only wished Mr. Hamilton's letter could arrive at once. He saw Ellen again himself twice in the five weeks, which elapsed between the discovery of her sin and the arrival of Mr. Hamilton's answer; but if kindness had so failed, it was comparatively easy to resist his well-intentioned, but in this case utterly mistaken sternness. He was in general so kind even in his judgments, that Mrs. Hamilton thought he must have some reason to believe Ellen so thoroughly hardened, and from his report of her was enabled to impart her husband's sentence with more firmness, than had she listened to her own kind, still loving heart.

It was as she and Mr. Howard had both expected. Ellen was no longer to remain at Oakwood, but to be placed under the care of a maiden lady, living in Yorkshire, a relation of Mr. Hamilton, and one who had occasionally visited Oakwood, and was, therefore, well known to Mrs. Hamilton, and to Ellis too, and regarded with such dislike by the latter, as to make her actually venture to entreat her mistress not to send Miss Ellen to her; she was sure it would break her heart. Now Miss Seldon was one of the worthiest women that ever breathed — honest, straightforward, truth-speaking literally to a fault, but as hard as she was true. Whether she ever had any feelings or not, Mrs. Hamilton, with all her penetration, never could discover; but the good she did was immense in practical benevolence, though the quick sympathy, the kindly word, the indulgent thought, seemed utterly unknown. She had no pity for faults or failings, always declaring forbearance and love were all folly; "if a branch were in the slightest degree decayed, cut it off; if the blight extend to the root, destroy it," she was fond of saying. As for youthful follies or errors, she had no patience with them, for never having been, or rather felt young herself, she could not understand the age in others. Ellis had not discrimination enough to discern the good which lay under this very disagreeable exterior; Mrs. Hamilton had; and suffering as she knew a residence with her must be to Ellen, if indeed she were really the character she had seemed in childhood — though the last few months had so contradicted it — she felt her husband had decided wisely, spite of the misery which still even the very thought of sending her orphan niece so completely from her, was to herself. Mr. Hamilton's letter read harshly, but his wife knew his high, almost stern principles; he had not seen Ellen's evident anguish; he could only judge from the relation which had been sent him, and all which that told was indeed against her. Of course he said, if she had confessed, and her confession in any degree pleaded for her, his wife would use her own judgment as to the period of her banishment; but he could not imagine any cause for her conduct sufficiently excusing, as to demand the avoidance of his sentence altogether.

Miss Seldon's last visit to Oakwood was sufficiently well

remembered by the young Hamiltons (though it was before their cousins had arrived from India) for them all — even Percy and Caroline, the most indignant against Ellen — to think of their father's sentence with the deepest regret, and with almost dread for its effect on Ellen.

"If she did but know her, she must speak," was Emmeline's exclamation. "I did not feel quite sure that I was my own happy self, all the time she was with us."

"The atmosphere was frozen twenty degrees below zero in all the rooms she frequented, though it was otherwise a hot summer," rejoined Percy; "and in Yorkshire —"

"Pray do not joke, dear Percy; I cannot bear to think of Ellen going away from us at all, much less to such a guardian, though I know she is very good," answered Herbert.

"Now, my good fellow, do not attempt to say a word for Nancy Seldon; she was the only person in the world I ever heard you acknowledge you disliked; so what must she be? Worthy! no doubt, or my father would not have trusted Ellen to her, but for any thing else —"

"Poor Ellen! she little knows to what her obstinacy is condemning her," rejoined Caroline; I wish she did, and then she might spare herself and mamma, too; though I fear even confession would not help her much now."

Mrs. Hamilton might and did think with them all, but she could not swerve from her duty. She wrote at once to Miss Seldon, not entering into particulars, but merely asking if she would consent to take charge of a relative, whose conduct demanded more rigid watchfulness and care, and an entire cessation of indulgence, than could be the case in the family circle at Oakwood. She and her husband had such perfect confidence in her, she said, that if she could oblige them by undertaking the duty, they knew, without any assurance on her part, that she would discharge it faithfully. The yearly sum they offered was large, because they wished their young relative to have all the comforts and appurtenances of a gentlewoman, and the advantages of the best education, the city near which she resided, could afford. Mrs. Hamilton had no doubt of the affirmative nature of the reply, for Miss Seldon owed the recovery of her fortune and position entirely to the exertions of Mr. Hamilton; and she had told him, once for all, that if she could but serve or oblige him in any way, great or small, it would make her far happier than she had ever been, or was likely to be in her solitary life. The letter written and despatched Mrs. Hamilton summoned Ellen once more to her presence.

The scene was again the library, where she had been writing, and the time nearing the short twilight of October. It was three weeks, rather more, since Sir Edward Manly's letter had been received, and Edward was, therefore, almost daily expected. The feelings with which his unhappy sister looked to his return it would be a vain attempt to define. At times the intense longing to see him again caused a wild, almost sick feeling of pleasure, that she might, perhaps, so soon do so; then came all that had passed, and she pictured his anger, his loathing — true it had been for him, but he had not thought of such a deed. He would, he must hate and spurn her, too; and the idea of meeting him became absolute agony. Then — and she shuddered in dread — would he think that he must acknowledge it was for him she had thus acted? and, if so, had she not betrayed instead of saving him? Incident after incident in their childhood rose before her, to give her hope that he would be silent now as then, and not betray himself; but these contending terrors, united with the constant though silent suffering of her banishment from all she loved, the utter hopelessness as to the end of this trial, had not been without effect on the outward frame. Ellis did not see it, from so constantly watching her, and from Ellen never refusing to take the exercise she desired her, and not making a single complaint as to the pain it was sometimes to walk, and always to swallow her meals; but as she stood opposite to her aunt, in the full light of the oriel window — her approach had been so noiseless, Mrs. Hamilton, who was bending over some papers, did not see her till she chanced to look up — the attenuation of form and feature was so very visible, that her aunt could not prevent herself from starting painfully, and the words with which she had intended to address her froze on her lips. It was with the utmost difficulty she refrained from folding her to her heart, and trying, by every means affection could devise, to soothe or remove that anguish, whatever its nature, far too deep and constant for one so very young; but how dared she do this, when, by this determined silence, Ellen so defied her authority, and seemed so resolved that neither severity nor kindness, nor her own sufferings should humble her spirit, though they had even affected her frame?

Conquering with a powerful effort the pleadings of affection, Mrs. Hamilton calmly entered on the subject for which she had summoned her, reading to her a greater part of her uncle's letter, hoping that its severity would spare her the pain of any additional remarks. Every word seemed to burn itself on

Ellen's brain. What she had hoped she knew not, for she thought she had never hoped at all; but the words, "No cause can be excusing enough to justify the entire setting aside this sentence," seemed by its agony to tell her that the thought *had* entered her mind, if the real cause were by any chance discovered would she be forgiven, and in time restored to confidence and love? And now it was over, even that hope was gone.

Mrs. Hamilton paused for a reply or an observation, but none came, and she continued impressively — "I can scarcely hope, Ellen, that as even the idea of sparing your only brother shame and misery, on his return home, expecting nothing but joy, after nearly three years' separation and exposure to danger, has had no effect in softening you, that your uncle's sentence will. Once I should have believed that only the thought of leaving me, and going to the care of a stranger, would have urged you to speak directly. I can believe this no longer; but as I wish you to be with Edward, at least part of his stay with us, I shall postpone your leaving us, one month from to-day. If, indeed, Edward's influence be such that, for his sake, you will make me a full confession and answer clearly and distinctly every question I put to you, your residence with Mrs. Seldon shall be limited to three, six, ten, or twelve months, according to the nature of the motive of this incomprehensible and, apparently most sinful conduct. If you leave us still obdurate, years will, in all probability, pass before we can feel sufficiently confident in the restored integrity and openness of your character to permit your return to us. The pain you are inflicting upon me it is useless to dwell upon. As the child of my only and most dearly loved sister, I have loved you, hoped for you, with little less intensity of affection than that I have borne toward my own; for I felt that, with the sole exception of your brother, I was the only being you had on earth united to you by ties of blood. How this conduct repays my love and care you must answer to yourself; I can only be sensible of bitter disappointment.

Again she stopped, evidently expecting a reply, but Ellen still remained silent. The short twilight of autumn had set in so suddenly, that Mrs. Hamilton was not aware her niece's cheek had become still paler, and that her white lips quivered repeatedly, as if she several times tried to speak, but could not. After a silence of some minutes, she said —

"If you are determined not to speak, Ellen, you may retire; I have told you all I wished to say, except that till you leave us, though you will still occupy your present rooms, and be still under Ellis's care, you are at liberty to employ yourself, and go about the house and grounds as usual."

Ellen turned to go, still in that unbroken silence; she had reached the low step dividing the upper part from the lower part of the room, and whether she did not see it, or from some other cause, the room suddenly reeled before her, and she fell heavily forward. To spring toward her, raise her tenderly, bear her to the nearest couch, though she so trembled herself at finding Ellen quite insensible, as to render the task unusually difficult, and to ring hastily for Ellis, was the work of a minute, but it was many minutes before their united efforts could bring back consciousness.

"I knew it would break her heart, poor lamb!" was Ellis's exclamation, in a tone of most unusual excitement; "thank God, thank God! Master Edward's coming home, and that she is not to go till he does."

"Have you so much confidence in his influence?" asked her mistress, as, unable to resist the impulse, she bent down and repeatedly kissed the cold brow and cheek, to which she was so earnestly striving to restore warmth, "God in mercy grant you may be right!"

"Right? Dear my lady!" (whenever Ellis was strongly moved, she always so addressed her mistress,) "I would stake your confidence in me, which is all my life's worth, if Master Edward is not at the bottom of it all, and that this poor child is sacrificing herself for some fancied danger to him! I saw enough of that work when they were young children, and I have noticed enough since she has been under my care."

"Edward!" repeated Mrs. Hamilton, so bewildered, as to stop for the moment chafing Ellen's cold hand; "Edward! bearing the high character he does; what can he have to do with it?"

"I don't know, my lady, but I am sure he has. Young men, ay, some of the finest and bravest among us, get into difficulties sometimes, and it don't touch their characters as their officers see them, and Master Edward was always so terrified at the mere thought of my master knowing any of his faults; but—hush! we must not let her know we suspect any thing, poor lamb; it will make her still more miserable. You are better now, dear Miss Ellen, are you not?" she added, soothingly, as Ellen feebly raised her hand to her forehead, and then slowly unclosed her eyes, and beheld her aunt leaning over her, with that same expression of anxious affection, which her illness had so often caused in her childhood. Sense, or rather memory, had not quite returned, and her first words were with a faint but happy smile —

"I am better, dear aunt, much better; I dare say I shall soon be well." But it was only a momentary forgetfulness; swift as thought came the whole of what had so lately passed — her uncle's letter, her aunt's words, and murmuring, in a tone how painfully changed! "I forgot — forgive me," she buried her face in the pillow.

"Ellen, my dear Ellen! why will you persist in making yourself and me so miserable, when a few words would make us happier?" exclaimed Mrs. Hamilton, almost imploringly, as she bent over her.

"Do not urge her now, dear my lady, she is not well enough; give her till Master Edward comes; I am sure she will not resist him," answered Ellis, very respectfully, though meaningly, as her look drew her mistress's attention to the shudder which convulsed Ellen's slight frame, at the mention of her brother.

Pained and bewildered more than ever, Mrs. Hamilton, after waiting till the faintness seemed quite gone, and thinking that if the restraint of her presence were removed, Ellen might be relieved by tears, left her, desiring Ellis to let her know in a short time how she was. The moment the door closed, Ellen threw her arms round Ellis's neck, exclaiming passionately —

"Take me away — take me away, dear Ellis; I cannot bear this room — it seems all full of misery! and I loved it so once, and I shall love it again, when I am miles and miles away, and cannot see it — nor any one belonging to it. Oh, Ellis, Ellis! I knew you were too kind. I was too glad and contented to be with you; it was not punishment enough for my sin — and I must go away — and I shall never, never see my aunt again — I know I shall not. Oh! if I might but die first! but I am too wicked for that; it is only the good that die."

And almost for the first time since her sin had been discovered, she gave way to a long and violent fit of weeping, which, though terrible while it lasted, as the anguish of the young always is, greatly relieved her, and enabled her after that day not to revert in words (the thought never left her till a still more fearful anxiety deadened it) to her uncle's sentence again.

Mrs. Hamilton sat for a very long time alone after she had left Ellen. Ellis's words returned to her again and again so pertinaciously, that she could not break from them. Edward! the cause of it all — could it be possible? — could it be, that he had plunged himself into difficulties, and afraid to appeal to his uncle or her, had so worked on Ellen as not only to make her send relief, but actually so to keep his secret, as to endure every thing rather than betray it? Circumstance after circumstance, thought after thought, so congregated upon her, so seemed to burst into being, and flash light one from the other, that her mind ached beneath their pressure. Ellen's unhappiness the day his last letter had been received, her sudden illness — had it taken place before or after Robert had lost the money? She could not satisfy herself, for her husband's sudden summons to Feroe, hasty preparations, and departure, had rendered all the month confused and unsatisfactory in its recollections. So intense was the relief of the idea, that Mrs. Hamilton feared to encourage it, lest it should prove a mere fancy, and urge softer feelings toward her niece than ought to be. Even the supposition made her heart yearn toward her with such a feeling of love, almost of veneration, for the determined self-devotion, so essentially woman's characteristic, that she resolutely checked its ascendency. All her previous fancies that Ellen was no ordinary child, that early suffering and neglect had, while they produced some childish faults, matured and deepened the capabilities of endurance and control, from the consciousness (or rather existence, for it was not the consciousness to the child herself) of strong feeling, returned to her, as if determined to confirm Ellis's supposition. The disappearance of her allowance; her assertion, that she was seeking Mrs. Langford's cottage, by that shorter but forbidden path, to try and get her to dispose of her trinkets, when the wind blew the notes to her hand — all now seemed connected one with the other, and confirmed. She could well understand, how in a moment of almost madness they might have been used without thought, and the after-effect upon so delicate a mind and conscience. Then, in contradiction to all this (a mere hypothesis raised on nothing firmer than Ellis's supposition) came the constantly favorable accounts of Edward; his captain's pride and confidence in him; the seeming impossibility that he could get into such difficulties, and what were they? The name of Harding rushed on her mind, she knew not why or how — but it made her tremble, by its probable explanation of the whole. A coarse or even less refined mind, would have either appealed at once to Ellen, as to the truth of this suspicion, or thought herself justified in looking over all Edward's letters to his sister, as thus to discover the truth; but in Mrs. Hamilton's pure mind the idea never even entered, though all her niece's papers and letters were in her actual possession. She could only feel to her heart's core with Ellis, "Thank God, Master Edward's coming home!" and pray earnestly that he might be with them, as they hoped and anticipated, in a few, a very few days.

CHAPTER VII.

THE LIGHT GLIMMERS.

THE earnest wishes and prayers of Mrs. Hamilton and her faithful Ellis were disappointed. The latter part of the month of September had been exceedingly stormy, and though there was a lull from about the 3d to the 9th of October, the equinoctial gales then set in with the utmost fury; continuing day after day, night after night, till the ear seemed almost to tire of the sound, and the mind, anxious for friends at sea, despair of their cessation. During the few calm days, the young party at Oakwood had scarcely been absent from the windows, or from that part of the park leading to the Plymouth road, above an hour at a time. Percy and Herbert rode over to Plymouth, but were told the frigate could not be in for a full week. The late storms must have detained her, though she was a fast-sailing craft. It was a great disappointment to them, for on the 10th of October college term began, and they were compelled to return to Oxford. The cause of their mother's intense desire for Edward's return, indeed, they did not know; but they were most impatient to see him, and they hoped, they did not exactly know what, with regard to his influence with Ellen. However, the day of their departure came, and still he had not arrived, and the storms had recommenced. Percy had gone to say good-by to Ellis, with whom Ellen chanced at that moment to be. Full of spirits and jokes, he determinately looked away from his cousin, took both Ellis's hands, and shook them with his usual heartiness.

"Good-by, dear Ellis. I wonder if I shall ever feel myself a man when talking to you. How many tricks I have played you in this room, and you were always so good-natured, even when one of my seat-crackers set your best gown on fire, and quite spoiled it; do you remember it? I do think you were nearly angry then, and quite enough to make you; and papa made me save up my money to buy you a new dress. I did not play such a practical joke in a hurry again."

Ellis laughed, and perfectly remembered it, and with another hearty good-by he turned away.

"You have forgotten your cousin, Mr. Percy," she said, disregarding Ellen's imploring look.

"When she remembers her duty to my mother, I will remember that she is my cousin," was his hasty answer, and he hurried from the room as Herbert entered. His good-by to Ellis was quite as warm as Percy's, and then turning to Ellen, he put his arm round her, kissed her cheek, and said, with impressive earnestness —

"God bless you, dear Ellen! I hope you will be happier when we meet again, and that it will not be so long before we do, as we fancy now;" and, affected almost to tears at the grateful, humble look she raised to his, he left her.

Overcome as much by the harshness of the generous, warm-hearted Percy, whom she so dearly loved, as by the gentle kindness of Herbert, Ellen remained for several minutes with her arms on the table, her face hid upon them. She thought she was quite alone, for Ellis had gone about some of her business, when she was startled by Percy's voice.

"I am a brute, Ellen, nothing less; forgive me, and say good-by. I can't understand it at all, but angry as I am with you, your pale face haunts me like a spectre, so we must part friends;" and as she looked hastily up, he kissed her warmly twice, and ran away without another word.

Days passed heavily, the gales seeming to increase in violence, and causing Mrs. Hamilton more terrible anxiety and vague dread than she allowed to be visible. The damage among the shipping was fearful, and the very supposed vicinity of the frigate to the Channel increased the danger. The papers every morning presented long lists of ships wrecked, or fatally dismantled, loss of crews or part of them, mails and cargoes due but missing; and the vivid recollection of the supposed fate of her own brother, the wretchedness of the suspense before the fate of his vessel was ascertained, returned to heighten the fears that would gain ascendency for her nephew, and for the effect of this terrible suspense on Ellen, more especially — if indeed she had endured all these weeks, nay, months, of misery for him.

At first Ellen seemed unconscious that there was any thing remarkable in the delay, the thought of her own departure being uppermost; but when the thought did press upon her, how it came she knew not — that of the given month the weeks were passing, and Edward had not arrived, and that there must be some reason for the long delay — storm, shipwreck death, all flashed upon her at once, and almost maddened her. The quiet calm of endurance gave way. She could not sleep at night from the tremendous winds; not even when Ellis had a bed put up in her room, and remained with her all night herself; she never complained indeed, but hour after hour she would pace her room and the passage leading to Ellis's, till compelled to cease from exhaustion; she would try steadily to employ herself with some difficult study, and succeed, perhaps, for half an hour, but then remain powerless, or recommence her restless walk. Mrs. Hamilton made several attempts without any apparent interference on her part, to get her to si occasionally with her and Miss Harcourt, and her cousins, but she seemed to shrink from them all. Emmeline, indeed, when once aware of the terrible trial she was enduring, would sit with her, drawing or working as if nothing had occurred to estrange them, and try to cheer her by talking on many topics of interest. Caroline would speak to her kindly whenever she saw her. Miss Harcourt alone retained her indignation, for no suspicion of the real cause of her silence ever entered her mind.

Poor Ellen felt that she dared not indulge in the comfort this change in her aunt's and cousins' manner produced. She wanted to wean herself quite from them, that the pang of separation might be less severe, but she only seemed to succeed in loving them more. One thought, indeed, at length took such entire possession of her mind, as to deaden every other: — it was the horrible idea that, as she had sinned to save Edward, perhaps, from merited disgrace, he would be taken from her; she never breathed it, but it haunted her night and day. Mr. Maitland saw her continually, but he plainly told Mrs. Hamilton while the cause of anxiety and mental suffering lasted he could do her no good. It was a constant alternation of fearful excitement and complete depression, exhausting the whole system. Repose and kindness — alas! the latter might be given, but the former, in the present position of affairs, how could it be insured?

The month of grace was waning; only two days remained, and Edward had not arrived, and how could Mrs. Hamilton obey her husband — whose every letter reiterated his hope that she had not been prevailed on to alter his sentence, if Ellen still remained silent — and send her niece from her? She came at length to the determination, that if another week passed and still there were no tidings, not to let this fearful self-sacrifice, if it really were such, last any longer, but gently, cautiously, tenderly as she could, prevail on Ellen to confide all to her, and promise, if Edward really had been erring and in difficulties, all should be forgiven for her sake, and even his uncle's anger averted. Once her determination taken, she felt better enabled to endure an anxiety which was injuring her almost as much as Ellen; and she turned to Ellis's room, which she had lately very often frequented, for she scarcely felt comfortable when Ellen was out of her sight, though she had full confidence in Ellis's care.

Ellen was asleep on a sofa, looking so wan, so haggard — so altered from the Ellen of five short months back, that Mrs. Hamilton sat down by her side, pondering whether she was doing right to wait even another week, before she should try to bring relief by avowing her suspicions — but would it bring relief? and, after all, was it for Edward? or, had she been allowing affection and imagination to mislead and soften, when sternness might still be needed?

Ellen woke with a start as from some fearful dream, and gazed at Mrs. Hamilton for a full minute, as if she did not know her.

"My dear Ellen, what is it? You have been sleeping uncomfortably — surely you know me?"

"I thought I was at — at — Seldon Grange — are you sure I am not? Dear aunt Emmeline, do tell me I am at Oakwood, I know I am to go, and very soon; but I am not there now, am I?" and she put one hand to her forehead, and gazed hurriedly and fearfully round her, while, with the other, she held tightly Mrs. Hamilton's dress. There was something alarming both in her look and tone.

"No, love, you are with me still at Oakwood, and you will not go from me till you have been with Edward some little time. You cannot think I would send you away now, Ellen?"

The soothing tone, her brother's name, seemed to disperse the cloud, and bursting into tears, she exclaimed —

"He will never come — I know he will never come — my sin has killed him?"

"Your sin, Ellen, what can that have to do with Edward?'

"Because," the words "it was for him" were actually on her lips; but they were checked, and, in increasing excitement, she continued — "Nothing, nothing, indeed, with him — what could it have? But if he knows it — oh, it will so grieve him; perhaps it would be better I should go before he comes — and then, then, he need not know it; if, indeed, he ever comes."

"I do not think you quite know what you are saying, my dear Ellen; your uncomfortable dream has unsettled you. Try and keep quiet for an hour, and you will be better. Remember, suffering as this dreadful suspense is, your brother is still in a Father's gracious keeping; and that He will listen to your prayers for his safety, and if it be His good pleasure, still restore him to you."

"My prayers," answered Ellen, fearfully. "Mr. Howard said, there was a barrier between Him and me, while I would not confess; I had refused His mercy."

"Can you confess before God, Ellen? Can you lay your whole heart open before Him, and ask Him in his infinite mercy, and for your Saviour's sake, to forgive you?"

"I could, and did do so, answered Ellen, returning Mrs. Hamilton's earnestly inquiring look, by raising her large, expressive eyes, steadily and fearlessly, to her face; "but Mr. Howard told me it was a mockery and sin to suppose God would hear me or forgive me while I refused to obey Him, by being silent and obdurate to you. That if I wished His forgiveness, I must prove it by telling the whole to you, whom His commandments desired me to obey, and — and — as I dared not do that, I have been afraid to pray." And the shudder with which she laid her head again upon the pillow, betrayed the misery of the fear.

"And is it impossible, quite impossible that you can confide the source of your grief and difficulty to me, Ellen? Will you not do so, even if I promise forgiveness, not merely to you, but to *all* who may have erred? Answer me, my sweet child; your silence is fearfully injuring your mind and body. Why do you fancy you dare not tell me?"

"Because, because I have promised!" answered Ellen, in a fearful tone of returning excitement, and, sitting upright, she clasped her hands convulsively together, while her cheek burned with painful brilliancy. "Aunt Emmeline — oh, do not, pray do not speak to me in that kind tone! be harsh and cold again, I can bear it better. If you did but know how my heart and brain ache — how they long to tell you and so rest — but I cannot — I dare not — I have promised."

"And you may not tell me whom you have promised?" replied Mrs. Hamilton, every former thought rendered apparently null and vain by these words, and painfully disappointing her; but the answer terrified her.

"Mamma — I promised her, and she stands by me so pale, so grieved, whenever I think of telling you," answered Ellen, clinging to Mrs. Hamilton, but looking with a strained gaze of terror on vacancy. "I thought I must have told you, when you said I was to go — to go to Seldon Grange — but she stood by me and laid her hand on my head, and it was so cold, so heavy, I don't remember any thing more till I found you and Ellis leaning over me; but I ought not to tell you even this. I know I ought not — for look — look, aunt Emmeline! — don't you see mamma — there — quite close to me; oh, tell her to forgive me — I will keep my promise," and shuddering convulsively, she hid her face in her aunt's dress.

Mrs. Hamilton was dreadfully alarmed. Whatever the foundation, and she had no doubt that there was some, and that it really had to do with Edward and his poor mother's mistaken partiality, Ellen's imagination was evidently disordered. To attempt obtaining the truth, while she was in this fearful state of excitement, was as impossible as cruel, and she tried only to soothe her to composure; speaking of her mother as happy and in Heaven and that Ellen had thought of her so much, as was quite natural in her sorrow, that she fancied she saw her.

"It is not reality, love; if she could see and speak to you, I am sure it would be to tell you to confide all your sorrow to me, if it would make you happier."

"Oh, no, no — I should be very wicked if it made me happier; I ought not even to wish to tell you. But Mr. Myrvin told me, even when mamma went to Heaven, she would still see me, and know if I kept my promise, and tried to win her love, by doing what I know she wished, even after she was dead; and it was almost a pleasure to do so till now, even if it gave me pain and made me unhappy; but now, now, aunt Emmeline, I know you must hate me; you never, never can love me again — and that — that is so hard to bear."

"Have you forgotten, my dear Ellen, the blessed assurance, there is more joy in Heaven over one sinner that repenteth, than over ninety-and-nine who have not sinned? and if our Father in Heaven can so feel, so act, are His creatures to do less? Do you think, because you have given me pain, and trouble and disappointment, and compelled me to use such extreme severity, and cause you so much suffering, that it will be quite impossible for me to love you again, if I see you do all you can to win back that love?"

Ellen made no answer; but the alarming excitement had so far subsided, as to raise the hope that quietness would subdue it altogether. Mrs. Hamilton remained with her till she seemed quite calm, and would not have left her then, but she had promised Caroline to drive with her into T— that afternoon, to make some purchases; Emmeline and Miss Harcourt were spending the day at Greville Manor, and her daughter depending on her, she did not like to disappoint her. But the difficulty to think of other things, and cheerfully converse on comparatively indifferent topics, was greater than she had ever found it. That Ellis's surmise was correct, she had no longer the smallest doubt. Ellen was sacrificing herself, not merely for the love she bore her brother, but from some real or imaginary promise to her poor mother. What its exact nature was, she could not indeed satisfy herself, but that it had something to do with concealing Edward's faults seemed to flash upon her, she hardly knew how. Ellis's words "that she had seen enough of that work when they were children," returned to her, and various incongruities in Ellen's character and conduct which she had been unable to reconcile at the time, all seemed connected with it. But to arrive at the truth was much more difficult than ever; still, how could she send Ellen away? and yet, if still silent, would mere surmise satisfy her husband? There was but one hope, one ray of light — Edward's own honor, if indeed he were permitted to return; and even while driving and talking with Caroline, her heart was one fervent prayer that this might be, and the fearful struggle of her devoted Ellen cease.

Her aunt's gentle and unexpected kindness had had such a beneficial effect on Ellen, that, after her early dinner, about three o'clock, she told Ellis she would go in the school-room, and try and read there for an hour; she knew all the family were out, and therefore would be quite undisturbed. Ellis willingly acquiesced, rejoicing that she should seek any change herself, and advised her, as it was such a mild, soft afternoon, after the late storms, to take a turn on the terrace, on which a glass-door from the school-room opened; it would do her good. Ellen meant to take her advice, but as she looked out from a window over a well-remembered landscape, so many painful thoughts and recollections crowded on her, that she lost all inclination to move. She had not stood there for many weeks, and it seemed to her that the view had never looked so very lovely. The trees all had the last glories of autumn — for it was early in November — the grass was of that beautiful humid emerald which always follows heavy rain, and though the summer-flowers had all gone, the sheltered beds of the garden, lying beneath the terrace, presented many very beautiful still. The end of the terrace, a flight of stone steps, overlooked the avenue, leading from the principal lodge to the main entrance, and where Ellen stood, she could distinguish a few yards of the path where it issued from some distant trees. She gazed at first, conscious only that she was banished from it all, and that, however long her departure might be deferred, she must go at last, for her uncle's mandate could not be disobeyed; but gradually her eye became fixed as in fascination. A single figure was emerging from the trees, and dressed in the uniform of a midshipman—she was sure it was! but it was a figure so tall, so slim, his step so lingering, it could not be Edward, most likely some one of his messmates come to tell his fate. He was taller even than Percy, but so much slighter, so different to the boy from whom she had parted, that, though her heart bounded and sunk till faintness seemed to overpower her, she could not convince herself it was he. With an almost unconscious effort she ran out, through the glass-door to the steps of the terrace she could now see him distinctly, but not his face, for his cap was low over his forehead; but as he approached, he paused, as if doubting whether to go up to the hall door, or the well-known terrace, by which he had always rushed into the school-room, on his daily return from Mr. Howard's; and as he looked hastily up, his cap fell back, and his eyes met Ellen's. A wild but checked scream broke from her lips, and all was an impenetrable mist till she found herself in her brother's arms, in the room she had quitted, his lips repeatedly pressing her cheek and forehead, and his voice, which sounded so strange—it did not seem like Edward's, it was so much more deep and manly—entreating her to speak to him, and tell him why she looked so ill; but still her heart so throbbed she could not speak. She could only cling close to him and look intently in his face, which was so altered from the happy, laughing boy, that had he not been, from his extreme paleness and attenuation of feature, still more like their mother when she was ill, his sister would scarcely have known him.

"Dearest Ellen, do speak to me; what has been the matter, that you look so pale and sad? Are you not glad to see me?"

"Glad! oh, Edward, you cannot know how glad; I thought you would never, never come, the storms have been so terrible; I have been ill, and your sudden appearance startled me, for I had thought of such dreadful things, and that was the reason I could not speak at first; but I am sure you are as pale as I am, dear, dear Edward; you have been wounded—have you not recovered them yet?"

"My wounds, Ellen! oh, they were slight enough; I wished and tried for them to be severer, to have done for me at once, but they would not, they only bought me praise, praise which maddened me!"

"Sir Edward," murmured Ellen, in a low, fearful voice, "how did he part with you?"

"As he has always treated me, a kind, too kind father! oh, Ellen, Ellen, if he did but know the deceiving villain that I am!"

"Would he indeed not forgive, Edward, if he so loves you? not if he knew all, the temptation, the —"

"Temptation, Ellen! what excuse ought there to be in temptation? Why was I such a fool, such a madman, to allow myself to be lured into error again and again by that villain, after I had discovered his double face, and I had been warned against him, too? Why did I so madly disregard Mr. Howard's and my uncle's warning letters, trusting my self-will and folly, instead of their experience? Brave! I am the veriest coward that ever trod the deck, because I could not bear a sneer!"

"And he? are you still within his power?" inquired Ellen, shrinking in terror from the expression of her brother's face.

"No, Ellen, no; God forgive me — I have tried not to rejoice; the death was so terrible, so nearly my own, that I stood appalled, and, for the first time these two years, knelt down to my God for pardon, mercy to repent. The lightning struck him where he stood, struck him beside me, leaving the withering smile of derisive mockery, with which he had that moment been regarding me, still on his lips. Why, and where had he gone? he, who denied God and his holy Word, turned the solemn service into mockery, and made me like himself — and why was I spared? Oh, Ellen, I have no words to describe the sensation of that moment!" He stopped, and shuddered, then continued, hurriedly, "Changed as I am in appearance, it is nothing to the change within. I did not know its extent till now that I am here again, and all my happy boyhood comes before me; aunt Emmeline's gentle lessons of piety and goodness — oh, Ellen, Ellen, what have been their fruits? For two years I have given myself up to passion, unrestrained by one word, one thought of prayer; I dared, sinful madman as I was, to make a compact with my own conscience, and vow, that if I received the relief I expected from you, and was free from Harding, I would reform, would pray for the strength to resist temptation, which I had not in myself; and when, when the man that was despatched by Sir Edward from the shore, with the letters for the crew, sunk beneath the waves, bearing every despatch along with him, I cursed him, and the Fate, which had ordained his death. Ellen, Ellen! why was I saved, and Harding killed?"

"And you never received my letter, Edward? Never knew if I had tried to relieve you from Harding's power?" answered Ellen, becoming so deadly pale, that Edward forced himself to regain composure; the nature of his information causing such a revulsion of feeling in his sister as to deaden her to the horror of his words. For what had all this suffering been?

"I was sure you had, Ellen, for you always did, and I could trust you as I could myself. A sudden squall had upset the boat, and the man was so encumbered by a large great-coat, every pocket filled with letters and papers, that he sunk at once though every help was offered. I threw myself into the sea to save him, and Lieutenant Morley praised my courage and benevolence — little did he know my motive! Besides, Sir Edward told me there was an inclosure for me in my uncle's to him, and regretted he had not kept it to give it me himself — would to Heaven he had? Till Harding's death I was in his power; and he had so used it, that I had vowed, on our arrival in England, to abscond, hide myself forever, go I cared not where, nor in what character! But he is dead, and I am free; my tale need be told to none, and if I can I will break from this fatal spell, and redeem the past; but it seems, as if fiends urged me still to the path of evil! Would that I had but courage to tell all to Mr. Howard, I should be safer then; but I cannot — cannot — the risk is too great. Carriage wheels!" he added, starting up — "my aunt and Caroline; oh, how I rejoiced when they told me at the lodge that my uncle was not here!" And in his extreme agitation at the thought of meeting his aunt, he forgot his sister, or he might have been startled at the effect of his words.

CHAPTER VIII.

THE STRUGGLE.

Mrs. Hamilton had been told at the lodge of her nephew's arrival, and so powerful was her emotion, that she leaned back in the carriage, as it drove rapidly from the lodge to the Hall, without the power of uttering a word. Caroline was surprised, for his return seemed to her only a cause of rejoicing; she had no idea of the mingled dread and joy, the trembling, lest Edward had indeed deceived them all, and, if he had not, the redoubled mystery of Ellen's conduct. While he was absent she could think calmly on him as the cause of all, but now that he was returned, her heart seemed to turn sick with apprehension, and she had hardly strength to inquire where he was, and great was her surprise when she found his arrival was still unknown. Caroline's joyful exclamation as she ran into the school-room to put away some of her purchases, drew her there at once; and for the first five minutes the intense thankfulness that he was indeed safe and comparatively well—that whatever might be the secret change, his affection for her, to judge by the warmth and agitation of his embrace, was unchanged, and she had that to work on, alone occupied her mind and enabled her to regain her calmness.

"You do indeed look as if you wanted English air and home nursing, my dear boy," she said, after some little time had elapsed, and Edward had seated himself by her, his hand still clasped in hers; "Sir Edward was quite right to invalid you. Emmeline does nothing but talk of your wounds as making you a complete hero; I am unromantic enough to wish that you had brought me home more color and more flesh, and less glory; but, I suppose from being so pale, you are more like your poor mother than ever;" and she looked at him so earnestly, that Edward's eyes, spite of all his efforts, sunk beneath hers. He answered gayly, however, and, in reply to Caroline's numerous queries, entered into an animated description of their voyage home and the causes of their detention, in their being so often compelled to put into port from the fearful storms they had encountered, and time slipped away so fast that the dinner-bell rung before any one was prepared.

That Ellen should look paler than even when she had left her in the morning, and be still more silent, did not astonish Mrs. Hamilton; the agitation of meeting her brother was quite enough to occasion it; and she advised her to remain quiet while they were at dinner, that she might rejoin them afterward. She looked as if she had been so very lately ill, that Edward was not surprised at her having dined already; but many little things that occurred during the evening—her excessive quietness, the evident restraint between her and Caroline, and, he at first fancied, and then was quite certain, between her and his aunt, startled and perplexed him. She seemed restrained and shy, too, with him, as if in constant terror. Poor child! her aunt had advised quietness while alone, and her brother's words rung in her ears, till repose seemed farther off than ever. After all she had suffered before, and after the sending that fatal letter, it had never reached him: she had utterly failed in her attempt to save him. If she had, indeed, confided at first in Mrs. Hamilton, measures would have been taken, she was sure, to have secured him the necessary relief, for whenever her uncle had sent him his allowance it was through Sir Edward, not encountering the risk of the loss of the letter. There had been times when, in the midst of her sufferings, Ellen could realize a sort of comfort in the idea that she had saved Edward and kept his secret; but where was this comfort now? All she had endured, all she was still to endure, was for nothing, worse than nothing; for if Edward knew her sin, feeling that it had brought him no good, and given up, as she felt he must be, to unrestrained passion, or he could not have given vent to such fearful sentiments, she actually trembled for its effect upon him and his anger on herself. She had sometimes fancied that, perhaps, his errors were not so great as he believed them, that he would confess them when he found only his kind, indulgent aunt at home, and so peace and hope gradually dawn for both him and her. All her wish, her hope now was that Mrs. Hamilton could be prevailed upon not to tell him what she had done, for whether it made him think he ought to confess himself its cause or not, its effect on him would be so terrible, that she felt any additional suffering to herself could be better borne.

With these thoughts, no wonder she was silent, utterly unable to subdue them as she wished, and evince natural interest in all that had occurred to Edward; and tell him all that had happened to herself during their long separation. Caroline, however, was so animated; and when Emmeline and Miss Harcourt returned, unable to comprehend what they could possibly be sent for a full hour earlier than usual, the astonishment and delight at seeing Edward, prevented any thing like a pause in conversation, or unnatural restraint. His cousins found so much to tell as well as to listen to, about Percy and Herbert, as well as themselves; and Emmeline made Edward tell her such minute particulars of their engagements with the pirates, and how he was wounded, and what Sir Edward said to him, that Mrs. Hamilton, anxious as she was — for the longer she was with her nephew, the more convinced she was that he could not meet her eye, and that his gayety was not natural — could not help being amused in spite of herself.

Engrossed with thought how to arrive at the truth, for which she ardently longed, she entered the library, when the prayer-bell rung, with her children; quite forgetting, till she had taken the place at the reading-desk, which, in the absence of her husband and sons, she always occupied herself, that she had intended to desire Ellen to resume her usual place by Emmeline, wishing to spare her any additional suffering the first night of Edward's return, and to prevent any painful feeling on his part. It was an oversight, but it vexed her exceedingly. She looked hastily round, in the hope of being in time, but Ellen was already in her place, though she had evidently shrunk still more into the recess of the lower window, as if longing for its massive curtains to hide her, and her face was buried in her hands. Mrs. Hamilton would have been still more grieved, if she had seen, as Ellis did, the beseeching, humble look, which, as they entered, Ellen had fixed upon her, and that her pale lips had quivered with the half-uttered supplication, which she failed in courage to fully pronounce. Edward appeared too wrapped in his own thoughts to notice it then; and as his aunt's gentle but impressive voice fell on his ear, the words, the room, the whole scene so recalled the happy, and comparatively innocent past, that it was with difficulty he could restrain his feelings, till the attitude of kneeling permitted them full vent in tears, actual tears, when he had thought he could never weep again. The contrast of his past and present self, rendered the one more brightly happy, the other more intensely dark than the actual reality. The unchecked faults and passions of his early childhood had been the sole cause of his present errors; but, while under the gentle control of his aunt and uncle, and Mr. Howard, he had not known these faults, and, therefore, believed they had all come since. He longed intensely to confide all his errors, all his remorse, to Mr. Howard, whom he still so dearly loved; but he knew he had not courage to confess, and yet hated himself for his cowardice.

Only too well accustomed to control, he banished every trace of tears (from all save the eye rendered even more than usually penetrating from anxiety) as he arose, and became aware, for the first time, that Ellen was not where he was accustomed to see her. He kissed her fondly as she hurriedly approached him; but perceiving she left the room with merely a faint good-night to the rest of the family, and no embrace, as usual, from Mrs. Hamilton, he darted forward, seized his aunt's hand, and exclaimed —

"What is the matter with Ellen, aunt Emmeline? Why is

she so changed, and why is your manner to her so cold and distant? and why did she kneel apart, as if unworthy to join us even in prayers? Tell me, for pity's sake!"

"Not to-night, my dear Edward. It is a long tale, and a painful one, and I rely on *you* to help me, that Ellen and myself may be again as we have been. It is as much pain to me as to her that we are not. To-morrow, I promise you, you shall know all. You have had excitement enough for to-day, and after your exhausting voyage must need rest. Do not fancy this an evasion of your request; I have longed for your return to influence Ellen, almost as much as for the happiness of seeing you again."

Edward was compelled to be satisfied and retire; but though he did feel sufficient physical exhaustion, for the comfort of his room to be unusually luxurious, his sleep was restless and disturbed by frightful dreams, in which, however varied the position, it always seemed that he was in danger, and Ellen sacrificing herself to save him.

On retiring for the night, Mrs. Hamilton discovered a note on her dressing-table. She thought she knew the writing, but from tremulousness it was so nearly illegible, that it was with great difficulty she deciphered the following words:

"I am so conscious I ought not to address you, know so well that I have no right to ask any favor from you, when I have given you so much trouble and pain, that I could not have asked it, if you had not been so very, very kind this morning. Oh! aunt Emmeline, if indeed you can feel any pity for me, do not, pray, do not tell Edward the real reason of my banishment from Oakwood; tell him I have been very wicked — have refused to evince any real repentance — but do not tell him what I have done. He is ill, unhappy at having to resign his profession even for a few months. Oh! spare him the misery of knowing my sin. I know I deserve nothing but severity from you — I have no right to ask this — but, oh! if you have ever loved me, do not refuse it. If you would but grant it, would but say, before I go, that in time you will forgive me, it would be such comfort to the miserable — ELLEN."

Mrs. Hamilton's eyes filled with tears; the word "*your*" had evidently been written originally, but partially erased, and "*the*" substituted in its stead, and she could not read the utter desolation of one so young, which that simple incident betrayed, without increase of pain; yet to grant her request was impossible. It puzzled her — for why should she so persist in the wish expressed from the beginning, that Edward should not know it? unless, indeed — and her heart bounded with the hope — that she feared it would urge him to confess himself the cause, and her sacrifice be useless. She locked up the note, which she would not read again, fearing its deep humility, its earnest supplication, would turn her from her purpose, and in praying fervently for guidance and fitful sleep, her night passed.

For some time after breakfast the following morning, Edward and his aunt were alone together in the library. It was with the utmost difficulty, he suppressed, sufficiently to conceal, the fearful agitation which thrilled through every nerve as he listened to the tale he had demanded. He could not doubt the use to which that money had been applied. His sister's silence alone would have confirmed it; but in that hour of madness — for what else is passion unrestrained by principle or feeling? — he was only conscious of anger, fierce anger, against the unhappy girl who had borne so much for him. He had utterly forgotten the desperate words he had written. He had never received the intended relief. Till within a week, a short week of his return, he had been in Harding's power, and as Ellen's devotion had saved him nothing, what could it weigh against the maddening conviction, that if he had one spark of honor remaining, he *must* confess that he had caused her sin? Instead of saving, she had betrayed him; and he left his aunt to seek Ellen, so evidently disturbed and heated, and the interview itself had been so little satisfactory in softening him, as, she had hoped, to win him to confession at once, for she had purposely spoken as indulgently of error and difficulty as she could, without betraying her strengthened suspicions, that if she had known how to do so, she would have forbidden his seeing Ellen till he was more calm.

Unhappily, too, it was that part of the day when Ellis was always most engaged, and she was not even in her own room, so that there was no check on Edward's violence. The control he had exercised while with his aunt but increased passion when it was removed. He poured forth the bitterest reproaches — asked how she could dare hope relief so obtained, would ever have been allowed to reach him? — what had she done but betrayed him? for how could he be such a dishonored coward as to let her leave Oakwood because she would not speak? and why had she not spoken? — why not betrayed him at once, and not decoyed him home to disgrace and misery?

Passion had so maddened him that he neither knew what he said himself, nor heard her imploring entreaties not to betray himself and she never would. She clung to his knees as she kneeled before him, for she was too powerless to stand, reiterating her supplication in a tone that ought to have recalled him to his better self, but that better self had been too long silenced, and infuriated at her convulsive efforts to detain him, he struck her with sufficient force to make her, more by the agony of a blow from him, than the pain itself, loose her hold at once, and darted from the room.

The hall door was open, and he rushed through it unseen into the park, flying he neither knew where nor cared, but plunging into the wildest part. How he arrived at one particular spot he knew not, for it was one which, of all others, in that moment of excitement, he would gladly have avoided. It was a small glade in the midst of the wood, shelving down to the water's edge, where he and Percy, with the assistance of Robert, had been permitted to erect a miniature boat-house, and where Edward had kept a complete flotilla of tiny vessels. There were the trees, the glade, the boat-house still, ay, and the vessels, in such beautiful repair and keeping, that it brought back the past so vividly, so overpoweringly, from the voiceless proof which it was of the affectionate remembrance with which he and his favorite tastes had been regarded, even in his absence, that he could not bear it. He flung himself full length on the greensward, and as thought after thought came back upon him, bringing Ellen before him, self-sacrificing, devoted, always interposing between him and anger, as she had done from the first hour they had been inmates of Oakwood, the thought of that craven blow, those mad reproaches, was insupportable; and he sobbed for nearly an hour in that one spot, longing that some chance would but bring Mr. Howard to him, that he might relieve that fearful remorse at once; but utterly unable to seek him of himself.

Edward's disposition, like his mother's, was naturally much too good for the determined pursuit of evil. His errors had actually been much less grave, than from Harding's artful representations he imagined them. He never indulged in passion without its being followed by the most agonized remorse; but from having pertinaciously banished the religion which his aunt had so tried to instil, and been taught by Harding to scoff at the only safe guide for youth, as for every age, God's holy Word, he had nothing whereon to lean, either as a comfort in his remorse, a hope for amendment, or strength for self-conquest; and terrible indeed might have been the consequences of Harding's fatal influence, if the influence of a home of love had not been still stronger.

Two hours after he had quitted his aunt, he rejoined the family, tranquil, but bearing such evident traces of a mental struggle, at least so Mrs. Hamilton fancied, for no one else noticed it, that she still hoped she did not exactly know what, for she failed in courage to ask the issue of his interview with Ellen. She contented herself with desiring Emmeline to tell her cousin to bring her work or drawing, and join them, and she was so surprised, when Emmeline brought back word that Ellen had said she had much rather not, that she sought her herself.

Ellen's cheeks, in general so pale, were crimson, her eyes in consequence unnaturally brilliant, and she looked altogether so unlike herself, that her aunt was more anxious than ever; nor did her manner, when asked why she refused to join them, when Edward had so lately returned, tend to decrease the feeling.

"Emmeline did not say *you* desired it, or I should have known better than disobey," was her reply, and it was scarcely disrespectful; the tone seemed that of a spirit, crushed and goaded to the utmost, and so utterly unable to contend more, though every nerve was quivering with pain. Mrs. Hamilton felt bitter pain that Ellen at length did indeed shrink from her; that the disregard of her entreaty concerning her brother appeared so to have wounded, that it had shaken the affection which no other suffering had had power to move.

"I do not *desire* it, Ellen, though I wish it, she replied, mildly; "you are of course at liberty to act as you please, though I should have thought it most natural that, not having been with Edward so long, you should wish to be with him as much as possible now he is at home."

"He will not wish it; he hates me, spurns me, as I knew he would, if he knew my sin! To-day I was to have gone to Seldon Grange; let me go at once! then neither he, nor you, nor any one need be tormented with me any more, and you will all be happy again; let me go, aunt Emmeline; what should I stay for?"

"If you wish it, Ellen, you shall go next week. I did not imagine that under any circumstances, you could have expressed a desire to leave me, or suppose that it would make me particularly happy to send you away."

"Why should it not? you must hate me, too, or — or you

would not have refused the only — only favor I asked you before I went," answered poor Ellen, and the voice, which had been unnaturally clear, was choked for the moment with sobs, which she resolutely forced back. Mrs. Hamilton could scarcely bear it; taking her ice-cold hands in both hers, she said, almost tenderly —

"You have reason to condemn me as harsh and cruel, Ellen; but time will perhaps explain the motives of my conduct, as I trust and pray it will solve the mystery of yours; you are not well enough to be left long alone, and Ellis is so much engaged to-day that I do wish you to be with me, independent of your brother's society. If you so much prefer remaining here, I will stay with you, though of course, as Edward has been away from us so long, I should wish to be with him also."

It was almost the first time Mrs. Hamilton had ever had recourse in the management of her family to any thing that was not perfectly straightforward; and though her present motives would have hallowed much deeper stratagems, her pure mind shrunk from her own words. She wished Ellen to be constantly in Edward's presence, that he might not be able to evade the impulse of feeling and honor, which the sight of such suffering, she thought, must call forth; she could not bear to enforce this wish as a command, when she had already been, as she felt — if Ellen's silence were indeed self-devotion, not guilt — so cruelly and so unnecessarily severe. Ellen made neither reply nor resistance, but, taking up her work, accompanied her aunt to the usual morning-room, from which many a burst of happy laughter, and joyous tones were echoing. Caroline and Emmeline were so full of enjoyment at Edward's return, had so many things to ask and tell, were so perfectly unsuspicious as to his having any concern with his sister's fault, that if they did once or twice think him less lively and joyous, than when he left home, they attributed it simply to his not having yet recovered the exhausting voyage and his wounds. Miss Harcourt, just as unsuspicious, secretly accused Ellen as the cause of his occasional abstraction: her conduct was not likely to pass unfelt by one so upright, so honorable, and if he had been harsh with her, as from Ellen's fearfully shrinking manner, and complete silence when they were together, she fancied, she thought it was so deserved, that she had no pity for her whatever.

The day passed briskly and happily enough, in *seeming* to Mrs. Hamilton and Edward, in reality to all the other members of the party — but one. The great subject of regret was Mr. Howard's absence; he might be back at the rectory that evening, and Emmeline was sure he would come to see Edward directly. As the hours waned, Ellen became sensible of a sharp and most unusual pain darting through her temples, and gradually extending over her forehead and head, till she could scarcely move her eyes. It had come at first so suddenly, and lasting so short a time, that she could scarcely define what it was, or why she should have felt so suddenly sick and faint; but it increased, till there was no difficulty in tracing it, and before prayer-time, had become such fearful agony, that, if she had not been inured to pain of all kinds, and endowed with extraordinary fortitude and control, she must more than once have betrayed it by either giving way to faintness, or screaming aloud. She had overheard Mrs. Hamilton desire Robert to request Mr. Maitland to come to Oakwood as soon as he could, and not hearing the reply that he was not expected home till late at night, expected him every moment, and thought he would give her something to relieve it, without her complaining.

Edward had asked his cousins for some music, and then to please Emmeline, had sketched the order of their engagement with the pirates, and no one noticed her, for Mrs. Hamilton's heart was sinking with disappointed hope, as the hours passed, and there was no sign to prove that her surmise was correct, and if it were, that the truth would be obtained.

The prayer-bell rung, and as they rose, Edward's eyes, for the first time since she had joined them, sought and fixed themselves on his sister's face. The paroxysm of pain had for a few minutes subsided, as it had done alternately with violence all day, but it had left her so ghastly pale, that he started in actual terror. It might have been fancy, but he thought there was the trace of his cowardly blow on her pale forehead, raised, and black, and such a feeling of agony and remorse rushed over him, that it was with difficulty he restrained himself from catching her in his arms, and beseeching her forgiveness before them all; but there was no time then, and they proceeded to the library. Every step Ellen took appeared to bring back that fearful pain, till as she sat down, and then knelt in her place, she was sensible of nothing else.

The service was over; and as Mrs. Hamilton rose from the private prayer, with which each individual concluded his devotions, her nephew stood before her, white as marble, but with an expression of fixed resolution, which made her heart bound up with hope, at the very moment it turned sick and faint with terror.

Several of the lower domestics had quitted the library before Edward regained voice, and his first word, or rather action, was to desire those that remained to stay.

"My sister has been disgraced, exposed before you all," he exclaimed, in a tone of misery and determination, that so startled Miss Harcourt and his cousins, they gazed at him bewildered, "and before you all must be her exculpation. It was less for her sin than her silence, and for the increased guilt which that appeared to conceal, you tell me, she has been so severely treated. Aunt Emmeline, *I* am the cause of her silence — I was the tempter to her sin — I have deceived my commander, deceived my officers, deceived you all — and instead of being what you believe me, am a gambler and a villain. She has saved me again and again from discovery and disgrace, and but for her sin and its consequences would have saved me now. But what has sin ever done but to betray and render wretched? Take Ellen back to your love and care, aunt Emmeline, and tell my uncle, tell Sir Edward the wretch I am!"

For a full minute after these unexpected, startling words there was silence, for none could speak, not even Emmeline, whose first thought was only joy, that Ellen's silence was not so guilty as it seemed. Edward had crossed his arms on the reading-desk, and buried his face upon them. The instantaneous change of sentiment which his confession excited toward Ellen in those most prejudiced can scarcely be described; but Mrs. Hamilton, now that the words she had longed for, prayed for, had been spoken, had scarcely strength to move. Address Edward she could not, though she felt far more pity toward him than anger; she looked toward Ellen, who still remained kneeling, though Ellis stood close by her, evidently trying to rouse her, and with a step far more hurried, more agitated than her children or household had ever seen, she traversed the long room, and stood beside her niece.

"Ellen," she said, as she tried to remove the hands which clasped the burning forehead, as if their rooted pressure could alone still that agonizing pain, "my own darling, devoted Ellen! look up, and forgive me all the misery I have caused you. Speak to me, my child! there is nothing to conceal now, all shall be forgiven — Edward's errors, difficulties, all for your sake, and he will not, I know he will not, cause you wretchedness again; look up, my poor child; speak to me, tell me you forgive me."

Ellen unclasped her hands from her forhead, and looked up in Mrs. Hamilton's face. Her lips moved as if to speak, but in a moment an expression of agony flitted over her face, a cry broke from her of such fearful physical pain, that it thrilled through the hearts of all who heard, and consciousness deserted her at the same moment that Mr. Maitland and Mr. Howard entered the room together.

CHAPTER IX.

ILLNESS AND REMORSE.

It was indeed a fearful night which followed the close of our last chapter. Illness, sufficient to occasion anxiety, both in Herbert and Ellen, had been often an inmate of Oakwood, but it had merely called for care, and all those kindly sympathies, which render indisposition sometimes an actual blessing, both to those who suffer and those who tend. But illness, appearing to be but the ghastly vehicle of death, clothed in such fearful pain that no control, even of reason and strong will, can check its agonized expression, till at last, reason itself succumbs beneath it, and bears the mind from the tortured frame, this is a trial of no ordinary suffering, even when such illness has been brought about by what may be termed natural causes. But when it follows, nay, springs from mental anguish, when the sad watchers feel that it might have been averted, that it is the consequence of mistaken treatment, and it comes to the young, to whom such sorrow ought to be a thing unknown, was it marvel that Mrs. Hamilton, as she stood by Ellen's bed, watching the alternations of deathlike insensibility with paroxysms of pain, which nothing could relieve, (for it was only the commencement of brain fever,) felt as if she had indeed never known grief or anxiety before. She had looked forward to Edward's confession bringing hope and rest to all; that the aching head and strained nerves of her poor Ellen, only needed returning love, and the quietness of assured forgiveness for herself and Edward, for health and happiness gradually to return; and the shock of such sudden and terrible illness, betraying, as it did an extent of previous mental suffering, which she had not conceived as possible in one so young, almost unnerved her. But hers was not a character to give way; the anguish she experienced might be read in the almost stern quiet of her face, in her gentle but firm resistance to every persuasion to move from Ellen's bed, not only through that dreadful night, but for the week which followed. The idea of death was absolute agony; none but her God knew the struggle, day after day, night after night, which she endured, to compel her rebellious spirit to submission to His will, whatever it might be. She knew earth's dearest, most unalloyed happiness could not compare with that of Heaven, if indeed it should be His pleasure to recall her; but the thought *would not* bring peace. She had no reason to reproach herself, for she had acted only as imperative duty demanded, and it had caused her almost as much misery as Ellen. But yet the thought would not leave her, that her harshness and cruelty had caused all the suffering she beheld. She did not utter those thoughts aloud, she did not dare give words to that deep wretchedness, for she felt her only sustaining strength was in her God. The only one who would have read her heart, and given sympathy, strength, comfort, without a word from her, her husband, was far away, and she dared not sink; though there were times when heart and frame felt so utterly exhausted, it seemed as if she must.

Mr. Howard's presence had been an inexpressible relief. "Go to Edward, my dear friend," she had said, as he lingered beside the bed where Ellen had been laid, longing to comfort, but feeling at such a moment it was impossible; "he wants you more than any one else; win him to confide in you, soothe, comfort him; do not let him be out of your sight."

Not understanding her, except that Edward must be naturally grieved at his sister's illness, Mr. Howard sought him, and found him still in the library, almost in the same spot.

"This is a sad welcome for you, Edward," he said, kindly laying his hand on his shoulder, but do not be too much cast down. Ellen is very young, her constitution, Mr. Maitland assures us, is good, and she may be spared us yet. I came over on purpose to see you, for late as it was when I returned from Exeter, and found you had arrived, I would not defer it till to-morrow."

"You thought you came to see the pupil you so loved," answered Edward, raising his head, and startling Mr. Howard, both by his tone and countenance. "You do not know that I am the cause of my poor sister's suffering, that if she dies, I am her murderer. Oh, Mr. Howard," he continued, suddenly throwing himself in his arms, and bursting into passionate tears, "why did I ever leave you? why did I forget your counsels, your goodness, throw your warning letter to the winds? Hate me if you will, but listen to me — pity me, save me from myself.'

Startled as he was, Mr. Howard, well acquainted with the human heart, its errors, as well as its better impulses, knew how to answer this passionate appeal, so as to invite its full confidence and soothe at the same time. Edward poured out his whole tale. It is needless to enter upon it here in detail; suffice it, that the artful influence of Harding, by gradually undermining the good impressions of the home he had left, had prepared his pupil for an unlimited indulgence in pleasure, and excitement, at every opportunity which offered. And as the Prince William was cruising off the coast of British America, and constantly touching at one or other of her ports, where Harding, from his seniority and usefulness, and Edward, from his invariable good conduct, were often permitted to go ashore; these opportunities, especially when they were looked for and used by one practised in deceit and wickedness, were often found. It does not require a long period to initiate in gambling. The very compelled restraint, in the intervals of its indulgence, but increased its maddening excitement, and once given up to its blind pursuit, Harding became more than ever necessary to Edward, and of course his power over him increased. But when he tried to make him a sharer and conniver in his own low pleasures, to teach him vice, cautiously as he thought he had worked, he failed; Edward started back appalled, and though unhappily he could not break from him, from that hour he misdoubted and shrunk away. But he had given an advantage to his fell tutor, the extent of which he knew not himself. Harding was too well versed in art to betray disappointment. He knew when to bring wine to the billiard-table, so to create such a delirium of excitement, that Edward was wholly unconscious of his own actions; and once or twice he led him into scenes, and made him sharer of such vicious pleasures, that secured him as his slave; for when the excitement was over, the agony of remorse, the misery, lest his confiding captain should suspect him other than he seemed, made him cling to Harding's promises of secrecy, as his only refuge, even while he loathed the man himself. It was easy to make such a disposition believe that he had, in some moment of excitement, done something which, if known, would expel him the Navy; Edward could never recall what, but he believed him, and became desperate. Harding told him it was downright folly to think about it so seriously. It was only known to him, and he would not betray him. But Edward writhed beneath his power; perpe tually he called on him for pecuniary help, and when he had none, told him he must write home for it, or win it at the billiard-table, or he knew the consequences; and Edward, though again and again he had resolved he would not touch a ball or cue, (and the remorse had been such, that he would no doubt have kept the resolve, had it not been for dread of betrayal,) rather than write home, would madly seek the first opportunity, and play, and win perhaps enough, all but a few pounds, to satisfy his tormentor, and for these he would appeal to his sister, and receive them, as we know; never asking, and so never hearing, the heavy price of individual suffering at which they were obtained.

The seven or eight months which had elapsed before his last fatal appeal, had been occasioned by the ship being out at sea. Sir Edward had mentioned to Mr. Hamilton, that Edward's excellent conduct on board had given him a longer holiday on shore, when they were off New York, to which place he had been despatched on business to the President, than most of his companions. Edward thought himself safe, for Harding had been unusually quiet; but the very day they neared land, he told him he must have some cash, sneered at the trifling sum Edward had by him, told him if he chose to let him try for it fairly, they should have a chance at billiards for it; but if that fail, he must pump his rich relations for it, for have it he must. Trusting to his luck, for he had often won, even with Harding, he rushed to the table, played, and as might be expected, left off, owing his tormentor fifty pounds. Harding's fiendish triumph, and his declaration that he must trouble him for a check to that amount, signed by the great millionaire, Arthur Hamilton, Esq., goaded him to madness. He drank down a large draught of brandy, and deliberately sought another table and another opponent, and won back fifteen; but it was the last day of his stay on shore, as his enslaver knew, and it was the wretchedness, the misery of his heavy debt to the crafty, merciless betrayer of his youthful freshness and innocence, who had solemnly sworn if he did not pay it by the next letters from his home, he would inform against him, and he knew the consequences, which had urged that fearful letter to Ellen, from which all her suffering had sprung. Edward was much too young and ignorant of the world's ways to know that Harding no more dared execute his threat against him, than he could put his own head in the lion's mouth. His remorse was too deep, his loathing of his changed self too unfeigned, to believe that his errors were not of the heinous, fatal nature which Harding taught him to suppose them; and the anguish of a naturally fine noble, independent spirit may be imagined. All his poor mother's lessons of his uncle's excessive sternness, and determined pitilessness, toward the faults of those less firm and worthy than himself, returned to him, completely banishing his own experience of that same uncle's excessive kindness. The one feeling had been insensibly instilled in his boyhood, from as long as he could remember, till the age of twelve; the other was but the experience of eighteen short months. Oh, if parents would but think and tremble at the vast importance of the first lessons which reach the understanding of the young beings committed to their care! Let them impress TRUTH, not prejudice, and they are safe. Once fix a false impression, and they know not, and it is well, perhaps, they do not, the misery that tiny seed may sow.

Mr. Howard listened with such earnest, heartfelt sympathy, such deep commiseration, that his young penitent told him every error, every feeling, without the smallest reserve; and in the long conversation which followed, he felt more comforted, more hopeful of himself, than he had done for long, long months. He told, with such a burst of remorseful agony, his cruelty to his devoted sister, that Mr. Howard could scarcely hear it unmoved, for on that subject there seemed indeed no comfort; and he himself, though he would not add to Edward's misery by confessing it, felt more painfully self-reproached for his severity toward her than his conduct as a minister had ever excited before.

"Be with me, or rather let me be with you as much as you can," was Edward's mournful appeal, as their long interview closed; "I have no dependence on myself — a weak, miserable coward! longing to forsake the path of evil, and having neither power nor energy to do so. I know you will tell me, pray — trust. If I had not prayed, I could not have confessed — but it will not, I know it will not last."

"It will, while enduring this heavy trial of your poor sister's terrible illness, and God's infinite mercy may so strengthen you in the furnace of affliction, as to last in returning joy. Despair, and you must fall; trust, and you will hope and struggle — despite of pain or occasional relapses. Your faults are great, but not so great as Harding represented them — not so heavy but that you can conquer and redeem them, and be yet all we have believed you, all that you hoped for in yourself."

"And my uncle —" said Edward, hesitatingly.

"Must be told; but I will answer for him that he will be

neither harsh nor unjust, nor even severe. I will write to him myself, and trust to convince him that your repentance, and resolution are sufficiently sincere, to permit you a second trial, without referring to Sir Edward. You have done nothing to expel you from your profession; but it depends on yourself to become truly worthy of its noble service."

There was much in the sad tale he had heard to give hope, and Mr. Howard longed to impart its comfort to Mrs. Hamilton; but he felt she could not listen. While day after day passed, and the poor sufferer for another's errors lay hovering between life and death, reason so utterly suspended, that even when the violent agony of the first seven days and nights had subsided into lethargic stupors, alternating with such quiet submission and gentle words, that, had it not been for their wandering sense, one might have fancied intellect returning; still reason was absent — and, though none said it aloud, the fear would gain dominion, that health might return, but not the mind. The first advice had been procured — what was distance, even then, to wealth? — every remedy resorted to. Her luxuriant hair cut close, and ice itself applied to cool that burning, throbbing pain; but all had seemed vain, till its cessation, at the end of seven days, somewhat renewed Mr. Maitland's hope.

Not one tear had Mrs. Hamilton shed, and so excessive had been her fatigue, that Miss Harcourt and her children trembled for her; conjuring her, for their sakes, for her husband's, to take repose. Mr. Maitland's argument, that when Ellen recovered her senses (which he assured her now he had little doubt she would eventually,) she would need the soothing comfort of her presence still more than she could then, and her strength must fail before that — if she so exhausted it — carried more weight than all the rest; and her daughters had the inexpressible relief of finding that when, in compliance with their tearful entreaties, she did lie down, she slept, and slept refreshingly, for nature was exhausted. There was much of comfort in those days of trial, which Mrs. Hamilton fully realized, when Ellen's convalescence permitted her to recall it, though at the time it seemed unnoticed. That Caroline's strong mind and good heart should urge her to do every thing in her power to save her mother trouble, even to entreat Ellis and Morris to show her, and let her attend to the weekly duties with them, and accomplish them so earnestly and well, that both these faithful domestics were astonished and delighted, was not surprising; for hers was a character to display its better qualities in such emergencies. But that Emmeline should so effectually rouse herself from the overwhelming grief, which had at first assailed her at Ellen's fearful sufferings and great danger, as to be a comfort alike to her mother and Edward, and assist Caroline whenever she could, even trying to be hopeful and cheerful for others' sakes, till she actually became so, *was* so unexpected, from the grief she had indulged in when she parted from her father, that it did surprise. To be in the room with Ellen had so affected her at first, that she became pale, and so evidently terrified, that Mrs. Hamilton half desired her not to come, especially as she could do no good; and Mrs. Greville and Mary had tried to prevail on her to stay with them, but she would not hear of it.

"If I can do no good, can neither help mamma in nursing Ellen, nor do as Caroline does, I can, at least, try to comfort poor Edward, and I will not leave him. If I am so weak as not to be able to endure anxiety and sorrow without showing it, it shall not conquer me. No, no, dear Mary; come and see me as often as you like, but I cannot leave home till mamma and Ellen and we are all happy again!"

And she did devote herself to Edward, and so successfully — with her gentle sympathy with his grief, her tender feeling toward his faults, her conviction of her father's forgiveness, her unassuming but heart-breathing piety, which, without one word unduly introduced of a subject so holy, for she felt herself much too lowly and ignorant to approach it — yet always led up his thoughts to God, and from one so young, so humble, and, in general, so joyous, had still greater effect in confirming his returning religious hope, than had his teachers been only those who were older and wiser than himself. However miserable he might be before she came, he looked to her society, her eloquence, as comfort and hope; and soon perceiving this, she was encouraged to go on, though quite astonished — for she could not imagine what she had done to deserve such commendation — when Mr. Howard, one day meeting her alone, took both her hands in his, and with even unusual fervor bade God bless her! — for young, lowly as she was, she not only comforted the erring, but raised and strengthened the penitent's trembling faith and hope.

Poor Edward! harder than all seemed to him his aunt's silence. He knew his sister entirely engrossed her — ill as Ellen was, it could not be otherwise; but he passionately longed only for one word from her: that she forgave him the misery she was enduring. Not aware that such was his feel ing, conscious herself that her sole feeling toward him was pity, not anger, and looking to herself alone as the cause of her poor child's sufferings, she did not think for a moment that he could imagine her never referring to his confession originated in displeasure.

Ten or twelve days had so passed, when one afternoon, completely exhausted with two nights' watchfulness — for though nurse Langford and Fanny were in constant attendance on Ellen, she could not rest if she heard that harrowing cry for her, even though her presence brought no comfort — she went to lie down for a few hours on a couch in her dressing-room. Caroline had taken a book, though with not much inclination to read, to sit by her, and watch that her sleep should not be disturbed. How in those moments of quiet did she long for her father! feeling intuitively how much heavier was her mother's trial without his loved support. He had been written to by them all since Edward's confession. Mrs. Hamilton had done so in Ellen's room, only to beseech him to write forgivingly, forbearingly to the unhappy cause of all. She did not dare breathe her feelings, even on paper, to him, convinced that if she did so, control must give way, and she was powerless at once; but her husband knew her so well that every suppression of individual emotion betrayed, more forcible than the most earnest words, all she was enduring.

Caroline had kept her affectionate vigil nearly two hours, when Edward's voice whispered, "Miss Harcourt wants you, dear Caroline; let me take your place, I will be quite as watchful as yourself; only let me stay here, you do not know the comfort it will be."

To resist his look of pleading wretchedness was impossible. She left him, and Edward drawing a low stool to the foot of the couch, as if not daring to occupy his cousin's seat, which was close by the pillow, gazed on the mild, gentle features of his aunt, as in their deep repose they showed still clearer the traces of anxiety and sorrow, and felt more keenly than ever the full amount of misery, which his errors and their fatal concealment had created. "Why is it," he thought, "that man cannot bear the punishment of his faults without causing the innocent, the good, to suffer also?" And his heart seemed to answer, "Because by those very social ties, the strong impulses of love for one another, which would save others from woe, we may be preserved and redeemed from vice again, and yet again, when, were man alone the sufferer, vice would be stronger than remorse, and never be redeemed."

Mrs. Hamilton woke with that painful start which long watchfulness always occasions, and missing Caroline, yet feeling as if she were not alone, her eyes speedily fixed themselves in some surprise on the figure of her nephew, who, unable to bear the thoughts the sight of her exhaustion produced, had bent his head upon the couch. Inexpressibly touched, and glad of the opportunity to speak to him alone, she called him to her, and there was something in the tone that encouraged him to fling himself on his knees by her side, and sob like an infant, saying, almost inarticulately —

"Can you, will you ever forgive me, aunt Emmeline? Your silence has almost broken my heart, for it seemed to say you never could; and when I look at my poor Ellen, and see how I have changed this happy home into sorrow and gloom, and sin, for it is all my work — mine, whom you have loved, treated, trusted, as a son — I feel you cannot forgive me; I ought to go from you; I have no right to pollute your home."

"Hush, Edward! do not give utterance or indulgence to any such thoughts. My poor, unhappy boy! your errors have brought such fearful chastisement from the hand of God himself, it is not for me to treat you harshly. May His mercy avert yet severer trial! I will not hear your story now; you are too agitated to tell it, and I am not at this moment strong enough to hear it. I am satisfied that you have confided all to Mr. Howard, and will be guided by him. Only tell me how came you first to apply to Ellen? Did the thought never strike you, that in sending relief to you, she might be exposing herself to inconvenience or displeasure? Was there no consideration due to her?"

"I never seemed to think of her, except as glad and willing to help me, at whatever cost to herself," was his reply. "I feel now the cruel selfishness of the belief — but oh, aunt Emmeline, it was fostered in me from my earliest childhood, grew with my growth, increased with my years, received strength and meaning from my poor mother's utter neglect of her, and too indulgent thought for me. I never thought so till now, now that I know all my poor sister's meek and gentle worth, and it makes me still more miserable. I never could think her my equal; never could fancy she could have a will or wish apart from mine, and I cannot trace the commencement of the feeling! Oh! if we had been but treated alike! but taught to so love each other, as to think of each other's happiness above our own, as you taught my cousins!"

"Do you know any thing of the promise to which poor Ellen

so constantly refers?" inquired Mrs. Hamilton, after gently soothing his painful agitation.

He did not; but acknowledged that from the time they had become inmates of Oakwood, Ellen had constantly saved him from punishment by bearing the panalty of his faults; recalling numerous incidents, trifling in themselves, but which had always perplexed Mrs. Hamilton, as evincing such strange contradictions in Ellen's childish character, and none more so than the disobedience which we related in our second part, and which Edward's avowal of having himself moved the flower-stand, now so clearly explained. He said, too, that Mr. Howard had thought it necessary, for Ellen's perfect justification, to examine her letters and papers, but that all his appeals to her had been destroyed but one — his last fatal inclosure, the exact contents of which he had so utterly forgotten, written, as they were, in a moment of madness, that he shuddered himself as he read it. He placed the paper in Mrs. Hamilton's hand, conjuring her not to recall her forgiveness when she read it; but she must see it, it was the only amends he could make his poor Ellen, to exculpate her fully. Was it any wonder it had almost driven her wild? or that she should have scarcely known the means she adopted to send him the relief, which, as he deserved, had never reached him.

Mrs. Hamilton read the letter, and as thought after thought rose to her mind, connecting, defining, explaining Ellen's conduct from her fifteenth birth-day, the day she received it, to the discovery of her sin, and her devoted silence afterward, trifling incidents which she had forgotten returned to add their weight of evidence, and increase almost to agony her self-reproach, for not seeing the whole before, and acting differently. She remembered now Ellen's procrastination in writing to Edward, the illness which followed, and could well understand her dread lest the finding the notes should be traced to that day, and so throw a suspicion on her brother, and her consequent firmness in refusing to state the day she had found them.

That long interview was one of inexpressible comfort to Edward; but though his unfeigned repentance and full confession gave his aunt hope for him, it did but increase her individual trial, as she returned to Ellen's couch, and listened to wanderings only too painfully explained by the tale she had heard.

CHAPTER X.

MISTAKEN IMPRESSIONS ERADICATED.

It was the seventeenth day of Ellen's illness, and for six-and-thirty hours she had slept profoundly, waking only at very long intervals, just sufficiently to swallow a few drops of port wine, which Mr. Maitland had ordered to be administered if she woke, and sunk to sleep again. It was that deep, still, almost fearful repose, for it is so like death, which we can scarcely satisfy ourselves is life, except by holding a glass at intervals to the lips, to trace if indeed it receive the moisture of the breath. And nurse Langford, Mrs. Hamilton, and Edward had, through these long hours, watched and scarcely stirred. For they knew that on her waking hung hope or misery, return of intellect, or its confirmed suspension. Mr. Maitland had particularly wished Edward to be with her when she recovered her senses, that his presence might seem as natural as either of her cousins; but he warned him that the least display of agitation on his part, or reference to the past, in her exhausted state, might be fatal to her. It was quite the evening. Widow Langford had lighted the lamp, and sat down by the fire, scarcely able to breathe freely, from the intensity of her hope that Ellen would recover. And if such were her feelings, what were Edward's and Mrs. Hamilton's? The former was kneeling on the right of the bed, his eyes alternately fixed on his sister, and buried in the coverlid. Mrs. Hamilton was on the opposite side, close to Ellen's pillow, the curtain drawn so far back, that the least change on the patient's countenance was discernible. Hour after hour had so passed, the chimes that told their flight were scarcely heard by those anxious watchers. It was about eight o'clock, when a slight movement in Ellen made her aunt's heart to throb, as almost to deprive her of breath; her eyes unclosed, and a smile, such as Mrs. Hamilton had not seen for weeks, nay, months circled her lips.

"Dear aunt, have I been ill? It seems such a long, long time since I have seen you, and my head feels so strange, so light; and this room, it is my own, I know, but I feel as if it did not belong to me, somehow. Do make my head clear, I cannot think at all."

"Do not try to think yet, darling. You have been very, *very* ill, and to endeavor to think might hurt you. Strength will soon return now, I hope, and then your head will be quite clear again," returned Mrs. Hamilton, quietly and caressingly, though she so trembled with the change from sickening dread to certain hope, that she herself scarcely knew how she spoke at all.

"But what made me so ill, aunt? I feel as if it were some great pain; I cannot remember any thing clearly, but yet it seems as if I had been very unhappy — and that — that you did not love me any more. Did any thing make me ill? Was it really so?"

"That I did not love you, my Ellen! Indeed, that was only fancy. You were very unhappy, as we were all, for Edward did not come as soon as we expected him, and the storms were very dreadful, and we feared his ship might have been wrecked, or cast ashore, somewhere very far off, where we could not hear of him; and when you saw him, and knew he was safe, the anxiety and pain you had undergone, made you ill; you know a little thing will do that, dearest."

"But is he really safe, aunt Emmeline? Where is he?"

"Close by you, love. He has been as watchful and anxious a nurse as I have been. Poor fellow, you have given him a sad welcome, but you must make up for it, by-and-by."

Ellen looked languidly, yet eagerly round, as her aunt spoke, and her gaze fixed itself on her brother, who was struggling violently to suppress the emotion which, at the sound of her voice, in connected words, nearly overpowered him; and still more so, when Ellen said, more eagerly than she had yet spoken —

"Dear Edward! come and kiss me, and do not look so sad. I shall soon get well."

He bent over her, and kissed her repeatedly, trying in vain to say something, but he felt so choked, he could not; and Ellen held his hand, and looked earnestly, searchingly in his face, as if trying painfully to define the vague thoughts and memories which seemed all connected with him and with pain, but which would not take a distinct form. Her eye wandered from him for a moment to nurse Langford, who had come to the foot of the bed, and that seemed another face connected with the blank past, and then it fixed itself again on Edward, and her pale face so worked with the effort of thought, that Mrs. Hamilton became alarmed. She saw, too, that Edward was growing paler and paler, and trembled for the continuance of his control. Taking Ellen's hand gently from his, and arranging her pillow at the same time, so as to turn her face rather from him, she said, playfully —

"You have looked at Edward long enough, Ellen, to be quite sure he is safe at home. So now I shall be jealous if you give him any more of your attention and neglect me ; you must take some nourishment, and try to go to sleep again, for I must not have you try your strength too much."

"If I could but remember clearly," answered Ellen, sadly ; "it is all so vague — so dark — but I do not think it was only because he did not come, that made me so unhappy."

"You are not going to be disobedient, dearest," replied Mrs. Hamilton, firmly, though fondly, as she hastily signed to Edward to leave the room, which he most thankfully did, never stopping till he reached his own, and tried to thank God for His great mercy, but could only sob. "I told you not to think, because to do so might retard return of strength, and indeed you must try and obey me; you know I am very peremptory sometimes." And the fond kiss with which she enforced the command seemed to satisfy Ellen, whose natural submissiveness, combined with excessive physical weakness, caused her to obey at once, and not attempt to think any more. She took the required nourishment with returning appetite, and soon afterward fell quietly and happily to sleep again, her aunt's hand closely clasped in hers.

From that day, all fear of disordered intellect departed, and, gradually, the extreme exhaustion gave way before Mr. Maitland's judicious treatment. Strength, indeed, returned so slowly and almost imperceptibly, that it was necessary to count improvement by weeks, not days. And when, six weeks after her first seizure, she was thought well enough to be carried to Mrs. Hamilton's dressing-room, and laid on a couch there, it was a source of gratitude and rejoicing to all. But Mr. Maitland and Mrs. Hamilton soon saw, with intense anxiety, that with physical strength, memory and thought had both fully returned, and that their consequence was a depression so deep, as effectually to retard her perfect recovery. She seemed to shrink from all attention, all kindness, as utterly undeserved, even from her cousins. She would look at Edward for half an hour together, with an expression of suffering that made the heart actually ache. At times she would receive Mrs. Hamilton's caressing and judicious tenderness as if it were her only comfort, at others, shrink from it, as if she had no right to it.

"This will never do," Mr. Maitland said, about ten days after Ellen's removal into her daily quarters, and finding she was losing ground; "there is something on her mind, which must be removed, even if to do so, you refer to the past. She remembers it all too clearly, I fear, so our not alluding to it does no good. You must be the physician in this case, my dear Mrs. Hamilton, for I am powerless."

But though she quite agreed with him, how to approach such a very painful subject required no little consideration; but, as is very often the case, chance does that on which we have expended so much thought.

One afternoon Ellen lay so still, so pale, on her couch, that Mrs. Hamilton bent over her to listen if she breathed, saying, as she did so, almost unconsciously —

"My poor Ellen, when shall I have the comfort of seeing you well and happy again?"

Ellen hastily unclosed her eyes, for she was not asleep — it had been only the stupor of painfully-engrossing thought, rendering her insensible to all outward things, but her aunt's voice aroused her, and it seemed an inexpressible relief to feel they were quite alone. Trying to rise, and clasping her hands, she said, in a tone of strong excitement —

"Oh, aunt Emmeline, how can I be happy — how can I be well — when I think — think — that if it had not been for my sin, and the misery it brought on me, Edward might be safe still? no one need have known his errors. I tried to save — and — and I have only betrayed, and made him wretched. All I suffered was for nothing, worse than nothing!"

"Thank God, you have spoken, my dear child! I felt as if I dared not introduce the subject; but now that you have yourself, I think I shall be able, if indeed you will listen to me patiently, Ellen, to disperse the painful mists, that are still pressing so heavily on this poor little heart and brain," she said, fondly, though seriously, as she put her arm round Ellen, to support her as she sat up. "I do not tell you it is not a natural feeling, my love, but it is a wrong one. Had your sin, in consideration of its being, as I am now convinced it was, wholly involuntary — for in the fearful state of mind Edward's desperate letter occasioned, you could not have known or thought of any thing, but that relief seemed sent to your hand — had it on that account been permitted so far to succeed, as to give him the aid he demanded, and never have been traced to you, it would have confirmed him in the path of guilt and error, and poisoned your happiness forever. When you recall the agony, almost madness you felt, while burdened with the consciousness of such an act, how could you have borne it, if it had continued through months, perhaps years? You shudder; yet this must have been the case, and Edward would have persisted in error, if your sin had been permitted to succeed. Its detection, and the sufferings thence springing, terrible as they have been to you, my poor child, have saved him; and will, I trust, only bring securer happiness to you."

"Saved him!" repeated Ellen, half starting up, and scarcely hearing the last words — "saved Edward!"

"Yes, dearest, by leading him to a full confession, and giving him not only the inexpressible comfort of such a proceeding, but permitting him to see, that great and disappointing as his errors are, they can be conquered. They are not of the irremediable, guilt-confirming nature, that he was taught to suppose them from Harding's own most guilty ends, and so giving him hope and resolution to amend, which a belief that amendment is impossible, entirely frustrates. Do not fear for Edward, my own love; he will give you as much pride and comfort as he has anxiety and grief; and you, under God's merey, will have been the cause. It is a hard lesson to learn, and yet, Ellen, I think one day, when you can look back more calmly on the last few months, you will acknowledge with me, that great as your sufferings have been, they were sent in love both to him and to you."

"If they have saved him — saved him from a continuance in error, and so made him happy! — Oh, aunt Emmeline, I can think so now, and I will try to bear the rest? but why," she added, growing more excited, "oh, why have you been so good, so kind? Why did you not continue cold and distant? I could bear it better, then."

"Bear what, love? What have you more to bear? Tell me all without reserve. Why should I be cold, when you deserve all my love and kindness?"

"Because — because, am I not to go to Seldon Grange, as soon as I am strong enough? Uncle Hamilton said, there could be no excusing cause demanding a complete avoidance of his sentence. I thought it was pain enough when you first told me; but now, now every time I think about it, it seems as if I could not bear it."

"And you are not called upon to bear it, my dear child. Is it possible you could think for a moment that I could send you away from me, when you have borne so much, and been treated with far too much severity already? Did I not tell you that the term of your banishment depended entirely on the motive of your silence, and do you think there was no excuse in your motive, my Ellen, mistaken as it was? Is self-devotion to be of no more account to me, than it seemed to you? Come, smile, dearest; I promise you, in your uncle's name and my own, you shall never leave us, unless it be of your own free will and pleasure, a few years hence."

Ellen did try to smile, but she was too weak to bear this complete removal of a double burden without an emotion that seemed more like pain than joy. She laid her head on her aunt's shoulder, and wept without restraint. They were the first tears she had shed since her illness, and Mrs. Hamilton thanked God for them. She did not attempt to check them, but the few words she did speak, told such affectionate sympathy, such perfect comprehension of that young heart, that Ellen felt as if a mountain of lead were dissolving from her.

"And now, my Ellen, that I have relieved you of a painful dread, will you ease my mind of a great anxiety?" inquired Mrs. Hamilton, nearly an hour afterward, when Ellen seemed so relieved and calmed, that she could talk to her without fear.

"You look surprised; but it is a subject you alone can explain, and till it is solved, I shall never feel that your happiness is secure. What is this promise, to which in your illness you so constantly referred, and which, I fear, has strengthened you in the system of self-sacrifice for Edward's sake, in addition to your love for him?"

A deep flush rose to Ellen's transparent cheek and brow, as she answered, falteringly —

"Ought I to tell you, dear aunt? You do not know how often, how very often I have longed to ask you, if to keep it made me do wrong — whether I ought to break it? And yet it seemed so sacred, and it gave poor mamma such comfort!"

"When did you make it, love? Its import I need not ask you, for you betrayed it, when you knew not what you said, and it was confirmed by your whole conduct. To shield Edward from blame or punishment, by never revealing his faults?"

"Was it wrong?" murmured Ellen, hiding her conscious face.

"Wrong in you! no dearest; for you were too young to know all the pain and evil it was likely to bring. Tell me when, and how, it was taken; and I think I can prove to you that your poor mother would have recalled it, had she had the least idea of the solemn hold it had taken upon you."

Thus encouraged, Ellen narrated the scene that had taken place in widow Morgan's cottage just before Mrs. Hamilton arrived; and her mother's fears for Edward, and dread of Mr

Hamilton, which it was very evident, and now more than ever, had extended to both her children. She said that Mr. Myrvin's assurance, that her mother could see, and would love her in Heaven, directly following the promise, had given it still more weight and solemnity. That at first she thought it would be very easy to keep, because she loved Edward so dearly; but she had not been long at Oakwood before it made her very unhappy, from its constant interference with, and prevention of, her obedience and duty to her aunt; that it had often caused her violent headaches, only from her vain attempts to satisfy herself as to that which she ought to do. When Edward first went to sea, and all seemed so right and happy with him, of course she became happier than she had ever been before. Then came his difficulties, and her conviction that she must save him and keep his secret. That her reason and her affection often urged her to confide all to her aunt, certain that she would not harshly condemn Edward, but would forgive and help him far more effectually than she could; but she dared not, for whenever she thought thus, the figure of her mother rose before her, seeming to reproach and threaten her for exposing the child she so dearly loved, to disgrace and ruin; and this was so vivid, so constant, during his last appeal, that she thought she must be going mad; that nothing but the dread of not being firm enough to keep Edward's secret, had withheld her from confessing her sin at once to her aunt, especially when her uncle had so solemnly denounced it as theft, and that when it was discovered it seemed actual relief, though it brought such severe punishment, for she knew no suffering for her could be too severe.

The tale, as Ellen told it, was brief and simple enough, and that there was any merit in such a system of self-devotion never seemed to enter her mind for a moment; but to Mrs. Hamilton it revealed such an amount of suffering and trial, such a quiet, systematic, heroic endurance, that she unconsciously drew that young delicate being closer and closer to her, as if her love should protect her in future from any such trial; and from what had it all sprung? — the misery of years, at a period when life should be so joyous and so free, that care and sorrow flee it as purely and too briefly happy to approach? From a few thoughtless words, from a thoughtless, partial mother, whose neglect and dislike had pronounced that disposition cold, unloving and inanimate whose nature was so fervid, so imaginative, that the utmost care should have been taken to prevent the entrance of a single thought or feeling too precocious, too solemn for her years. It may be urged, and with truth, that to an ordinary child the promise might have been forgotten, or heedlessly laid aside, without any harm accruing from it, but it was from not caring to know the real character of the little being, for whose happiness and virtue she was responsible, that the whole mischief sprung; and it is this neglect of maternal duty against which we would so earnestly warn those who may not have thought about it. It is *not enough* to educate the mind, to provide bodily necessaries, to be indulgent in the gift of pleasure and amusement, the *heart* must be won and taught; and to do so with any hope of success, the character must be transparent as the day; and what difficulty, what hinderance, can there, or ought there to be, in obtaining this important knowledge to a mother, from whose breast the babe has received its nourishment, from whose arms it has gradually slipped away to feel its own independence, from whose lips it has received its first lessons, at whose knee lisped its first prayer? How comparatively trifling the care, how easy the task to learn the opening disposition and natural character, so as to guide with gentleness and love, and create happiness, not for childhood alone, though that is much, but for youth and maturity.

All these thoughts passed through Mrs. Hamilton's mind as she listened to her niece, and looked at the pale, sweet face lifted up to hers in the earnestness of her simple tale, as if unconsciously appealing for her protection against the bewildering and contending feelings of her own young heart. How she was effectually to remove these impressions of years, indeed she knew not; her heart seemed to pray for guidance that peace might at length be Ellen's portion, even as she heard.

"You could scarcely have acted otherwise than you have always done toward Edward, my dear Ellen, under the influence of such a promise," she said; "your extreme youth, naturally enough, could not permit you to distinguish, whether it was called for by a mere impulse of feeling in your poor mother, or really intended. But tell me, do you think it would give me any comfort or happiness if I could see Emmeline act by Percy as you have done by Edward? To see her suffer pain and sorrow, and be led into error, too, sometimes, to conceal Percy's faults, and prevent their removal, when, by the infliction of some trifling pain, it would save his exposing himself to greater?"

"But it seems so different with my cousins, aunt; they are all such equals. I cannot fancy Emmeline in my place. You have always loved them all alike."

"And do you not think a mother ought to do so, dearest?

"But how can she, if they are not all equally deserving? I was so different to Edward; he was so handsome and good, and so animated and happy; and I was always fretful and ill, and they said so often naughty; and he used to fondle poor mamma, and show his love, which I was afraid to do, though I did love her so *very* much, (the tears started to her eyes,) so I could not help feeling he must be much better than I was, just as I always feel all my cousins are, and so it was no wonder poor mamma loved him so much the best."

"Have I ever made any difference between Edward and you, Ellen?" asked Mrs. Hamilton, conquering, with no small effort, the emotion called forth by Ellen's simple words.

"Oh, no, no!" and she clung to her in almost painful emotion. "But you are so good, so kind to everybody; you would love me, and be kind to me as poor papa was, because nobody else could."

"My dear Ellen, what can I do to remove these mistaken impressions? I love you, and your father loved you, because you have qualities claiming our love quite as powerfully as your brother. You must not imagine because you may be less personally and mentally favored, that you are *inferior* to him, either in the sight of your Heavenly Father, or of the friends and guardians He has given you. And even if such were the case, and you were as undeserving as you so wrongly imagine yourself, my duty, as that of your mother, would be just the same. A parent does not love and guide her children according to their individual merits, my dear Ellen, but according to the fountain of love which, to enable her to do her duty, God has so mercifully placed in her heart; and therefore those who have the least attractions and the most faults, demand the greater cherishing to supply the place of the one, and more careful guiding to overcome the other. Do you quite understand me, love?"

Ellen's earnest face, on which joy and hope seemed struggling with doubt, was sufficient answer.

"All mothers do not think of their solemn responsibility in the same light; and many causes — sad recollections and self-reproaches for her early life, and separation in coldness from her father and myself, might all have tended to weaken your mother's consciousness of her duty, and so, without any fault in yourself, my Ellen, have occasioned her too great partiality for Edward. But do you remember her last words?"

Ellen did remember them, and acknowledged they had so increased her affection for her mother, as to render the promise still more sacred to her.

"I feared so, dearest; but it is just the contrary effect which they should have had. When she called you to her, and blessed and kissed you as fondly as she did Edward, she said she had done you injustice, had failed in her duty to you, and it so grieved her, for it was too late to atone for it then; she could only pray to God to raise you up a kinder parent. I have tried to be that, for her sake, as well as your own; and will you not acknowledge, that if she had been spared to love and know your affection for her, she could no more have borne to see you suffer as you have done for Edward, than I could my Emmeline for Percy? Do you not think, when she had learned to feel as I do, which she had already begun to do, that she would have recalled that fatal promise, and entreated you not to act upon it? What has it ever done but to make you so painfully suffer, lead you often into error, and confirm, by concealment, Edward's faults?"

Ellen's tears were falling fast and freely, but they were hardly tears of pain. Her aunt's words seemed to disperse a thick mist from her brain and heart, and for the first time, to satisfy her that she might dismiss the painful memory of her promise, and dismiss it without blame or disobedience to her mother.

Mrs. Hamilton had begun the conversation in trembling, for it seemed so difficult to accomplish her object without undue condemnation of her sister; but as Ellen, clasping her arms about her neck, tried to thank her again and again, for taking such a heavy load from her heart, saying that she would still help Edward just the same, and she would try to guard him and herself from doing wrong, that her mother should love her still, she felt she had succeeded, and silently, but how fervently, thanked God.

"But will you tell me one thing, aunt Emmeline? Why, if the promise were mistaken, and poor mamma would have wished it recalled, did I always seem to see her so distinctly, and fancy she so desired me to save Edward from my uncle's displeasure?"

"Because you have a very strong imagination, my love, increased by dwelling on this subject; and in your last trial your mind was in such a fearful and unnatural state of excitement, that your imagination became actually diseased. It was not at all surprising; for much older and stronger, and wiser persons would have experienced the same, under the same pressure of grief, and terror, and remorse. But what can I do, to cure this morbid imagination, Ellen?" she continued, playfully; "sentence you, as soon as you get well to a course of mathematics, six hours each day?"

"I am afraid my poor head will be more stupid at figures than ever," replied Ellen, trying to smile, too.

"Then I suppose I must think of something else. Will you follow Emmeline's example, and tell me every thing, however foolish or unfounded it may seem, that comes into this little head — whether it worries or pleases you? You have nothing, and you will have nothing ever again, I trust, to conceal from me, my dear Ellen; and if you will do this, you will give me more comfort individually, and more security for the furtherance of your happiness, as far as my love can promote it, than any other plan."

Her playfulness had given place to renewed earnestness, and Ellen, as if in the very thought of such perfect confidence dwelt security and peace, so long unknown to her, gave the required assurance so eagerly and gratefully, that Mrs. Hamilton was satisfied and happy.

CHAPTER XI.

THE LOSS OF THE SIREN.

From that day, Ellen's recovery, though a sad trial of patience both to the young invalid and her affectionate nurses, was surely progressive, without any of those painful relapses which had so tried Mr. Maitland's skill before. She no longer shrunk from the society of her relations, receiving Caroline's and Miss Harcourt's many kind attentions with surprise indeed, for she could not imagine what could have so altered their feelings toward her, but with that evident gratitude and pleasure, which encourages a continuance of kindness. Emmeline was always kind, but it was indeed happiness to feel she might talk with and share her amusements, as in former days; and that, instead of thinking she ought not to receive her aunt's affection, the only thing she asked in return was her full confidence. The inexpressible rest to poor Ellen which that conversation gave is not to be described. It was so blessed, so soothing, that it seemed too unnatural to last, and the secret dread that her uncle would not feel toward her and Edward as her aunt did was its only alloy. Edward, too, was cheerful, and almost happy when with her: and a long conversation with Mr. Howard, which that worthy man insisted upon having as soon as she was strong enough, to remove the false impressions which his severity had given, and which never ceased to grieve and reproach him, caused his almost daily visits to be anticipated by her with as much gladness as they had before brought dread.

"And now that anxiety for Ellen is at an end, I must have you take more care of yourself, Mrs. Hamilton. Your husband's last injunctions were, that I should never pass a week without calling once or twice at Oakwood to know how all was going on, and what would he say to me if he could see you now?"

"He little thought how my strength would be tried, my good friend, and so will quite acquit you. I assure you that, physically, I am perfectly well" — (the worthy doctor shook his head most unbelievingly) — "but even with one great anxiety calmed, there remains another, which every week increases. It is more than double the usual time of hearing from my husband. We have never had any answer to the letters detailing Ellen's danger and Edward's return, and the answers have been due a full month."

"But the weather has been so unusually tempestuous, it may have been impossible for the Siren to ply to and fro from Feroe to Scotland, as Hamilton wished, and no ships are likely to touch at those islands in the winter. I really think you need not be anxious on that score; none but Arthur Hamilton's head could have contrived your hearing as regularly from such an outlandish place as you have done. No news is good news, depend upon it. He may be anxious on your account, and returning himself."

"God forbid!" answered Mrs. Hamilton, turning very pale; "better the anxiety of not hearing from him than the thought of his being at sea in this season."

Oakwood had resumed its regular happy aspect, though Ellen was still up-stairs. Morris and Ellis had once more the happiness of their beloved mistress's superintendence, and proud were they both, as if Caroline had been their own child, to show all she had done, and so unostentatiously, to save her mother trouble when she had been too anxious to think of any thing but Ellen; and the mother's heart swelled with a delicious feeling of gratitude to Him who, if in making her so acutely sensible of her solemn responsibility had deepened and extended *anxiety*, had yet in the same measure heightened and spiritualized *joy*. The fruit was indeed worth the nurture, though it might have been often washed with tears. Intensely anxious as she felt herself, as did also Mr. Howard and Mr. Maitland, and, in fact, all Arthur Hamilton's friends, she yet tried to sustain the spirits of her children, for the young men had evidently grown anxious on the subject too. It was not unlikely that the seas round Feroe, always stormy, should prevent any ship leaving the island, and the young people eagerly grasped the idea: so painful is it to youth to realize a cause for anxiety; but even they, at times, grew unconsciously sad and meditating, as the usually joyous season of Christmas and New Year passed, and still there was no letter. Ellen and Edward both in secret dreaded the arrival of the answer to the latter's confession; but still their affection for Mrs. Hamilton was too powerful to permit any thought of self interfering with the wish that her anxiety might be calmed.

In January the weather changed; the tremendous winds gave place to an almost unnatural calm, and to such excessive mildness and closeness of atmosphere, that it affected the health of many who were strong, and not only made Ellen very languid, but frequently recalled those dreadful headaches which were in themselves an illness. Business called Mr. Howard to Dartmouth near the end of the month, and he prevailed on Edward to accompany him, for whenever his sister was more than usually suffering his gloom redoubled. The first few days were so fine that the change renovated him; Mr. Howard declared it was the sight of old ocean, and Edward did not deny it; for though it was good for the permanence of his repentance and resolution to amend, to have the influence of his home sufficiently long, his spirit inwardly chafed at his detention, and yearned to be at sea again, and giving proof of his determination to become indeed a British sailor.

The third day of their visit, the lull and heaviness of the air increased so strangely and closely, for January, as to seem almost portentous. Edward and Mr. Howard lingered on the beach; the well-practised eye of the former tracing, in many little things unseen to landsmen, the slow, but sure approach of a fearful storm.

"It is strange for the season, but there is certainly electricity in the air," he said, directing Mr. Howard's attention to ridges of white-fringed clouds floating under the heavens, whose murky hue was becoming denser and denser; and ever and anon, as lashed by some as yet silent and invisible blast, the ocean heaved and foamed, and gave sure evidence of approaching fury; "there will be, I fear, a terrible storm to-night; and look at those birds," (several sea-gulls were skimming along the waves almost bathing their white plumage in the blackened waters), "strange how they always herald tempest! Emmeline would call them spirits of the blast, revelling in the destruction it foretells!"

"It is approaching already," rejoined Mr. Howard, as a long hollow blast moaned and shivered round them, followed by the roar of a mountainous wave bursting on the beach. "God have mercy on all exposed to its fury!" and he gladly turned more inland, while Edward remained watching its progress with an almost pleasurable feeling of excitement, only wishing he could but be on the sea, to enjoy it as such a storm deserved to be.

As the day drew to a close it increased, and as darkness set in, its fury became appalling. Blasts, long and loud as the reverberation of artillery, succeeded one another with awful rapidity, tearing up huge trees by the roots, and tiles from the roofs. Now and then, at distant intervals, blue lightning played through the black heavens, betraying that thunder had mingled with the wind, though it was impossible to distinguish the one sound from the other; and as the gusts passed onward, streaks of white and spots of strange unnatural blue gleamed through the gloom for a moment's space, leaving deeper darkness as they disappeared. The ocean, lashed to wildest fury, rolled in huge mountains of troubled waters, throwing up showers of snowy foam, contrasting strangely with the darkness of earth and heaven, and bursting with a sound that deadened for the time even the wild roar of the blast. To read or even to converse, in their comfortable quarters in the hotel, which overlooked the sea, became as impossible to Mr. Howard as to Edward. About eleven o'clock, however, the wind suddenly veered and lulled, only sending forth now and then a long sobbing wail, as if regretful that its work of destruction was even checked; but the sea raged with equal fury, presenting a spectacle as magnificent, as awful, and giving no appearance of a calm. A sharp report sounded suddenly from the sea — whether it was the first, or that others might have been lost in the tumult of the winds and waves, who might answer? Another, and another, at such rapid intervals, that the danger was evidently imminent, and Edward started to his feet. Again — and he could bear it no longer. Hurriedly exclaiming, "They are signals of distress and close at hand! Something must be done; no sailor can sit still, and see sailors perish!" he rushed to the beach, closely followed by Mr. Howard, who was resolved on preventing any mad attempt. Crowds of fishermen and townsmen had congregated on the beach, drawn by that fearful sound, which, by the light from the guns seemed scarcely half a mile distant; and yet so perilous was the present appearance of the ocean, that to go to their assistance seemed impossible. Suddenly, however, Edward's voice exclaimed, with the glad and eager tone of perfect confidence, "They can be saved! — a strong boat and two willing rowers, and I will undertake to reach the vessel, and bring the crew safe to shore. Who among you," he continued, turning eagerly to the group of hardy fishermen, "will be my assistants in this act of common humanity? who possesses willing hearts and able hands, and will lend them?"

"No one who cares for his life!" was the sullen answer from one of those he addressed, and the rest stood silent, eyeing, half disdainfully half admiringly, the slight figure of the young sailor, revealed as it was, in the fitful light of the many torches scattered by the various groups along the beach. "It is well for boys to talk, we cannot expect old heads on young shoulders; but not a boat with my consent leaves the harbor to-night; it would be wilful murder."

"I tell you I will stake my life on the venture," answered Edward, his passion rising high. "Am I speaking to sailors, and can they hesitate when they hear such sounds? Give me but a boat, and I will go by myself: and when you need aid, may you find those to give it! you will scarce dare ask it, if that vessel perish before your eyes. Lend me a boat, I say, fitted for such a sea, and the lender shall be rewarded handsomely. If there be such risk, I ask none to share it; my life is my own, and I will peril it."

It would have made a fine scene for a painter, that young, slight form and boyish face, surrounded by those weather-beaten men, every countenance expressing some different emotion, yet almost all unwilling admiration; the torches' glare, so lurid on the pitchy darkness; the sheets of foam, rising and falling like showers of dazzling snow; the craggy background; and, out at sea, the unfortunate vessel, a perfect wreck, struggling still with the fast-rising waters. Mr. Howard saw all, but with no thought of the picturesque, his mind was far otherwise engaged.

"By Neptune! but your honor shall not go alone! I have neither parent, nor sister, nor wife to pipe for me, if I go; so my life must be of less moment than yours, and if you can so peril it, why should not I?" exclaimed a stalwart young fisherman, advancing, and Edward eagerly grasped his rough hand, conjuring him to get his boat at once, there was not a moment to lose; but the example was infectious, and an old man hastily stepped forward, declaring the youngsters had taught him his duty, and he would do it.

"Great God! what do they say?" exclaimed Edward, as his younger companion hastened down the beach to bring his boat to the leeward of the cliff, to launch it more securely, and a rumor ran through the crowds, whence arising it was impossible to discover. "The Siren — Captain Harvey — my uncle's ship! — and he must be in her — she would never leave Feroe without him. What foundation is there for this rumor? let me know, for God's sake!"

But none could tell more than that a vessel, entering the harbor just before the gale, had hailed the Siren, about twenty miles distant, and she seemed laboring heavily, and in such a distressed state that a very little would finish her. Not a word escaped Edward's lips, which grew for the moment blanched as marble. Mr. Howard, to whom the rumor had brought the most intense agony, for not a doubt of its truth would come to relieve him, was at his side, grasping his hand, and murmuring hoarsely —

"Edward, my poor boy, must your life be perilled too? — both — both — this is awful!"

"Let me but save *him*, and if I perish it will be in a good cause. Tell aunt Emmeline, I know she will comfort my poor Ellen; and that the boy she has saved from worse misery than death, did all he could to save her husband! and if I fail" — he stopped, in strong emotion, then added — "give Ellen this, and this," he cut off a lock of his hair with his dirk, and placed it and his watch in Mr. Howard's trembling hand. — "And now, my friend, God bless you and reward you, too!" He threw himself a moment in Mr. Howard's arms, kissed his cheek, and, darting down the beach, leaped into the boat, which was dancing like a nutshell on the water. It was several minutes, ere they could succeed in getting her off, the waves seeming determined to cast her back; but they were fairly launched at length, and then they heeded not that one minute they rode high on a mountain wave, seeming as if nothing could save them from being dashed in the abyss below; the next were buried in a deep valley, surrounded by huge walls of water, threatening to burst and overwhelm them. For a boat to live in such a sea at all seemed miraculous; and old Collins always declared that unless some angel sat at the helm with Edward, no human arm could have taken them in safety. If it were an angel, it was the pure thought, the faith-winged prayer, that he might be the instrument, in the Eternal's hand, of turning aside death and misery from that beloved home, in which even his errors had been met with *love*, and conquered by *forgiveness.*

With every effort, and they were such as to bid the perspiration stream down the face and arms of those strong men, and almost exhaust Edward, for he took an oar in turn, it was full an hour from their leaving the shore before they reached the ship. She had ceased firing, for by the lights on shore they had discovered the boat's departure, and watched her progress by the lantern at her head, as only those can watch who feel, one short hour more, and their ship will float no longer!

Collins was spokesman, for Edward, as they grappled the boat alongside, had sunk down for the moment powerless by the helm; roused, however, effectually by the answer —

"The Siren — bound to Dartmouth — from Feroe — owner Arthur Hamilton, passenger — now on board — nine in crew."

"In with you all then — that is Captain Harvey's voice, I'll be sworn; the rumor was only too true."

"Ay, old Collins!" returned the Captain; "we thought to perish in sight of our own homes; now, Mr. Hamilton, not a man will stir till you are safe!"

His companion leaped into the boat without reply, and, sinking on one of the benches, drew his cloak closely round his face. Peril was indeed still around him, but compared with the — even to that Heaven-directed heart — terrible struggle of beholding death, rising slowly but surely round him in the water-filling ship, almost within sight and sound of his home, his beloved ones, the mere *hope* of life seemed almost overpowering. The crew of the hapless Siren quickly deserted her. Captain Harvey was the last to descend, and, as he did so, a block of iron, loosened from its place, fell cornerwise, and struck sharply on Edward's forehead, almost stunning him for the moment, as he watched the Captain's descent. He felt the blood slowly trickling down his temple and cheek; but he was not one to be daunted by pain: he resumed his station at the helm in unbroken silence, only speaking when directions were absolutely necessary, and then only in a few brief sailor-terms. They had scarcely proceeded a third of their way, when the waters boiled and foamed as tossed by some strange whirlpool, and it required all Edward's address and skill as steersman to prevent the frail boat from being drawn into the vortex. The cause was soon displayed, and every heart shuddered, for ten minutes later, and help would indeed have been in vain. The unfortunate vessel had sunk—been swallowed up in those rushing waters; the suction of so large a mass, producing for a brief interval the effect of a whirlpool. The silence of awe and of intense thankfulness, fell on the heart of every man, and more than all on his who had so far recovered his first emotion as to gaze wonderingly and admiringly on the boyish figure at the helm, whose voice was utterly unknown, and whose features the fitful light, and the youth's steadfast gaze on his rowers, prevented his tracing with any certainty.

The crowds had increased on the shore, watching with intense eagerness the return of the boat; but the expectation was too deep for sound, silence almost portentous reigned. A huge sea had concealed her for several minutes, and Mr. Howard, who during these two long hours had remained spellbound on the beach, groaned aloud in his agony; again she was visible, driven on with fearful velocity by the tide, nearer, nearer still. He thought he could distinguish the figure of his friend: he was sure he could hear the voice of Edward, urging, commanding, directing a landing somewhere, in contradiction to the opinion of others. They were within a dozen yards of the shore, but still not a sound of gratulation was heard. Every eye was fixed, as in the fascination of terror, on a wave in the distance, increasing in size and fury as it rapidly approached. It neared the boat—it stood impending over the frail thing as a mighty avalanche of waters—it burst; the boat was seen no longer, and a wild and terrible cry sounded far and near along the beach!

CHAPTER XII.

FOREBODINGS.

The whole of the day Mrs. Hamilton had vainly tried to shake off a most unwonted gloom. Convinced herself that it was greatly physical, from the unusual oppressiveness of the weather relaxing the nerves, which had so many months been overstrained, yet her thoughts would cling to Mr. Maitland's words, that her husband might be coming home himself; but if the accounts of Ellen's danger and Edward's confession had recalled him, he ought to have arrived full two or three weeks previous. The gale that swept round her — the awful and unnatural darkness — the remarkable phenomena, at that season, of lightning — and the long, loud thunder-claps * which inland could be fearfully distinguished from the gale, appalled the whole household; and therefore it was not much wonder that the vague idea of her husband's having left Feroe, and exposure to such a tempest, should become in that fearful anxiety almost a certainty of agony. It was well, perhaps, that her unselfish nature had an object to draw her in some slight degree out of herself, for her firmness, her trust beyond the accidents of earth, all seemed about to fail her, and make her for the time being most wretched. As the storm and closeness increased, so did Ellen's feverish restlessness; her nerves, not yet fully restored, felt strung almost to torture with every flash, and clap, and blast. She tried to laugh at her own folly; for, though often terrified, when a little child, at the storms in India, those of England had never affected her at all, and she could not understand why she should feel this so childishly. But argument is of little moment in such cases; and Mrs. Hamilton, satisfying her that she could no more help her present sensation than her physical weakness, tried to soothe and amuse her, and in so doing partially cheered herself. She did not leave her till past midnight; and then desiring Mrs. Langford to sit up with her till she was comfortably asleep, retired to her own bed-room. Never since her husband's absence had its solitude felt so vast — so heavily oppressive; thought after thought of him thronged her mind till she fairly gave up the effort to struggle with them. "Will his voice ever sound here again, his heart give me the support I need?" rose to her lips, as she gazed round her, and the deep stillness, the gloom only broken by a small silver lamp, and the fitful light of the fire, seemed but a solemn answer. She buried her face in her clasped hands, and the clock struck two before that inward conflict permitted her once more to lift up heart and brow in meek, trusting faith to Him who still watched over her and her beloved ones; and after an earnest, voiceless prayer, she drew her little table, with its books of devotion, to the fire, and read thoughtfully, prayerfully, for another hour, and then sought her couch. But she could not sleep; the wind had again arisen, and fearing to lie awake and listen to it would only renew her unusual agitation, she

* These storms, as occurring in Devonshire, in both January and February, are no creation of the imagination; the author has heard them herself, and more than one officer in the Preventive Service has mentioned them as occurring during the night-watches, and of awful violence.

rose at four, dressed herself, and throwing on a large shawl, softly traversed the passage, and entered her niece's room; finding her, as she fully expected, as wakeful and restless as herself, with the addition of an intense headache. She had persuaded nurse Langford to go to bed, but the pain had come on since then, and made her more restless and feverish than before. She could not lie in any posture to get ease, till at last, about six o'clock, completely exhausted, she fell asleep, sitting almost upright in her aunt's arms, her head leaning against her, as she stood by the bed-side. Fearing to disturb her, Mrs. Hamilton would not move, desiring the morning prayers to be said without her, and Miss Harcourt and her daughters not to wait breakfast, as she would have it with Ellen when she awoke. That she was stiff and exhausted with three hours' standing in one position, she did not heed, perhaps scarcely felt, for woman's loveliest attribute, that of a tender and utterly unselfish nurse, was hers to perfection. But she did not refuse the cup of chocolate Caroline brought her herself, and with affectionate earnestness entreated her to take.

"You look so fatigued and so pale, dearest mother, I wish you would let me take your place; I would be so quiet, so gentle, Ellen would not even know her change of nurses."

"I do not doubt your care, love, but I fear the least movement will disturb this poor child, and she has had such a restless night, I want her to sleep as long as she can. Your thoughtful care has so refreshed me, that I feel quite strong again, so go and finish your breakfast in comfort, dearest."

Caroline very unwillingly obeyed, and about a quarter of an hour afterward, Mrs. Hamilton was startled by the sound of a carriage advancing with unusual velocity to the house. It stopped at the main entrance, and she had scarcely time to wonder who could be such very early visitors, when a loud scream, in the voice of Emmeline, rung in her ears; whether of joy or grief she could not distinguish, but it was the voice of her child, and the already tortured nerves of the wife and mother could not bear it without a sensation of terror, amounting to absolute agony. She laid Ellen's head tenderly on the pillow, watched over her, though her limbs so trembled she could scarcely support herself, saw with intense relief that the movement had not disturbed her quiet sleep, and calling Mrs. Langford from an adjoining room, hastily descended the stairs, though how she did so, and entered the breakfast-room, she always said she never knew. Many and eager and glad voices were speaking at once; the very servants thronged the hall and threshold of the room, but all made way for her.

"Arthur! — my husband!" she did find voice to exclaim but every object but his figure reeled before her, and she fainted in his arms.

It was some time before she recovered, for mind and frame had been too long overtasked; and Mr. Hamilton, as he clasped her in his arms, beseeching her only to speak to him, and gazed on her deathlike countenance, felt in a moment that great as his anxiety had been for her, he had not imagined one half she had endured. His voice — his kiss — seemed to rouse the scattered senses, even more effectually than Miss Harcourt's anxiously proffered remedies; but she could not speak, she only looked up in his face, as if to be quite, quite sure he had indeed returned; that her vague fancies of danger, even if they had foundation, had merged in the most blissful reality, that she was no longer *alone;* and leaning her head on his bosom, was only conscious of a thankfulness too deep for words; a repose that, since his departure, she had not known for a single day. Neither she nor her husband could believe that it was only six months since they had been separated. It seemed, and to Mrs. Hamilton especially, as if she must have lived through years in that time, it had been so fraught with sorrow.

"Not one word, my own dearest! and only these pallid cheeks and heavy eyes to greet me. Must I reproach you directly I come home, for, as usual, not thinking enough of yourself; forgetting how precious is that self to so many your husband above all?"

"Nay, papa, you shall not scold mamma," said Emmeline, eagerly, as her mother tried to smile and speak in answer. "She ought to scold you, for not sending us one line to prepare us for your unexpected presence, and frightening us all by coming so suddenly upon us, and making mamma faint, as I never saw her do before. Indeed I do not like it, mother darling!" continued the affectionate girl, kneeling down by her mother, and clinging to her, adding, in a suppressed, terrified voice, "It was so like death."

Mrs. Hamilton read in a moment that Emmeline's playfulness was only assumed to hide strong emotion; that she was trying very hard for complete control, but so trembling, that she knelt down, literally because she could not stand. It was such a proof of her endeavor to profit by her mother's gentle lessons, that even at that moment it not only gave her the sweetest gratification, but helped her to rouse herself.

"Indeed, I think you are perfectly right, Emmy," she said, quite in her usual voice, as she pressed her child a moment to her, and kissed her cheek, which was almost as pale as her own. "I will not submit to any scolding, when papa himself is answerable for my unusual weakness; but as we wanted him so *very* much, why, we will be lenient with him, and only keep him prisoner with us for some time to come. But get him breakfast quickly, Caroline, love; such an early visitor must want it. When did you arrive, dearest Arthur?" she added, looking earnestly in his face, and half wondering at the expression upon it, it seemed to speak so many things; "surely not this morning? You were not at sea in yesterday's awful storm?"

"I was indeed, my Emmeline; can you bear to hear it, or have you been agitated enough already? I have been in danger, great danger, but our Father's infinite mercy has preserved me to you all, making the instrument of my preservation so young a lad and slight a frame, I know not how sufficiently to bless God, or to thank my preserver."

Mrs. Hamilton's hand closed convulsively on her husband's; her eyes riveted on his countenance as if she would grasp his whole meaning at once, but little did she guess the whole.

"I did not come alone," he added, striving for composure, and even playfulness, "though it seems I was such an important personage, as to be the only one seen or thought about."

"By-the-by, I did see, or fancied I saw, Edward," rejoined Caroline, who, at the news of her father having been in danger, had left the breakfast-table, unable to keep away from him, even that short distance, but neither she, nor either of the others, connecting her cousin with Mr. Hamilton's words, and not quite understanding why he should have so interrupted the most interesting subject. "He has gone to see Ellen, I suppose, and so we have missed him. Was he your companion, papa? How and where did you meet him?"

"Let him answer for himself!" replied Mr. Hamilton, still determinately hiding his feeling under a tone and manner of jest, and leaving his wife's side for a moment, he drew Edward from the recess of the window, where all this time he had been standing quite unobserved, and led him forward.

"Good heavens! Edward, what have you been about?" exclaimed Miss Harcourt, and her exclamation was echoed by Caroline and Emmeline, while Mrs. Hamilton gazed at him in bewildered alarm. He was deadly pale, with every appearance of exhaustion, and a most disfiguring patch on his left brow, which he had tried in vain to hide with his hair.

"You have been fighting."

"Only with the elements, Miss Harcourt, and they have rather tired me, that is all; I shall be well in a day or two. Don't look so terrified, dear aunt," he answered, with the same attempt at jest as his uncle, and throwing himself lightly on an ottoman by Mrs. Hamilton, he laid his head very quietly on her lap.

"Fighting — and with the elements? Arthur, dearest Arthur, for pity's sake tell me the whole truth at once; it cannot be —"

"And why should it not, my beloved?" (there was no attempt at jest now.) "He to whom your care has preserved a sister — whom your indulgent love has given courage to resolve that error shall be conquered, and he will become all we can wish him — whom you took to your heart and home when motherless — God has mercifully made the instrument of saving your husband from a watery grave, and giving back their father to your children!"

"To be associated in your heart with other thoughts than those of ingratitude, and cruelty, and sin! Oh, aunt Emmeline, I cannot thank God enough for permitting me this great mercy," were the only words poor Edward could speak, when the first intensity of his aunt's emotion was in some degree conquered, and she could look in his young face, though her eyes were almost blinded with tears, and putting back the bright hair which the rain and spray had so uncurled, as to lay heavy and damp upon his pale forehead, she imprinted a long, silent kiss upon it, and looking alternately at him and her husband, seemed powerless to realize any other thought.

Mr. Hamilton briefly, but most eloquently, narrated the events of the previous night, dwelling only sufficiently on his imminent peril, to evince the real importance of Edward's extraordinary exertions, not to harrow the feelings of his listeners more than need be. That the young officer's determined opposition to the almost angrily expressed opinions of Captain Harvey and old Collins as to the better landing-place, had saved them from the effects of the huge wave, which had burst like a water-spout a minute after they had all leaped in safety on shore, almost overwhelming the projecting sand to which Collins had wished to direct the boat, and so proving at once Edwards's far superior nautical knowledge, for had they steered there, the frail bark must inevitably have been upset, and its crew washed by the receding torrent back to sea. Harvey and Collins acknowledged their error at once, and looked eagerly for Edward to say so to him, but he had vanished the moment they had achieved a safe landing, to Mr. Hamilton's annoyance, for he had not the least suspicion who he was, and only longed to express, if he could not otherwise evince his gratitude, Collins and Grey refusing the smallest credit, declaring that if it had not been for this young stranger officer, of whom they knew nothing, not even his name, not a man would have stirred; that for any fisherman or mere ordinary sailor to have guided the boat to and from the sinking vessel, in such a sea, was so impossible, that no one would have attempted it; old Collins ending, with the superstition of his class, by a declaration, that his disappearance convinced his already more than suspicion, that it was some good angel in a boy's likeness; for Arthur Hamilton would never have been permitted so to perish: an explanation, Mr. Hamilton added, laughingly, that might suit his Emmy, but was rather too fanciful for him. However, his young preserver was nowhere to be found, but, to his extreme astonishment, and no little relief (for now that he was so near home, his anxiety to hear of all, especially Ellen, whom he scarcely dared hope to find alive, became insupportable,) Mr. Howard suddenly stood before him, grasping both his hands, without the power, for a minute or two, to speak. Mr. Hamilton overwhelmed him with questions, scarcely giving him time to answer one before he asked another. They had nearly reached the hotel, when Captain Harvey's bluff voice was heard exclaiming—

"Here he is, Mr. Hamilton; he is too exhausted to escape our thanks and blessings now. What could the youngster have tried to hide himself for?"

But before Mr. Hamilton could make any rejoinder, save to grasp the young man's hands strongly in his own, Mr. Howard said eagerly—

"Oblige me, Captain Harvey; take that boy into our hotel, it is only just round the corner; make him take off his dripping jacket, and give him some of your sailor's stuff. He is not quite strong enough for his exertions to-night, and should rest at once."

Captain Harvey bore him off, almost carrying him, for exertion and a variety of emotions had rendered him faint and powerless.

"Do you know him, Howard? who and what is he?" But Mr. Howard did not, perhaps could not reply, but hurried his friend on to the hotel; and entered the room, where, having called for lights, and all the ingredients of grog-punch, which he vowed the boy should have instead of the brandy and water he had called for, they found Edward trying to laugh, and protesting against all coddling; he was perfectly well, and he would not go to bed, and could not imagine what right Captain Harvey had to be a sailor, if he thought so much of a storm, and a blow, and a wetting.

"Nor should I, if you were sailor-rigged; but what business have you with this overgrown mast of a figure, and a face pale and delicate as a woman's?"

And so like his dying mother it was, that Mr. Hamilton stood for a moment on the threshold, completely stupefied. We leave our readers to imagine the rest; and how Captain Harvey carried the seemingly marvellous news that the brave young officer was Mr. Hamilton's own nephew, over the town, and in every fisherman's hut, in a miraculously short space of time.

We may as well state here at once, to save farther retrospection, that Mr. Hamilton, by the active and admirable assistance of Morton, had, after a three months' residence at Feroe, perceived that he might return to England much sooner than he had at first anticipated; still he did not like to mention even the probability of such a thing to his family, till perfectly certain himself. Morton never ceased persuading him to name a period for his return, knowing the comfort it would be to his home; but Mr. Hamilton could not bear the idea of leaving his friend in his voluntary banishment so many months sooner than they had reckoned on. When, however, the letters came from Oakwood, detailing Edward's return, and the discoveries thence proceeding, his anxiety and, let it be owned, his extreme displeasure against his nephew, prompted his return at once. Morton not only conquered every objection to his immediate departure, but tried, and in some measure succeeded, to soften his anger, by bringing before him many points in Mr. Howard's letter, showing real, good, and true repentance in the offender, which a first perusal of a narrative of error had naturally overlooked. The seas, however, were so fearfully tempestuous and the winds so adverse, that it was impossible either to leave Feroe, or get a letter conveyed to Scotland, for a full fortnight after the Siren's last voyage. Nothing but the extreme urgency of the case, increased by the fact that the detention of the Siren at Wick had given Mr. Hamilton a double packet of letters, but the second, though dated ten days later, gave the same hopeless account of Ellen, could have made him attempt a voyage home in such weather; yet he felt he could not rest, knowing intuitively the misery his wife must be enduring, and scarcely able to bear even the thought of what seemed most probable, that Ellen would be taken from her, and the aggravated trial it would be. The voyage was a terrible one, for length and heavy gales. More than once they wished to put into port, that Mr. Hamilton might continue his journey by land, but their only safety seemed keeping out at sea, the storm threatening to dash them on rock or shoal, whenever in sight of land.

By the time they reached the Land's End — they had come westward of England, instead of eastward, as they went — the vessel was in such a shattered and leaky condition, that Captain Harvey felt and acknowledged, she could not weather out another storm. The calm that had followed the heavy gales, gave hope to all; even though the constant shiftings of the wind, which was now not more than what, in sailor's parlance is called a cat's-paw, prevented their making as much way as they desired. At length they were within twenty miles of Dartmouth, and not a doubt of their safety disturbed them, until the darkening atmosphere, the sullen rise and suppressed roar of the billows, the wind sobbing and wailing at first, and then bursting into that awful gale, which we have before described, banished every human hope at once. The rudder snapped; every half-hour the water gained upon the hold, though every man worked the pumps. There was not a shred of canvas, but the masts, and yards, and stays bent and snapped like reeds before the blast. To guide her was impossible; she was driven on — on — till she struck on a reef of rock about a mile, or less, perhaps from Dartmouth. Then came their signals of distress, as a last lone hope, for the crew of the Siren were all too good seamen to dare believe a boat could either be pushed off, or live in such a sea. Their wonder, their hope, their intense thankfulness, when it was discovered, may be imagined. The rest is known.

"And how did you get this disfiguring blow, my dear Edward?" inquired his aunt, whose eyes, it seemed, would turn upon him, as if impossible to connect that slight figure with such immense exertions — though some time had passed, and a social, happy breakfast, round which all still lingered, had enabled them to subdue too painful emotion, and only to be conscious of the most deep and grateful joy.

"Pray do not call it disfiguring, aunt; I am quite proud of it. Last night I could have dispensed with such a striking mark of affection from the poor Siren, though I really hardly felt it, except that the blood would trickle in my eye, and almost blind me, when I wanted all my sight and senses too. But this morning Mr. Howard has made such a kind fuss about it, that I think it must be something grand."

"But what did you hide yourself for, Ned?" demanded Emmeline, all her high spirits recalled. Her cousin hesitated, and a flush mounted to his forehead.

"It was fear, Emmeline; absolute fear!"

"Fear!" she repeated, laughing; "of what? of all the bogies and spirits of the winds and waves, whose wrath you dared, by venturing to oppose them? Nonsense, Edward! you will never make me believe that."

"Because you do not know me," he answered, with startling earnestness. "How can your gentle nature understand the incongruities of mine? or loving your father as you do, and as he deserves, comprehend the dread, the belief in his unpitying sternness to youthful error, which I imbibed from my childhood? He held — he holds — my fate, forgiveness or exposure, and how could I meet him calmly? Emmeline, Emmeline, if I had been but as morally brave as I may be physically, I should have had nothing to dread, nothing to hide. As it is, uncle Hamilton, judge, act, decide as you would if I had not been the undeserved means of saving you — it will be the best for me;" and, rising hurriedly, he left the room before any one could reply.

"But you will forgive him, papa; you will try him again; and I am sure he will be morally brave, too," pleaded Emmeline; her sister and Miss Harcourt joining in the entreaty and belief, and Mrs. Hamilton looking in his face without uttering a word. Mr. Hamilton's answer seemed to satisfy all parties.

Ellen meanwhile had awoke, quite refreshed, and all pain gone, been dressed and conveyed to her daily quarters, the events of the morning entirely unknown to her; for though the joyful news, spreading like wildfire through the house, had reached Mrs. Langford's ears, and made her very happy, she had quite judgment enough, even without a message to that effect from her mistress, to keep it from Ellen till carefully prepared.

"What can I say to my little Ellen for deserting her so long?" inquired Mrs. Hamilton, playfully, as she entered her room, about twelve o'clock, after a long private conversation with her husband.

"I wish you would tell me you had been lying down, dear aunt; it would satisfy me better than any other reason."

"Because you think it would do me the most good, dearest. But look at me, and tell me if you do not think I must have been trying some equally efficacious remedy." Ellen did look and so radiant was that kind face with happiness, that she was startled.

"What *has* happened, aunt Emmeline? You have heard from my uncle," she added, her voice trembling. "What does he say? — will he —"

"He says, you must summon all your smiles to greet him, love; for he hopes to be with us very, *very* shortly, so you will not wonder at my joy?"

Ellen tried to sympathize in it; but Mrs. Hamilton soon saw that her perhaps natural dread of what should be her uncle's judgment on her brother and herself, prevented all pleasurable anticipation of his arrival, and that the only effectual way of removing it was to let them meet as soon as possible.

CHAPTER XIII.

FORGIVENESS.

THREE days after Mr. Hamilton's arrival, a cheerful party assembled in his wife's dressing-room, which, in its elegant appurtenances — signs as they were, of a most refined and beautiful taste — certainly deserved a higher appellation; but boudoir, Percy had always declared, did not harmonize at all with the old English comforts of Oakwood, and he would not have a French word to designate his mother's room especially. Ellen was on her sofa, working; Edward, who she thought had only returned that morning, at her side, reading; Caroline and Emmeline, drawing, the one with some degree of perseverance, the other with none at all. It seemed as if she could not sit still, and her wild sallies, and snatches of old songs, repeatedly made Miss Harcourt look up from her book, and Mrs. Hamilton from her work, surprised.

"Emmeline, I *cannot* draw," exclaimed Caroline, at length, "you are making the table as restless as yourself."

"Why can you not say it was moved by an irresistible sympathy? It is most extraordinary that you will still speak plain matter-of-fact, when I am doing all I can to make you poetical."

"But what am I to poetize on now, Emmeline? — the table, or yourself? because, at present, they are the only subjects under consideration, and I really cannot see any thing very poetical in either."

"Not even in *me*, Lina?" archly replied Emmeline, bending

down so that her face should come before her sister, instead of her copy, which was a very pretty, small marble figure. "Now, if you were not the most determined piece of prose in the world, you would find poetry even in my face.

> "For, lo! the artist no more gazed
> On features still and cold;
> He stood, bewilder'd and amazed,
> As living charms unfold.
>
> "As if touch'd by yon orient ray,
> The stone to life had warm'd;
> For round the lip such bright smiles play,
> As never sculptor form'd.

There, Caroline, that is what you ought to have *felt*. If I can make poetry on my face — "

"Poetry on yourself! Why, Emmeline, I thought you were repeating a verse of some old poet, with which I am unacquainted. I really beg your pardon. I did not know your favorite Muse had dubbed you follower as well as worshipper."

"Nor did I till this moment. She feared for her reputation near such a lover of prose as you are, and so touched me with inspiration. I am exceedingly obliged to her; but even if I failed to make you poetical, Caroline, you might have emulated Cowper, and instead of singing the 'Sofa,' sung the 'Table.' Indeed I think a very pretty poem might be made of it. Look at the variety of tasteful and useful things laid on a table — and there it stands in the midst of them, immovable, cold, insensible, just like one on whom we heap favors upon favors, and who remains so wrapped in self, as to be utterly indifferent to all. Now, Caroline, put that into rhyme, or blank verse, if you prefer it; it is a new idea, at least."

"So new," replied her sister, laughing, "that I think I will send it to Percy, and request him to turn it into a Greek or Latin ode; it will be so much grander than my English version. You have so astonished mamma, Emmeline, by your mad mood, that she has actually put down her work."

"I am so glad!" replied Emmeline, springing to her mother's side; "I like other people to be as idle as myself."

"But there is a medium in all things, young lady," answered her mother, half-gravely, half in Emmeline's own tone; "and I rather think your conscience is telling you, that it is not quite right to desert one Muse for another, as you are doing now."

"Oh, but my drawing must wait till her Muse inspires me

again. Poetry does not always come, and her visits are so delightful!"

"Then I am afraid you will think me very harsh, Emmeline; but delightful as they are, I must not have them always encouraged. If you encourage the idea of only working when the fit of inspiration comes upon you — in plain words, only when you feel inclined — you will fritter life away without one solid thought or acquirement. You think now, perhaps, habituated as you are to employment, that this is impossible; but you are just of an age to demand very strict watchfulness over yourself to prevent it. Now that you are emerging from the routine of childhood's lessons, and too old to be compelled to do that which is right, and — rendering your task of control more difficult — more susceptible to poetry, and what you term inspiration, than ever, you must try and infuse a little of Caroline's steady, matter-of-fact into your poetry, instead of almost despising it, as so cold and disagreeable. Now, do not look so very sad, and so very serious, love, and jump at the conclusion that I am displeased, because I speak seriously. I love your joyousness far too dearly to check it, or wish you to do so, especially in your own family; but just as you have learned the necessity of, and evinced so well and so feelingly, control in emotions of sorrow, my Emmeline, so I am quite sure you will trust my experience, and practise control, even in the pleasant inspiration of poetry and joy."

Emmeline sat very quiet for several minutes; she was just in that mood of extreme hilarity which renders control excessively difficult, and causes the last check upon it to be felt as harsh and unkind, and almost to bring tears. She was not too perfect to escape from feeling all this, even though the person who had caused it was the mother she so dearly loved; but she did not give way to it. A few minutes' hard struggle, and the momentary temper was so conquered, that, with an even more than usually warm kiss, she promised to think quite seriously on all her mother said; and, an effort far more difficult, was just as joyous as before.

"I have made so many mistakes in my drawing, mamma, I really do not think I can go on with it to-day; do let me help you, I will take such pains with my work, it shall be almost as neat as yours; and then, though my fingers are employed, at least I may go on talking."

Mrs. Hamilton assented, telling her she might talk as much as she pleased, with one of those peculiar smiles of approval which ever made Emmeline's heart throb, for they always told her, that the thoughts and feelings, and secret struggle with temper, which she imagined must be known only to herself, her mother by some mysterious power had discovered, and rewarded.

"Edward what are you so deep in?—'Fragments of Voyages and Travels'—I thought it was something much *deeper* than that by the deep attention you are giving it. You should dip in oceans, not in fragments of water, Ned."

"I did not feel inclined for the exertion," he replied, smiling.

"Do you know," she continued, "when I first read that book, which I did merely because I had a lurking sort of affection for a handsome cousin of mine who was a sailor, I was so charmed with the tricks you all played in the cockpit, that I was seized with a violent desire to don a middy's dress, and come after you; it would have made such a pretty story, too; but I did not think mamma and papa would quite approve of it, so I desisted. Should I not make a very handsome boy, Edward?"

"So handsome," he replied, again smiling, "that I fear you would not have preserved your incognita half an hour, especially with those flowing curls."

"My dear Emmeline, do tell me, what has made you in this mood?" asked Ellen; "last week you were so sad, and the last three days you have been—"

"Wild enough to frighten you, Ellen; ah, if you did but know the reason."

"You had better satisfy her curiosity, Emmy," said Mrs. Hamilton, so meaningly, that Emmeline's ready mind instantly understood her. "Tell her all that did occur in that awful storm three days ago, as poetically and lengthily as you like; no one shall interrupt you, if you will only be very careful not to exaggerate or alarm."

Edward gave up his seat to his cousin, and Emmeline launched at once into a most animated description of the storm and the shipwreck, and the rescue; cleverly contriving so to hide all names, as to elude the least suspicion of either the preserved or the preserver having any thing to do with herself, Ellen becoming so exceedingly interested, as to lose sight of the question which at first had struck her, what this could have to do with Emmeline's wild spirits.

"You do not mean to say it was his own father he saved?" she said, as her cousin paused a minute to take breath; "your tale is becoming so like a romance, Emmy, I hardly know how to believe it."

"I assure you it is quite true; only imagine what my young

hero's feelings must have been, and those of the family, to whom he gave back a husband and a father!"

"I should think them so intense, so sacred, as to be hardly joy at first, and scarcely possible to be imagined, even by your vivid fancy, Emmy."

"I don't know, Ellen, but I think I *can* imagine them; you may shake your head, and look wise, but I will prove that I can by-and-by. But what do you think of my hero?"

"That I should like to know him, and admire him quite as much as you can desire — and who told you all this?"

"One of the principal actors in the scene?"

"What, has your *penchant* for any thing out of the common way reached Dartmouth, and old Collins brought you the tale?"

"No," replied Emmeline, laughing; "guess again."

"William Grey?"

"No."

"One of the rescued crew who may know my aunt?"

"Wrong again, Ellen,"

"Then I cannot guess, Emmeline; so pray tell me."

"You are very silly, Ellen; were not Mr. Howard and Edward both at Dartmouth at the time? why did you not guess them? Not that I had it from either."

"Edward!" repeated Ellen, "did he know any thing about it?"

"More than any one else, dearest," answered Mrs. Hamilton, cautiously, but fondly; "put all Emmeline's strange tale together, and connect it with my happiness the other morning, and I think your own heart will explain the rest."

"More especially with this speaking witness," continued Emmeline, playfully putting back Edward's hair, that Ellen might see the scar. She understood it in a moment, and clasping her arms round her brother's neck, as he knelt by her, tried hard to prevent emotion, but could not, and burst into tears.

"Tears, my little Ellen; I said I would only be greeted with smiles," exclaimed a rich, deep voice, close beside her, and before she had time to fear his presence, she felt herself clasped with all a father's fondness in her uncle's arms; her head resting on his shoulder, and his warm kiss on her cheek.

"Edward!" was the only word she could speak.

"Do not fear for him, my dear Ellen; true repentance and a firm resolution to amend are all I ask, and if his future conduct really prove them, the errors of his youth shall be forgotten, as if they had never been."

"And — and —"

"I know all you would say, my dear child. I did think there could be no excuse, no palliation, for your sin; but even if I still wish the temptation had been resisted, you have indeed suffered for it, more than the harshest judgment could desire; let it be forgotten as entirely and as fully as it is forgiven."

In a very few minutes Ellen's composure was so fully restored, and her heavy dread so subsided, that the relief seemed to her almost a dream. Could it be possible that it was the relative she had pictured as so harsh and stern, and pitiless to youthful error, who had drawn a chair close by her sofa, and caressingly holding her hand in his, and looking so kindly, so earnestly, in her altered face, was trying to amuse her by telling her so many entertaining things about Feroe and Mr. Morton, and his voyage home, and alluding to her brother's courage, and prudence, and skill, in such terms as almost brought the tears again? Mr. Hamilton was inexpressibly shocked at the change which mental and bodily suffering had wrought in his niece. There is always something peculiarly touching, and appealing to the best emotions, in youthful sorrow or suffering of any kind; and her trial had been such an aggravated one — combining such agonized remorse, for an act, which the harshest judgment, knowing all points of the case, could scarcely pronounce as other than involuntary, with the most heroic, but perfectly unconscious self-sacrifice, and not only terror for her brother's fate, but an almost crushing sense of misery for his faults, that the pallid face, and frame so delicately fragile, had still deeper claims for sympathy and cherishing than even when caused by ordinary illness. The loss of her unusually luxuriant hair, except the soft bands which shaded her face, visible under the pretty little lace cap, made her look much younger than she really was, and so delicately transparent had become her complexion, that the blue veins were clearly traceable on her forehead, and throat, and hands; the dark, soft lash seemed longer than before, as it swept the pale cheek, the brow more pencilled, and the eye, whether in imagination, from her friends knowing all she had endured, or in reality, was so expressive of such deep, quiet feeling, that the whole countenance was so altered and so improved, that it seemed as if the heavy, sallow child was rapidly changing into one of those sweet, lovable, heart-attracting girls, who, without any actual beauty, can never be passed unnoticed.

At Ellen's request, Mrs. Hamilton had, as soon as she was strong enough, read with her, morning and evening, the devotional exercises which were read below to the assembled family

Mrs. Hamilton soon perceived, and with no little pain, that Ellen shrunk from the idea of being well enough to rejoin them, in actual suffering. Here again was an effect of that same vivid imagination, of whose existence, until the late events, in one so quiet, seemingly so cold, Mrs. Hamilton had not the least idea of. Ellen had been so long accustomed to be silent as to her feelings in fact carefully to conceal them, that much as she might wish and intend to be unreserved, her aunt feared it would cause her some difficulty to be so, and she could not hope to succeed in controlling imagination, unless she were. That night, however, Ellen's unreserved confidence gave her hope. When the devotional exercises, in which she had joined with even more than usual earnestness and fervor, were concluded, she said, with almost Emmeline's confidence, as she laid her hand on her aunt's —

"I am so very, very happy to-night, dear aunt, that I am afraid I do not think enough of what is past. I did so dread my uncle's return — so tremble at what his sentence would be on Edward and myself, that even your kindness would not remove the weight; and now, that I have found it all so groundless, and he is so kind — so indulgent, I am so relieved, that I fear I must have thought more of his anger than the anger of God. My sin remains the same in His sight, though you and uncle Hamilton have so fully forgiven it, and — and — I do not think I ought to feel so happy."

"Indeed, my dear Ellen, I think you may. Our Heavenly Father is still more merciful than man, as Mr. Howard so clearly proved to you, in the long conversation you had with him. We know, by his Holy Word, that all he asks is sincere repentance for sin, and a firm conviction that in Him only we are made sufficiently righteous for our penitence to be accepted. I believe, Ellen, that His forgiveness was yours, long before I could give you mine, for He could read your heart, and saw the reason of your silence, and all the remorse and suffering, which, from the appearances, against you, I might not even guess; and that, in His compassionating love and pity, He permitted your increased trial; ordaining even the failure of the relief to Edward, to convince you, that, not even in such a fearful case as yours, might error, however involuntary, prosper. I can trace His loving providence even in the fact of your finding one more note than you wanted, that discovery might thence come, which, without such a seeming chance, was, humanly speaking, impossible. He has shown compassion and love for you and Edward, in the very sufferings He ordained.

So do not check your returning happiness, fearing it must be unacceptable to Him. Try to trace all things, either of joy or sorrow, to Him. Associate Him with your every thought, and believe me, my own Ellen, your very happiness will both draw you nearer to Him, and be an acceptable offering in his sight."

Ellen listened eagerly, gratefully; she felt as if, with every word Mrs. Hamilton said, the film of doubt and vague fancies was dissolving from her mind, and, after a short pause, she said —

"Then you do not think, aunt Emmeline, my inability to pray for so long a time, was a proof that God had utterly forsaken me? It made me still more wretched, for I thought it was a sure sign that I was so irredeemably wicked, He had left me to the devices of my own heart, and would never love or have mercy on me again. Even after you had quite forgiven me, and proved to me my promise was a mistaken one and not binding, I still felt the difficulty to pray, and it was so painful."

Such inability is very often so entirely physical, my dear Ellen, that we must not think too much about it. Our simple duty is to persevere, however little satisfactory our devotions; and put our firm trust in our heavenly Father, that He will heal us, and permit His countenance so to shine upon us again, as to derive *comfort* from our prayers. Your inability before your illness was the natural consequence of Mr. Howard's severe representations, which he has since assured me, he never would have used, if he could have had the least idea of the cause of your silence. You, my poor child, were suffering too much, from a complete chaos of conflicting feelings and duties, to be able to realize this, and I am not at all astonished, that when you most yearned for the comfort of prayer and trust, the thought that by your silence you were failing in your duty to me and so disobeying God, should utterly have prevented it. Since your severe illness the inability has been entirely physical. As strength and peace return, you will regain the power, and realize all its comfort. Try, and under all feelings trust in and love God, and do not be too much elated, when you can think seriously and pray joyfully, nor too desponding when both fail you. In our present state, *physical* causes alone, so often occasion these differences of feeling in hours of devotion, that if we thought too much about them, we should constantly think wrong, and be very miserable. Try and prove your desire to love and serve God, in your *daily conduct* and *secret thoughts*, my Ellen, and you will be able to judge of your spiritual im provement by *action* and *feeling*, far more truly and justly than by the mood in which you pray."

The earnestness of truth and feeling was always so impressed on Mrs. Hamilton's manner, whenever she addressed her youthful charge, that her simplest word had weight. Happy indeed is it when youth — that season of bewildering doubt and question, and vivid, often mistaken fancies, and too impetuous feeling — has the rich blessing of such affectionate counsels, such a friend. Why will not woman rise superior to the petty employments and feelings too often alone attributed to her, and endeavor to fit herself for such a thrice blessed mission; and by sympathy with young enjoyments — young hopes — young feelings, so attract young affections, that similar counsels, similar experiences, may so help and guide, that the restless mind and eager heart quiesce into all the calm, deep, beautiful characteristics, which so shine forth in the true English wife — the true English mother!

A fortnight after Mr. Hamilton's arrival, Ellen was well enough to go down stairs for part of the day, and even to read and write a little. She was so very anxious to recommence her studies, which for many months had been so painfully neglected, that it was a great trial to her, to find her head was not yet strong enough for the necessary application. There were many, very many privations and trials, attendant on convalescence after so severe an illness, known only to Ellen's own heart, and to her aunt's quick sympathy; and she very quickly learned in them the meaning of Mrs. Hamilton's words regarding religion in conduct and feeling, as well as in prayer. She tried never to murmur, or dwell on the wish for pleasures which were denied her, but to think only on the many blessings which surrounded her. It was not an easy task so to conquer natural feeling, especially as the trial and its conquest was often known only to herself; but the earnest wish, indeed, to become holy in daily conduct, as well as in daily prayer, never left her mind, and so enabled her at length fully to obtain it.

If Mrs. Hamilton had wanted evidence of her husband's public as well as domestic worth, she would have had it fully now. His danger and his preservation once known, letters of regard and congratulation poured upon him, and Montrose Grahame made a journey down to Oakwood expressly to welcome back, and express his individual gratitude for his friend's safety to his youthful preserver. But Edward so shrunk from praise or admiration, that his uncle, rejoicing at the feeling, would not press him, as he had first intended, to accompany him to Ox ford, where he went to see his sons. Percy rated him soundly in a letter for not coming. Herbert seemed, as if he could only think of his father's danger, and thank God for his safety, and for permitting Edward to be the means. So great was the desire of Mr. and Mrs. Hamilton to re-assemble all their happy family once more, before Edward left them, that the young men made an exception to their general rule, and promised to spend Easter week at home. It was early in March, and anticipated by the home party with the greatest delight.

CHAPTER XIV.

THE RICH AND THE POOR.

"We have had such a delightful excursion, mamma. Ellen, how I do wish you could have been with us!" joyously exclaimed Emmeline, as she ran into the usual sitting-room, one of those lovely afternoons, that the first days of March so often bring, promising spring long before she really comes. "It is such a picturesque cottage, and Dame Collins, and Susan, and a host of little ones, look so nice, and so clean, and so pretty, and happy; it does one's heart good to look at them."

"Are you sure you cannot find another adjective to apply to them, Emmy? You have heaped so many together, that it is a pity you cannot find a few more."

"But they really do look so comfortable, and are so grateful for all you and papa have done for them: Emmeline's description for once, is not too flowing," rejoined the quieter Caroline, who had followed her sister into the room.

"And were they pleased with your visit?" asked Ellen.

"Oh, delighted! particularly at our making their pretty little parlor our dining-room, and remaining so long with them, that they could show us all their comforts and conveniences, without any bustle."

"Mrs. Collins is really a sensible woman. Do you not think so, mamma?" inquired Caroline.

"Yes, my dear. She has brought up her own large family and her poor orphan grandchildren so admirably, in the midst of their extreme poverty, and bears such a name for kindness among her still poorer neighbors, that I truly respect and ad mire her. She is quite one of those in whom I have often told you some of the very loftiest virtues are to be found; and yet to see her, as she trudges about in her homely, humble fashion, never dreaming she is doing or has done any thing remarkable in her hard-working life, who would suspect it?"

"Only look, Ellen, how beautifully our collection will be increased," continued Emmeline, who just at that moment was only alive to pleasure, not to contemplation, even of goodness, in which she much delighted, and pouring into her cousin's lap a basket of beautiful shells and other marine treasures. "Papa has just given us a new cabinet in time, though he only thought of it as a place for his Faroe curiosities. To think of his remembering our tastes even there!"

"But where did you get these from?"

"Why, the children were playing with some, which were so perfect, I could not help admiring them, and Mrs. Collins was in a bustle of pleasure that I liked any thing so trifling, because she could gratify me, and she made me take all these, adding, that her good man would be sure to look out for some more for us; for when I told her they not only pleased me, but my poor invalid cousin, who was Edward's sister, you should have seen how her eyes sparkled."

"Oh, you have quite won the dame's heart, Emmy!" said Miss Harcourt. "What with talking to her, and to Susan, and playing with every one of the children, and making them tell you all their plays and their schooling, and then gathering you a nosegay, telling them it should adorn your room at home!"

"And so it shall," gayly interrupted Emmeline; "I desired Robert to put them in water directly, for they were very pretty, and I like them better than the best bouquet from our green-house."

"I do not quite agree with you, Emmeline," said Caroline, smiling.

"Not you, Lina, who ever thought you would? by-the-by, I never saw you so agreeable and natural in a poor man's cottage in my life. What were you saying to Dame Collins?" actually holding her hand, and something very bright shining in your eye."

"Dear Emmy, do not run on so," whispered Ellen, as she noticed Caroline's cheek crimson. Emmeline was at her side in a moment, with an arm round her neck.

"Caroline, dear, forgive me. I did not mean to tease you; only it was unusual, was it not?"

'I was trying to tell Mrs. Collins all I thought of her husband's share in saving our dear father, Emmy. I forgot all of folly and pride then."

"You are very seldom proud now, dearest Lina, and I was the foolish one not to have guessed what you were saying, with out tormenting you. Mamma, do you know I have such an admirable plan in my head?"

"First tell mamma," interrupted Caroline, "that William Grey has chosen to be a partner with Collins in the more extended fishing and boating business, which papa has secured them, instead of entering into business by himself; this has been settled since you were there, I think."

"Yes, my dear, I did not know it; but Mrs. Collins must like it, for she regretted very much that her sons were all scattered in different trades, and her little grandson, whose taste pointed to the sea, was not old enough to go out with his grandfather."

"But only listen to my plan, mamma, dear! William Grey and Susan Collins cannot possibly see much of each other, without falling in love; and they will make such an industrious, pretty couple, and papa will give them a cottage to themselves, and I will go to their wedding!"

"Just such a plan as I should expect from your giddy brain, Emmy. But how do you know that Grey has any desire for a wife?"

"Oh, because Edward said he could not help remarking, even in the midst of that awful scene, how mournfully he said he would bear a hand, for he had neither mother, sister, nor wife to pipe for him; now, if he married Susan, he would have a very pretty wife to lament him."

"Poor Susan, I fancy she would rather not become his wife, if it be only to mourn for him, Emmy; rather a novel reason for a marriage, certainly."

"Oh, but mamma, dear! you know that I don't mean exactly and only that; somebody to be interested for, and love him. No one can be happy without that."

"Susan was telling me, mamma, how thankful she is to you, for finding her and her sister employment, that they might be able to help the family," rejoined Caroline. "I was quite pleased with her manner of speaking, and she blushed so prettily when Miss Harcourt praised the extreme neatness of her work."

"Ah, mamma, if you could but hear all they say of you!' again burst forth Emmeline, who it seemed could not be quiet, going from one subject to another with the same eager zest;

"if you had but heard the old dame tell her astonishment and her pride, when she saw you enter their former miserable hut, and sitting down on an old sea-chest, invite her to tell, and listened to all her troubles, just as if you had been her equal, and left such comfort and such hope behind you, as had not been theirs for many a long day. She actually cried when she spoke, and so did I, because she spoke so of *my* mother. Oh, mother, darling, how proud your children ought to be, to belong to one so beloved, so revered by the poor, and the rich too, as you are!"

"Flatterer!" playfully answered Mrs. Hamilton, laying her hand caressingly on her child's mouth, as she knelt in sport before her. "I will not hear such praise, even from you. Believe me, darling, to win love and respect is so easy, so delightful, that there is no merit in obtaining it. We ought only to be thankful, when granted such a station and such influence as will permit extended usefulness and thought for others, without wronging our own."

"Yes; but, mamma, many people do a great deal of good, but somehow or other they are not beloved."

"Because, perhaps, in their earnest desire to accomplish a great deal of good, they may not think quite enough of *little* things, and of the quick sympathy with other persons' feelings, which is the real secret of winning love, and without which, sometimes even the greatest benefit is not valued as it ought to be. But did you see old Collins himself?"

"He came in just before we left, and was so delighted to see papa sitting in his ingle-nook, and only wished Edward had been there too."

"And where is your father?" asked Mrs. Hamilton. Did he not return with you?"

"Yes, but Edward wanted him, and they are in the library. I am quite certain there is some conspiracy between them; these long private interviews bode no good. I shall scold papa for being so mysterious," said Emmeline.

"I rather think he will return the benefit, by scolding you for being so curious, Emmy. But here is Edward, so the interview to-day has not been very long."

"Has papa been telling you old Collins's naval news, Ned?" And, without waiting for an answer, she continued, "that there is a fine seventy-four, the Sea Queen, preparing at Plymouth, to take the place of your old ship, and send back Sir Edward Manly and the Prince William. Now do not tell me you know this, Edward, and so disappoint me of the rare pleasure of telling news."

"I am sorry, Emmy, but I have known it for some weeks."

"And why did you not tell us?"

"Because I did not think it would particularly interest you, until I could add other intelligence to it." He stopped, and looked alternately at Mrs. Hamilton and Ellen, as if asking the former whether he might proceed.

"And can you do so now, my dear Edward?" she replied, understanding him at once. "Ellen is too anxious for your advancement to expect, or wish you always to remain with her. Have you your appointment?"

"Yes, aunt. My uncle's letter to the admiralty brought an answer at last. It came while he was out, and has been tantalizing me on the library-table for four hours. But it is all right. As the Prince William is returning, and I am so anxious to be still in active service, I am permitted, though somewhat against rule, to have a berth in the Sea Queen. I am sure it is all uncle Hamilton's representations, and I am so thankful, so glad!"

"To leave us all, again, you unfeeling savage!" exclaimed Emmeline, trying to laugh off the universal regret at this announcement. Ellen had looked earnestly at her brother all the time he spoke, and then turned her face away, and a few quiet tears trickled down her cheek. Edward's arm was very quickly round her, and he whispered so many fond words and earnest assurances, united with his conviction that it would still be a whole month, perhaps more, before he should be summoned, as he had leave to remain with his family till the Sea Queen was ready to sail, that she rallied her spirits, and, after remaining very quiet for an hour, which was always her custom when she had had any struggle with herself, for the frame felt it — though neither word nor sign betrayed it — she was enabled fully to enjoy the grand delight of the evening — Percy's and Herbert's arrival.

Easter week was indeed one of family joy and thankfulness, not only that they were all permitted once more to be together, but that the heavy clouds of sin and suffering had rolled away from their roof, and pleasure of the sweetest and most enduring because most domestic kind, reigned triumphant. Percy's astonishment at Edward's growth, and the alteration from the handsome, joyous, rosy boy, to the pale, almost care-worn looking youth (for as long as Ellen bore such vivid traces of all she had endured for his sake, and was, as it were, the constant presence of his errors, Edward tried in vain to recover his former spirits,) was most amusing.

"You are all deceived," he would declare; "one of these days you will discover you have been receiving a spurious Edward Fortescue, and that he is as much a pretender as his namesake, Charles Edward."

"Then he is no pretender, Percy. He is as truly the son of Colonel Fortescue, as *Prince* Charles was the grandson of James. Now don't begin a civil contest directly you come home; you know you and I never do agree on historical subjects, and we never shall; you hate Mary the great, great, great grandmother of Prince Charles, and I love her, so we must be always at war."

"Stuart-mad, as usual, Tiny! but if that really be Edward, I wish he would just look a boy again, I don't like the change at all; poor fellow!" he added, to himself, "it is not much wonder."

The days passed much too quickly. Emmeline wished a dozen times that the days would be twenty-four, instead of twelve hours long. The weather was so genial that it added to enjoyment, and allowed Ellen the delight, known only to such prisoners to sickness as she had been, of driving out for an hour or two at a time, and taking gentle walks on the terrace, and in the garden. The young men were to return on the Monday, and on the Saturday previous a little excursion had been planned, to which the only drawback was that Ellen was not quite strong enough to accompany them: it was to visit Alice Seaton, whom we mentioned in a former chapter. Mr. Hamilton had succeeded in finding her brother a lucrative employment with a lawyer in one of the neighboring towns, a few miles from where she and her aunt now lived, enabling young Seaton to spend every Sabbath with them; and Alice now kept a girls' school on her own account, and conducted herself so well as never to want scholars. It had been a long promise to go and see her, the drive from Oakwood being also most beautiful; and as she and her brother were both at home and at leisure the last day in Easter, it had been fixed upon for the visit. Percy was revelling in the idea of driving his mother and Miss Harcourt in a new barouche, and the rest of the party were to go on horse-back. But a dispute had arisen who should stay with Ellen, and Edward insisted upon it, it was his right; and so they thought it was agreed.

"I wish, dear Percy you would prevail on Edward to accompany you," pleaded Ellen, fancying herself alone with him, not seeing Herbert, who was reading at a distant table.

"I wish, dear Ellen, you were going with us," he answered, mimicking her tone.

"But as I cannot, make him go. It always makes him more unhappy when I am prevented any pleasure, than it does myself; and I cannot bear to keep him by me four or five hours, when this lovely day, and the exercise of riding, and, above all, your company, Percy, would make him, at least for the time, almost his own merry self, again."

"Thanks for the implied compliment, cousin mine," replied Percy, with a low bow.

"Reward me for it, and make him go."

"How can I be so ungallant, as to make him leave you alone?"

"Oh, I do not mind it, I assure you!" I am well enough to amuse myself now; I cannot bear you all giving up so many pleasures as you have done for me; I am so afraid of getting selfish."

"You selfish, Ellen? I wish you were a little more so; you are the most patient, devoted little creature that ever took woman's form. You have made me reproach myself enough, I can tell you, and I owe you a grudge for doing so."

"Dear Percy, what can you mean? If you knew how hard I find it to be patient, sometimes, you would not praise me."

"I mean that the last time I was at home, I was blind and cruel, and added to your sufferings by my uncalled-for harshness, and never had an opportunity till this moment, to say how grieved I was — when the truth was known."

"Pray do not say any thing about it, dear Percy," entreated his cousin, the tears starting to her eyes, as he kissed her warmly; it was only just and natural that you should have felt indignant with me, for causing aunt Emmeline so much misery, and alloying all the enjoyment of your holidays. I am sure you need not reproach yourself; but will you make Edward go?"

"If it really will oblige you, Ellen; but I do not half like it." And he was going very reluctantly, when he met Herbert.

"You need not go, Percy," he said smiling; "my ungracious cousin would not depute me as her messenger, but I made myself such, and so successfully that Edward will go, Ellen."

"Dear Herbert, how can I thank you enough! he will be so much happier with you all."

"Not with me," said Herbert, archly, "for I remain in his place."

"You!" repeated Ellen, surprised; "indeed, dear Herbert, it must not be. I shall do very well alone."

"Ungracious still, Ellen! what if I have been looking all the morning for some excuse to stay at home, without owning to my mother the truth — that I do not feel to-day quite equal to riding? If your looks were as ungracious as your words, I would run away from you into my own room; but as they are rather more gratifying to my self-love, we will send them all away, and enjoy our own quiet pleasures and your little drive together, Nell."

Whatever Ellen might have said to convince him she could be happy alone, the beaming look of pleasure on her countenance, satisfied all parties as to the excellence of this arrangement; and happy, indeed, the day was. Herbert seemed to understand her unexpressed feelings so fully; and that always makes the charm of conversation, whatever its subject. We do not require the *expression in words* of sympathy — it is an indescribable something that betrays its existence. Favorite authors — and Herbert was almost surprised at Ellen's dawning taste and judgment in literature — the delights of nature after a long confinement, as if every flower were more sweet, every bit of landscape, or wood, or water more beautiful, and the many holy thoughts and pure joys springing from such feelings, were all discussed, either cosily in their sitting-room, or in their ramble in the garden; and after Ellen's early dinner, which Herbert shared with her as lunch, she proposed, what she knew he would like, that her drive should be to Greville Manor, and they might spend a full hour with their friends, and yet be back in time. Herbert assented gladly; and the warm welcome they received, Mrs. Greville's kind care of Ellen, and Mary's eager chat with her and Herbert, and the number of things they seemed to find to talk about, made the hour literally fly; but Herbert, enjoyable as it was, did not forget his charge, and drove her back to Oakwood while the sun still shone bright and warmly: and when the party returned, which they did only just in time to dress for dinner, and in the wildest spirits, the balance of pleasure at home and abroad, would certainly have been found quite equal.

Ellen still continued quietly to lie down in her own room while the family were at dinner, for she was then sufficiently refreshed to join them for a few hours in the evening. Percy and Emmeline, at dinner that day, kept up such a fire of wit and mirth, that it was somewhat difficult for any one else to edge in a word, though Edward and Caroline did sometimes contrive to bring a whole battery against themselves. Just as the dessert was placed on the table, however, sounds of rural music in the distance, advancing nearer and nearer, caused Percy to pause in his wild sallies, and spring with Edward to the window, and their exclamations soon compelled all the party to follow their example, and send for Ellen to see the unexpected sight too. Banners and pennons floated in the sunshine, and the greater part of the nautical inhabitants of Dartmouth were marshalled in goodly array beside them, headed by Captain Harvey and his crew, with Collins in the midst of them; they were all attired in the new clothing which Mr. Hamilton had presented to them; and a fine picture Percy declared old Collins's head would make, with his weather-beaten, honest-speaking face, the very peculiar curls in which his really yellow hair was twisted, and the quid of tobacco, from which, even on this grand occasion, he could not relieve his mouth and cheek. A band of young men and girls surrounded the first banner, which, adorned with large bunches of primroses and violets up the staff, bore the words, "Hamilton and benevolence;" and among them Emmeline speedly recognized William Grey and Susan Collins, walking side by side, she looking down and smiling, and he so earnestly talking, that she whispered to her mother with the greatest glee, that her plan would take place after all. Then came a band of sturdy fishermen, chums and messmates of Collins, and then a band of boys and girls, from all Mr. Hamilton's own village schools, decked in their holiday attire, and holding in their hands tasteful garlands of all the spring flowers they could muster, and bearing two large banners, one with the words, "Fortescue forever! All hail to British sailors!" and the other a representation of the scene on the beach that eventful night, and the sinking vessel in the distance. The workmanship was rude indeed, but the effect so strikingly descriptive, that Mrs. Hamilton actually shuddered as she gazed, and grasped, almost unconsciously, the arm of her nephew as he stood by her, as if the magnitude of the danger, both to him and her husband, had never seemed so vivid before.

The windows of the dining-room had been thrown widely open, and as the rustic procession came in sight of those to whom their whole hearts tendered homage, they halted; the music ceased, and cheer on cheer resounded, till the very echoes of the old park were startled out of their sleep, and sent the shout back again. Percy was among them in a moment, singling out old Collins, whom he had tried repeatedly to see since his visit home, but never found him, and grasped and shook both his hands with the full vehemence of his character, pouring out the first words that chose to come, which better expressed his grateful feelings to the old man than the most studied speech. William Grey had already received substantial proofs of his gratitude, and so he had then only a kind nod, and a joke and look at the pretty, blushing Susan, which said a vast deal to both, and seemed as if he quite seconded Emmeline's plan. Mingling joyously with all, he had bluff words, after their own hearts, for the men, smiles for the maidens, and such wild jokes for the children, as lost them all decorum, and made them shout aloud in their glee. Herbert seconded him quite as well as his quieter nature would allow. Edward had hung back, even when his name was called out lustily, as if he could not bear such homage.

"Join them, my boy; their humble pleasure will not be half complete without you," whispered Mrs. Hamilton, earnestly, for she guessed his thoughts. "Remember only at this moment the large amount of happiness you have been permitted to call forth. Do not underrate a deed which all must admire, because of some sad thoughts; rather resolve — as you can and have resolved — that the alloy shall be burned away, and the true metal alone remain, for my sake, to whom you have given such happiness, dear Edward."

The cloud dispersed from brow and heart in a moment; and he was in the midst of them, glad and buoyant almost as Percy, while the cheer which greeted him was almost overpowering to his sister, so much humble, yet earnest feeling did it speak.

"You really should have given us timely notice of your intentions, my good friend," said Mr. Hamilton, warmly grasping Captain Harvey's hand. "At least we might have provided some substantial refreshment after your long march, as I fear we have but slender fare to offer you, though Ellis and Morris are busy already, I am happy to see."

And urged on by their own delight at this homage both to their master and his young preserver, who had become a complete idol among them, a long table was speedily laid in the servants' hall, covered with a variety of cold meats, and bread and cheese in abundance, and horns of cider sparkling brightly beside each trencher. Fruit and cakes eagerly sought for by Emmeline, were by her distributed largely to the children, who remained variously grouped on the lawn, their glee at the treat heightened by the sweet and gentle manner of its bestowal.

Captain Harvey and his mate, Mr. Hamilton entertained himself, introducing them to his family, and especially Ellen, who, as the sister of Edward, found herself regarded with an interest that surprised her. Percy brought in old Collins and Grey, both of whom had expressed such a wish to see any one so nearly belonging to the brave young sailor; and her manner of receiving and returning their greeting, thanking them for the help they had so efficiently given her brother, made them still prouder and happier than before. After an hour and a half of thorough enjoyment — for their humble homage to worth and goodness had been received in the same spirit as it had been tendered — the procession marshalled itself in the same order as it had come; and rude as the music was, it sounded, as Emmeline declared, really beautiful, becoming fainter and fainter in the distance, and quite picturesque the effect of the banners and pennons, as they gleamed in and out the woody windings of the park, both music and procession softened in the mild, lovely twilight of the season.

CHAPTER XV.

A HOME SCENE, AND A PARTING.

"CAROLINE! Emmeline! come to the music-room, for pity's sake, and give me some delicious harmony," exclaimed Percy, as soon as lights came, and the excitement of the last two hours had a little subsided. "Sit quiet — unless I have some amusement for my ears — I neither can nor will. I will have some music to lull my tired senses, and a waltz to excite my wearied frame."

"And rest your limbs," said Edward, dryly.

"Don't you know, master sailor, that when fatigued with one kind of exercise, the best rest is to take another? Now I have been standing up, playing the agreeable, for two mortal hours, and I mean to have a waltz to bring back the stagnant circulation, and to be pleased for the fatigue of pleasing. Caroline and Emmeline, away with you both. Ellen, love, I will only ask you to come with us, and be pleased, too. Be off, Edward, no one shall be my cousin's cavalier but myself; Herbert has had her all day. Take my mother, if you like. Father, escort Miss Harcourt. That's all right, as it always is, when I have my own way!"

His own way, this time, gave universal satisfaction. The talents of his sisters had been so cultivated, as a means of enhancing home-happiness, and increasing their own resources, that their musical evenings were always perfect enjoyment

Caroline, indeed, improved as she was, still retained her love of admiration sufficiently, to find still greater enjoyment in playing and singing when there were more to listen to her, than merely her own family, but the feeling, in the security and pure atmosphere of Oakwood, was kept under control, and she could find real pleasure in gratifying her brothers, though not quite to the same extent as Emmeline.

Percy, after comfortably settling Ellen, threw himself on the most luxurious chair that he could find, stretched out his legs, placed his head in what he called the best position for listening and enjoying, and then called for duets on the harp and piano, single pieces on both, and song after song, with the most merciless rapidity.

"Your sisters shall neither play nor sing to you any more," his mother, at length, laughingly, said, "unless you rouse yourself from this disgracefully idle fit, and take your flute, and join them."

"Mother, you are lost to every sensation of mercy! after all my exertions, where am I to find breath?"

"You have had plenty of time to rest, you lazy fellow; letting your sisters fatigue themselves, without remorse, and refusing your share," expostulated Edward. "Caroline, Emmeline, take my advice, and strike! don't play another note."

"You young rebel! teaching my sisters to revolt against the authority of such an important person as myself. However, I will be condescending for once; Tiny, there's a love, fetch me my flute."

It was so very close to him as he approached the piano, that his sister comically took his hand, and placed it on it, and two or three very pretty trios were performed, Percy declared with professional *eclât*.

"Now don't go, Percy, we want your voice in a song. Emmy, sing that pretty one to your harp, that we wish papa so much to hear; Percy and I will join, when wanted."

"Caroline, I have not the genius to sing at sight."

"Oh, you have often! and the words will inspire you. Come, Herbert, we want you, too; Edward's singing voice has deserted him, or I should enlist him also. Emmeline, what are you waiting for?"

"I cannot sing it, dear Caroline; do not ask me," answered Emmeline, with a confusion and timidity, which, at home, were perfectly incomprehensible.

"Why, my little Emmy, I am quite curious to hear this new song do not disappoint me!" said her father, encouragingly.

"But after Caroline I cannot sing worth hearing," still pleaded Emmeline.

"My dear child, I never heard you make such a foolish excuse before; your mother and myself never find any difference in the pleasure that listening to your music bestows, however one performer may be more naturally gifted than the other."

"I declare I must sing it if it be only for the mystery of Tiny's refusing," said Percy, laughing. "Come, Bertie — a MS. too — what a trial for one's nerves."

The words, however, seemed sufficiently satisfactory for them readily to join in it. Emmeline still hesitated, almost painfully; but then gathering courage, she sat down to her harp, and, without any notes before her, played a few bars of one of those sweet, thrilling Irish melodies, so suited to her instrument, and then commenced her song, the sweetness of her voice, and clearness of articulation atoning well for her deficiency in the power and brilliancy which characterized her sister. The words were exceedingly simple, but sung with deep feeling, and heart-appealing as they were, from the subject, we hope our readers will judge them as leniently as Emmeline's hearers.

EMMELINE'S SONG.

"Joy! joy! No more shall sorrow cloud
The home by Love enshrined:
The hearts in Care's cold fetters bow'd,
Now loveliest flowers have twined;
And dove-eyed Peace, with brooding wing,
Hath made her dwelling here;
And Hope and Love sweet incense fling,
To welcome and endear.

"He has return'd! — and starless night
No longer o'er us lowers.
Joy! joy! The future is all bright
With rosy-blossom'd hours.
What gladness with our Father fled!
What gladness he'll restore!
He has return'd, through perils dread,
To bless his own once more!

"Joy! joy! Oh let our voices raise
Their glad and grateful lay,
And pour forth thanksgiving and praise
That grief hath passed away!
That he was snatch'd from storm and wave
To dry pale Sorrow's tear;
Restored! his home from woe to save —
Oh! welcome, Father dear!"

Emmeline's voice had at first trembled audibly, but seeming

to derive courage from her sister and brother's accompaniment, which, from their knowledge of music, was so beautifully modulated as to permit her sweet voice to be heard above all, and every word clearly distinguished, it became firmer and more earnest as she continued, till she forgot every thing but the subject of her song. For full a minute there was silence as she ceased, but with an irresistible impulse Mr. Hamilton rose from his seat, and, as Emmeline left her harp, he clasped her in his arms.

"How can I thank you, my Emmeline, and all my children, for this fond greeting?" he exclaimed, with more emotion than he generally permitted to be visible. "Where could you find such appropriate words? What! tears, my little girl," he added, as, completely overcome by the excitement of her song and her father's praise, Emmeline most unexpectedly burst into tears. "What business have they to come when you have given your parents nothing but pleasure? Drive them away, love; what! still no smile? We must appeal to mamma's influence, then, to explain and soothe them."

"Where did you get them, Tiny? explain, for I am positively faint from curiosity," comically demanded Percy, as Emmeline, breaking from her father, sat down on her favorite stool at her mother's feet, and hid her face in her lap. Mrs. Hamilton laid her hand caressingly on those soft curls, but though she smiled, she did not speak.

"She will not tell, and you will none of you guess," said Caroline, laughing.

"You are in the secret, so out with it," said Edward.

"Not I; I am pledged to silence."

"Mother, dear, tell us for pity," pleaded Herbert.

"I can only guess, for I am not in her confidence, I assure you," she replied, in the same playful tone, and raising Emmeline's lowered head, she looked a moment in those conscious eyes. "Dictated by my Emmeline's affectionate little heart, they were found in this pretty shape, in the recesses of her own fanciful brain — is not that it, dearest?"

"There, Emmy, I knew mamma would find it out, however we might be silent," said Caroline, triumphantly, as her sister's face was again concealed.

"Emmeline turned poet! Angels and ministers of grace defend me! I must hide my diminished head!" spouted Percy. "I thought at least I might retain my crown as the poet of the family, and to be rivalled by you — a light-footed fawn — wild gazelle — airy sprite — my especial Tiny! it is unbearable!"

"But we must all thank you, notwithstanding, Emmy," continued Herbert.

"Ah, but I have very little to do with it; the arrangement, of the words to the air, and the accompaniment, are Caroline's; I could not have done that," said Emmeline; her tears changed to her most joyous smiles.

Percy and his father turned directly to Caroline, the former with a Sir Charles Grandison's bow, the other with a most affectionate kiss; and her mother looked at her with such an expression of gratified pleasure, that she could not help acknowledging to herself, such pure enjoyment was not to be found in the praise and admiration of strangers.

"Now, Emmeline, you have still a mystery to explain," said Edward. "Why did you not own your offspring, instead of, by silence, almost denying them?"

"And here I really cannot help you," answered Mrs. Hamilton; "I cannot imagine why my Emmy should conceal a fact that could only give pleasure to us all."

"I think I know," said Ellen, timidly; "Emmeline was thinking of all you said about controlling an impulse, and not always encouraging that which she termed inspiration, and perhaps she thought you did not quite approve of her writing, and so wished to conceal it."

"How could you guess so exactly, Ellen?" hastily answered Emmeline, forgetting, in her surprise at her cousin's penetration, that she betrayed herself.

"Because I should have felt the same," said Ellen, simply.

"Then I must have explained myself very badly, my dear children, or you must have both misunderstood me. I did not mean you to neglect such an enjoyment as poetry, but only to keep it in its proper sphere, and not allow it to take the place of resources, equally intellectual, but which have and may still cost you more patience and labor. Poetry is a dangerous gift, my dear child; but as long as you bring it to the common treasury of Home, and regard it merely as a recreation, only to be enjoyed when less attractive duties and studies are completed, you have my full permission to cultivate — and try, by the study of our best authors, and whatever other help I can obtain for you, to improve yourself in it. No talent that is lent us should be thrown aside, my Emmeline; our only care must be, not — by loving and pursuing it too intensely — to *abuse* it; but I must not lecture you any longer, or Percy's patience will fail; I see he has placed Miss Harcourt already at the piano, and Edward and Caroline are ready for their waltz."

"And so I transform one Muse into another," exclaimed Percy, who, in his sister's absorbed attention, had neared her unobserved, and catching her round the waist, bore her to the upper end of the room, and a minute afterward she was enjoying her waltz, with as much childish glee, as if neither poetry nor reflection could have any thing to do with her.

"Why is poetry a dangerous gift, dear aunt?" inquired Ellen, who had listened earnestly to all Mrs. Hamilton had said.

"Because, my love, it is very apt to excite and encourage an over-excess of feeling; gives a habit of seeing things other than they really are, and engenders a species of romantic enthusiasm, most dangerous to the young, especially of our sex, whose feelings generally require control and repression, even when not joined to poetry. To a well-regulated mind and temper, the danger is not of the same serious kind as to the irregulated, but merely consists in the powerful temptation it too often presents to neglect duties and employments of more consequence, for its indulgence. There is a species of fascination in the composition of even the most inferior poetry, which urges its pursuits, as giving so little trouble, compared to the perseverance necessary for music and drawing, and such a vast amount of pleasure, that it is difficult to withdraw from it. This is still more strongly the case when the young first become conscious of the gift, as Emmeline is now. As she gets older, and her taste improves, she will not be satisfied with her efforts, unless they are very superior to the present, and the trouble she will take in correcting and improving, will remove a great deal of the too dangerous fascination attending it now; still I am not anxious, while she retains her confidence in my affection and experience, and will so control the enjoyment, as not to permit its interference with her other more serious employments."

Ellen listened eagerly, and they continued conversing on many similar topics of interest and improvement, till the prayer bell rang, and startled her into the recollection that she had always retired nearly an hour before, and so had avoided entering the library, which she still quite shrunk from. Percy stopped his dance, which he had converted from a waltz into a most inspiring gallopade, the last importation, he declared, from Almack's; Miss Harcourt closed the piano; and Herbert paused in his conversation with his father. Nothing like gloom ever marked the signal for the hour of devotion, but lighter pleasures always ceased a few minutes before, that they might better realize the more serious thought and service.

Mrs. Hamilton had never ceased to regret the disgrace she

had inflicted on Ellen, in not permitting her to retain her own place with the family, at least in the hours of devotion, for it seemed more difficult to remove that impression than any of her other trials. Returning her niece's startled look with one of the sincerest affection, she said —

"You will remain with us to-night, my dear Ellen, will you not?"

"If you wish it, aunt."

"I do wish it, dearest, most earnestly. It is so long since I have had the happiness of seeing all my children round me in this solemn hour, and till you join us, I can not feel quite sure that you have indeed forgiven an act of severity, which, could I but have suspected the truth, I should never have inflicted."

"Forgiven! — you!" repeated Ellen, in utter astonishment, but rising instantly. "Aunt Emmeline, dear aunt Emmeline, pray, do not speak so; why did you not tell me your wish before? I would have conquered my own disinclination to enter the library, weeks ago; indeed, indeed, it only seemed associated with my own guilt and misery."

Mrs. Hamilton drew her arm fondly in hers, refusing for her the aid of either of the young men, who had all hastened toward her, and led her herself to the library, and to her usual place beside Emmeline. Many an eager but respectful look of affectionate admiration was directed toward her by the assembled household, the greater part of whom had not seen her since the night of Edward's confession; and the alteration in her appearance, the universal sympathy which her dangerous illness and its cause had called forth, even in the humblest and most ignorant — for it is the *heart*, not the *mind*, which is required for the comprehension of self-devotion — her very youth seeming to increase its magnitude, had inspired such a feeling of love, that could she have known it, would have prevented that painful sensation of shyness.

Many, many thoughts thronged her mind, as her uncle's impressive voice fell on her ear; thoughts which, though they prevented her following the words of the prayers, and caused the tears, spite of every effort, to stream through her slender fingers, yet turned into thankfulness and praise, ere the service ceased, that, fiery as the ordeal had been, she could still recognize a hand of love, and bless God, not only for the detection of her involuntary sin, but for every pang she had endured.

The next day was Sunday, bringing with it all sorts of quiet, sober pleasures of its own, only alloyed by the thought that it was the last day of Percy's and Herbert's visit The following morning they started for Oxford, Mr. Hamilton and Edward intending to accompany them part of the way, and then to proceed to Ashburton, where the former had business, and then make a little tour through Plymouth home. The next day was so beautifully fine and genial, that Emmeline declared it would do Ellen the greatest possible good to go with her a few miles out of the park, to see a waterfall she had lately discovered, and which she had been longing for Ellen to see, as Caroline would not admire it as much as it deserved. Miss Harcourt accompanied them, and on their return, its beauties were described to Mrs. Hamilton in the most animating strain; Emmeline declaring the air was more deliciously fresh, the trees more green, the sky more brilliantly blue, than they had ever been before; and that the very sound of the water, as it dashed down a black rock, and threw up spray, which the rays of the sun rendered so beautifully iridescent, as to seem like a succession of rainbows, was a whole volume of poetry in itself.

"And what extraordinary vision do you think that silly cousin of mine chose to fancy she saw coming down the Ashburton road, mamma? Actually the apparitions of papa and Edward. She will persist in the fancy. Miss Harcourt and I could only see two men on horseback, at too great a distance for any identity to be recognized — but it must be their wraiths, if it be, for they had no idea of coming home to-day."

"I am sure I was not mistaken, Emmeline," said Ellen (whom her aunt now observed looked agitated and flushed); "and they were riding so fast, something very pressing must have recalled them."

"And you are frightening yourself at shadows, my dear! but indeed I think you must be mistaken, for your uncle told me, he should be particularly engaged to-day," said Mrs. Hamilton.

"She is not mistaken, though," exclaimed Caroline, who was standing at one of the windows; "for here they both are, true enough, and riding quite fast down the avenue. However, the mystery will soon be solved."

Mr. Hamilton and Edward entered almost immediately afterward, the latter evidently very much agitated, the former so tranquil and cheerful that the momentary anxiety of his wife was calmed directly. He laughed at their bewilderment, and said that an important letter had reached him at Ashburton, summoning him to Plymouth, and so he thought he would just see how all was going on at Oakwood first. This was not at all a satisfactory reason from Mr. Hamilton. Edward evidently tried to answer Ellen's inquiries quietly, but he could not, and exclaiming, "You tell her, my dear uncle! I cannot," ran out of the room. Mr. Hamilton instantly changed his jesting manner, so far as quietly and affectionately to seat his niece beside him, and tell her, cautiously and kindly, the real cause of their unexpected return. Orders had been sent to the Sea Queen, to sail much sooner than was expected, and therefore he had deferred his business, and returned with Edward directly.

"It is a trial, my dear Ellen, a very hard one just now, under all circumstances; but I am sure you will bear it with fortitude, for Edward's sake. The only drawback to his happiness in being again permitted to follow his profession, is the thought of the trial, it will be to you."

"But when must we part? When must he leave Oakwood?" was all poor Ellen could ask; but in such a tone of quiet sorrow, her uncle could not for the moment reply.

"The Sea Queen leaves Plymouth, wind permitting, the end of the week, but — Edward must be on board to-morrow."

A low cry escaped involuntarily from Ellen's lips, as she buried her face on the cushion of the couch where she was sitting, and an exclamation of surprise and regret broke from all. Mrs. Hamilton felt it almost as much as Ellen, from not only her own unspoken anxiety, as to whether indeed his home influence would save him from temptation in future, but that she could enter into every thought and feeling which in Ellen must so aggravate the actual parting — always a sorrow in itself. After a few minutes Ellen raised her head, and, though her cheek was perfectly colorless, every tear was checked.

"Tell Edward he need not fear my weakness, dear Emmeline," she said, trying hard to speak quite calmly. "Only beg him to come to me, that we may spend the little time we have together; I will be as cheerful as himself." And, effort as it was, she kept her word; so controlling sorrow, to enter into his naturally glad anticipations, that her brother felt as if he could not love, nor venerate her enough.

He was obliged to leave Oakwood (accompanied by his uncle) so early the next morning that all his preparations had to be completed by that night. Ellis's activity, though she could not endure the idea of his going, speedily and satisfactorily settled that matter. Robert Langford, who had only regained his natural light-heartedness since Ellen had taken her usual place in the family, always declaring his carelessness had been the origin of all her misery, was another so active in his service, that Edward had only to give a hint of any thing he wanted, even if it could only be procured at some distance, and it was instantly obtained.

The hours wore on, the evening devotions were concluded, but still the family lingered in the library: there seemed so many things to say, for Mr. Hamilton and Miss Harcourt would not let the conversation flag, and Edward would talk and laugh, as if he were only going from home for a few days. Midnight chimed, but still Mrs. Hamilton felt as if she could not give the signal for separation: but when one struck, there was a general start, and an unanimous declaration it could not be so late.

"I assure you it is," Mrs. Hamilton cheerfully said; "and poor Edward will get no sleep, if we do not separate at once. He must certainly send you a box of artificial roses, for this unusual dissipation will bear all the natural ones away. Ellen, love, I must be cruel enough to resist that pleading look; remember, your full strength has not yet returned."

She spoke kindly, but firmly, and there was a general move. Edward, laughingly, promised to send his cousins the very best box of rouge he could procure at Plymouth, and wished them good night as gayly as if they should meet as usual the next morning. Once only his voice faltered — "Ellen, love, good night! My own sister, God in Heaven bless you!" were all he said the last sentence escaping as if involuntarily, as if he had merely meant to say good night; and for more than a minute the brother and sister were clasped in each other's arms. There were tears in Mrs. Hamilton's eyes, and her husband's were most unwontedly dim, for words were not needed to reveal to them the trial of that moment to those two young hearts. To Ellen's especially, for her lot was woman's — to *endure* until time should prove the reality of Edward's resolution, and mark him indeed the noble character his disposition so fondly promised. His was active service, the banishment of *thought* by *deed.* Breaking from her brother, and not daring to address either her aunt or uncle, lest her control should fail her too soon, Ellen hastened from the room.

"Go to her, aunt Emmeline; oh, tell her I will never, never cause her to suffer again!" implored Edward, as soon as he could speak, and clasping his aunt's hand. "She has been struggling with herself the whole evening for my sake, and she will suffer for it to-morrow, unless she give it vent, and she will weep less painfully if you speak of comfort."

"She will be better alone a little while, my dear boy; young as she is, she knows where to seek and find comfort, and her tears would flow more freely, conscious only of the presence and healing of her God. I shall not part from you now. Ellis wanted me for some directions about your things, and I will come to you in your room afterward."

Mrs. Hamilton knew the human heart well. When she went to Ellen, the paroxysm of natural sorrow had had vent, and her sympathy, her earnestly expressed conviction that the trial of beholding error and remorse in one so beloved would not occur again, could bring comfort. The tears indeed might still have flowed the faster, perhaps, at the voice of kindness, but there was healing in them; and when her aunt left her to go to Edward, she sent him a fond message that she was better, and in a few days would be happy, quite happy for his sake.

It was late before Mrs. Hamilton quitted her nephew. We will not repeat all that passed between them, all that that fond watchful relative so earnestly, so appealingly said. Not much in actual words of counsel had she ever before addressed to him, feeling that that duty was better performed by Mr. Howard and his uncle. She had simply tried to influence him by the power of love, of forbearance, of sympathy with his remorse, and pity for his errors. In the wretchedness, the fearful anxiety, Ellen's danger and painful illness had occasioned herself individually, she had never spoken, or even let fall a sentence which could reproach him as the cause of all; and, therefore, now that she did give her anxious affection words, they were so spoken, that her nephew never forget them.

"I feel now," he had said, near the conclusion of their interview, "as if nothing could tempt me to err again; but oh, aunt Emmeline, so I thought when I left home before; and its influences all left me as if they had never been. It may be so again and — and — are there not such doomed wretches, making all they love best most miserable?"

"Not, indeed, if they will take their home influences with them, my beloved boy. They deserted you before because, by the insidious sentiments of a most unhappy man, your religion was shaken, and you flung aside with scorn and misbelief the *only safety* for the young — God's most Holy Word. The influences of your home are based on that alone, my Edward. They appear perhaps to the casual observer as only love, indulgence, peace, and the joy springing from innocent and happy hearts; but these are mere flowers springing from one immortal root. In God's Word alone is our safety, there alone our strength and our joy; and that may be yours still, my boy, though far away from us, and in a little world with interests and temptations of its own. Take this little Bible; it has been my constant companion for eighteen years, and to none but to yourself would I part with it. If you fear your better feelings failing, read it, be guided by it, if at first only for the sake of those you love; I do not fear, but that very soon you will do so for its own sake. It bears a name within it which I think will ever keep it sacred in your care, as it has been in mine."

Edward opened it eagerly, "Charles Manvers!" he exclaimed; "My own sailor-uncle, whose memory you have so taught me to love. It is indeed a spell, dear aunt, and you shall never regret a gift so precious. But how came it yours?"

"He came to me just before starting for his last trip, entreating me to exchange Bibles with him, that in our most serious moments we might think of each other. It was such an unusually serious speech for him, that it seemed to thrill me with a vague foreboding, which was only too soon realized. I never saw him again; and that little book indeed increased in value."

Her voice faltered, for even yet the memory of her brother was so dear to her that she could never speak of him without emotion. Edward reiterated his eager assurance that it should be equally valuable to him, adding —

"I have often had strange fancies about uncle Charles, aunt, and longed for the command of a ship, to scour the coast of Algiers, and learn something more about the Leander. Somehow or other, I never can believe he was drowned, and yet to think of him as a slave, is terrible."

"And not likely, my dear boy; think of the lapse of years. But painful as it is, we must separate, Edward; I must not detain you from rest and sleep any longer. Only give me one promise — if ever you are led into temptation and error again, and it may be — for our strongest resolutions sometimes fail us — write to me without the smallest hesitation, openly, freely; tell me all, and if you need aid, ask it, and I will give it; and, if it be possible avert your uncle's displeasure. I have no fear that, in telling you this, I am weakening your resolution, but only to prevent one fault becoming many by concealment — from dread of anger, and therein the supposed impossibility of amendment. Remember, my beloved boy, you have a claim on me which no error nor fault can remove; as, under providence, the preserver of my husband, I can *never* change the anxious love I bear you. You may indeed make me very miserable, but I know you will not; you *will* let me look on your noble deed with all the love, the admiration, it deserves. Promise me that, under any difficulty or error, small or great, you will write to me as you would have done to your own beloved mother, and I shall have no fear remaining."

Edward did promise, but his heart was so full he could not restrain himself any longer, and as Mrs. Hamilton folded him to her heart, in a silent but tearful embrace, he wept on her shoulder like a child.

CHAPTER XVI.

THE BIRTHDAY GIFT.

Brightly and placidly, as the course of their own beautiful river, did the days now pass to the inmates of Oakwood. Letters came from Edward so frequently, so happily, that hope would rest calmly, joyously, even on the thought of him. He never let an opportunity pass, writing always to Mrs. Hamilton (which he had scarcely ever done before,) and inclosing his letters to Ellen open in hers. The tone, the frequency, were so changed from his last, that his family now wondered they had been so blind before in not perceiving that his very seeming liveliness was unnatural and overstrained.

With Ellen too, Mrs. Hamilton's anxious care was bringing in fair promise of success — the mistaken influences of her childhood, and their increased effect from a morbid imagination, produced from constant suffering, appearing, indeed, about to be wholly eradicated. Anxious to remove all sad associations connected with the library, Mrs. Hamilton having determined herself to superintend Ellen's studies, passed long mornings in that ancient room with her, so delightfully, that it became associated only with the noble authors whose works, or extracts from whom, she read and revelled in, and which filled her mind with such new thoughts, such expansive ideas, such calming and earnest truths, that she felt becoming to herself a new being. Lively and thoughtless as Emmeline she could not now indeed become — alike as their dispositions naturally were; but she was more quietly, enduringly happy than she had ever remembered herself.

There was only one alloy, one sad thought that would intrude, causing a resolution, which none suspected; for, open as she had become, she could breathe it to none but Ellis, for she alone could assist her, though it required many persuasions and many assurances, that she never could be quite happy, unless it was accomplished, which could prevail on her to grant it. Ellen knew, felt more and more each week, that she could not rest till she had labored for and obtained, and returned into her aunt's hands the full sum she had so involuntarily appropriated. The only means she could adopt demanded such a seeming interminable period of self-denial, patience, and perseverance, that at first as Ellis represented and magnified all connected with it, she felt as if, indeed, she could not nerve herself for the task, much as she desired to perform it; but prayer enabled her to face the idea, till it lost its most painful aspect, and three months after Edward's departure she commenced the undertaking, resolved that neither time nor difficulty should deter her from its accomplishment. What her plan was, and whether it succeeded, we may not here inform our readers. Should we be permitted to resume our History of the Hamilton Family, both will be revealed.

Greatly to Caroline's delight, the following October was fixed for them to leave Oakwood, and, after a pleasant tour, to make the long anticipated visit to London. There would then be three or four months' quiet for her to have the benefit of masters, before she was introduced, and Mrs. Hamilton fondly hoped, that the last year's residence at home, fraught as it had been with so much of domestic trial, and displaying so many hopeful and admirable traits in Caroline's disposition, would have lessened the danger of the ordeal of admiration and gayety which she so dreaded for her child — whether it had or not, a future page will disclose.

To Emmeline this arrangement was a source of extreme regret, individually, in which Ellen now quite sympathized. But Emmeline had never forgotten her mother's gentle hint, that too great indulgence of regret or sorrow becomes selfishness, and she tried very hard to create some anticipation of pleasure, even in London. Ellen would not look to pleasure, but merely tried to think about — and so, when called upon, cheerfully to resign that which was now so intensely enjoyable — her studies with her aunt — and so benefit by them as to give Miss Harcourt no trouble when she was again under her care; as she knew she and Emmeline must be, more than they had been yet, when Caroline's introduction, and their residence in London, would take Mr. and Mrs. Hamilton so much from domestic pursuits and pleasures, and, even when at home, compel them to be so frequently engrossed with a large circle of friends, and all the variety of claims on their attention and time, which a season in London includes.

It was again the 7th of June, and Ellen's birthday. Accustomed from the time she became an inmate of Oakwood to regard the anniversary of her birth in the same serious light as

Mrs. Hamilton had taught her cousins — as a day of quiet reflec tion, as well as of thankfulness and joy, as one that, closing and recommencing another year of their individual lives, taught them that they were becoming more and more responsible beings — it was not much wonder that Ellen, the whole of that day, should seem somewhat less cheerful than usual. She had indeed had many sources of thankfulness and joy during the past year, but a heart and mind like hers could not recall its principal event without a return of sorrow. Mrs. Hamilton would not notice her now unusual sadness until the evening, when perceiving her standing engrossed in thought beside one of the widely-opened windows, near which Caroline was watering some lovely flowers on the terrace, she gently approached her, and, putting her arm round her, said, fondly —

"You have thought quite seriously and quite long enough for to-day, my dear Ellen; I must not have any more such very silent meditations. That there is something to regret in the retrospect of the last year, I acknowledge, but you must not let it poison all the sources of thankfulness which it brings likewise."

"It was not of my past conduct, I was thinking at this moment, aunt Emmeline — it was — "

"What, love? tell me without reserve."

"What I never, never can return in the smallest degree, all I owe to you," replied Ellen, with a sudden burst of emotion, most unusual to her controlled and gentle character; "I never can do any thing to evince how gratefully, how intensely I feel all the kindness, the goodness you have shown me from the first moment you took me to your home — an unhappy, neglected, ailing child, and this year more, more than ever. My own poor mother left me in my dangerous illness, and what have you not done to give me back not merely physical, but mental health? Day and night you watched beside me, forgetting all the care, the misery, my conduct had caused you, only thinking, only seeking, to give me back to health and happiness. Oh, aunt Emmeline, your very household can evince gratitude and love, in the performance of their respective duties — I can do nothing, never can. If I only could."

"Do you remember the fable of the lion and the mouse, my dear Ellen, and Miss Edgeworth's still prettier story on the same subject?" replied Mrs. Hamilton, more affected than she chose to betray, though she drew her niece closer to her, and kissed her fondly. "I hope I shall never be caught in a net, nor exposed to such horrors and danger as poor Madame de

Fleury in the French Revolution; but for all that, and unlikely as it seems now, my dear child, you may have many an opportunity to return all that you so gratefully feel you owe me. Do not let any such thought worry you; but believe me, when I assure you that affection and confidence are the only return I require, united, as they are in you, with such an earnest desire, and such persevering efforts to become all your best friends can wish you."

She was interrupted by the entrance of Emmeline, with a small parcel in her hand.

"Mamma, this has just arrived from Exeter for you; with an apologizing message from Mr. Bennet, saying, it should have been here last night, as he promised, but he could not get the articles from London in time. I am so very curious as to what it possibly can be, that I would bring it to you myself."

"Any other time I would punish your constant curiosity, Emmeline, by refusing to gratify it. I cannot do so now, however, for I should punish myself as well. I did want it most particularly this morning; but I am glad it was not delayed till the day was quite over. Your uncle and I did not forget your birthday, my dear Ellen, though it seemed so." And opening the parcel as she spoke, a very pretty jewel-case appeared, containing the watch, cross, and all the other trinkets Ellen had placed in Mrs. Langford's hand, and never had had the courage to inquire for, and the few her aunt had kept for her, but so prettily arranged and beautifully burnished, that she would scarcely have known them again.

"Did you never feel any curiosity as to the fate of your trinkets, my love, that you have never asked about them?"

"I knew they were in better hands than my own," replied Ellen, with a quivering lip. "I felt I had no further right to them, after attempting to part with them."

"I know there are some very painful associations connected with these trinkets, my dear Ellen, and, therefore, I would not return them to your own care, till I could add to them a birth-day-gift," and, lifting the upper tray, she took out a gold chain, and a pair of bracelets of chaste and beautiful workmanship—"that the sad memories of the one may be forgotten in the pleasant thoughts of the other. I have only one condition to make," she added, in an earnest lower tone, as Ellen tried to speak her thanks, but could only cling to her aunt's neck and weep. "If ever again you are tempted to dispose of them, dearest, promise me to bring them to me, for my valuation first."

"You shall be put into fetters at once, Ellen," said Emmeline, joyously, as her cousin gave the required promise, so eagerly, that it was evident, she felt how much security dwelt in it. "Mamma, make her put them on; I want to see if she looks as interesting as Zenobia did in her golden chains."

"I think you might find a prettier simile, Emmeline," replied Mrs. Hamilton, smiling, as she granted her request, by throwing the chain round Ellen's neck, and fastening the bracelets on her wrists.

"So I can, and so I will," replied the lively girl, altering, without the smallest hesitation, the lines to suit her fancy —

"For thee, *rash girl*, no suppliant sues;
For thee may vengeance claim her dues,
Who, nurtured underneath our smile,
Repaid our cares with treacherous wile.

. . . . . .

Dishonoring thus thy loyal name,
Fetters and warders *thou must claim*.
The chain of gold was quick unstrung,
Its links on that *fair neck were* flung;
Then gently drew the glittering band,
And laid the clasp on Ellen's hand."

THE END.

THE DAYS OF BRUCE.

A Story from Scottish History.

BY GRACE AGUILAR.

With Illustrations. 2 vols., 12mo. Cloth, $2.00.

"We have had an opportunity of observing the interest it awakens in different classes of readers, and in no instance has it failed to rivet attention, and to induce a high estimate of the author's powers. Miss Aguilar was evidently well read in the times of Bruce. It is long since we met with a work which combines so happily the best qualities of historical fiction."—*Eclectic Review.*

"The life of the hero of Bannockburn has furnished matter for innumerable tales in prose and verse, but we have met with no records of that famous era so instructive as 'The Days of Bruce.'"—*Britannia.*

"'The Days of Bruce' was written when, in the vigor of intellectual strength, Grace Aguilar was planning many things, and all for good; it was, we know, her especial favorite; it is full of deep interest."—*Mrs. S. C. Hall, in Sharpe's Magazine.*

"It is a volume which may be considered as solid history, but is nevertheless entertaining as the most charming novel ever produced by genius. Sir Walter Scott's name as an author would not have been disgraced by it had it appeared on the title-page instead of Grace Aguilar."—*Bucks Chronicle.*

"This deeply-interesting romance—a composition of great eloquence, written with practised polish and enthusiastic energy. We are not surprised at the eloquence, the warmth, and the pathos with which Grace Aguilar paints love-passages; but we are astonished at the fire and accuracy with which she depicts scenes of daring and of death."—*Observer.*

"The tale is well told, the interest warmly sustained throughout, and the delineation of female character is marked by a delicate sense of moral beauty. It is a work that may be confided to the hands of a daughter by her parent."—*Court Journal.*

"Every one who knows the works of this lamented author, must observe that she rises with her subjects. In 'The Days of Bruce' she has thrown herself into the rugged life of the fourteenth century, and has depicted the semi-civilization of the period in a manner that is quite marvellous in a young woman. Grace Aguilar always excelled in her delineations of female character, while the skill she evinces in the illustration of the historical personages, and her individualization of the imaginary ones, might at once entitle her to a birthplace among historical novelists."—*Ladies' Companion.*

"Her pen was ever devoted to the cause of virtue; and her various publications, exhibiting the beauties and enforcing the practice of the 'tender charities' of domestic life, have, we doubt not, recommended themselves to the hearts of numbers of her countrywomen. The work before us differs from the former publications of its author, inasmuch as it is in fact an historical romance, for this species of writing the high feeling of Grace Aguilar peculiarly fitted her; many of the scenes are very highly wrought; and while it will fix in the reader's mind a truthful idea of the history and style of manners of 'The Days of Bruce,' it will also impress upon him a strong sense of the ability and noble cast of thought which distinguished its lamented author."—*Englishwoman's Magazine.*

New York: D. APPLETON & CO.

"We look upon 'The Days of Bruce' as an elegantly-written and interesting romance, and place it by the side of Miss Porter's 'Scottish Chiefs.'" —*Gentleman's Magazine.*

"A very pleasing and successful attempt to combine ideal delineation of character with the records of history Very beautiful and very true are the portraits of the female mind and heart which Grace Aguilar knew how to draw. This is the chief charm of all her writings, and in 'The Days of Bruce' the reader will have the pleasure of viewing this skilful portraiture in the characters of Isoline and Agnes, and Isabella of Buchan."—*Literary Gazette.*

"What a fertile mind was that of Grace Aguilar! What an early development of reflection, of feeling, of taste, of power of invention, of true and earnest eloquence! 'The Days of Bruce' is a composition of her early youth, but full of beauty. Grace Aguilar knew the female heart better than any writer of our day, and in every fiction from her pen we trace the same masterly analysis and development of the motives and feelings of woman's nature. 'The Days of Bruce' possesses also the attractions of an extremely interesting story, that absorbs the attention, and never suffers it to flag till the last page is closed, and then the reader will lay down the volume with regret."—*Critic.*

HOME SCENES AND HEART STUDIES.

By GRACE AGUILAR.

WITH ILLUSTRATIONS.

One volume, 12mo. Cloth. Price, $1.00.

The Perez Family.
The Stone-Cutter's Boy of Possagno.
Amete and Yafeh.
The Fugitive.
The Edict; a Tale of 1492.
The Escape; a Tale of 1755.
Red Rose Villa.
Gonzalvo's Daughter.
The Authoress.
Helon.
Lucy.
The Spirit's Entreaty.
Idalie.
Lady Gresham's Fete.
The Group of Sculpture.
The Spirit of Night.
Recollections of a Rambler.
Cast thy Bread upon the Waters.
The Triumph of Love.

New York: D. APPLETON & CO.

www.ingramcontent.com/pod-product-compliance
Lightning Source LLC
LaVergne TN
LVHW020059110826
845151LV00001B/25
9781425544850